INVISIBLE JUSTICE

INVISIBLE JUSTICE

A
KYLE MCMANN & GRAHAM KURLAND
MEDICAL THRILLER

GARY BROWN, MD

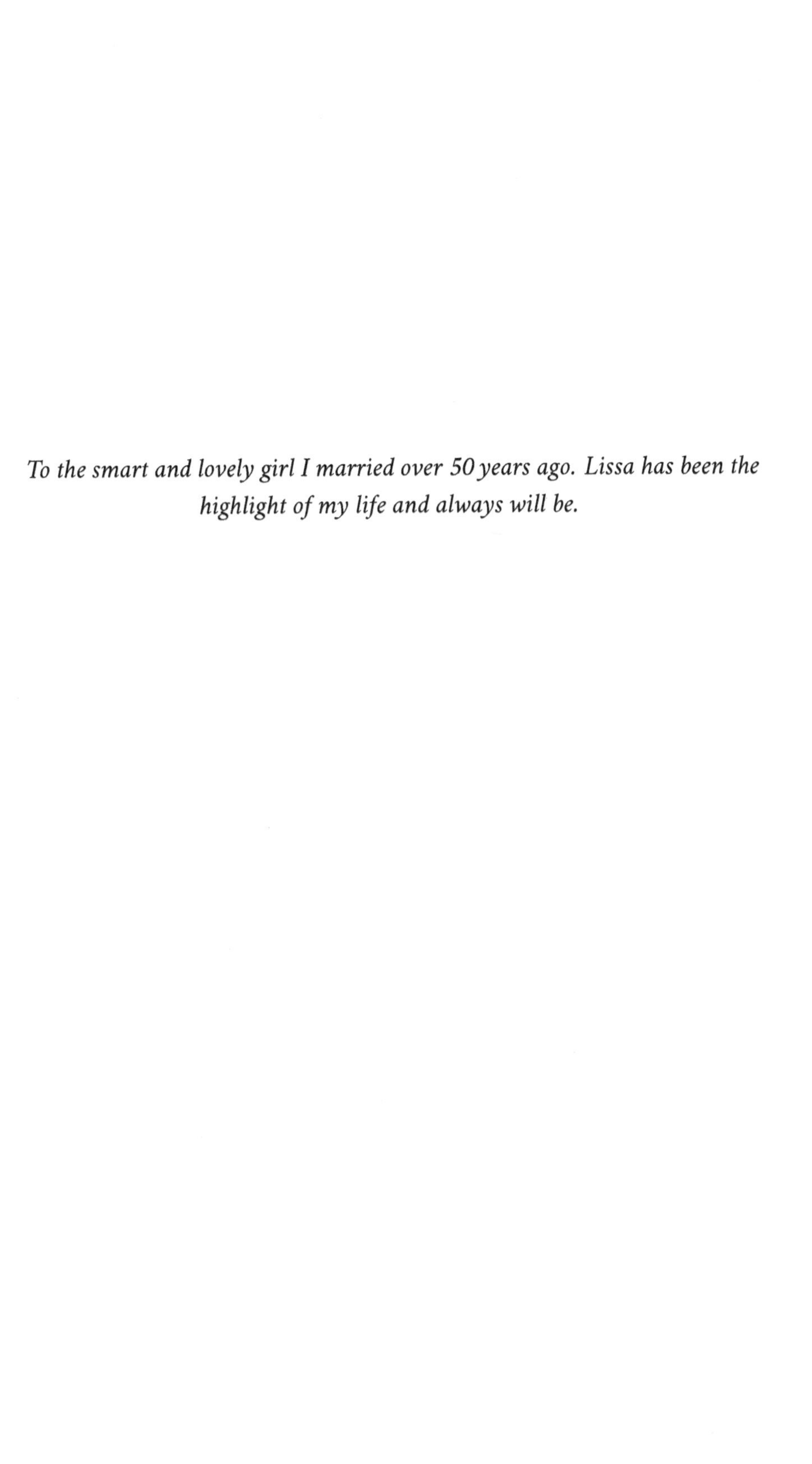

To the smart and lovely girl I married over 50 years ago. Lissa has been the highlight of my life and always will be.

"Illnesses do not come upon us out of the blue. They are developed from small daily sins against Nature. When enough sins have accumulated, illnesses will suddenly appear."

—HIPPOCRATES

Contents

Praise for Invisible Justice

"Dr. Gary Brown has created a rip-roaring "Dexter with Doctors" thriller, using his deep-dive knowledge of medical catastrophes, hard-earned as they were by one of America's top eye surgeons, from slicing into eyeballs for decades. It's so much fun to watch brilliant medical minds figure out how to murder, with as much pain as humanly possible, evil bastards who prey on the innocent. There's a fantastic love story between two hot yet damaged doctors trying to find love in a world full of blood, guts, death, and the miraculous saving of lives. This is the kind of book you keep thinking about as you go through your day and can't wait to get back to, just to see who dies next and in what excruciating way they bite the dust, knowing full well that the events are not natural."—**Henry Sterr**y, bestselling author of *Chicken*

"Dr. Gary Brown blends his considerable medical acumen with gripping storytelling ability to take the medical thriller to new heights. Gary is an artistic master who entertains, educates, and tantalizes our intellect... I can't wait for the next book."—**Timothy W. Olsen**, M.D. Professor and Consultant of Ophthalmology, Mayo Clinic, Chair Emeritus, Emory University Founder, iMacular Regeneration, LLC

"Gary, I found your book wonderful...I just kept turning the pages. I couldn't stop. I wanted to know what happened next?...What happened next?...What happened next?...It unfolds in a really good way. I like that being a doctor, you have access to that kind of information. And your protagonist is a woman. She ends up joining this thing called the Tribunal, which is kind of like a—we talked about this earlier—*Dexter on Steroids*—as she gets the bad guys. I like reading thrillers, whether they're legal or in this case medical. I think you've done a really great job. So, congratulations on your book."—**Jack Canfield**, author of *Success Principles* and the co-author of the Chicken Soup for the Soul™ series with over 600 million sales.

Chapter One

Outside the Surgical Emergency Room

Grady Memorial Hospital, Atlanta, Georgia

Kyle McMann groaned as she paced on the Grady Memorial Hospital Emergency Room ramp, her eyes tracking the incoming ambulance. She prayed this wasn't another twenty-five-year-old—her exact age—stiffened by rigor mortis, still cradling her crying infant son in her arms. She was haunted by the mother's lifeless stare that sent shivers down her spine. Obviously, some evil bastard shot her close up as she held her baby.

Kyle had picked the short straw, as per usual. She was starting her career as an intern in the Surgical Emergency Room of Grady, the Mount Everest of U.S. shock-trauma centers.

Unlike most hospitals that had one ER, this godforsaken medical behemoth had three: the Surgical ER, the Medical ER, and the Pediatric ER. Each had its own unique variants of traumatizing trauma.

It was dark by nine p.m. on Thursday, July 5th, and she shielded her eyes from the strobing reds and blues. It was her job to screen the incoming "clients."

Though not specified in the hospital bylaws, inherent in the mission of the lowest of the low on the professional totem pole was ramp duty.

Aka processing the worst of the worst and pronouncing the dead bodies dead.

Didn't get much grimmer than that.

Her mind flashed back to this morning's thirty-one-year-old basketball phenom with bacterial meningitis. A day ago, a vibrant human being. Now approaching his maker with a devastated brain failing on a respirator despite the efforts of the best infectious disease minds on the planet.

She'd been there for five days, and already it was wearing her out.

Facing the families.

The tears.

The sobbing.

Parents collapsing.

It was like everyone fell from the tree of horrors and hit each branch on the way down.

Her fight or flight reflex kicked in, and she sprinted to the ambulance, sharp brown eyes focused, runner's body whipping towards the EMS vehicle, coughing out the black exhaust that smacked her face-on and splayed her middle-parted chestnut brown hair in both directions. Staying on the driver's side, she peered in as the BLS 911 Emergency Ambulance backed into the ramp.

"What is it?" she shouted as the driver rolled down his window.

"Bad one, doc. Bleeding like a stuck pig. A bunch of kids worked him over with bats and knives. You want to get in here fast."

Kyle's heart sank as she ran back and yanked open the rear door. She jumped in before the van came to a full stop.

Blood.

And more blood.

A vampire's wet dream.

On the sheets. The floor. Smeared on the windows.

"Come on!" she shouted to the half-panicked tech staring at the abdomen. "Let's get him inside."

The two front EMTs ran around back and pulled the stretcher out. The group slammed through the steel and glass doors into the ER.

"WAIT A MINUTE!" Ellen Chu, the hard-as-a-rock head nurse, blocked their path and held up her hand. "What's going on?"

Kyle spoke up from behind. "Let 'em through. We're going to Trauma, stat."

She pushed the stretcher, sweeping Ellen aside, then looked back over her shoulder. "And call Eli."

The Trauma Room was halfway down the hall. It was larger than the rest, so more people could fit in to stabilize the endless stream of broken bodies in this war zone.

Kyle slipped in before the men and slapped the trauma room table. "Here. Let's move him. One, two, *three.*"

They lifted the patient from the stretcher using the draw sheet underneath him.

He was light. *Must be a kid*, Kyle thought.

She peered into the open abdomen. The wound stretched all the way across the belly.

"Oh, man," she cried as she catapulted back.

An arterial pumper squirted blood into the air, hitting her directly in the right eye.

Everything she learned drained from her mind.

She went from flight/fight to freeze.

All she could see was that fountain of red shooting up from the patient's pulsating bowel.

Where the hell was Eli?

Her stomach dropped from the sheer helplessness of it all.

Think, dammit. THINK!

Ellen poked her head around the corner.

Kyle looked up from the bowel, snapped out of her stupor, and wiped blood from her face with the arm of her white lab coat.

"Where's Eli?"

"I told him to get his ass down here stat." Ellen looked at the spurting blood, then back at Kyle and said, like it was the most obvious thing in the world: "Shouldn't we start an IV?"

"Yeah, yeah, uh, good idea." Kyle shook her head and mentally kicked herself. Four years of working her ass off, and she couldn't even think of an IV? What kind of a moron was she?

"I'll put in the IV," Ellen said hard and fast, "but you've gotta get that bleeder, or he won't last until Eli gets here." The ambulance attendants backed off while Ellen tossed Kyle a large Kelly clamp, then ransacked the drawers for an IV.

"Kyle?!" she barked, "C'mon, let's go."

Kyle faced the patient, ready to save his life.

Then she froze. Again.

Sure, she'd been through the surgical rotation, but only as a second or third assistant. She'd read all the books. But books didn't shoot blood at you while you tried to stop them from dying.

It was her first week in the ER, for fuck's sake.

She wasn't even a real doctor yet. Real doctors knew what they were doing.

"Kyle, SNAP OUT OF IT!" Ellen shouted.

"Okay, sorry…" Kyle muttered as she sprang out of her stupor.

She pulled on a pair of surgical gloves and yanked the suction catheter from the wall. The long plastic tube slurped the liquid blood and dark clots from the open wound to expose a glistening bowel.

There it was.

The base of the bleeder.

She took the Kelly clamp and went for it.

Blood splattered her face again.

Now it was in her left eye.

What if he had AIDS?

Or hepatitis?

"Damn!" She missed.

The blood was pooling.

And the bleeder was going down again.

In another second, it would disappear below the surface of a new red pond.

She went for it once more, holding her right wrist to steady her hand.

"Gotcha, you little bastard."

"What's going on?"

Kyle squinted to keep more blood from rolling into her eyes as she growled at Eli, finally strolling in like the cool customer he was. "Nice of you to stop by."

The second-year surgery resident leaned over to inspect the wound. "Looks to me like you're doin' a-okay to me, Newby."

A clot dislodged from another severed vessel.

Blood spewed two feet and caught Eli in the cheek. "Okay, well, maybe you do need a little help from your friends."

He wiped his face with a green towel and snapped on a pair of tan gloves. "Kyle, gimme the suction catheter. I'll work here. You put a second IV in his other hand. Ellen, call the OR. Tell them we're coming up stat."

Kyle was happy to slide aside. She grabbed the patient's right hand and smacked the back of it a half dozen times to raise a vein. It was no easy matter considering the scar tissue covering the vessels.

Strange. She'd given her little brother a scar like that once. Brian had been chasing her in the house, and she slammed the bathroom door on his hand as hard as she could.

The poor kid. She remembered it like it was yesterday. She'd cried for nights when she saw the skin torn back and the tears running down his little pink cheeks.

She stared at the patient's face.

Except there was no face.

No pink cheeks. Nothing close to normal human features. Only bloated purple lips, swollen shut eyes, and the disfigured pulp left by the vicious stomping. His facial bones had to be fractured beyond recognition.

Eli clenched his teeth, his casual nonchalance gone. "Son of a bitch!"

"What? What's the matter?" Kyle asked.

"Every time I grab a damn vessel, another pops up." Even Eli, the king of chill, was sweating. Something he rarely did. "We've gotta get this bowel fixed, or we won't have to worry about the rest of him."

Ellen careened around the doorway corner on one hand. "They gave us the okay. Said to bring him right up."

"Unlock this stretcher. LET'S GO!!!" Eli threw another clamp on the exposed gut.

The trio wheeled the stainless-steel stretcher as fast as they could into the main corridor of the ER, then down the dim hallway, with Kyle sprinting at the side.

She looked down at the abdomen. Blood was oozing everywhere. She ran ahead and punched the erratically blinking, red "UP" button. Twice. Three times. Four…Eli, Ellen, and the patient arrived in seconds.

Kyle's foot tapped on the floor, and she bit her lower lip as she stared at the patient's hand. Was she going to lose this one, too?

Her mind disassociated as she waited for the clanking elevator. She needed to stop after work to stock up on Fritos. Brian was visiting on Monday. Just out of tenth grade, this was his first solo trip by train. It was a wonder Mom let him come, especially for two days. She hated being alone since Dad died. But she'd finally relented when he expressed such a strong interest in Emory University. He so wanted to follow his big sister's path, only on the veterinary side.

"No pulse," Ellen said as she felt the patient's neck and looked up from the head of the stretcher with wide eyes.

Eli reached for a confirming feel, then looked back toward the ER, hesitant for a moment.

"We gotta get him to the OR," he decided. "Kyle, you pump. I'll breathe him."

Kyle jumped onto the stretcher and straddled the patient with her legs, half-standing, taking care not to put weight on the open abdomen.

Knees flexed, she pushed down on his chest with both palms, counting off one-per-second thrusts that forced blood through his oxygen-starved body.

One of the clamps slipped, and blood squirted, spraying the crotch of her white house officer's pants over and over.

She kept going.

Unless they got this poor kid's heart started again, he'd be a brainstem preparation in ten minutes.

Eli sighed deeply and shook his head. "Not good, guys. Where's a phone to call a code?"

He glanced left, then right. "Not even a fucking phone?" Cells were useless down here.

Ellen scowled and ran back to the ER, mumbling something unintelligible, though her tone needed no explanation.

"I don't think I'm pumping him well," Kyle said between heavy breaths.

"Why not?" Eli asked.

"There's no support under his back."

"God DAMNIT!"

Eli dropped the breathing mask, pushed the stretcher against the wall for stabilization, and pulled a sideboard out from underneath. "Turn him so I can put this under."

Kyle stopped her thrusts and, standing on the stretcher with her back against the wall, lifted the left side of the patient's body while Eli tried to slip the flat board underneath. The awkward position set off horrific pounding in her head, but not before she had him halfway over.

"Almost. Just a little more."

The patient's shirt slipped up.

The birthmark!

The brown oval over his right kidney!

Kyle's shocked mouth dropped open. Instead of pulling harder, she dropped him.

The patient fell back on Eli and the board with a thud.

Kyle's head snapped back and slammed against the hard tile wall abutting the stretcher. She could hear a crack as her head bounced.

The birthmark. The mark on his back—Brian's mark.

And with the hand scars?

NOOOOO!!!

Eli yanked his right hand out from between the board and the stretcher and shook it.

"Kyle! What the hell are you doing? Why'd you let go?"

The board crashed to the ground.

Kyle climbed down and grabbed the side of the stretcher, her head exploding with the worst pain she'd ever felt.

Eli held his hand and grimaced. "What's wrong with you? Get moving, or he's gonna die."

"I—I can't. I just can't, I'm not, I don't… I just can't…"

"Why not?"

"I-I can't."

"Jesus Christ!" Eli uttered.

Then he shouted, "HELP, STAT!!! WE NEED HELP DOWN HERE!!!" He hit a red wall alarm and climbed onto the stretcher. He pumped with his good hand while Kyle hugged the wall for support.

Brian.

Dear God, NOOOOO!

What was he doing here four days early? He never showed up anywhere early in his entire life.

Personnel poured from the stairways and into the hallway.

Eli jumped off and ran down the corridor, waving at the people pushing the stretcher back to the ER.

"Come on, move it, MOVE IT!"

Kyle stumbled after them in a daze. The seat of her pants dripped blood that splattered down to her green and white Nikes. Normally, the wetness would've driven her crazy. Now she watched and felt a cold nothingness.

While her head throbbed with an excruciating ache.

As if it were on fire.

People ran past.

Someone was shouting in the distance.

Bodies crowded the main ER.

Their faces were blurs.

She stopped outside the door to Trauma. Inside, it was alive with a flurry of activity, but the noises were far away.

Kyle stood alone, the Ghost of Christmas Past, looking in on people illuminated by the powerful overhead beams.

As she stood there wobbling, the noise stopped.

Suddenly, the frenzied motion ceased.

White coats and pants came out singly and in pairs, silent, their heads hanging low.

Eli came last, biting his lower lip.

Only the solitary monotone of the cardiac monitor echoed through the door.

Kyle dropped back against a wall and slid to the ground, a hand pressing into each temple to try and hold in the jackhammer pounding inside her head.

Her mental and physical pains faded as she passed out into a black void.

Chapter Two

Seven Years Later

Pennsylvania Hospital, Eighth Street, Philadelphia, Pennsylvania

Graham Kurland, 6' 5", 230 pounds of sinew and muscle, strolled in the Pennsylvania Hospital parking lot like the former Purple Heart winner he was, a world-class warrior who'd traded his weapons for a scalpel and become a rising star surgeon of the medical world, as well as a renowned transplant researcher. If you looked closely, you could see his assurance and graceful gait almost concealed the limp he'd had after a grenade's shrapnel shredded his leg.

He was greeted by the occasional nurse who flirted, or a doctor who was in awe and/or jealous of the famous Dr. Kurland. But no matter how much attention he got—professional or personal—none of it ever went to his head. He either didn't know or care how brilliant and easy on the eyes he was.

He was excited about the surgery he was scheduled to perform. A double renal artery in a recipient kidney. Much more difficult to implant than a single renal artery. So his XXL brain was working out each detail, making contingencies for everything that could go wrong. The donor kidney had two arteries supplying it, rather than the typical one. This anomaly made it more difficult to connect the donor kidney into the kidney recipient. Couldn't be done without a great team. They were very good. But were they great? He thought so.

This was his last year of internal medicine residency. He had already finished his surgical residency and would be one of the select few in the country with Boards in Surgery *and* Medicine. He couldn't have done it without his photographic memory. And his years as a kill-or-be-killed warrior. And a CEO who turned his dead father's business into a cash cow. While raising his teenage brother.

BAM!

A car backfired loudly, like a shot being fired just outside the hospital.

Suddenly, Graham was in the middle of a raging battle in the desert outside Kandahar, missiles and bullets flying. Eddie Severs, his ride-or-die best friend, was by his side. Eddie took one step towards him, and the whole world exploded as he stepped on an IED.

Graham was thrown back, even as he saw Eddie blow up, blood and flesh flying as he screamed in agony and horror.

Graham felt a hand on his shoulder, and he whipped around, fists clenched, fire in his eyes, face full of rage, in full fight mode.

He snapped back to reality when he saw he was face-to-face with Nurse Beth Kelly, a fifty-something veteran of twenty-five years at Penn, the sweetest, kindest soul here. She was looking horrified at Graham's hard, furious face, his body spring-loaded and ready to kill.

The look of terror on Nurse Kelly's face jolted Graham back to sanity. He saw what he was doing and was overcome with shame and embarrassment. He forced his face into a disarming, charming grin.

"Sorry, Beth, oh my God, you scared the bejesus outta me. My apologies, I get a little wonky sometimes. I didn't mean to scare you. I'm really sorry."

Beth's face changed from scared to neutral to thoughtful to understanding to kind. She nodded and smiled her sweet smile. "PTSD," she said with an understanding nod. "My husband served in Desert Storm. Gee willikers, I know trauma's a killer. I hope to heck you're getting help."

"Oh yeah, I went through the program, I just get a little sketchy when I hear, uh..."

"Loud noises? Like a gunshot. Or a car backfiring?" she gave him a wry little smile. "I get it."

"Thanks, Beth, I really appreciate that. Maybe we could keep this, uh, you know..."

She made a funny little locking-her-lips-with-a-key gesture and did a slightly silly mock whisper. "What happens at Penn stays at Penn."

Graham laughed.

Beth laughed.

"Shall we?" Beth nodded and gestured towards the hospital.

"Yes, we shall," Graham said with his trademark aw-shucks animal magnetism as they walked through the parking lot and into the rest of their lives.

Chapter Three

Society Hill

Philadelphia, Pennsylvania

Kyle McMann jogged in her blue Penn State sweatshirt and white shorts, trying to shake the dread in her head and the pain in her heart as the scene of her bloody brother dying in front of her while she froze played in an endless loop in her tortured brain.

She kicked into a sprint past a Philadelphia Society Hill colonial cloaked in brick and light blue shutters, focusing on the anger instead of the pain. The cowardly monsters who'd tortured and murdered Brian were never caught. They got away scot-free. And it still haunted Kyle, day and night. It was a cool day in July, and she watched the kids play street hockey on cobblestoned-lined Delancey Street.

"Outta the road, ya crazy bitch!" A South Philly welcome combined with a horn blasting from a black Chevy flying down Seventh Street that nearly sideswiped her.

She jumped out of her skin, breathing hard, heart pounding as she glanced at the black snake tattoo on the hairy forearm while the driver gave her a one-fingered salute out the window.

"Asshole!" she fired back, shaking her fist and returning a middle finger at the cloud of black smoke and clanking muffler.

Hadn't she just sworn she wasn't going to lose it again? You'd think she'd have better self-control. She sighed deeply, trying to calm the rage coursing through her.

She took a deep, deep breath and stared at a Philadelphia Horse-Drawn Carriage Tour horse dutifully pulling its wagon as it turned the corner.

A teenage boy stickhandled a street hockey puck. He shot the rubberized disc hard. It flew into the trunk of a gray Toyota, christening it with a dent.

He looked so much like her brother Brian. The ragamuffin haircut, the Flyer's sweatshirt with the red "10" on the back. The same build. Even the voice.

And there it was again, the palpable, inescapable ache that lived just below the surface of her every waking hour. The tears came, but she bit her lip, choking them back down.

So young, so alive, so…

"Can I help you, lady?" the youth said, facing her straight on.

"Uh, no. Sorry, I just thought…"

She took off at a brisk clip, jogging along the docks. Her runs were an escape from the sleep-deprived life-and-death stress of the hospital. And the recurring misery of knowing she had killed her own brother because she failed to do her job. But even that was becoming more difficult now that she was only getting out once or twice a week.

More and more her legs felt like lead, her lungs as if they might explode, and her side ached like combat boots were stomping on her gut.

Maybe now that she was approaching thirty-three, she was finally middle-aged. She couldn't say she hadn't been expecting it.

She saw herself reflected in a plate-glass window as she ran past. Five-feet-eight-inches. Sweet dimples, a smattering of freckles, and soft brown eyes just a shade darker than her hair. Full lips, complete with a cupid's bow pattern on the upper. She was fit, with sculpted arms and a tight core.

But her chin was totally wrong, too narrow at the bottom. It highlighted the fact that her mouth was too wide. And her ears were way too big.

She thought she was a Plain Jane, even though her friends insisted she was a natural beauty.

Still, most people thought she was just out of college.

She reminded herself to have an attitude of gratitude. After her cerebral aneurysm ruptured when Brian died in the ER, she was lucky to be alive.

Two months in the hospital, then another four in rehab. Kyle had a lot of time to think about the scumbags who beat her brother to death. They were never identified or caught. None of them spent one second in prison for their evil deed. She was sure they kept torturing and killing, bringing death and heartache to other families. That fact kept relentlessly circling around and around in her mind for all these years. No closure. No consequences, no justice.

Despite this, she did well in physical therapy and was able to take her internship a year late. Even though for six months, she felt like collapsing by mid-afternoon. She still had chronic nerve pain in her legs. And the all-too-frequent, often blinding headaches. But that was nothing compared to the patients she saw every day who were suffering tortures of the damned as they lay on death's doorstep.

She stopped to run in place on Spruce, waiting for the light to turn.

"Hey, sweetie, need help?"

Now what?

Kyle spun around with a closed fist, ready to do battle.

To her surprised delight, she spied a half-shaven panhandler. Sitting on a makeshift orange crate chair outside the Seven-Eleven, his two remaining teeth stood out at angles to their normal position. His navy wool jacket was threadbare, with moth holes and multicolored stains.

"Joshua…" She smiled. "You scared me."

"I scared you?" He looked hurt.

Kyle leaned over and patted him on the arm. "Sorry. I just had a bad day."

"I could tell."

"My face?"

"Written all over, Doc. Don't let it get you, though. Some days you're the windshield, and some days you're the bug. But it all evens out in the end."

Kyle smiled. "How's that ulcer?"

Joshua patted the stump of his left leg. "Fine. Real fine."

"You call me if it acts up."

"You know it."

She pulled a five-dollar bill from her sweatshirt and handed it over, accompanied by a big, sweet smile.

"Thanks, Doc."

"My pleasure."

She might be having a bad day, but seeing Joshua sitting on that wooden fruit crate, both legs amputated above the knee, put everything into perspective. Every day was a rough one for him. But he was always so positive—at least on the outside. She realized she could learn a lot from good old Joshua.

Kyle left with a wave as the light changed and sped past the crumbling Colonial Mikvah Burial Ground.

It was a miracle she wasn't lying under one of those headstones herself, considering the whip-sawing bouts of depression.

Razor blades, pills, a hose from the muffler to the car—she'd thought about them all. She was ready to be done with the past. But clearly, the past was not ready to be done with her. She was determined to move on with her life and work as hard as she could to make the world a better place.

Since she was appointed as the new Chair of the Infectious Disease Department last month, there was barely a second to breathe. But it was something to be proud of. Few docs her age could claim to be a full professor at a metropolitan teaching hospital, much less a departmental chair. Of course, the fifty-odd peer-reviewed papers she'd published didn't hurt.

But the fact that she was a woman and a chairman? Unheard of at stodgy Pennsylvania Hospital. Letting her in must have been like bringing a kangaroo to a picnic for the old farts on the Executive Council. An awe-inspiring collection of freeze-dried fossils. Half of them still thought women should be renting oxygen from men.

And Chairman?

What about using the right term? Chairwoman? Or even Chairperson? Wouldn't the old boys' club love that?

And if they didn't?

Well, they could sit on it and twirl.

No matter, all the years of work above and beyond the call of duty had paid off. While her friends partied, she'd spent countless evenings and weekends in the lab, writing her articles, and climbing her way up the mountain of success.

But it wasn't just about recognition. It was knowing that her life meant something. That her work had advanced medical knowledge and improved people's lives. It was the grateful smiles and hugs from people like the Russillos when she pulled little Alyssa from the death grip of E. coli sepsis. Those were what made it worthwhile. Gave her a purpose as she tried to make amends for failing once when it counted most. Never mind that she had an aneurysm rupture and spent the next two months in the neurosurgical ICU. She'd never let her patients down again, not as long as she had a breath in her body. She wasn't about to sit by and watch someone else's little brother die.

Success, of course, had not come without cost. Her childhood girlfriends had long since married and had children. Some were even divorced. They all said they envied her achievements. But achievements didn't run down the hall laughing and wrap happy little arms around her neck. Or keep her bed warm at night.

There was no time for dating. She'd also become more and more picky. It was so hard to find a decent man who didn't wrinkle his nose and change the subject to the Phillies every time she talked about her work.

Worse yet, the recent promotion was just one more accomplishment she had no one to share with. Many a Saturday night over the past year, she'd sat on her sofa alone with a bottle of Chardonnay and wondered what the point of it all was.

Her cell rang and derailed her train of thought. She stopped and pulled it from her pocket.

David.

"Hello?" she said.

"Kyle. How are you?"

"Good, thanks. What's up?"

"I wondered whether you were free on Friday?"

"I'm sorry. I have to put together a talk."

"Really? Don't you ever stop to do something fun?"

"I enjoy what I do."

"Gimme a break."

"Goodbye, David."

"You're turning into an old maid professor."

"Thanks for the call. Have a nice life."

She disconnected.

Maybe it was rude of her to hang up like that. But still…

David, the man of her dreams. On paper, anyway. Intelligent, investment banker, Stanford MBA. Perfect spouse material, according to a global expert, Joanne Susac, in Pathology. She'd certainly ridden the train enough times to know.

But "supportive" didn't exist in David's dictionary. He refused to take her job, her career, her calling, seriously. He wanted a trad wife. It was one thing to be old-fashioned, but this man was stuck in the twentieth century, when a woman was required to stay at home and be a broodmare. For a smart guy, he didn't have the common sense of a moth.

Frankly, she was relieved that it was over.

She kicked a small stone and sent it spinning to the curb.

It was hard to believe more than five years had passed since cancer had taken Mom. They'd always been so close. Had such great talks. Shared everything.

Now there was no one to confide in, no one to care, no one to worry whether she came home by midnight.

Or at all.

She sent another stone flying, stubbing her toe in the process.

Maybe hers was meant to be a solo flight. Perhaps she should be a fatalist and accept it.

But why? She'd never accepted change well…

Why had she gone to Atlanta in the first place?

If only Brian hadn't come, if only she could turn back time and change those last few moments. The ache of his absence gnawed at her in ways that words failed to capture, leaving a hollow echo where laughter and love once lived. Every memory seemed sharper at dusk, each regret a heavy stone she carried alone.

Damn him.

And damn her brain for spiraling into misery over and over again.

She looked down Spruce Street and slowed to a walk, grabbing her left side to dull the stabbing pain. Ignoring the chronic pain in her legs. She did four miles, barely, but she made it.

As her breathing slowed down, she walked down the brick walk and past the stairwells to the basements of the rowhomes. She had a flash of the young medical student found dead weeks ago, crumpled up at the bottom of one of the stairwells. There were no leads, and the perpetrator had never been caught. In all likelihood, she would never be caught. One more brutal killing of an innocent young woman. Her blood boiled all over again, knowing yet another scumbag would rape and murder, escape justice, and go unpunished.

There was no one in sight.

No dogs.

No kids.

No cabs.

No one.

Even Society Hill seemed lonely and distant today. At least a cool breeze felt good on her face.

Brian's death could have been yesterday. Again, she fantasized about making the devils who'd tortured her brother suffer the way they'd made him suffer. Smash their teeth in with a baseball bat. Crack their skulls with a crowbar. Or maybe have them splayed out in an operating theater and destroy them surgically the way they'd destroyed her brother. Over and over, she'd dreamed of confronting and dissecting them into little pieces. But every time she'd wake up in a sweat just as she cut them open and watched them writhe in misery.

How many other lives had they ruined?

How many other innocents agonized over loved ones lost and maimed by those monsters?

If there was any justice in the world, they'd all burn in hell for a hundred years.

But what could she do to make them pay?

"Outta the road, bitch!" came the familiar Philly voice from the black Chevy zooming up from behind.

She picked up a baseball-sized rock, turned, and threw it as hard as she could, then screamed with glee as her missile cracked his windshield.

Then she felt a tightness constrict her head, like a vice-like grip was squeezing her brain. She heaved a frustrated sigh.

And prayed it wasn't another aneurysm.

Chapter Four

Pennsylvania Hospital ER

Eighth Street, Philadelphia, PA

Four huge men who looked like they could open beer cans with their eyeballs thrust a stretcher with an old man on it into the Pennsylvania Hospital Emergency Room as a loud BANG disrupted the stillness of the last Sunday night in August.

The elderly man was laid out on the stretcher, silent and still, vacant eyes staring ahead.

"We need a fuckin' doctah?" Ralph "Rocco" DiNunzio, the behemoth at the stretcher's head, thundered. Sweat dampened his jowls, which were both covered by a heavy five o'clock shadow that extended well down his bulldog neck. "NOW!!!"

"Sir, I'll be with you in just a—"

"I said NOW!"

The angry giant leaned over the desk and grabbed the pencil-thin receptionist on each side of his collar. His huge hands encircled the little man's neck as he yanked the receptionist's face close. So close that his lengthy nose hairs touched the clerk's lips.

"You get a doctor here NOW, or yer gonna look like Humpty friggin' Dumpty!"

"Y-yes sir."

The receptionist backed off with terrified staccato steps as the huge brute released him. He grasped the phone, hands shaking so badly that he had to hit the four numbers to get the resident.

The big man scowled from across the desk, an intermittent tic twitching up the left side of his mouth. At least six-four and barrel-chested, he had tree-trunk forearms and black chest hair poking out from his white polo shirt.

"Today, not yestuhday! My uncle needs help NOW! I want da bes' doctor in dis GOD DAMN HOSPITAL!!!"

He poked a massive, blunt finger into the receptionist's chest as a not-so-gentle reminder that he meant business. And that this business was life-and-death.

"Doctor Kurland's on his way, sir." The receptionist clerk retreated to the farthest corner of his cubicle and averted his eyes as he absent-mindedly leafed through a random stack of papers between glances.

The big man turned his attention to the stricken man lying on the stretcher. "Hang awn, Uncle Frank. It'll be erright, I swear."

Stacey Thomas, the evening charge nurse, caught the commotion from the other end of the ER and rushed over. Wearing a white blouse and light blue slacks, her shoulder-length red hair was pulled back by a scrunchie of the same color.

"I'm Nurse Thomas," she said sharply to the pissed-off ogre head man.

"Ralph DiNunzio. Mr. Mancini's nephew and I need you—"

She looked over the patient. "No trauma, right?"

"No, he's jus'…I mean, look at him, can't you see he's fucked up, what is wrong wichew people?"

"You need to lose the attitude, or I will call security, and they will escort you from the premises. Do you understand?"

The mammoth thug started to retort, but Stacey shut him down with a fierce look and a menacing point of her finger.

"Good," she said. "Then let's move him to a room." Stacey motioned to an orderly, and together they transferred the comatose old man to a larger stretcher. He was feather light.

The big man, with his huge, dubious coterie close behind, shadowed them like a bunch of 'roided up attack dogs from the waiting area down a corridor to a side room.

"What happened?" Nurse Thomas asked as she put a blood pressure cuff on in the room.

"We jus' found him in bed," DiNunzio said with an unequivocal South Philly accent. "I got home after 'lebben an' went up to tawk to him about some urgent business. He usually goes to bed early, so I hadda wake him up."

"And?"

"He woul'n't wake up. When he finally did, he coul'n't see, and he was burnin' up all over."

"How was he earlier today?"

"Fine."

Stacey glanced toward DiNunzio's three ferocious ghouls outside the door. A spiritually challenged and morally bankrupt group, if she'd ever seen one. At least they stayed in the corridor, apparently content to let DiNunzio manage the executive activities.

She felt the pulse. Seventy-two and regular. Normal.

The blood pressure was 120/80. Perfect.

Stacey stuck a small cone in the man's ear. Ninety-nine temp, nothing to write home about.

She pulled apart the old man's shirt and examined his upper torso. He looked like he'd spent a week naked in the Sahara.

The EKG technician wheeled in his machine and pasted wire leads onto Mancini's chest and arms.

Normal tracing. Good rate. Regular rhythm.

Stacey bit her lower lip and jotted down her findings.

What was this?

Nothing like she'd seen before, that was for sure.

DiNunzio glared and growled. "Well, what the fuck's wrong wit' him?"

"I'm not sure."

"Is it a stroke?"

"I doubt it."

"How do ya know?"

"Stroke patients usually don't look like this. They don't exhibit burns or whatever this is on his chest. They have numbness, weakness, and slurred speech. Your uncle needs testing."

DiNunzio moved closer and closer. Until he was seriously invading her personal space.

"Pardon me," she said as she put her fingers on Mancini's neck. "Do you mind?"

"What?"

"You need to back off," Stacey said with a sting that made the gangster retreat.

DiNunzio backed off. "Fine. Butchoo betta get me doctah PRONTO, or we are gonna have a fuckin' problem, Capiche?"

Stacey looked beyond the doorway and caught a white coat.

Graham Kurland.

Thank God. He'd figure this out fast. He was the smartest doc in the hospital. By leaps and bounds.

Graham entered the room with his country-boy smile. His hands were buried deep in the pockets of a white lab coat that read *Chief Resident*. He still moved like the former All-State tight end he was in high school. His dark brown hair was frazzled, no surprise since it was well after midnight. He suppressed a deep yawn as he turned his head and emphasized his square chin covered with fine fuzz from skipping a day of shaving.

"Sorry, crazy day at the House of Madness," he apologized. "What's up, Stace?"

"Thanks for coming so fast. This is Mr. Mancini. And his nephew, Mr. DiNunzio."

"I'm Ralph DiNunzio," Rocco said, like everyone knew he was King of South Philly.

Graham looked at DiNunzio, saw who he was, then said in a low, calm voice packed with power, "Graham Kurland." Turning back to Stacey, he asked, "What's the history?"

"He came in approximately ten minutes ago. He was found like this around eleven tonight. Apparently, he was asymptomatic earlier in the day."

"Is he conscious?"

Mancini opened his eyes.

Graham leaned down. "Sir, what happened?"

No answer.

The eyes shut.

Graham glanced at DiNunzio. "Does he have a hearing problem?"

"He hears fine. Look, doc, you gotta fuckin' do something-"

Graham cut him off with a tight glance and a raised finger.

DiNunzio shut up.

Graham took a penlight from his lab coat pocket, pulled up Mancini's right lid, and shone the bright light on it. The black pupil in the center stood still. Same for the left.

DiNunzio moved around to the other side of the stretcher, facing Graham.

Though the room temperature was a comfortable seventy degrees, beads of sweat rolled down his cheeks.

"Are you da the bes' doctor in this place?"

Graham looked up. "Right now I am."

"Mr. Mancini's an important man," DiNunzio said.

"We're all important men."

"A *very* important man. An' I' wawnin' you…"

Graham stared daggers that withered the thug. A West Point grad and former captain in the storied 75th Ranger Regiment until he met up with a Taliban grenade, he had a zero bullshit policy. He moved with an assurance and graceful gait that almost concealed the limp he'd had after a grenade shrapnel shredded his leg.

"What's da story wit' his eyes?" DiNunzio demanded.

"At the moment they're not working," Graham said. "He's blind, at least for now."

"Madre di Cristo. Fix him!"

"It might be a good idea to find out why. You think?" he said, like he was talking to a dim child as he stared down DiNunzio.

The big man twitched, then backed off.

Graham picked up the chart and scanned Stacey's scribble.

"Where's the EKG?"

Stacey handed him the paper sheet.

"Doesn't appear to be cardiac."

"I thought the same," she said.

DiNunzio moved closer and shook a finger in Graham's face. "Look, lemme make dis clear. I don' want no amat'uhs on his case."

Graham's jaw tightened so hard that Stacey could swear she actually heard it. He saw himself rearing back and hammering this creep with a thunderous right hook to the jaw. The feel of the jawbone cracking, reverberating through his fist up his arm and down his spine. The joy of watching the bully's knees buckle and plummet like a tree falling and landing on the floor with a thud.

But he'd learned how to control the wild PTSD triggers. So he took a deep cleansing breath, he excused himself, and walked out into the main corridor.

Stacey saw exactly what was happening, and she knew Graham well enough to see he needed to give himself a little time out. Clearly, he didn't want to confront this creep and lay him out in front of his uncle. She was also sure he'd have the receptionist clerk alert the cops.

This DiNunzio SOB was a loose cannon if there ever was one. The words, the gestures, the whole demeanor. She'd seen his kind before, more than once.

Graham came back with an LED gooseneck and a cool, calm little grin on his extremely pleasing face. "Let's get this very important gentleman's clothes off," he said.

They pulled and cut off Mancini's clothing, and Stacey put a gown on him. The old blind man was scalded from head to toe, every square inch of his body redder than the sunburn from hell. His chest was forming large blisters, while the ones on his neck were already dark, meaning they were loaded with blood.

"What would do dat?" DiNunzio said. "Scahlet fever?"

"Interesting thought," Graham mumbled, "but that's usually kids."

"He looks like he's been bahbecued."

Graham ignored him, but he was right. Barbecued with a flamethrower. He bent over and peered at the skin up close. The areas without blisters were covered with thousands of red dots, a few larger than the head of a pin.

"Flat," he said as he felt them with the tips of his fingers.

"Possibly a rash?" Stacey asked.

"That's what I was thinking. At least where he's not blistered."

Mancini's lips were swollen as well.

"Stace, give me the light, will you please?"

Stacey shone a gooseneck lamp into Mancini's mouth, and Graham opened it. The entire inside lining was swollen.

"Sir, open your eyes," Graham said distinctly.

Mancini's lids fluttered, then opened. His eyes were fire engine red, the inner corners crusted with yellow-green pus.

"That's some case of pink-eye," Stacey whispered. "Almost like gonorrhea."

"What de fuck?" DiNunzio stomped his foot. "No fuckin' way. You tellin' me my Uncle Frank got clap in his eyes?"

"No," Graham said with exaggerated patience. "I seriously doubt it. But eyes with gonorrhea can look like this. Were they red this morning?"

"White as a baby's ass."

"That's very white," Graham said as he pulled out his stethoscope and listened to the lungs, then gave the liver a quick feel and tapped on the lower abdomen. "The bladder's distended. We'll have to catheterize him." He snapped on a rectal glove and squeezed some clear K-Y jelly onto the index finger.

"Stace, let's roll him over."

Stacey pulled him halfway over, while Graham lifted the sheet, pulled apart Mancini's buttock cheeks, and inserted his finger.

Despite his lethargic condition, Mancini winced and went rigid. Small wonder. The pink anal tissues were terribly swollen and badly blistered.

Graham took a stool sample for blood, then removed the soiled glove partway and shot it into the contamination pail slingshot fashion.

Looking at Stacey, he said, "We need blood work. Let's get a stat CBC and differential, a comprehensive metabolic panel, and an arterial blood gas. We should plug in an IV, too. Five percent dextrose and a quarter normal saline at 150 cc an hour."

Stacey hung up a plastic bag of IV solution, then punctured the man's left arm for blood while Graham tackled the right for the IV. He passed a thin plastic catheter into a vein, taped it, and connected its open end to the clear fluid hanging above.

Mancini didn't notice.

"I'll get the intern down here to finish the work-up," Graham said as he left for the front desk. "Why don't we catheterize him and send a urine specimen for chromatography. I doubt he's been poisoned, but you never know." Graham gave her a chummy smile.

"No, Dr. Kurland, you never do," Stacey said with a wry grin. "By the way, congrats on the double kidney."

"I had a great team," Graham deflected the praise with a shrug.

"But every great team needs a great star," she nodded like she knew exactly what she was doing and wasn't going to let him get away with not accepting her congratulations.

"Well," he said with a little nod. "Thank you."

Stacey grabbed a sterile catheterization tray from the glass cabinet on the wall and pulled a ceiling-mounted curtain around the patient. She heard Graham say a few words to the nephew as he left, but missed the drift.

She was one hundred percent sure, nonetheless, that he told Gigantor to back off.

Placing a blue tray on Mancini's chest, Stacey drew back the sheet to expose his penis. She put on sterile gloves, draped plastic with a hole centrally for the organ, then pulled back the uncircumcised foreskin. The accumulated sebum looked like rotten cottage cheese and had a spoiled milk odor that activated her gag reflex. Luckily, she knew how to shut that down quickly. She wiped the rancid mess away, then bathed the organ with Betadine solution.

The greased catheter slid in several inches until it met resistance. Mancini stiffened until she felt a pop as the plastic tube passed through his enlarged prostate.

Yellow urine flowed like a raging river. She saved several ounces in a sterile plastic cup for urine chemistry and a culture for bacteria, then connected the catheter to clear tubing that went to a plastic bag.

She hung the bag over the side of the stretcher and was stunned that it filled above the 1,000 cc mark, well over a quart. More than twice the normal bladder capacity.

Good thing the poor man was out of it. The pain had to be unbearable.

Stacey pulled back the surrounding curtain, only to discover DiNunzio glowering from the doorway. He seemed less agitated, but his stare made her shiver. It was like he was looking at her naked.

"What the fuck's goin' on. How's he doin'?" DiNunzio demanded.

Stacey took a breath and said, "He's stable for now. And most certainly in a lot less pain." She pointed to the bulging urine bag, then set the used catheter tray on the counter. "We'll be sending him to the floor and running a battery of more tests."

"I want 'im to have da best care money can buy."

"Don't worry. Dr. Kurland is the Chief Resident, and he is the best we've ever had. And Dr. McMann is the attending doctor on call. She'll be in charge. There's definitely no one better."

"So, what's wrong wit' him?"

"We're not sure yet, but the blood tests will help us make a determination."

"I heard da doc say pois'nin'."

"That's just speculation. But the lab work will be exhaustive and guide our diagnosis."

DiNunzio pulled his wallet from his back pocket and handed her a card. "Cawll me da secon' dere's a change in Mr. Mancini's condition."

"Of course."

"I'm gonna leave two men here wit' him, 'roun' da clock."

"They don't allow that."

"Who's dey?"

"You'll have to take that up with the hospital nursing supervisor."

"Den get 'er, God dammit."

Stacey sighed, reminded herself to stay professional, then dialed the number and handed the receiver to DiNunzio. She took Mancini's blood pressure and pulse, while DiNunzio barked like a rabid dog and had a terse conversation with her superior.

While doing busy work, she eavesdropped: "Senator Fumio…" "Yeah, da one on da Hospi'l Board… " "Hey, Mr. Mancini's life is *always* in danger…"

From what she heard, it sounded like DiNunzio's muscle would be staying.

Oh, happy day.

She stared at Frank Mancini's peaceful face.

Who the hell is this guy?

DiNunzio turned to leave, then stopped and looked her straight in the eyes with a glare that would curdle milk.

"Listen, Sweetcheeks. You tell da staff. No screw-ups. Or else." He ran a finger across his throat. International symbol for: I'll cut your fucking throat. "Youz got dat?"

Stacey nodded as goose bumps sprinted up and down her arms.

DiNunzio furiously strode out. She'd hustle the paperwork. With any luck, Mancini would be out of the ER in thirty minutes, tops.

And again she asked herself:

Who the hell is this guy?

Chapter Five

Pennsylvania Hospital ER

Eighth Street, Philadelphia, PA

Ralph DiNunzio snarled as he gunned his black Cadillac Escalade and it screeched out from the Emergency Room parking lot, dipping its chrome hubcaps halfway into a water-filled pothole. The splash threw an inescapable eight-foot wave at the face of a man in a worn three-piece suit about to enter the hospital.

"Jackass!"

"Yeah. Tell me about it." The uniformed Philadelphia cop next to the brown three-piece snickered as he watched the man brush off the filthy water.

Graham spied the two men and met them by the front door. "Gentlemen, thanks for coming. I'm Doctor Kurland."

"Sergeant Franco Rossi, Detective Division, Metro Police." The man in the brown suit looked up from his soaked suit to meet Graham's outstretched hand, then nodded over to the man next to him. "Officer Ryan."

The uniform remained silent, acknowledging Graham's greeting with a small nod.

"So, what's the problem here?" Rossi asked.

"Some mobbed-up joker came in with his uncle, scared the holy crap outta everybody, and threatened the staff. He and one of his thug buddies just pulled out when you were walking in." He looked at Rossi's suit. "They left a couple of other goodfellas."

"Uh huh."

"Anyway, security here tonight is a bunch of older fellows, and I thought they'd have a tough time if these assclowns caused trouble."

Rossi stuck his hands in his pockets and tried to suppress a yawn. "You get a name?"

"DiFabio… No. Uh, hang on…DiNunzio."

"Ralph DiNunzio?" Rossi said like he's been shocked with a cattle prod. "He's the patient?"

"No. The obnoxious nephew."

"Who's the patient?"

"Frank Mancini."

Rossi's eyes popped as he let out a low whistle, raised his eyebrows, and mouthed: *No shit.* "Where's he at?"

"Right inside."

Now Graham had the same thought as Stacey.

Who the hell is this guy?

"Can I see him?"

"Sure. We're just waiting for lab tests." Graham led the men to Mancini's ER bedside as DiNunzio's two associates quietly skulked down the hall.

Rossi looked at the sleeping man, and a satisfied grin brightened his dour mug.

Graham heard the guy give a little chuckle.

"You know who this is?" Rossi asked.

"I haven't the foggiest," Graham replied, even more curious. "Is he related to the Pope? Or maybe Tony Soprano?"

"Frank Mancini is one of the biggest hoodlums on the East Coast. He runs organized crime in Philly and South Jersey like that dictator, Kim Jock Face, the North Korean piss pot. He kills, extorts, tortures, I'm talking sick twisted shit."

"We've been after this SOB for years, but never got the goods on him. The sucker makes Jeffrey Dahmer look like a Cub Scout. And that bastard was a serial killer who ate his victims." Rossi smiled and rocked on his heels. "And now look at him, the miserable son-of-a-bitch."

Mancini opened his eyes and lifted his head in the direction of the new voice. Just as quickly, it collapsed back into the pillow, eyes staring lifeless, dead ahead.

Graham was shocked by the pleasure these two took in another man's suffering. "Sergeant, this man's in terrible pain. No matter who he is or what terrible things he's done, we treat everyone here with respect and humanity, and I expect you to honor that while you're here."

Rossi held up his hand to cut him off. His smile had vanished.

"I'm sorry, Doctor…Kurland, isn't it?"

"Yes."

Rossi motioned Graham to step outside the exam room.

"I'm not as heartless as I sounded. Let me tell you more to put it into perspective. One of our boys on the force, a good kid named Gleason, on narco undercover, stumbles onto Mancini's crew selling narcotics to high school kids. Nice way to make a buck, right? Mancini's thugs nabbed him, beat him senseless, then doused him with gasoline and burned him alive."

"That's awful. I'm certainly sorry, but everyone deserves—"

"Hear me out, Doc. They burned this kid over ninety-five percent of his body and then threw him in a dumpster. Left him for dead. By the time we found him the next day, he was covered with scabs that were oozing the worst crap you ever smelled. It would gag a maggot. Doc, I've seen some inhuman shit in my day, but this was the worst."

Graham couldn't quite figure out why this sounded so familiar.

Rossi took a deep breath. "And you know who gave the orders? That poor old man lying there in terrible pain."

"What happened to Gleason?"

"The doctors worked on him. How they got all those worms, or whatever they were, off him, I don't know. Anyway, they did. I watched that poor kid every day for five weeks, and I prayed to the Holy Mother for him to die. The suffering was… ungodly. I was happy when he vomited up half his blood and took his last breath. Then I only had to worry about his wife and little boy."

Rossi looked down, then up again at Graham. "Ya know why I had to worry about his wife and kid?"

"No."

"Because the bastard has families killed, too. Just to drive home the point that you DO NOT FUCK with Frank Mancini."

"When was this?"

"About four months ago."

"Was Gleason blind, too?"

"God damn right. The bastards gouged out his eyes with the flip top from a Fanta soda can. Never saw a thing again… How'd you know?"

"I took care of him."

Graham's shoulders collapsed as he felt sick to his stomach. No wonder the story sounded so familiar. He remembered being asked to see Gleason in consultation on the Gastroenterology Service last Spring.

The case was imprinted in his brain. Skin grafts, agonizing pain, screams, the putrid stench of infected flesh. He tacitly agreed. The young cop would have been better off if he'd died straightaway. Finally, mercifully, a gastric stress ulcer, the kind you get with a terrible burn, eroded into a blood vessel in his stomach and bled him dry.

"If this man and his thugs did all that, why aren't they in jail?" Graham asked, already suspecting the answer.

Rossi sneered. "Money. Get yourself a good enough lawyer, and you can get away with anything. Think about it. The kid couldn't identify anyone in a line-up. How are you gonna get witnesses to testify? Or a jury to convict someone like that? They're just law-abiding people who'd be scared to death of Mancini. Literally."

"I get it," Graham said. His brother Cody was a cop. Until some wretched scumbag shot him in the back and put a 9 mm copper-jacketed slug through his heart. His cop buddies turned the psychopath into a piece of Swiss cheese. But, oddly enough, it didn't stop Graham's agony one bit. There wasn't a day that he didn't miss Cody.

"But don't let that guide your treatment any," Rossi said with enough sarcasm to indicate that he wouldn't mind one bit if Mancini died a slow, miserable death.

Graham looked dead serious as he said, "Heal the sick and do no harm."

"That's the Hypocritic Oath, right?"

"Hippocratic."

"Maybe not in this case," Rossi said, "'cause if this rat fuck lives, more innocent people die."

Graham started to argue, then thought better of it, and walked back to Mancini. Rossi followed him in.

Mancini was peacefully sleeping. Hard to believe this frail old man was responsible for everything Rossi claimed. But having lived through armed combat for too many years, Graham knew you truly could never judge a book by its cover. He had a vivid flash of the young officer's tortured body and grimaced as the foul, haunting smell flooded through him. He could absolutely imagine DiNunzio and his thugs doing all that and more.

But how could anyone gouge out another human's eyes and then burn him alive? Shouldn't they suffer the way they'd made that kid suffer?

Graham knew he had to push aside his loathing. It seemed impossibly hard, but he was a man of honor who took his life-and-death oath very seriously.

And there was still something they were missing medically in the old bastard. This is exactly the kind of thing that would obsess Graham day and night until he solved the puzzle.

The hamster wheel in his brain was interrupted by the wall phone ringing.

"Lab, Dr. Kurland." The front desk clerk said.

"Thanks." He propped the phone against his shoulder with his chin. "Kurland here."

Graham's eyes popped open as he scribbled some numbers on Mancini's chart and whispered:

"Whoa!"

The receiver slipped from his chin and bounced off the floor. He yanked it up by the cord and put it back to his ear. "Did I hear that correctly? His pH is six point eight? Are you sure?" Graham listened, shook his head, and said, "Okay, thanks." Then hung up.

"Is that bad?" Rossi mouthed.

"Normal pH is seven point four. I've never seen a number that low in someone who's still alive."

Graham studied Mancini, his brain firing on all cylinders. This is the part he loved. Putting symptoms together endlessly until he heard something inside the lock click, a door in his mind opening, and he saw the blinding truth of a solution. Excitedly, he beckoned to Stacey, who walked in wheeling an automated intravenous setup.

"Stace, come here. Look at him. See anything abnormal?"

"Well, he's beet red, he's covered with blisters and pustules, he can barely move, he's confused, he's..."

"No, no. Look at his respirations."

"Not unusual. Maybe a little fast."

"Exactly. If his severe acidosis was caused by something like diabetic coma, they'd be deep and rapid."

"True. What do you conclude from that?"

"I don't know, but it's amazing he's still breathing. Let's hook up a line with sodium bicarbonate."

Rossi looked on while Stacey rummaged through the cabinet for the bicarb.

"Now this is justice," the cop said in a low voice.

Graham ignored the comment. But maybe he was right. There was a good chance he'd actually be saving lives if he let this torturous murderer die.

But he just couldn't. So he turned Mancini's head, held his lids open with one hand, and shone a flashlight into his eyes with the other and said:

"Look at this."

"What? What is it?" Stacey said with a bottle of clear fluid in hand. She and Rossi both moved closer for a better look.

"His pupils. They're large. Still fixed and no response."

"Nothing," she agreed.

"Sir, can you see my light?" Graham held the beam an inch from Mancini's eyes.

No response.

"SIR, CAN YOU SEE MY LIGHT?" Graham repeated the same, only louder.

With great effort, Mancini whispered, "I can't see squat."

Graham pocketed the flashlight and pulled a hand-held ophthalmoscope from the instrument rack on the wall. He looked into the back of each eye. "His optic nerve heads are swollen. Out of sight swollen. Pun intended."

"Increased intracranial pressure?" Stacey asked, as she looked, too.

"Good thought, Stace, that's why you're such a fan favorite around here."

"Thank you, Dr. Kurland," she said with a happy grin.

"Pressure on the brain looks like that, but it usually doesn't decrease vision for weeks to months. I can also see the retinal blood vessels pulsating. That frequently usually goes against high intracranial pressure."

Graham's brain started whirling again.

What the hell was this?

What if it were contagious?

They couldn't risk ignoring that.

But Graham also knew how quickly increased pressure in the brain could kill. It could push the brainstem out through the bottom hole in the skull, the foramen magnum. If that happened, they wouldn't have to worry about a low pH. His respiratory center would be crushed, and breathing would become an instant memory. This evil bastard would die on his watch.

In his mind's eyes, he saw his brother dead on the coroner's table. His fists clenched, his jaw tightened, and he wanted to punch something as hard as he could.

He let out a deep sigh.

Do no harm. That was his code. But to this ungodly abomination? The empty hole in Graham's soul ached.

In the end, he was a doctor. He couldn't ignore his duty. He had to do his job.

So back to the grindstone. Get more medical facts and more social history on Mancini the Murderer.

"Stace, let's get him up for magnetic resonance tomography of the brain to be sure. As soon as the bicarb is running." Graham picked up a phone. "I have a tickle, an itch, a hunch. But we need more tests. Grab extra tubes for blood work–blood cultures too."

"I'll give neurosurgery a heads up about the intracranial pressure. If that's what it is, he's their problem, not ours."

"If not," Graham said, "he's ours for better and for worse. We take him up to the Sixth Floor Medical ICU ASAP."

Stacey could hear Graham's preference by the tone of his voice.

He'd rather let the scumbag rot to death.

Chapter Six

Pennsylvania Hospital

Philadelphia, PA

"I hear the blind guy with the surface-of-the-sun blisters is a big-time mobster who'd kill your mom if there was a nickel in it," Harry Turner, the medicine intern assigned to the Mancini's case, breathlessly addressed Graham on the Sixth Floor just as Frank Mancini arrived by stretcher from Magnetic Resonance Imaging.

Graham gritted his teeth and pulled Harry aside. "Harry, if you talk like that about patients, we are gonna have a serious problem. Do you wanna have a serious problem with me?"

"Oh, yeah, sorry, no, actually you are the last person in the world I wanna have a problem with–"

"That's the smartest thing you've said in a long time, Harry." Graham leaned in and whispered confidentially. "Even though he *is* a big-time mobster who *would,* in fact, kill your mom if there was a nickel in it."

"Really?" Harry asked wide-eyed.

Graham put his finger in front of his lip. "Mum's the word."

Harry nodded, happy to be in on the skinny. Having just turned twenty-six, Harry was ten years younger than Graham. Abe Lincoln-tall and beanpole thin, disheveled red hair and matching freckles that numbered more than the dollars in the national debt. Congenitally good-natured,

Harry was always in a rush. To the lab. To microbiology. For conferences. Graham just wished he'd hurry up and get organized.

"It's a fascinating, strange case, I've never seen anything like it," Graham said with a puzzled tilt of his head. "A seventy-year-old man who was fine until this evening, when he developed a world-class big-time rash and suddenly went blind. His labs aren't all back yet, but he has a pH of six point eight."

"Sweet! What are you thinking?"

"Not sure yet. His optic nerves were massively swollen. I assumed increased intracranial pressure. But his cranial MRI was normal. So that's not it. We're back to GO, do not collect two hundred dollars."

"Is that bicarb hanging?"

"Yes. Check his pH again in about an hour in case he needs more."

Harry scanned the computer record and flipped through the pages. "With that kind of acidosis, is this guy in diabetic coma?"

"Already checked. He's not diabetic," Graham said without looking up from the hospital staff directory. He ran his finger down the page.

"Kyle, Kyle… Here it is. McMann, Kyle. 926-3033."

Just seeing her name made a warm wave of well-being wash through Graham. As he dialed her number, he had a flash of her working on a patient, completely absorbed, a top drawer world-class professional, at the top of her game, making a save on a patient who should've died. Then that look of joyful rapture that he knew all so well. That magical high of saving a life. He'd caught her eye right then, and they'd shared that moment that only a doctor in the trenches can appreciate. Her eyes were so bright and shiny that she glowed like the universe was shining a spotlight on her.

"Dr. Kurland, uh…"

Graham's blissful reverie was interrupted, and he sprang back into action, dialing the number on his cell. A click followed the fifth ring.

"Hello?" Her voice, dusky with sleep, sent a little shiver through him.

"Hi, Kyle, it's Graham Kurland. I'm sorry I woke you, but I desperately need your big brain."

A muffled yawn with a little chuckle. *Totally adorable*, Graham thought.

A big, sleepy smile crept across her face. He'd been on her radar for months. She knew this was probably a medical consultation and not a booty call. But a girl could dream, couldn't she?

"Sure, big guy, always happy to talk with you."

She meant it, he could tell, and he couldn't stop a smile from erupting all over his face.

Graham reiterated Mancini's history and clinical signs.

When he said *Mancini*, Kyle's heart stopped, and she had to stop a gasp of terror from jumping out of her mouth. Graham Kurland was a combination genius and bloodhound. When he got a sniff of a trail, he was relentless. The call went from dream to nightmare in a flash. She'd have to tiptoe through this minefield if she didn't want to blow herself and her friends up.

"Does he…have a fever?" she asked, trying to sound calm and measured.

"Not really. Oral temp's ninety-nine."

"How about the rest of his vitals?" She stalled while she tried to figure out a way of gently directing him away from the source of Mancini's affliction without making it obvious she was doing so.

"Not bad. Pulse of eighty, respirations eighteen. The crazy thing is, he's got a pH of six point eight."

"Wow. There aren't many things causing that degree of acidosis. Are his kidneys okay? Renal failure can do it." That might lead him down another path.

"They seem to be. Hold on a second." Graham flipped a couple of pages to the lab blood tests. "They're fine. His creatinine's normal."

"Scratch that idea." Graham Kurland had a reputation for being for a reason. She was going to have to tap dance as fast as she could to get him off their trail. "How about diabetes?"

"I thought of that. Glucose is 110. Couldn't be better."

Kyle yawned again to cover as her brain searched for a viable explanation for Mancini's bizarre series of symptoms.

"We thought maybe a metabolic screen for toxic agents," Graham said.

Kyle's central nervous system went haywire. This could be catastrophic. "What are you thinking about?"

"Wood alcohol, methanol poisoning. It can cause severe acidosis. Blindness too. I saw a case as an intern."

"Seems highly unlikely," she said in what she hoped was her most convincing voice.

"Yeah, you're probably right," he conceded.

"But let me know when the results come back." She knew she had to stay one step ahead of Graham. Which sounded frankly impossible given what a pro's pro the man was.

"Excellent," she sighed with deep relief. She'd managed to direct him away from them. For now. Good. "I guess great minds do think alike."

"Thanks. If that's the case, we'll give him an ethanol drip and stay with the sodium bicarb. Right?"

"Uh-huh. Run in that alcohol."

Graham shook his head. The ultimate paradox, drinking alcohol to combat the harmful effects of wood alcohol. But it made sense when you knew ethanol gobbled up the enzymes that turned the wood alcohol into poisonous formaldehyde.

It also gave you a nice drunk when it went in by vein. Not that Mancini would appreciate that right now.

"Get the lab values back ASAP," Kyle said. "If it's methanol, you should start peritoneal dialysis too."

"Thanks, Kyle. We'll get moving on it. I'll call you if anything new comes up. Sorry to wake you."

"That's okay. But that rash doesn't usually go along with the methanol. Get the dermatologists to check it out in the morning."

"Already did. Thanks again."

"You bet. Goodnight."

"Yeah, thanks, maybe, uh…" he was this close to asking her to get a beverage, or a meal, or anything really. Luckily, his cerebral cortex stopped that idea, reminding him what a boneheaded move that would be in the middle of a consult.

"What is it?" she asked, torn between imagining how nice it would be to get an invitation from the man and how weird it would be to get one right now. And thinking maybe this could be a good excuse to stick close to the good Dr. Kurland. If she played it right, it could be a win-win situation. Keep herself and her friends safe. And maybe spark a flame in Graham.

"Oh, nothing, it can wait. Go back to sleep, and thanks again, you're a lifesaver. Literally."

"Always happy to help, anytime, seriously," she said, imagining his big hands on her. That was the first thing she noticed about him when she watched him stitch up a vascular tear with shocking expertise. Those hands. Huge, strong, skilled.

As she hung up the phone, a sweet, dreamy smile took over her face while she descended back into sleep, hoping he'd be guest-starring in her dream.

She was such a sweetheart. Smart as a whip. Always ready to help, no matter how busy. Or how asleep.

Graham made an addition to his to-do list: ask Dr. Kyle McMahon out. Pronto. If not sooner.

He turned to his intern, Harry. "Get the setup for peritoneal dialysis. We need a couple of large plastic catheters, solutions, and an IV pole. Then call the lab to push them on that toxin screen. I think we've got methanol poisoning."

"Awesome, dude. Where'd he get that?"

"Who knows? Homemade booze, antifreeze, Sterno. Any number of places."

Graham and Harry walked in to see Mancini in the ICU next to the nurses' station. He'd need to be watched carefully after dialysis.

The procedure wasn't technically difficult. They'd push a large needle with a surrounding plastic tube, the catheter, through the stomach muscles into the abdominal cavity. Then they'd take out the needle and run fluid in and out through the catheter, over and over. The methanol would ooze into the fluid from the countless blood vessels in the bowel until it was mostly extracted.

Calculating the amount and composition of the fluid actually took longer than the insertion of the catheter. Graham looked at the numbers he'd scribbled on his notepad, then double-checked. He sat on the bed to speak with Mancini, while the nurse and Harry gathered the equipment.

"Mr. Mancini?"

No reply.

"Mr. Mancini!"

"Eh?" A raspy whisper.

"Mr. Mancini, did you drink any alcohol tonight?"

No answer.

"Mr. Mancini, wake up."

Graham shook him lightly. "Mr. Mancini!"

Harder.

Damn. No lid flutters. Nothing.

Forget it. They could explain when he came back around. This was an emergency.

Graham stuck his head outside the cubicle. "Harry, get in here quick, will you? He's getting worse. Any word from the lab?"

"They just called. Spot on, Sherlock. His methanol level was off the wall. Whatever made you think of that?"

"Sheer genius, Doctor Watson. Let's get going."

Graham turned to the young ICU nurse, adjusting Mancini's EKG leads.

"Lynn, give the pharmacy a call, please. Tell them we need an ethyl alcohol drip, STAT."

Harry pulled back the cover to expose Mancini's abdomen. He looked up at Graham and shrugged. "You know, ah, I've never done one of these before."

"Don't worry. A monkey can do it. Well, a trained monkey. Let's prep him first. We'll go just off midline in the lower left quadrant."

Harry gloved and scrubbed the exposed skin with brown Betadine solution, while Graham set up the needle and catheter.

"Alright, I think we're ready," Harry said, looking less than his usually confident self. "It's as sterile as it's going to get."

Harry injected a small amount of xylocaine under the skin, two inches below the navel. He raised a circular white welt an inch across. Even if he slipped back into reality, Mancini shouldn't feel much.

Harry held the needle over the welt and looked up. "Sure, you don't want to do the honors?"

"You got this, Harry, you're the man. Well, you're *a* man anyway." Graham said with a funny little shrug.

Harry laughed, releasing a ball of tension in his belly.

Just what the doctor ordered. Graham smiled, nodding with calm reassurance. "You got this, Harry, just go slowly until you feel a pop, then stop. That means you're into the peritoneal cavity surrounding the bowel."

"Okay."

Harry's hands trembled until he rested them on the patient's body. He positioned the stiletto-like needle perpendicular to Mancini's abdomen, then thrust forward, hard at first to penetrate the tough, reddened skin. He then slowly pushed it in with care, several inches, almost to the hilt.

"Uh, I still haven't felt a pop. This guy's so thin that I should be out of his back by now."

Graham leaned over Mancini's belly. Harry was right. They should have been well through the abdominal wall.

"Keep going, slowly. Any second you'll feel it."

"I'm meeting resistance. It feels hard." Harry looked up. "I think I've hit bone."

"Give a little suction and see what you get."

Harry pulled on the syringe attached to the catheter. Brown ooze flowed into the line. "Oh, shit."

Harry had that right.

Graham made an involuntary fist but stopped the impulse to chastise Harry.

It could only be one thing—liquid feces. Harry had perforated the bowel. Bacteria-laden shit waste would seep into the surrounding, sterile peritoneal cavity like Genghis Khan's hordes.

Not only did Mancini have a potentially lethal skin disease, on top of methanol poisoning. Now there was a decent chance they'd given him life-threatening bacterial peritonitis as well.

Harry stared in horror at the violated abdomen. "Sorry, I, Jesus, what is wrong with me, I'm such a–."

"Stop!" Graham said with as much empathy as he could muster. "Pull it out. We've got to try again. Why don't I take a shot?"

He moved two inches to the left of the original site. The needle penetrated the abdominal wall with a pop.

"I'm so sorry, Graham. I don't know what I did wrong, I—"

"Everyone makes mistakes, why shouldn't you? You know what that's from?"

"No," Harry mumbled, drowning in shame.

"Big Bird sings it on Sesame Street," Graham said, deadly serious.

Harry smiled. Then he laughed. Just what the doctor ordered.

"Be the canary. Forget it. It's as much my fault as yours. Could have happened to anybody with his screwed-up skin. In the meantime, we need antibiotics. Put him on eighty mg of rifaximin. It should kill the gram-negative bacteria that get out of the bowel. But we'll also get daily blood cultures."

"You got it."

"I'll ask the bowel surgeons to look and see if they want to sew up the perforation. Don't feel bad, okay? The more patients you treat, the more you'll realize that shit happens. In this case, literally."

Another smile from Harry.

"Yeah." It was hard for Harry to appreciate the unintended pun.

"Thank you, Graham. For real."

"My pleasure. Promise me that one day you'll pass it forward to some eager newbie who messes up and won't stop punishing himself."

"I promise," said Harry, like he really meant it.

Graham walked back to the front desk. His cerebral cortex weighed all the evidence and came up with a conclusion. Right now, they should just watch. The hole would most likely close on its own. But since he was on a medicine rotation, protocol meant that he should contact the surgeons. Because if Mancini got worse, it would be in the surgical ballpark.

Damn.

The bowel was a bacteriological zoo, home to over thirty trillion bacteria.

Some of the worst microbes known to man lived in the gut. With just that little prick, millions, make that billions, escaped into the surrounding sterile peritoneal cavity where the stomach and intestines lay.

And of all people. A gangster with a pathological nephew the size of Rhode Island.

Or he could do everyone a favor and just let the sick fuck die.

Well, nobody ever said medicine was perfect.

They had to fix it. They'd faced worse problems than this.

But it was hard to remember when.

Chapter Seven

South Philadelphia, PA

2:58 am

Protected in the shadows from the South Philadelphia streetlight, Nate Champion and Randy White, both topping 6'3", buff and ripped, decked out in dark nylon running pants and black hoodies, surveyed the two-story, late 19th-century brownstone.

From a distance, they appeared identical. But if you looked close up, you'd see that Nate was the color of milk chocolate and had a nasty scar behind his left jawbone, while Randy had skin like a peach and ice-blue eyes so sharp it almost hurt to look at them. They seemed to be the kind of guys who could kill with one finger.

Because they were.

The brownstone stood undistinguished among its neighbors. A bare ten feet separated it from a twin on the right, and the same distance from a small grocery on the left. Located across the street, the architecture was the same turn of the nineteenth century.

If you'd put ten Philadelphia houses in a police line-up, you would have never picked this plain-Jane one as the home of a mob chieftain. But a low profile had always been a priority for Frank Mancini. Opulent ostentation was best left to the country estate, out of view of the public eye.

The last rays of the setting moon reflected off parked cars, waxing and waning with the clouds. Except for the occasional low-pitched hum of an eighteen-wheeler heading for the food distribution center on Oregon Avenue, the street was dead.

Nate and Randy leaned their heads together. Nate pointed to a back door in the left alley. Randy nodded his head in agreement.

Nate stepped from the safety of the shadows and crossed the street in a flash, a small satchel under his arm. In an instant, the darkness between the buildings and his matching complexion swallowed him up. Slowing as he silently approached the back door, he stopped to adjust his earwig.

"All quiet," he said in a low voice.

"Here too, Nate," his lookout said. "Go for it."

Randy adjusted his night vision goggles, then reached into the satchel and removed two thin metal rods from it. He inserted them into the lock and rotated until there was a soft click.

It was quiet in the kitchen.

No burglar alarms.

No flashing lights.

Not even a dog.

This house didn't need them. The mere knowledge of who lived there was more than enough protection. Only a fool with a death wish would attempt to penetrate or violate Frank Mancini's home.

But the two ex-Navy Seals were no fools. And they did not share a death wish.

The rooms were dark. Nate was familiar with the interior from his previous visits, but even so, he crept toward the front with extreme care. From the kitchen in the back, through the dining room, to the living room by the street.

He looked out a window, caught a moving shadow, and pulled back.

Hell. A damn dog scavenging garbage.

Nate picked the lock on the liquor cabinet, studied the bottles in the case, and frowned.

"Bad news," he whispered to his partner out on the street, "it's not here."

"You're kidding."

"I wish."

"Keep looking. No way we're leaving empty-handed."

"All quiet upstairs?"

"Copy that."

Nate turned his back to the front window, looked at the center stairway through the doorway to his left, and then straight ahead. The kitchen was on the other side of the dining room. He could still make it through both rooms and out the way he came.

Should he try?

It was now or never.

But that damn bottle…

The light switched on in the foyer at the bottom of the stairway and lit up part of the living room where he stood. Nate disappeared into the shadows toward the dining room and froze.

Footsteps were already at the bottom of the stairs.

Too late for escape through the dining room and kitchen.

Was she headed for the living room? Or would she go back to the kitchen through the center hallway?

Emily Mancini stopped and yawned at the bottom of the stairs. Nate held his breath until she rounded the corner and continued through the center hall into the kitchen. She picked up a telephone and punched in a number.

"Helen, it's me. I couldn't sleep. Ralph hasn't called about Frank. I wondered if you'd heard anything."

The receiver almost exploded in Nate's ear. "Nate, you okay?"

He didn't dare speak. Instead, he pressed the silent button on his watch. One buzz meant mission still in progress, two signaled abort, and three meant get me the hell out ASAP.

Mrs. Mancini hung up the phone, opened the refrigerator, then slammed the door shut.

From his view at the edge of the living room shadows, Nate was surprised at her appearance. Slender, dark hair, attractive. Unlike Mancini, she wasn't anywhere near seventy. It was a stretch to think she was fifty. Not at all what he'd expected for the old man's spouse. The trophy wife?

Nate remained silent and statue-still, hoping to God she wouldn't wander into the living room.

Damn it all. Go back to bed.

The two previous trips had gone so well, the last only seventy-two hours ago.

The ticking of the mantel clock sounded thunderous in the otherwise silent house. Nate's heart pounded, two beats per click, the sound radiating up to his ears. It was so loud he was afraid she could hear it too. He took three deep breaths and told himself not to go all *Tell Tale Heart*.

The noise in the kitchen stopped.

Nate stiffened.

Where was she?

He strained for a clue as he plastered his back against the wall.

Mrs. Mancini stepped into the dining room and then the living room, where Nate was.

This was it.

He was finished.

He clutched his satchel against his chest in the shadows, trying to decide what to do with her.

But she walked right past him, across the room to the front window.

Nate tried to disappear. He failed. He struggled to push himself further into the wall, a useless endeavor. She was ten feet away, staring out onto the street. He was still as a rock.

"You son of a bitch," she whispered. "The people whose lives you destroyed. God is giving you justice."

She turned and looked right at Nate. "You bastard."

Did she see him?

Did he dare move?

Did he dare not?

He tensed, ready to spring.

But he held, praying she hadn't adjusted to the darkness.

She walked back toward the dining room and kitchen. Right past him.

He let out a long breath, his heart thumping through his chest, the beats so fast he couldn't count them.

The kitchen light dimmed, then disappeared. He could hear her footsteps going from the kitchen, through the center hallway, and up the stairs. Finally, the light in the bottom foyer went out.

Nate was drenched in sweat. His pits were soaked.

He continued the search hard and fast, sparing no cabinet or drawer, taking great care to leave everything looking untouched.

What if they couldn't find it? There was a good chance they'd all be fucked. What would the consequences be?

He was down to the last cabinet and thinking maybe God wasn't on their side.

He opened the door, and his heart skipped a beat. There it was. His Holy Grail. A bottle of Johnny Walker Blue. Mancini's favorite, the bottle he shared with no one. At two hundred bucks a fifth, it was the prince of scotches. At least the evil old bastard had taste.

He held the bottle up to the light of his flashlight and smiled. A quarter gone. This was it. He opened his brown satchel and removed a substitute duplicate filled to a similar level.

No one would ever know.

Nate left through the back door but stopped in the alley when he heard a car on the street. He leaned into the shadows against the wall.

What now?

He strained around the corner for a peek.

A dark Cadillac had pulled up to the curb. Ralph DiNunzio, Mancini's nephew and now capo, climbed out from the front passenger seat and spat a two-ouncer onto the sidewalk. He didn't recognize the other three, probably soldiers in the organization.

Great. Just freaking great.

The guy was a prick on steroids. A violent prick to boot. With a .44 magnum hair trigger, he had the compassion of a black widow in heat.

"Stay low, Nate," Randy said. "I'm here if you need me."

Nate leaned back and heard them walk up to the front porch a dozen feet away. The group stopped in unison. There was a click, a spurt of light, then the smell of cigarette smoke.

"Lou, I got dis weird feelin' 'bout my uncle."

"Whaddaya mean?"

"There's lotsa people who'd like to see Frank Mancini get whacked."

"True. But I t'ink he hadda stroke. Don'choo?"

"Stroke patients don't look like dat. Dey said so at da hospi'l."

"Dey don't know everyt'ing. Same t'ing happ'ned to my Uncle Cosmo. He woke up blind one mornin', never saw nuttin' again."

DiNunzio tapped his finger on his lips. "Maybe."

"You don' believe me, do ya?" Lou asked.

"Nope."

"Yer paranoid, Ralph."

"Dat's my job. Anywayz, dey said at da hospital dat strokes don't cause no bad rashes or burns. People usually get numb or weak. Keep yer ears open. Squeeze as many balls as you need to. I'm gonna have a tawk wit' a buddy of mine, Jerry Frondizio. He's dis hotshot internis' at Harvard. Gemme his number firs' t'ing in da mawnin'."

"Sher t'ing, bawss."

DiNunzio rang the doorbell, then smacked the cigarette out of a minion's hand. The butt hit the sidewalk and sent up a shower of red sparks. "Stinking weed," he hissed. "What the fuck's wrong wichew?" he hissed, "You know how she hates 'em,"

The porch light switched on, and the door opened.

"Em'ly," DiNunzio said. "Frank's in da hospital. Dey're stabilizin' him now."

"Come in, please." Mrs. Mancini ushered the four men inside.

Nate waited for a nanosecond, then bolted out of the shadows. Discovery meant he might have to terminate the entire group. Particularly since these lowlifes lived in a vengeful world, cutting off limbs, heads, and genitals for a lot less than what they were doing.

Chapter Eight

Pennsylvania Hospital

Philadelphia, PA

Kyle's head throbbed with a migraine from Hades as she tried to stop thinking about Graham Kurland discovering their plot and exposing them to the world. And DiNunzio. She called the lab and found out the results of the methanol test, but knew the source was untraceable.

Graham was working with her this morning, and she was scared. But also excited. Maybe they'd take their flirtation to the next level. The thought brought a smile to her eyes, and her head calmed a little.

It was their day to be at the Medical Clinic, a Jekyll and Hyde misnomer if ever there was one. It was slowly falling apart, and Kyle knew it needed an internal head-to-toe makeover.

The outside waiting area was Lord and Taylor chic—royal blue carpeting complemented by rose wallpaper and French impressionist reprints. To further throw them off guard, the enticing fragrance of a potpourri wafted through the air.

Main Line clientele were seated on the plush beige sofas, along with their less financially blessed South and North Philly counterparts. Overhead, the soft tones of Mozart drifted from the ceiling speakers at a pleasing decibel level.

But beyond the glass doors lay the domain of the exam rooms. Half a dozen, all clones courtesy of a thrifty administrator with the aesthetics of a drill sergeant, they boasted astonishing austerity.

Each room had a large, round generic business clock with an ivory face and oversized hands to remind you that time was just creeping by. There was a single wooden chair, and a black examination table covered with starched white paper. Stainless steel stirrups, compliments of a sixteenth-century Inquisition overseer, waited for the next victim.

No other furniture, only a sad pseudo-porcelain sink and a dispenser with urine-colored soap mounted on the wall. The only saving grace was in Room Two. Somehow, a Rockwell painting of an adorable small towhead with her dolly in the office of the kindly family doc managed to sneak in and hang lopsidedly on the plaster wall.

Every two weeks, staff members donated a morning to instruct the fledgling physicians on their internal medicine rotations. It was hard not to smile at their naiveté. They were smart kids. They just hadn't mastered the crossover from books to clinical practice. She remembered those uncomfortable days all too well. Being unprepared, freezing as she faced the catastrophe of her brother's bloody death. So she made damn sure she hadn't let anything slip through the cracks.

It was Kyle's turn to teach. Today, it was third-year medical students for the Intro to Physical Exam—shining lights, poking, probing into every possible orifice. They learned by doing it on each other so they could appreciate what it was like to walk in a patient's shoes.

She sighed as she imagined Graham Kurland striding in with her this month. He was the finest Chief Resident she'd seen in her three years here. Staff and peers all agreed. Brilliant, empathetic, with a work ethic from the Industrial Age, he was modest and humble as the day was long, despite it all. And yes, she had to admit, a dishy dreamboat to boot.

They'd been lucky to get him at Pennsylvania Hospital, particularly with how Mass General gave him the hard sell. He was one of a long line of superb house officers from the military, actually a decorated ex-Army Ranger, with multiple medals. Team players, they were enthusiastic, respectful, ready to take calculated risks, yet firm when necessary. Also unshakeable, even when the shit was flying thick and fast. And always willing to give a hundred and ten percent.

Speak of the Devil, there he was. Their eyes locked, and she felt a jolt in her brain, heart, belly, and several other regions. He tried to hide how happy he was to see her. He failed.

"Dr. McMann," he said with mock formality as he nodded his unkempt head. "So pleased to see you."

"Dr. Kurland," she said with the same playful faux formality, like they were in on the same joke, "The pleasure is all mine."

And then it hit her. She had to stop him from getting to the bottom of Mancini's malady. No matter what the cost.

She hid the pain that bolted back into her skull. She was good at hiding her pain. She'd been doing it ever since she believed she'd killed her brother Brian with her gross negligence.

"Everything okay?" Graham asked with a sweet smile.

"Never better," Kyle lied. "Did you get the lab results back? For the methanol?"

"Yes, they were positive," he said. "But the dermatology thing is still a mystery."

She suppressed a deep sigh of relief that he hadn't figured out what was going on. Yet. "Any change in his condition?"

"He's deteriorating," Graham said. "He's a real...piece of work."

"Is he?" Kyle said like she didn't already know.

"Oh yeah," Graham said. "The worst."

"Shall we?" she asked.

"We shall," he replied, eyes shining bright.

The students generally separated into male and female groups for the practical sessions. It wasn't hard to stay detached and relate to patients in a professional manner. It was a whole different ball of wax, however, when you were on the receiving end of a pelvic or prostate exam from a classmate, particularly when they were the opposite sex.

Graham worked with the four men in one room while Kyle took the three women across the hall.

The women finished early, so Kyle walked over to check on the men, stopping by the Ladies' Room first to splash water on her face and put on a fresh coat of lip gloss. Just because she sat at the top of the food chain didn't mean a girl couldn't look her best. And if she was being brutally honest, she wanted to look her best for the one and only Dr. Graham Kurland.

While plotting about how to gently lead him away from curing Mancini and let the scumbag die slowly and painfully.

The male students, all in their socks and undershorts, looked up with nervous smiles. Kyle felt like she had just stepped into a men's locker room. A little grin slipped onto her lips. She quickly made it disappear.

She spotted Graham as he spotted her, and he shot her a little grin of his own. She felt a flock of butterflies fluttering in her stomach.

"How're we making out here?" she asked him.

"Great," Graham said, then turned to his half-clad students. "You men feel ready to face genitals in all kinds of distress?"

They snickered, chuckled, smiled, and mumbled that they were indeed.

"Questions?" he asked.

None were forthcoming.

"Troops dismissed," Graham said. She gave him the nicest smile he'd gotten all week.

They thanked him and began to re-robe themselves.

"Good," Kyle said. "Let's go see the man you called me about last night."

"Sure." He stepped out with her for a few seconds.

"How's he doing?" she asked.

"Not great. He's in the ICU." Graham gave a frown that displayed his small, mild cleft lip scar. He was self-conscious about it, for sure. Little did he know that the Pennsylvania Hospital female contingent, to a person, agreed it accentuated his military mystique and made him even hotter than he already was.

She found her eyes lingering on his hands again, imagining them on her skin. She took a breath and reigned herself back in. Take care of business, get Mancini to the morgue, and then navigate her way into Dr. Kurland's good graces and big, handsome hands.

"Let's go now," Kyle said. "I'm in kind of a rush."

Warm weather and packed elevators, always such a pungent combination. Kyle held her breath as the elevator rose at an inch per second, then gasped for air when the doors opened on the Sixth Floor.

They entered the ICU. Graham printed several pages from Mancini's chart on the computer, and together they headed down to his room.

"Any improvement?" Kyle asked.

"Some." Graham flipped a couple of pages as they walked, then entered the room. "The dialysis helped, though he's still confused. But they say he's better than last night."

Kyle stood over the patient. "Mr. Mancini?"

Nothing.

Even in the dim light, the man looked like he'd been on the receiving end of a neutron blast. Mancini turned toward her with a directionless look.

She waved an inch in front of his open eyes.

Not even a blink.

Kyle rested her hand on his shoulder. "Mr. Mancini."

"Yeah?"

"Mr. Mancini, this is Dr. McMann. Do you know where you are?"

"Where?"

"In Pennsylvania Hospital. What year is it?"

"Fifty-two."

She looked at Graham skeptically. "Better?"

Graham shrugged. "At least he's talking."

Kyle pointed to Mancini's chest, where his hospital gown parted. "What did the dermatologists say about his skin?" She thought for a moment and had a flash of what might lead Graham down the wrong path. And Mancini to his grave. "I'd guess toxic epidermal necrolysis."

"Good guess. They thought the same. I've never seen a case."

This was better by the minute. "You never want to. I had a couple during my residency." Kyle turned her head and softened her voice. "Unfortunately, they both died from severe infection."

"There's no history of drug use, though. Doesn't that make you wonder?"

"Somewhat. But I've seen this in patients who never touched a drug in their life." Kyle bit her lower lip. Toxic epidermal necrolysis was often drug-related, most commonly coming from the use of sulfonamide drugs. "Were the derm people convinced?"

"Not a hundred percent. But they said it was pretty classic."

"They're the experts."

Graham leaned closer to inspect the skin. "The lighting's different here. But I think there's a change from last night…"

He walked to the blinds, opened them wider, then returned to the bedside.

"Definitely more blisters." He lifted the gown and pointed to Mancini's left thigh. "That area was diffusely red last night. Now it's raised as well."

Kyle grimaced as the light hit her eyes and the headache blasted into her cranium.

"You okay?" Graham asked with obvious concern.

"Yeah, just a headache, I'm fine."

"Are you?"

She loved the care in his voice.

"Yes." She gave him a smile to reassure and thank him, then got back to work. "But this points us back to toxic epidermal necrolysis. Skin changes can just be the tip of the iceberg if blisters are already developing. Let's get dermatology back again. Anything else I should know?"

Graham stepped back from the bedside and avoided her gaze. "There is one other thing…"

"What's that?"

"When we put in the peritoneal catheter for dialysis, we perforated his bowel."

Kyle grabbed his arm and pulled him into the hallway. "Run that by me again?" she said in a loud whisper.

"We perforated his bowel with the inserting stylet."

"That's what I thought you said. How do you know?"

"Liquid feces came back through the catheter. No excuses. It was my fault."

"You did that?" she asked with disbelief dripping from her voice.

"Well," he waffled, "it was my intern, but I was in charge, so…"

"Harry?" she asked.

"I'd rather not say," he said, though it was obvious he was covering for his young charge. Kyle loved how he took the bullet for the mistake of his underling. Yup, the buck stopped with Dr. Kurland. "Then what?"

"We reinserted it. He has antibiotics running in the infusion fluid."

"Oh boy."

She sounded sad, but she was gleeful inside. No way would this douchebag survive a perforated bowel, on top of the shitstorm she'd unloaded on him. Talk about adding insult to injury. She walked back to Mancini and pressed on his stomach. Not a normal soft belly, but not the rock-hard feeling of bacterial peritonitis… yet. She pulled the sheet back up over his body, then turned away.

"I just hate it when things like that happen." *Except to evil bastards like this one.* "We'll have to watch him like a hawk." She rested her palm on the back of Graham's hand.

Again, a jolt of pheromones bolted through her.

He loved how her hand felt on his.

Then they remembered they were at work and pulled back.

"Did you call the surgeons?' She stopped and realized what she'd said. "Sorry, you're a surgeon."

"I called them anyway. For political correctness. They'll be by soon."

"Let me know what they say."

"I will. I think they'll just watch. We have him on antibiotic therapy, and he appears to be responding."

"Good."

Kyle headed toward the door, then stopped and turned. Graham was biting the inside of his cheek and needlessly checking Mancini's pulse.

She could see how much he cared. Even for a scumbag like Mancini.

She felt something warm melting inside her.

"Come here." She nodded from the doorway.

Graham walked over.

"You and Harry both did your best. Some days you unscrew your navel, and your butt falls off. It happens. We'll get through this together. Okay?"

"Thanks, Kyle. I appreciate that."

"We're a team. You know that better than anyone. And Harry learned a valuable lesson today.

"Yeah," Graham said. "Don't fuck it up.

"Words to live by," Kyle smiled.

At least Graham was a quality act. The highest quality.

"Here, give me a hug."

They embraced for a glorious five seconds.

Kyle's head stopped aching.

Graham sighed like he wished it could last forever.

She stared into his eyes for a blissful second before turning what could have been a soft kiss into a sudden one-eighty back toward the office.

And the headache was back with a vengeance. Pushing on the pain-wracked, quarter-sized spot over her left temple, hammering at DEFCON 1, she wondered when her skull would explode into confetti.

Peritonitis.

From their procedure.

Damn!

Ben Franklin, Pennsylvania Hospital's founder, said there were only two things certain in life: death and taxes.

True.

But there was a hidden third one in medicine:

WHEN YOU WERE CAPTAIN OF THE SHIP,

ALL SHIT ROLLED DOWNHILL…

TO YOU.

Chapter Nine

Pennsylvania Hospital

Philadelphia, PA

Harry Turner suppressed a retch as another sheet of Mancini's outermost layer of skin, the epidermis, hung from his outstretched hand.

He'd been trying to reattach it to its underlying skin layer, the blood-vessel-filled dermis, when it separated from the old man's upper arm. Without the protective epidermis, armies of gas-producing bacteria marauded through the remaining vulnerable layers in a headlong drive to sweeter internal organs.

At least the sloughing was painless, or Harry would have heard about it in a big way.

It had been three weeks since they admitted Mancini. His dialysis was finished, and it looked like he wouldn't have complications from the bowel perforation, thank goodness. The surgical team had agreed with Graham that the hole in the bowel would close on its own. And it did. But Harry hadn't slept more than an hour straight until then.

Graham never told him until yesterday, but he noticed similarities in Harry's behavior to that of men in the field who had just shot their first enemy. Post-traumatic stress syndrome, complete with nightmares, guilt, easy startling, alterations in arousal, and overall numbness.

Generally, the most easy-going kid on the block, Harry had practically ripped off a new nurse's head for giving a drug an hour late. And not even a critical one. Then he'd felt guilty and couldn't stop apologizing. Fortunately, Graham also gave Harry some coping mechanisms that would help him deal with his PTSD. He had full faith that Harry would use the techniques and learn to manage his disorder.

Mancini was still stone blind but had regained his mental faculties, much to Harry's dismay. Hard to be an abusive racist or threatening torture and painful violence when he was out of touch with reality. The vicious verbal violence was now unbearable. But he knew that part of the job was learning how to bear it.

Harry stared at the confluent red sores that were once covered by skin on Mancini's trunk and limbs. Green pus oozed from all but the most recent lesions, and they reeked like meat rotting in a garbage heap.

The bandages and antibiotic creams were losing the battle to repel a massive onslaught by Pseudomonas aeruginosa, the dreaded bacterial species that made an all-you-can-eat smorgasbord of burn victim flesh. Its enzymes sliced through tissues like Superman on crystal meth.

Mancini groped for Harry before grasping his forearm with a gnarled hand.

"Doc, how'm I doin'?" he asked with a thick, old-world accent.

Harry cleared his throat. "I'd say it, uh, looks about the same as yesterday."

Mancini shook the railing and the bed. "The same? You're full of it, asshole. *Mangia merda e morire!*"

"Pardon?"

"Eat shit and die, you little *finocchio*! Get dem other doctuhs in here. Or my boys are gonna stomp yer bawlls like grapes."

Harry left the dressings half-finished and went to wash his hands. He did pity the man. On the other hand, the more he read about him, the more he despised him. His own father was one of the FBI's 91 "Service Martyrs," agents who died during an adversarial action. It happened when he was four, and Harry could hardly remember him.

Graham walked onto the floor and studied Harry, then joined him at the stainless-steel sink. He could feel how disturbed and rattled Harry was.

"You okay?"

"Yeah," Harry replied flippantly—and unconvincingly, "sure, absolutely."

"Really?" Graham asked like he already knew the answer to the question.

"Oh, uh," Harry paused, his shoulders dropping and the air draining out of him. "No, not really."

"What's going on?"

"It's Mancini. He looks like hell, smells like a cesspool, and now he's threatening me."

"Jesus Christ!" Graham exploded.

"Maybe that's who we should call. He may be the only one who can stop his fucktards from doing something unpleasant to my family jewels."

"I've had it with this bullshit. Come on. Let's straighten this shitbird out."

Graham strode into Mancini's room and stopped dead in his tracks. He swallowed twice, his anger bleeding out like a ruptured aorta.

"Mr. Mancini, it's Dr. Kurland. What's the matter?"

"Doc, you gotta take care of dis shit. I don' want no lackeys practicin' on me."

Harry opened his mouth but said nothing. Graham beat him to it.

"Sir," Graham said cold, hard, and sharp, "this is one of the finest hospitals in the country, and Dr. Turner is no lackey. He's my associate and a very talented doctor." He paused for effect. Harry basked in the praise. "Of course, if you'd like us to transfer you to another service, Dr. Turner and I would be more than happy to oblige."

Harry never heard Graham talk this way to a patient. But then Mancini was not a typical patient. Harry did want to help the man, but being threatened made an impossible job hopeless.

"I wanna see. If I ain't gonna get no better, I gotta get outta here. Now! *Avete capito?*"

"I understand. And I want you to know that we're doing our very best. We've gotten the methanol out of your system, but it's done considerable damage. In all honesty, Dr. Ramos, the ophthalmologist, thinks there's only a small chance you'll regain your vision."

Harry saw this for the teachable moment it was. Even though Mancini was the worst of the worst, Graham did not dash the man's last shred of hope. The one chance in a million that every patient clung to.

In fact, Harry had talked with Ramos. The man was stone blind. He couldn't see an A-bomb blast in a coal mine at midnight. It was as certain as time itself. But to crush him now would be like driving the stake deeper into Dracula's chest.

Mancini's shoulders slumped, and he dropped into his pillows. "Okay, doc, I'll see ya later." His voice trailed off to mumbling in Italian.

"One last thing," Graham said. "No more threats. No more abuse. No more of your nasty bullshit. We're doing the best anyone can. Dr. McMann and our team are some of the best doctors in the country. Any more of your bullshit and we're through with you. *Avete capito?*"

Mancini nodded and waved Graham out, acknowledging his agreement.

"Thanks for setting him straight," Harry said as they left the ICU.

"One day, you're going to see some douchebag abuse somebody working under you and do the same thing. We need to have each other's backs."

Harry was touched. Reassured. "Thanks."

"Mancini's a monster. And it's just a matter of time until those bacteria eat him up alive. They're digesting the skin right off his body, and they'll do the same to the rest of his organs."

"Maybe we should change the antibiotics," Harry suggested.

"Reasonable thought. But the bacterium's sensitive to gentamicin. It's not the antibiotic. It's like we're trying to hold back Niagara Falls with a fishnet. He has bacteria everywhere. When they get into tissues with poor blood supply, like cartilage, bone, and tendons, the drugs don't penetrate."

"I know."

Graham held open the double swinging doors at the entrance of the ICU for a regal woman in a gray skirt and white blouse.

"Mrs. Mancini," Graham said.

"Dr. Kurland, Dr. Turner. How's Frank? Is he any better?"

"I'm afraid he still can't see," Graham said. "The methanol's out of his system, but the optic nerves from his eyes to the brain are badly damaged beyond repair."

"Will he get *any* sight?"

"Very doubtful."

"I see."

"His skin is also breaking down further, and we're worried about the infection. I'm concerned overall."

The woman blinked but demonstrated no other external signs of distress. "Okay. Well, thank you, doctors. I think I'll go visit."

"Please call if you have any questions."

She nodded, and they watched her walk down the hall.

"Not what I'd call an outpouring of emotion," Harry commented.

"No doubt about that," Graham agreed.

"Think she's in denial?"

"Maybe. We see it often enough." Graham stopped and thought for a moment. "But maybe…"

Harry leaned in and whispered, "She doesn't give a shit."

"And who could blame her?"

Chapter Ten

Ninth Street by Wills Eye Hospital

Philadelphia, PA

The leaves were turning shades of red, orange, and yellow by the third week of September, and Mancini was closer to death by the hour. It had been over four weeks since his admission to the ICU, and the stream of relatives and friends had slowed until his wife and nephew were his only visitors.

Ralph DiNunzio slipped around the front curtain and entered his uncle's room unannounced. He stood by Mancini's bedside and watched him sleep. The old man seemed peaceful enough, but DiNunzio knew the blindness was killing him, even worse than the skin.

He was sinking into a solitary world and taking it out on anyone and everyone. Two days ago, Tommy Galotti had been slow returning from the lobby with a newspaper. Now, Tommy was two floors down, recovering from broken knees.

He didn't want to do it, but Frank had ordered it. And it made him happy, at least for an hour or two.

DiNunzio punched his cupped palm with a fist. Why did he want a fucking paper anyway? He couldn't even read it.

But blood was what counted. You were born into it, and you couldn't buy it for all the money in the world. Frank Mancini had looked after him for years. Now it was his turn to pay the old man back.

"Uncle Frank, I don't know who did this," DiNunzio whispered, "but I swear on my mudder's grave we'll get da bastards if it takes da res' of my life."

The police could find no evidence linking anyone to Mancini's dilemma. But DiNunzio knew better. It was the Carluccis, genetic bottom-feeders. No doubt about it. Though he lacked the evidence to throw the whole underworld into a bloody war, particularly when Cousin Vito in Chicago said to go slow.

Dr. McMann stepped into the room with three interns, stopping short as she caught DiNunzio's glare. She hid the great satisfaction he felt that Mancini was knocking on heaven's door. Or more likely, hell's door.

She stopped short as she was caught by DiNunzio's glare.

"Youze here to see my uncle?"

"Yes, we are." She came forward like the professional she was and extended her right hand.

DiNunzio hesitated, then shook it. "Can I talk to youze for a minute?" he said. "In private."

"Certainly. Let's step outside."

"What's goin' on here, Doc? I get cawled outta town for a week an' he's worse."

"I'm afraid he's developed a severe skin infection."

"What are dose oozin' scabs on his face?"

"They're covering pus."

"Will they get better?"

"I hope," she lied like she really meant it.

"Don't bullshit me, Doc, gimme da real story. How da ya know?"

"The reality is, I don't know. No one does. But we've got him on the strongest IV antibiotics known to kill the bacteria causing them."

"Why'z his arms and legs all bandaged up?"

"To keep in antibiotic ointment where he has no skin."

"He looks like shit."

"His condition is like someone with fourth-degree burns over ninety-five percent of their body."

DiNunzio's eyes narrowed. "BA burns, huh? So, what da fuck's gonna happen to 'im?"

"It's hard to say. He's extremely ill. And I don't know whether he's going to survive or not."

"I heard of a guy who had burns like dis. He gotta bad infection, den he t'rew up blood. Den he died."

"Burn patients can develop gastrointestinal bleeding. He's on medicines to try to prevent that."

"Doc, I tawked to a guy who knows a guy, and he said Frank prolly went blind from wood alcohol. But we had every bottle in his house tested. Awll normal. Any t'oughts?"

Kyle had to use every ounce of her composure to stop her face from revealing the shock and horror she was feeling. She had to nip this in the bud.

"Sorry, Mr. DiNunzio, but your guy's mistaken. We did all the tests. Methanol's untraceable. We haven't been able to find the original source of your uncle's sickness. I've racked my brain, but you can find it in paints, shellacs, antifreeze, poorly made booze, and any other number of chemicals. I haven't the foggiest."

"Den what's up wit' dis skin deal?" He shifted from one foot to the other.

"It's not the alcohol, but we don't know why he has it. It can happen from a severe allergy."

"He ain' got no alluhgies."

"That we know of. But people can become allergic to different things at any point during their lives. Sometimes, to entities we can't identify."

"Any way somebody coulda done dis to him?"

Kyle shook her head and lied like her life depended on it. "No. I don't see how."

"Uh huh."

"They would have had to expose him to something multiple times to create a bad allergy. Any new foods? New drinks? New smokes? Virtually anything."

"Un spaccapalle."

"You're right. It's a ballbuster. Only the good Lord knows."

DiNunzio's lips tightened. First, because he didn't realize she knew Italian. His mind raced back as he wondered whether he'd previously let anything slip.

And secondly, because he hadn't set foot in Saint Vincent's in years. Nonetheless, his devout Catholic mother had instilled a deep religious spark within him, a cinder that still smoldered. Maybe this was God's plan of retribution for the evil his uncle had done? The lives ruined? So many maimed, tortured, and killed.

He turned and headed to the elevator.

"Mr. DiNunzio," McMann called after him, "have I answered all of your questions?"

DiNunzio looked back. "Yeah. T'anks, Doc."

Despite all the thoughts churning through his head, he couldn't shake the similarities between his uncle's case and that narc cop six months back. It was like they followed the same script.

Coincidence?

No. Coincidences don't just happen.

He had to bring in some heavy hitters from the outside to help find the scumbags who did this.

To find them and rip their insides outside.

Chapter Eleven

Pennsylvania Hospital

Philadelphia, PA

By the final week of September, Mancini was a therapeutic disaster. Despite heroic efforts by the ICU staff, his condition deteriorated daily. His body fluids were in disarray with swelling in all limbs, and he was spiking intermittent fevers to a hundred and five. When he wasn't chilled to the bone under layers of blankets, he was sweating buckets. Except for the mummy-like bandages, he was naked.

Drs. Kurland and McCann stood outside the ICU in their white coats with other team members. They eyed each other for a moment and gave and received tiny, intimate nods that no one else noticed.

Both were torn. They wanted him dead.

But Graham was trying to save him. While Kyle was trying to kill him ASAP. Even as she looked like she was trying to keep him alive.

She turned ever so slightly and looked up at his sculpted cheeks. She couldn't wait til this shitstorm was over so she could begin the courting and sparking with Dr. Kurland.

"What do you think?" she asked him as casually as she could.

"So sad," he said. "But we've done everything medically possible."

Both knew all too well the outcome of severe sepsis. The bacteria that flourished in every crevice of his oozing, unprotected skin were marching relentlessly to the interior toward his organs, unless they were already infected. Even with maximum IV antibiotics, the infection was getting worse by the minute. And now the cultures showed enough other bacterial species to start a microbial zoo.

"I'm certainly glad you were on the case," Graham said softly. "It gives me confidence that we didn't miss anything."

"Ditto," she replied, feeling ever so slightly guilty about lying to his beautiful face. Reminding herself that she was on a mission to save lives by ending this one.

This was true. Chief Residents typically helped the interns and residents manage their cases, rather than give so much attention to one individual case. Though occasionally they did follow interesting individual cases closely. Graham managed to do both at the highest level. The fact that he was a huge Kyle McMann fan and wanted her support likely also played a role.

"I also know that you have more information in that big brain than a computer," she added with an admiring raise of her eyebrow.

They subtly exchanged smiles while the other physicians waited.

"I'll be in my office if you need me," Kyle said. "I know his uncle wanted us to resuscitate him under any circumstances, but I'll be in the background if that happens. There's nothing I can add. And I know you can handle DiNunzio, but if you want any help with him, I'm always here for you."

Graham understood. It was typically the junior house staff, the docs nearest in distance to patients whose hearts had stopped, who ran the cardiac codes to revive them. In most instances, the steps were standard.

She turned briskly and whisked away, a mixture of concern and longing on her face.

Graham turned his attention back to Mancini. The man's cheeks, forehead, and lids were all covered by scabs in different stages of maturity. Several hung by a thread, the green discharge at their bases preventing firm adhesions. Greenish-yellow mucus seeped from his beefy-red eyes, partway gluing the lids together over the sightless globes. The body bandages couldn't contain the overflow of pus, so the sheets were saturated with yellow-green secretions.

The stench of rotting flesh activated Graham's gag reflex. The foul odor came with a flashback of an Afghan village after a grisly Taliban massacre. His whole central nervous system went on high alert, and he had to use every bit of his mental strength to take a deep cleansing breath and pull himself back into the here and now.

Mancini seemed visibly unaffected by his own odor, no doubt immune to it as he continued to slip further from reality. The episodes of senseless babbling were now more norm than exception.

Harry turned away and took a deep breath as he removed the facial dressings and tossed them in the red "Infectious Waste" pail.

"How's his sodium?" Graham asked.

"One twenty-eight. He's losing it from every pore in his body."

"Albumin?"

"Same deal. It's "hard to keep up his blood pressure. I keep hanging more in the IV, but his skin—what's left of it—is leaking like a sieve. He also has had blood in his stool since yesterday."

"You think it's an ulcer?" Graham questioned.

"Could be. I ordered an upper GI series in radiology to check it out."

"Good."

Graham and Harry inspected the torso drainage, a mixture of pus, antibiotics, and sloughed skin. Harry brought his palm up to his forehead and shook his head from side to side. "Man, this is an abomination," he whispered.

Graham nodded and took out a pen to poke at the sticky mass. "It's amazing what the human body can endure. He's—"

They both jumped when Marlene, Mancini's daytime nurse, rushed into the room.

"I didn't realize you were here with him," she said.

"Why? What's wrong?" Graham asked.

"The cardiac monitor at the central station registered half a dozen irregular beats. Were you touching it?"

"No." Graham looked up at the green video screen over the patient's head.

She was right. Multiple premature ventricular contractions, some adjoined. A worrisome sign. And the pulse had increased to a hundred forty a minute.

Mancini awoke with a start. "Who's dere?"

"It's only your doctors and nurse, Mr. Mancini. This is Dr. Kurland."

"Doc, I ain't feelin' so good. My head's spinnin'…and I t'ink I crapped all ovah da bed."

Harry pulled down the top sheet. A putrid, maroon liquid covered the bottom sheet, smearing the bandages from Mancini's torso to his knees. The odor was distinctly more unpleasant than the rest of the debris. Both Harry and Marlene looked at Graham.

"Melena," Graham said, "bloody diarrhea. He's bleeding internally, probably from the duodenum. It's a Curling's ulcer."

"What causes it?" Marlene asked. "Acid?"

"In part. Bad burn victims also have decreased blood flow to the tissues. The inner lining of the stomach and bowel dies and sloughs off. Just like his skin."

"I thought this wasn't a burn," Marlene said.

"True," Graham said. "But it behaves like a burn."

"What now?" Harry asked.

"Open the IV all the way. Marlene, please get me a nasogastric tube and ice water. Harry, call the GI people down here so they can endoscope him. I'm going to pass a tube into his stomach and see if we can stop the bleeding with cold water in the interim."

Marlene returned in seconds with a nasogastric set-up. The clear plastic tube had the thickness of a pencil and was approximately two and a half feet in length. She squirted clear lubricating jelly on the end and handed it to Graham.

Mancini felt for Graham, his hand trembling. "Doc, what's goin' on?"

"Mr. Mancini, I want you to swallow while I pass this tube through your nose into your stomach."

"Wait a minute. Tell me what's goin' on first." He clutched Graham's arm.

Graham removed Mancini's hand and stared for a second. He might be half out of it, but the man had a right to know. "Mr. Mancini, you have severe bleeding from the gut. We have to stop it."

"Or what?"

"Or you could die."

Mancini blinked open his crusted lids, his face at first drained of expression. Terror then engulfed his blind eyes, which suddenly reflected the horror he was feeling inside.

Graham had seen the look too many times.

Within seconds, Mancini nodded and propped himself against the pillows. He followed directions, swallowing and gasping as Graham guided the nasogastric tube through his left nostril and down his throat.

"Don't worry, sir, we're making good progress," Graham said, then turned to Marlene. "Keep going."

"The GI folks will be up in ten minutes," Harry said. "What do you want me to do?"

"Start another IV and order four more units of blood."

Six inches of tubing remained when Mancini lurched forward with a violent retch. Projectile vomiting sprayed blood from his mouth to the far end of the bed.

"Jesus Mary an' Joseph!" Mancini rasped.

Another paroxysm twisted his body and sent a second flood past the end of the bed. He groped without purpose, yanking out the tube before a third wretch shook him.

"*Fottermi*! I'm dyin'!"

"Shit!" Graham scrambled to recover the nasogastric tube on the floor.

He rinsed it and tried to re-insert the tube, but Mancini couldn't hold still.

Marlene helped support Mancini's forehead, but he slipped from her grip, leaving her hands covered with green mucus and red-brown scabs.

Puddles of blood and coffee ground granules from Mancini's vomitus stained the sheets and dripped onto the floor.

With each additional spasm, the man's grasp on life ebbed.

Harry stabbed his arm three times to start another IV line.

Fluid poured into each arm, but nowhere close to the waves spewing out.

By the time the gastrointestinal team arrived, Mancini was unconscious. Graham hoped they could still slide their snakelike endoscope down his throat. These ulcers were often located just past the stomach. If they could get in there and cauterize it, they could stop the bleeding.

No sooner was the instrument in Mancini's mouth when the cardiac monitor began to flash and shriek. By some miracle, it stayed on.

More ICU staff ran into the room.

The monitor screamed louder.

"V-FIB!" someone yelled.

"Out with the endoscope!" Graham shouted. "Let's pump him."

Everyone assumed their positions in cardiac arrest mode.

Harry compressed Mancini's chest to force his heart to push blood through the body. The elderly man's brittle ribs cracked in rapid succession. With each thrust, another volume of blood spouted upward and outward from Mancini's mouth into the plastic breathing mask.

Harry and the team did their best not to get covered by the vile detritus, but couldn't avoid the disgusting muck.

After ten minutes, Graham nodded to Harry to stop. What were they saving anyway?

Mancini lay still, his shriveled body a mass of reeking, infected scar tissue. His open eyes stared at nothing.

A hush swept the room as they surveyed the havoc.

The cardiac monitor, exhausted by its explosive run, finally rested in peace.

The look of terror was still frozen on Mancini's face.

Kyle, having heard the commotion, rushed in at the exact moment.

She was so relieved that this man would never be able to hurt another man, woman, or child.

Chapter Twelve

Main Line

Berwyn, PA

The happy news of Mancini the mobster's death filled the opulent room as the setting sun cast eerie shadows through the tall French windows in the Berwyn Main Line estate house rooms and hallways. At the same time, it tickled the Waterford chandeliers, sending shimmering sparkles everywhere. The multiple Pennsylvania stone fireplaces sent out the aroma of burnt embers, while the central Seth Thomas clock dutifully ticked away the seconds.

Outside, the moisture formed irregular clouds and halos around lights standing as sentinels along the winding road to the house atop the hill. Gray doves cooed in the pines, and a trio of deer foraged in the garden.

The September Tribunal meeting was held, as always, on the last Friday evening of the month. Seven members sat around the rectangular mahogany table and listened while the eighth stood and spoke.

"The plan was most effective," Lionel C. Stenton said. Though approaching eighty, he still had the physique of a construction worker. With steel-blue eyes that matched his pin-striped suit, he could have easily passed for a Wall Street lawyer. He was, in fact, the son of a Philadelphia school teacher and had amassed a fortune from manufacturing industrial lasers. For him, vision was the art of seeing things that were invisible to others. The man was a financial and managerial genius who had parlayed his company to the top and joined the billionaire coterie decades before.

"He developed toxic epidermal necrolysis and shed the skin from every square inch of his body. As far as the blindness goes, they know it was methanol, but have no idea how he got it. And he died with the excruciating pain he inflicted on his victim.

"Outstanding," said Dr. Art Ramos, a stately man with a Hispanic accent. "And you're certain the drug can't be discovered?"

"Positive. His kidneys eliminated it early on. He had antibodies to it, but the chances of them being detected are nil."

"Good. Tell us the rest. I want to hear how the scumbag died."

The speaker was thin and trim and wore a grim but satisfied smile. "Mr. Mancini died from marked internal hemorrhaging. The equivalent of a burn and widespread infection caused him to develop a duodenal ulcer that bled without mercy. He vomited every last drop of blood, just like the young policeman he killed. I think you'll be happy to know he was aware of what was happening till the very end."

"All right!" Dr. Carlo Tursi said. A tall, thin, striking man with an excellent head of hair and an athletic build, dressed in a stylish gray suit, he pounded his fist on the table.

With that, everyone started celebrating their triumph.

"Wait a minute, Dr. Tursi. JUST A MINUTE!" Lionel C. Stenton, the senior statesperson at the end of the table opposite the speaker, raised his hand for silence. "We can revel in our success afterwards. We have more business first."

"Quiet!" hissed his assistant, Alden Booth, a slight, harmless-looking man with a pencil-slim mustache, a hook nose, and brown eyes that appeared magnified behind wire-rimmed gold spectacles.

The room quieted.

Stenton peered over bronze half-glasses perched in peril at the end of his nose. He turned to the two men seated to his right. "Nate, Randy, can we have an update?"

Nate Champion cleared his throat. "This probably isn't a big deal, but we thought you all should know. When we switched the alcohol bottles at Mancini's house, his wife almost saw me. Fortunately, that was not the case. There's one other thing, though."

All eyes fixed upon him. No one liked surprises.

"Ralph DiNunzio arrived just as I was leaving. I heard him talking to one of his men. He suspects foul play. And we know that he thinks his uncle may have been poisoned."

A pin dropping would have sounded like a grenade.

"He'd suspect foul play if his bowel movements didn't smell," Carlo Tursi wisecracked.

Laughter broke the tension.

"But no one else suspects anything. We just thought he was a loose cannon shooting off at the mouth," Nate added.

Stenton spoke again. "Tell us more, please."

"That's it," Nate insisted. "We don't have any more. They didn't know any specifics. Randy and I just think DiNunzio's a pathologically paranoid personality. Wouldn't you be if a whole galaxy of mobsters wanted to whack you in the most painful way possible?"

Shrugs, nods, and chuckles.

Stenton glanced over the group. "Is there *anything* we've left uncovered?"

No one answered.

"Good. But let me warn each of you that DiNunzio is a malicious viper. He's capable of extreme violence, particularly when he feels threatened." He looked at Champion and White.

"I agree," Nate said. "He's King Kong on steroids."

"Ditto," Randy White agreed. "If he even got a whiff, he'd go over Niagara Falls without a barrel for the chance to finish us off."

"Comforting," someone muttered from the far end of the table.

"We've got a tap on his phone," White said. "If anything comes up, Nate and I will get the news to everyone pronto. The text will say, '*Have a great day.*' If that shows up, call in immediately."

"Fine," Stenton said. "Further questions? Comments concerning Mancini?"

Silence.

"If not, this case is closed. We'll meet next month as usual. Before we go, however, I think we need a round of applause for the person who contributed the most to our success." He directed his attention to the speaker at the other end of the table. "Congratulations, Dr. McMann, for coming up with such an effective plan."

Kyle smiled at the applause. "Thank you."

Suddenly, the ongoing battle with her conscience faded away, and she knew she was doing the right thing.

Sure, it didn't bring her brother back, but it felt damn good knowing if there was a hell, scum-of-the Earth like Mancini were currently screaming there.

Chapter Thirteen

Wills Eye Hospital

840 Walnut Street, Philadelphia, PA

Darlene Pugh gave her sweet, sparkling sixty-five-year-old effusive smile to social worker Eva Corman, who supported her with one arm. Darlene's daughter took the other arm to guide Darlene down the hall to the Eighth-Floor elevator at Wills Eye Hospital.

Eva Corman returned the broad smile and patted Darlene on the arm. "As soon as we get you that motorized wheelchair, you'll be able to navigate like you're in at the Indy 500.... though I might slow it down a little."

"I'm so grateful. The other Social Service people talked about this forever. But you were the only one who took the time and made it happen." Despite central gray scars in Darlene's eye corneas from years of recurrent Herpes simplex infections, her eyes still beamed in her radiant face.

Darlene's daughter gave Eva a kiss on the cheek, and the mother-daughter pair entered the elevator, then turned around to face the doorway.

The small crowd in the immediate vicinity that overheard the conversation gave a small round of applause as the elevator door closed.

Eva mini-waved to all and walked back to her Social Service office. As if it had been pasted on, her smile fell off her face the second her windowless wooden door shut behind her.

Eva was barely forty-five. A five-foot-nine uber-babe, she still made a certain kind of man temporarily forget their name when she wore a low-cut dress and heels. But those features weren't often currency in the social service arena. So, she'd constructed the persona of the universal empathizer, the sweet sister of Mercy, who looked like she gave her heart and soul to the afflicted, the weak, and the meek.

When a bedridden widow shed a tear, Eva shed two. If a family was engulfed by sorrow, she was entrenched. When needed, she was Mother Teresa and Nelson Mandela rolled into one.

But at five p.m., her weekday work world stopped on a dime. Once she stepped into the Wills Eye Parking Lot, her smile turned into an inverted "U" frown until 8:30 am the next day. And her face morphed from pleasant to Wicked Witch of the West.

Eva unlocked the deadbolt to her third-floor condo overlooking the Delaware River in downtown Philly. She tossed her keys onto the coffee table, collapsed into the living room recliner, and pondered who her next client/victim should be.

The early October sun shone overhead, dust particles dancing in the currents. A whiff of bacon from breakfast still permeated the air, and the hum of the refrigerator competed with the afternoon rush-hour traffic on Front Street. Out on the sidewalk, school children discussed their critical affairs on the way home from the Delancey Street playground.

Eva struggled to her feet and stared at the kids passing in groups of three and four. Little bastards. Louder than hell.

Opening the window, she yelled at one of the more raucous groups. "Get the hell outta here, ya miserable little punks! Go scream outside your own windows!" She slammed the window shut, ignoring the middle finger responses.

Ambling into the bathroom, Eva blinked at her reflection in the mirror. Her neck-length black hair contrasted with her white skin below. God, she could use a little sun. But wasn't that bad for you, too? Seemed like everything good was bad for you these days.

She took a wad of tissue, wiped away the oil from her forehead and cheeks, then concentrated on her nose. Maybe she needed a few more foundation hits during the day to complement her Chanel *Chance* perfume. Looking and smelling the part of the pleasing social worker was essential to her financial well-being. Client trust was critical. And they had to like her to trust her.

She needed a fast two grand to keep Sid Weiss from repossessing that diamond necklace. When she asked him for another month, all she heard was, "Ha!"

She should have known. The little tightwad would sell his mother for a nickel.

Too bad the old Folkmans were dead broke. But how could she have known? Pure bad luck. From the way they kept their row home so nice, anyone would have thought they were in the money.

Nonetheless, things were looking up. Last month, she had the good fortune to be transferred to Wills Eye Hospital. It was like moving into the house where the goose that laid the golden frigging egg lived. It was a treasure trove, a veritable repository of blind homebound patients. Easier than grabbing candy from babies. How could those old blind people suspect, much less prove, they were being taken to the cleaners by the kindhearted social worker robbing them even more blind than they already were?

She was so good at what she did that she could steal their radios while the music was playing. It wasn't that hard to feign kindness when necessary, and, in a way, she did feel sorry for them. Well, maybe not sorry, but deep down she'd always feared she'd be afflicted by the possibility of some disabling disease.

Besides, there was patriotic precedent for what she did. The Golden Rule of American Business—*Do unto others before they do it unto you.*

Her metal file cabinet was filled with patient records, including the considerable batch she'd already copied from Wills Eye. She hauled herself back to the bedroom, pulled out the top drawer, and rummaged through the manila folders.

Where the hell was that thing?

She stopped for a moment to light up a Marlboro and took a few deep puffs. A drizzle had started, and she frowned at the annoying squeals of brakes as cars drove over the slick cobblestones. A good head-on would teach them a lesson.

She eventually pulled out the chart of the week. This would do just fine. She laid the smoking butt on top of the cabinet and flipped through the pages.

Nettie Johnson

Medical history: Seventy-seven-year-old African American female with insulin-dependent diabetes and diabetic retinopathy... legally blind.

Social history: Widowed for ten years, currently lives alone, no immediate family. Visiting nurse prepares insulin syringes weekly on Tuesdays.

Yes indeed, just fine. Alone in West Mount Airy, one of Philadelphia's upper-middle-class neighborhoods.

Eva belched gas from her last Diet Pepsi, settled into the living room TV chair, and gave a new Marlboro life with a few puffs. She excavated the inside of her right nostril with a pinkie and flicked her prize onto the matching green carpet.

Elderly woman. Blind. No family. Didn't get any easier than that. Maybe these Wills Eye people should all be her new targets. After all, she'd thought long and hard about how she could improve her efficiency. Calculated it down to dollars per hour.

Damn, it felt good to have a plan.

Chapter Fourteen

Mount Airy

Northwest Philadelphia, PA

Since all her friends were dead or infirmed, Nettie Johnson spent most of her waking hours devouring the audio of her favorite TV soaps.

She had trouble seeing the screen, of course, but she loved the plots. Sure, they were far-fetched, but what a great escape. Unlike the perpetually catastrophic doom and gloom newspaper headlines, she didn't have to feel bad for the sad, crazy, and damaged characters because she knew they were so phony.

She was still tired from Halloween the day before, but she enjoyed having the kids come to her door. Her days were the same from dawn to dusk, and she'd looked forward to it for weeks. The trick-or-treaters reminded her so much of Harold Jr. as a little tyke in his wizard costume.

Today was another exception. In addition to Janice Parker, her regular nurse at eleven a.m., a new social worker named Eva Corman from Wills Eye Hospital Social Services was coming at noon.

Nettie arranged and rearranged her furniture and decorations until everything was just right. Three years of blindness made it hard to function in unfamiliar surroundings. But in her own carefully constructed world realm, she navigated like a radar-guided 747 on cruise control. Each item had its place and was returned to that exact location.

Despite thirty years of diabetes, Nettie was still physically agile and mentally sharp. She's learned, with great difficulty, how to give herself the morning insulin injections. She'd pinch a small roll of wrinkled abdominal skin, then slip the tiny 31-gauge needle tip in and give herself the life-saving morning injections, just the way Janice showed her. She knew that missing even one day's insulin could bring on a diabetic coma.

The doorbell rang.

Nettie plumped a sofa cushion and rushed to answer it. It had to be Janice. She was always so prompt, the dear girl. Her arthritic fingers shook with excitement as she unlatched the oak door.

"Janice."

"Nettie, good to see you." Janice came in, and the two women hugged.

She knew Janice's busy schedule kept her moving, but she still liked to stop long enough for morning tea.

"How are things?" Janice asked, taking her usual seat on the sofa.

"Fine. Billy Lee, the grocery man, comes every Saturday. Little Teddy Brewster down the block is a garden wizard, and my eyes are better since my laser treatments at Wills Eye. So I can't complain."

"How about the injections?" Janice asked. "Any difficulties?"

"None. I feel better than I have in months."

"Good. But your diabetes is brittle. It isn't stable."

"I know."

"If you start sweating and shaking, your sugar is low. Pop in a candy fast. And if you're urinating more or thirstier, it's high. Call me right away."

"I will."

The two women talked while Janice checked Nettie's blood glucose after a finger needle stick, then filled each syringe with sixty units of Lantus insulin.

Within twenty minutes, Janice had finished her work and enjoyed her tea. She got up to leave.

"Thanks so much," Nettie said. "You know, I have another visitor today. She's coming at noon."

"Good. Who's that?"

"It's Ms. Corman, a social worker," Nettie said with a twinge of a drawl from her early days in the South Carolina low country. "Wills Eye Hospital is sending her to see how I'm doin'."

"I wonder why they didn't tell me?"

Nettie smiled. "You know red tape and all. The memo's probably in the mail."

"I'm sure you're right. Any problems, you can call me at the office or on my cell. What's the name of that social worker again?"

"Eva Corman," Nellie replied.

With a smile and a wave, Nettie closed the door and went back into the living room to tidy up for her next guest. It was barely 11:30, but she started lunch anyway. This was an occasion for fine China and Mother's silver. Only the best for her visitors.

With any luck, she could get this new woman to stop by more often.

Chapter Fifteen

Center City

Philadelphia, PA

Eva's tires squealed as she made a ninety-degree turn toward the exit of the underground parking lot beneath her condo.

She looked in her rearview mirror at the clouds of black smoke spewing from the tailpipe of her old Buick. Screw it. She passed a small blue Mercedes sedan draped in a plastic cover and smiled. Her precious baby was too conspicuous for today.

Eva's Buick emerged into the bright morning sun, and she made a right turn onto Pine. Blast-honking a blue-hair who dared to violate her personal space, she sent the car to the curb. Damned old ladies. So scrunched over that they couldn't see above the steering wheel. How the hell they ever had licenses was beyond her. If those Motor Vehicle flunkies did their jobs, the public wouldn't have to worry about them driving lethal weapons.

The late morning traffic was light before the midday scurry. So, she hopped onto the Schuylkill Expressway and bee-lined toward Northwest Philadelphia.

She smiled at the manicured lawns, trimmed hedges, and gleaming cars in their perfect driveways. In a few years, with more clients like this Johnson woman, she'd be able to retire to a neighborhood like this.

Reaching Nettie Johnson's house in thirty minutes, she parked in front.

The two-story fieldstone looked well-kept. Even the flowers in the side garden were arranged in ascending size from the sidewalk to the backyard. With a creak and a boom, she opened, then slammed her dented door shut. The street was quiet except for a pair of sparrows squabbling in a front maple.

Eva Corman took a deep breath, put on her sweetest smile, and rapped on the door.

"Who is it?" a muffled voice asked from the other side.

"Eva Corman. From Social Services at Wills Eye Hospital. I called the other day."

The inside door opened, and a small, wizened face peered through a crack, squinting as she tried to see Eva's face.

Eva beamed sweetness and light as she looked the old lady over. She was elated to see that the eyes were blind. She allowed herself a little devilish grin. They always pretended they could see.

"Mrs. Johnson, so very nice to see you," Eva said.

"Thank you for coming," Nettie opened the door further. "Please come in."

"Thank you," Eva purred as she scanned the surroundings like a hungry vulture. Silver candlesticks on the mantle.

Sterling. *Seventy, eighty bucks—easy.*

A gold cigarette lighter on the end table by the sofa. *A hundred bucks.* If that curmudgeon James at the pawnshop was in a good mood. Fat chance. More like *seventy-five.*

A whole set of fine china. *Five hundred bucks—at least.*

Although she couldn't see it, she guessed the bedroom was down the hall to the left. Older people always hid their cash and jewelry there. It gave them a false sense of security.

"Ms. Corman, it's awfully nice of you to come visit me," Nettie said.

"It's my pleasure, Nettie. I think we can help with your vision problems," she lied.

"That would be so nice."

Eva stared into the old woman's dark eyes. Definitely blind. A satisfied smile crept across her face. The hospital charts were right. This one had a lifetime membership in the white cane club.

Nettie excused herself to put the finishing touches on their lunch, leaving Eva to hone in on targets. She preferred to make several visits to gain a client's confidence, but that cheapskate Sid had her necklace on the top of his shit list. The bastard might send his goons to take it at any time.

She spied two family photographs in sterling silver frames on the fireplace mantle. Always a good subject for small talk, too.

Thirty bucks a pop,

She grinned as she slipped the frame into the big ass purse she always brought to home visits.

"Mrs. Johnson," she said as Nettie walked back in, "is that a picture of your family?"

"By the fireplace?"

"Yes."

"My husband and my little boy. Harold senior died in 1995. Do you know he was the first black investment banker in Philadelphia? I was so proud of him. Harold Junior passed away when he was only four years old." She sighed. "He drowned in a lake when we were visiting relatives in North Carolina."

Eva looked at the picture and rolled her eyes. Everyone had their sob story. *Cry me a river of crocodile tears!* she smirked. If she had to sit through one more of these, she was going to vomit. "I'm so very sorry," she said.

"Well, life must go on. And it has."

"True. In any event, I'm here to see if there's any way I can help you. You're receiving your social security benefits, aren't you?"

"Yes, I get them."

"I hope you have the money put away safely."

"My check's deposited directly in the bank."

"Smart idea."

So much for a big cash grab! Son of a bitch!

Eva felt like spitting.

They chatted through lunch, mostly about the symptoms of Nettie's brittle diabetes, until the elderly woman excused herself to visit the bathroom.

In ninety seconds, she'd rummaged through the living room, nabbed glass trinkets and the gold lighter, then resumed her sitting position.

And none too soon. A quick piss, to say the least.

Eva relaxed and assumed an air of faux empathy. Nothing over the top. The old woman would never suspect a thing.

Nettie almost collided with the end table. "Oh my. I just lose my bearings occasionally." She stiffened, staring at the far corner of the room.

"Ms. Corman?"

"Yes?"

"Why did you take my pictures of Harold and little Harold?"

Eva stiffened and straightened. *She heard!*

"I, uh, was just looking…looking at them and admiring your family."

"I doubt that," Nettie said. "Put the picture back, NOW! And the cigarette lighter, too."

Eva tried to remain calm, but her hands and knees were shaking. Sweat collected on her forehead as she fidgeted with her hair.

"What are you talking about, Nettie?" She forced a smile. "What makes you think I've taken anything?"

"You thought I was blind, didn't you? Well, I used to be. But I had laser treatments at Wills Eye, and I can see again."

"Oh, fuck me," Eva muttered to herself. The lazy bastards in Medical Records fell behind in recording the old woman's recent visits. What was she going to do now?

"I can hear like a cat, too," Nettie went on. "When you're blind, you use all your senses. Everything here has its own special sound when it's picked up. I thought you were just looking until I came out and saw the pictures gone. And your half-baked excuses. You might fool people who can't see anything. But not me. I've dealt with folks like you before."

Eva got up from the couch and wagged her finger in Nettie's face. "Listen, old woman, you're in no position to threaten me. If I were you, I'd forget this whole thing."

"Ms. Corman, I know your kind. They surround you like sharks when you're trying to scrape your way out of the gutter. You let them push you around once, and they never stop. They just keep coming back and back–till nothing's left."

"That's ridiculous."

"You think so? How many others have you done this to? I'm sure I'm not the first. And I bet I can find out real quick. What do you say to that, Ms. Corman?"

"Let's be reasonable. I don't think there's any cause for alarm here, Mrs. Johnson. We can work something out."

Eva licked her dry lips.

She needed time to think.

"I'm calling the police," Nettie announced, reaching for the phone.

Eva grabbed the old woman's spindly arm.

Nettie stood her ground.

"You old bitch," Eva sneered. "You're not doing me in." She towered over Nettie, who stood her ground despite being six inches shorter and fifty pounds lighter.

Eva shoved Nettie hard, and when she hit the floor, her right hipbone made a loud snap. Nettie tried to get up, but a crippling pain shot through her, her arms trembled, and she collapsed.

"You'll never get away with this," Nettie cried, clutching her hip and writhing on the floor.

"My dear, I've done nothing. You're old, and you had a little fall."

"Please help me. I can't move. It hurts so bad."

Eva circled her prey, enjoying her power over the helpless septuagenarian. She violently ripped out the telephone cord, took her cell phone, locked the windows, grabbed up the insulin syringes, and pulled down the shades. Fastening the dead bolt on the front door, she returned to her weeping, trembling victim.

"Please," Nettie begged. "Don't leave me like this."

Eva clenched her teeth and slowly shook her head. "You did this to yourself, old lady. You shouldn't've threatened me."

She watched Nettie struggle on the floor as the fierce pain made her bladder and bowels let go. Urine soaked the front of her dress. Driving her to incontinence. Eva smirked when the wet spot appeared at the front of Nettie's purple dress and the pungent odors of urine and feces permeated the room.

Eva quickly confiscated the rest of the valuables.

"Ms. Johnson, I'm afraid I must be going. It's been delightful visiting with you. But, as you know, I have other clients. Don't hesitate to call me if there's anything else I can do."

And with that, Eva left Nettie Johnson to die.

Chapter Sixteen

Nettie Johnson's Home

Mount Airy, Philadelphia

The world of pain pulsing out from her hip was numbing, so much so bad that Nettie couldn't think.

She watched the blur that was Eva Corman head for the back door, and raised her hand and pleaded one more time.

"Please…"

The figure waved her off. Nettie heard the click of the door locking before it slammed shut. Now, no one could enter unless they forced their way in. Eva's car door opened and shut, the engine turned over, and the vehicle sped down the street.

Nettie lay in her excrement, gathering her strength. She tried in desperation to pull herself up. The pain was too sharp, and she crumpled in a heap.

She dragged herself toward the hall telephone with her thin arms, pausing to rest after each small advance. At last, she made it to the end table with the phone. She reached and groped for it.

Oh Lord.

No dial tone. She saw the cord had been ripped out of the wall. And her cell was gone.

She buried her face in her arms and wept until her eyes were dry.

The slightest movement caused a spasm that rocketed from her hip down to her toes, up through her guts, and into her brain. It hurt so much that she vomited. And that made another bolt of agony jolt through her brain. She vomited again, but now it was dry heaves.

Taking short and fast breaths to quiet the retching, she managed to reduce the pain to a point where her brainstem's vomiting center was able to withstand the assault. She did her best to remain still. But the pain from lying in one position soon got worse than the one in her broken hip. She was cursed either way.

Darkness eventually crept into the living room. The small figure on the floor lay still, apart from the shivers of agony, as the pain ripped through her. It was warm, and she knew the tremors weren't from the temperature.

With no food in her stomach, the insulin was causing her blood glucose level to plummet. The only way to help it was to take in calories right away. She realized that the low sugar was making her vision more blurred.

Oh God.

The next step was a coma. Then death.

Unless she got immediate help.

She listened.

Silence.

There was nobody to call or check on her.

What a sad way to go.

Alone with no one to care.

She sobbed again on the floor, the vomitus six inches in front of her face.

Mobilizing her last ounce of strength, she palm-pulled the bile-colored liquid and solid chunks into her mouth and chewed until her jaw ached. The foul smell made her retch, but she kept it down.

If this wasn't hell, it was for sure in the same zip code.

Exhausted by the struggle to survive, she closed her eyes and mercifully passed out.

Chapter Seventeen

Eva Corman's Condominium

Center City, Philadelphia, PA

Eva Corman started at the noise. The cops were pounding on her door.

It was only a matter of time.

There it was again.

They had to be out there with flashing lights, guns, and loudspeakers.

She slowly got out of bed.

What in God's name was she going to do?

Eva rehearsed her lie.

Nettie Johnson was fine when she left her house, but I noticed she was very frail and having trouble walking and...

But she couldn't get past the first line without her mind clouding up.

She craned her neck to look out of her room.

Crap. Just a damn Venetian blind flapping in an open window!

She relaxed, rubbed her eyes, and yawned. She realized her nightgown was wet from sweating.

She'd been dreaming.

Actually continuing the latest nightmare she'd had all night about being discovered and ruined.

She glanced down at her bedside clock. Six am. Time to get up anyway.

She dressed in a flash and devoured two hard-boiled eggs on her way through the kitchen. Cleanup could wait. She had to know how the old woman was doing, or she'd go crazy.

Taking the exit from the garage on two wheels, she spun out onto the street. She put a hand to her temple and felt the throbbing. She'd already popped a half dozen Tylenol and two Percocet but knew she couldn't get rid of this headache until she found out about Nettie Johnson. With any luck, the old woman was dead.

But what if she'd been found and, God forbid, been rescued? Why had she been so impulsive and crazy? With the others, she'd been cautious, always flying under the radar. But she had a bad feeling about this one. Was she trying to get caught? No. She just had to take care of this and go back to being her usual careful self.

How long would it take the old woman to die? The diabetes should finish her fast, but with Eva's rotten luck, she could hang on for days.

The thirty-minute drive seemed to take like thirty days. Eva stopped her car with a jerk in front of a tall sycamore down the block and sat. She jumped when a chunk of bark from the tree landed on her hood. Taking several seconds to regain her composure, she leaned back in her seat to begin her vigil and lit up the first Marlboro of a virgin pack. She puffed it down to a butt in less than three minutes.

God damn.

She tapped her foot and twitched, glancing left, right, and into the mirror. No way could she just sit here for eight hours and not arouse suspicion. Fishing out another Marlboro, she pulled away from the curb for the first of endless passes and parks.

By noon, the butts were overflowing onto the floor. Two packs gone. Or was it three? No one had gone to Nettie's door. Not even the mail carrier. She knew she should wait until darkness, but she couldn't stand one more hour of driving by that damn house, or she'd scream. Besides, people would be coming home from work, and her car could attract attention.

"Screw it," she growled as she kicked open the car door and set out for Nettie's. Her heart was pounding as hard as her head. She forced herself to slow down and chill. Her stomach gurgled in concert, and she pushed on it to stop the noise.

This better not take long.

Chapter Eighteen

Nettie Johnson's Home

Mount Airy, Philadelphia

Nettie awoke to the morning light with pain that wracked the length of her body. Her first thought was that she would have been better off dead if the low glucose had taken her.

Excruciating cramps and stiffness from lying in one position on the floor were so bad that they exceeded the stabs in her hip.

But now there was the unquenchable thirst from her rising sugar.

Eating the vomitus had saved her life, but the insulin no longer had any effect. The ultra-high glucose was overwhelming her kidneys and drawing fluid from every bit of her body. The puddle of urine was spreading faster than it could dry.

She forced herself to recall all the good that had come her way over the years. And to remind herself of her faith. In the end, she knew someone would rescue her. She'd been praying Billy Lee would stop by with the groceries.

What day was it? Did I miss him?

Her mind was running away from her, and it was getting harder and harder to stay focused. Still, as the mantle clock ticked off each minute, she couldn't shut out the thought that life was ebbing from her tired old body.

If not for the scratching sounds at the window, Nettie Johnson wouldn't have opened her eyes again.

She was tired.

So tired.

"Thank you, Lord. Thank you for hearing me and sending someone," she whispered. She had no idea what time it was.

She tried to lift her head, but it fell back onto the floor.

The sound of a key in the back lock!

But then there were familiar footsteps approaching from the kitchen.

It was over.

"You're a tough old bat," Eva said. "But don't worry, it won't be much longer."

Nettie closed her eyes. "Oh, Lord, why?" she whispered. A violent retch shook her and sent burning vomitus out of the right side of her mouth. Even with the awful pain, she barely moved.

Eva walked past her into the bedroom, but was back in a minute. When she returned, Nettie could feel her scowling and staring. But what could she do? She was too weak to make a sound, much less move.

"The place smells like a cesspool. Now that I know you're gonna be dead in a couple of hours, my work is done here. Have a great day. I'm outta here!" Eva strutted triumphantly out, pausing to fart on her way to the door.

Nettie heard the finality of the key turn.

The only sound was the ticking clock.

She could only pray for herself and for the strength to forgive her tormentor.

Despite everything, she felt closer to God than ever. Soon—so very soon—she would enter His holy kingdom. Reunite with her husband and son.

She'd been feeling guilty that she was unable to attend church because of the diabetes, but now knew He didn't mind. He understood.

He loved her and was waiting for her.

Chapter Nineteen

Philadelphia City Hall

Center City, Philadelphia, PA

The judge had just left less than five minutes ago. Everyone else followed in hierarchical order. The empty Philadelphia City Hall courtroom seemed cold despite a comfortable seventy-two degrees. Janice Parker sat alone, numbed by the pronouncement of the jury.

Not guilty? How could that be?

Three days of testimony had left her body exhausted and her brain shattered. She could hear the voices of the Assistant DA and Eva Corman's lawyer outside in the hallway. They were laughing and making plans to meet for a drink at O'Grady's.

God, didn't it matter?

The whole thing was nothing more than a damn job to them. They didn't care who won or lost. Neither was about to lose sleep over some insignificant old Black woman.

It was impossible to believe this monster would not be convicted of murder. What had she been thinking? Corman was convicted of nothing. Not so much as a slap on the wrist.

So, what if the coroner couldn't tell the exact time of death? It had to be less than a week, since Janice was the one who found her the next Tuesday.

What about the neighbor across the street who testified he'd seen Eva Corman leave the Johnson house on two consecutive days? No big deal that he had one bad eye. The other one was good. For God's sake, they even found one of Nettie's silver picture frames in Corman's living room. If that wasn't circumstantial evidence, what was? Did they need a narrated video?

With his twisted legal lingo and confident smile, the smooth-talking defense attorney nullified every scrap of evidence. It was absurd, all of it. Why would Nettie ask Eva to return and visit her the next day? And, of course, when Eva saw her each day, she was fine?

Right.

The frame was even more absurd. Eva loved it so much that Nettie wanted her to have it.

And those fake tears running down her face? A crock of bullshit.

"Evidence inadequate—accidental fall—the burden of proof lies with the prosecution—the charge of murder cannot be substantiated."

Janice could only stare at the jury. And the judge? He was some alien life form. If this was justice, God help the poor person who got injustice.

Janice's stomach turned over as she remembered the instant she found Nettie more than two months ago. The dehydrated small body, alone at the end. The outstretched hand reaching for an insulin syringe, for water, a phone. Or just a friend. As far as she knew, she was one of the few friends Nettie had.

She pounded her clenched fist on the seat next to her. Why hadn't she called her at the end of the week like she usually did? Why? Why!

Janice wiped the tears from her face with the back of her hand and sniffed. Guilt was one thing, but the thought of that murderous woman going free was unfathomable. Who would be next? She could imagine little Stan Ericson, his crippled body pushed down the steep stairs of his basement. While Eva was snatching his dead wife's jewelry, he was saving for his granddaughter's sixteenth birthday.

Her stomach lurched again, and her eyes ached. She had to get up and away from this hellhole.

She stumbled out of her seat and kicked the exit door open, ignoring the hair in her eyes and the tears rolling down her cheeks.

Her mascara and makeup must be a wreck, but what the hell? She shuffled into the hall, looking for a fountain.

Without warning, her stomach turned inside out. She lunged toward the bathroom at the end of the hall and fell into the first stall.

Thrusting her head over the bowl, she confessed her soul into the toilet.

Her arms shook as she clutched the seat. But she refused to give in to unconsciousness. At least not in the damned Ladies' Room.

As suddenly as it had come, the wave passed. Janice fell back against the side of the stall and slid down to the floor. She gazed ahead, unaware of the small scraps of soiled toilet paper that surrounded her.

This wouldn't be the end of the book on Nettie Johnson's life.

Not if she had any say.

Chapter Twenty

Pennsylvania Hospital

Philadelphia, PA

Kyle bit her tongue until she tasted blood as she tried to suppress the monstrous yawn thundering from her toes. It was fine being the attending physician on morning rounds, but interns who ran on at the mouth to hear themselves speak were worse than a high colonic. She wondered how he'd react if she let out a primal scream. At least it would make *her* feel better.

"This one was transferred to the ICU from the ER at about eleven last night. She's a thirty-five-year-old woman who was found unconscious on the pavement by the police at Thirteenth and Locust. From the contusions on her face, arms, and chest, she appears to have been badly beaten."

Kyle knew the area well. Formerly a tough neighborhood, urban renewal had made inroads. The girl was probably a leftover hooker who crossed her pimp. They didn't last long alone on the streets.

"Unfortunately," Barclay said, "we don't have additional history."

"No ID?" Kyle asked.

"A credit card and driver's license."

"What's her name?"

"Janice Parker. We've tried to contact her family, but so far no success."

Kyle looked up in surprise. "Janice Parker?"

"Yes."

"Let me see that." She went to the computer and stared at the first page. The name was right, but this couldn't be the Janice Parker she knew.

The cohort entered the patient's ICU room.

Oh God, it was her.

Janice had taken care of any number of Kyle's homebound patients. What in heaven's name was she doing at Thirteenth and Locust?

"Go on," Kyle said, though she feared Barclay might drone on forever.

She wanted Graham Kurland on this case. Hell, she wanted Graham Kurland any way she could get him.

"Physical examination revealed a well-developed, well-nourished, unconscious white female. Her pulse was ninety and regular, and the blood pressure was one-twenty over eighty. Respirations were erratic at twenty per minute, and she was afebrile. External exam revealed multiple bruises on the face, chest, abdomen, and legs.

Kyle stared at the grotesque swelling of her face. Whoever did this must have fractured half of her facial bones. It was all too familiar.

"She had a large bruise of the right upper lid," Barclay continued, "as well as a hemorrhage from a laceration around the mouth and three broken teeth. Blood was present behind the left eardrum, suggesting a fractured skull. Her lungs sounded normal, and the cardiac exam was unremarkable. The abdomen was soft, and the pelvic exam revealed bruising and blood at the entrance to the vagina. There was also blood in the rectum."

"How about her neurologic status?"

"She's remained unconscious. When she arrived on the floor, she was unresponsive to voice and painful stimuli. I suspect her condition hasn't changed."

He reached inside the patient's hospital gown and grabbed the comatose woman's left nipple, twisting it a full 180 degrees. "See?"

Kyle's mouth dropped. "What are you doing?"

"Excuse me?"

"What if it were you and someone twisted your penis like a corkscrew?"

A female in the back of the group giggled.

Barclay lowered his head. "Sorry."

Kyle glared. *Abysmal idiot. Later, Barclay.*

She sighed. Was becoming an avenging vigilante turning her into a bad person?

But right now she needed to figure out what was going on here. Someone had destroyed a very good human being, and it made her blood boil. She'd have to make sure that the savage scumbag who did this paid the price. With interest.

She calmed herself and worried about how quickly she'd gone from fact-finding doctor to perpetrator of rogue and violent revenge. Another thought to table and investigate at a later date.

"What did the MRI show?" she asked. "Any blood?"

"No localized hematomas."

"Skull fractures?"

"Several."

"Then repeat it today. With fractures, there's always a minimum of microscopic bleeding. We need to make sure she doesn't have a late bleed."

"Will do."

"What else did the MRI show?"

"Diffuse brain swelling. I asked the neurosurgeon to see her, and he suggested we start intravenous steroids to decrease it. I loaded her with ten milligrams of IV dexamethasone and had the drip running at a milligram an hour."

Kyle flipped through the computer record. "Let's make sure we have a breathing monitor. A cardiac monitor, too. I don't like these irregular respirations."

"Okay," Barclay said, walking on eggshells, craning his neck to look down the hall. "Here's the neurosurgeon now."

Carlo Tursi, athletically thin and dressed in a different smart gray suit than he'd been wearing at their Tribunal meeting, walked with an assurance that almost concealed the limp he'd had since his injury. He was considered one of the finest neurosurgeons on the East Coast at the relatively young age of thirty-nine. And he liked everyone to know that.

"Hello, Dr. McMann…" He gave her a knowing look of intimacy that no one else would pick up on before he continued. "And folks." He smiled in response to the cacophony of greetings. "How's our patient?"

"I'm concerned about her irregular breathing, Dr. Tursi," Kyle said, ignoring his private personal quarter-smile. "Do you think she has damage to the respiratory center?"

Tursi pursed his lips. "I couldn't see it on the MRI, but we're still early. There's no reason to believe she's herniating and pushing the brainstem out through the foramen magnum to affect breathing. So, I think probably yes. I suspect she has a small contusion in the respiratory center."

Bruised brain tissue could easily explain the erratic breathing, but at least Janice wasn't herniating. Kyle had seen more than enough of that, swollen brain tissue and/or blood pushing the brain out of the skull through the foramen magnum, the hole at the bottom of the skull where the brain connected with the spinal cord. It was a surefire way to stop all breathing.

"My suggestion is to watch her and continue with the IV steroids," Tursi said. "There's a good chance she'll improve."

"To what extent?" Kyle asked.

Tursi shrugged. "Hard to say. Only time will tell."

"Thank you. I assume you'll follow her with us?"

"Of course. And I'll…see you soon," he said with a knowing nod. Then strolled out.

Kyle looked back at Janice, battered, beaten, and broken.

She vowed to get to the bottom of this.

And punish whoever was responsible.

Chapter Twenty-One

Fanelli's Restaurant

South Philadelphia, PA

Ralph DiNunzio contemplated the most painful way to exterminate whoever butchered his uncle as he leaned back in the brown leather chair and brought his third cigarette to life, defying the steel-hard rule his uncle had enforced at business meetings. Whether a meeting was family or multi-family, like this one, the rule had been inviolate. Uncle Frank Mancini would have deposited his ass on Christian Street for this.

He'd taken total control of the family since Mancini's tragic, painful, and untimely demise. And so far, the stakeholders were faring well. Nonetheless, the CEO position in this corporation had, at best, a tenuous half-life. Fraught with uncertainty in a violent world, it was subject to rapid and brutal changes.

Fifteen men from various families sat at the long oak table in the back room of Fanelli's restaurant in South Philly at ten p.m. The yellowed Venetian blinds were drawn, and the *Closed* sign hung out front. It was the week before Thanksgiving, and Christmas wreaths already graced the walls. Their pleasing fragrance complemented the agreeable aroma of the southern Italian cuisine.

Though DiNunzio lit up, no one else dared reach for a smoke. Instead, they stared straight ahead or fiddled with their drinks or napkins. The new patriarch cleared his throat and took a sip of Chianti, savoring it as he watched the others. He enjoyed how they squirmed when he stared each one down. Spineless worms, predictable as shit from a goose. Not one of them had his gonads. In another era, they'd be feudal serfs.

He slurped the rest of the wine and set the glass on the table. "Gentlemen, t'ank youze for comin'. I'll get right to da point. We still don't know da reason for my uncle's death. So we contacted one of da bes' pat'ologists from Boston to review da autopsy results." DiNunzio leaned forward. "And he t'inks Uncle Frank got poisoned."

Gasps and murmurs of astonishment filled the room. The implications were far-reaching.

Angelo Carlucci, head of the major rival family, flicked a piece of lint off the sleeve of his gray, three-piece Armani. "Why are you so sure, Ralph?"

"We know 'bout da wood alcohol, maybe just a bad batch of booze. But da doc thinks his condition came from another drug too." DiNunzio leaned forward in his seat and clasped his hands firmly on the table. He looked straight at Carlucci as he spoke.

"He examined awll da specimens and said he di'n't know of anything else it could be."

Carlucci stood up. "Ralph, I hope you're not implying that anyone here is connected with your uncle's unfortunate death."

"I'm not sayin' dat, Angie. I jus' want to see justice done if what the doctor says is true."

Carlucci clenched his jaw and stared at DiNunzio, who smiled. Carlucci was a prime suspect. He and Mancini had more than their share of confrontations in the past.

DiNunzio glanced at Carlucci's face and then followed the lines of his jacket. It was understood that one came unarmed to these meetings. Yet, in these unstable times, nobody could be certain the older rules were still sacred. Several men looked to their personal guards, who stood at respectful distances.

"God dammit, Ralph!" Carlucci punched his open palm with a closed fist.

"Frank and I had our disagreements. But I swear nobody in our family was involved."

The room hushed. Every man waited for DiNunzio's reply, each holding his breath. Even the smoke from DiNunzio's cigarette stopped its circuitous journey.

The guards stiffened, tense, ready to spring.

DiNunzio looked down, then up at Carlucci. He tapped his thick fingers and licked his stretched lips.

"I don't th'ink youze had anything to do wit' dis, Ang."

The group let out a sigh of relief. The Feds had been crawling up their asses with microscopes for the past year. And right now, war would be disastrous.

"I'm glad to hear that," Carlucci said, pulling on his lapels on his jacket as he sat. "So, who do you suspect?"

"I don' know. Dat's why I asked youze here. I need help from you and yer people, Angie. I need help from everyone in dis room."

"You got it, Ralph."

The others nodded their support.

"Good. And when we find 'em, I'll cut deir balls awff an' stuff 'them down deir throats."

A wave of agreement swept through the room

Ralph smirked. As he proclaimed, "Dey'll be begging us to kill them before we're done gettin' our pound of flesh."

Chapter Twenty-Two

Philadelphia's Main Line

Berwyn, PA

Kyle McMann was the first of the four docs and three other members of the Tribunal to hand off her execution vote on the next violent ghoul who'd escaped justice to Alden Booth, Stenton's fastidious assistant.

Despite the merry pre-Christmas atmosphere in the City, the tone was solemn at the monthly Tribunal meeting. It reminded Kyle of the Sunday prayer meeting at her childhood home just before a hellion of a tornado struck.

Lionel C. Stenton was seated at the head of the dining room table in his Berwyn manse. To Stenton's left was Booth's empty chair. In clockwise order, then came ex-SEALs Randy White and Nate Champion, ophthalmologist Art Ramos, anesthesiologist Lindsey Tate, neurosurgeon Carlo Tursi, and Kyle McMann.

Booth took Kyle's paper and added it to the others. He was a slight, harmless-looking man with a pencil-slim mustache, a hook nose, and brown eyes that appeared magnified behind wire-rimmed gold spectacles.

Art Ramos leaned over to Kyle. "A serious case of nerdis physiologicus. I hope it's not terminal."

"Sorry?"

"Booth," he whispered. "Doesn't he look like a mouse with glasses?"

Kyle coughed to cover her giggle. Trust Art to lighten the mood.

Stenton glared.

Booth was the most compulsive person Kyle had ever met. A former psychologist, he had relinquished his career to become Stenton's aide. The man was competent. He just lacked sensitivity for other humans.

She imagined a "humph" as his little mouth frowned if he'd heard Art's comment. She pictured him with sharp little whiskers and choked down another laugh. Art was spot on.

Stenton surveyed the others from his seat. Booth stopped beside Tursi and folded his arms across his chest.

"Dammit, man, stop hovering," Tursi snapped. "You're enough to make coffee nervous."

Booth dropped his arms and folded his hands. He was pushy and demanding in his position as Stenton's chief exec, but he wasn't a fool.

Tursi cast the final vote, and Stenton took the returns. "You've all reviewed the case," Stenton said, "and I trust your decisions merit careful thought." He leafed through the papers, one by one.

Kyle reflected upon the events that led to the final vote, wondering if anyone had doubts. Or was there some small piece of evidence she'd forgotten?

Janice came out of her coma after ten days. At first, she spoke with a ratchet-like voice that made conversation impossible. Two weeks later, she was able to tell her story in bits and pieces.

She'd followed Eva after the trial, mustering the courage to confront her at her apartment. When Janice pressed for the lurid details, she got them. Because Eva had no intention of letting her leave with them.

Janice's biggest mistake was underestimating her opponent. Eva had freakish strength and knew how to use it. She struck the first blow, a vicious shot to Janice's face. After that, everything was a blur.

Kyle could only piece together the rest. It was night, and Eva knew she had to finish in short order. She'd pummeled Janice's body with her boots until she stopped breathing, then assumed her victim was dead. In any case, she took the corpse a dozen blocks away—in a wheelchair?—and deposited it in an alley off Thirteenth Street.

It was a clever cover-up, but she'd made one serious mistake. Janice wasn't dead. She was in severe shock, the fine-line limbo between life and death.

Kyle had called in the police after she learned the details, but the hearing was a joke. Janice was no stalker, although you wouldn't know it from the courtroom actions.

The DA obviously knew what he was talking about when he said the case was weak. There was no evidence that Janice had even been in Eva's apartment. No DNA, no blood, hair, or bits of skin. Eva played the eraser game well.

And now Janice was deteriorating again, so much so that coherent speech had slipped away. Kyle groaned when she heard the diagnosis.

Encephalomalacia.

Thousands of little bubbles in the brain where bruised tissue was breaking down. There was only one way for her to go. And there was nothing they could do about it.

"No witnesses," "lack of evidence," "with a reasonable degree of certainty," all spewed from Eva's attorney like bile.

Kyle felt like wringing his neck in that kangaroo court. Add that idiot judge to the list, too, the same one as at Eva's last trial. She didn't know for sure, but she suspected Eva was not above dalliances when necessary. The body language was there.

It had been six weeks since Eva had brutally pummeled Janice. And over three months since Nettie Johnson's death. Despite the time, Kyle could see the vivid details fresh in the mind of each person at the table.

Stenton looked up.

"Guilty."

Kyle bowed her head, happy invisible justice was going to be served. The vote was unanimous. From her point of view, no sentence would be too severe. The woman was a vile ogre.

The others sat stone still. A great weight was lifted now that the decision was made. Tursi shot a glance toward Kyle, and their eyes met, neither showing emotion.

"The floor's open for discussion," Stenton said.

Kyle raised her hand.

"Yes?"

"I've given this considerable thought."

"We're listening."

"I propose a tiered method of retribution for Eva Corman, something appropriate for the agony she caused Nettie Johnson, Janice Parker, and who knows who else. But I'll need help, however."

She turned to Lindsey Tate.

Tate was a distinguished-looking Black man. Completely bald except for a semicircular rim of gray-black hair that started just above his ears, he had a small mustache of similar shading that complemented his effusive smile. He was an anesthesiology prodigy who had risen from the ranks with a fistful of academic honors, holding both a PhD in pharmacology and an MD from Jefferson Medical University.

"What can I do?" he asked, his voice deep and resonant.

"I need a purified preparation of streptozotocin."

"You said streptozotocin?"

"Yes."

"That's an unusual one."

"Can you get it?"

"I think so."

"Excellent. And there's one other."

"What's that?"

"Kuru virus."

"Good grief! That's deadly material." Tate took off his glasses and rubbed his forehead. "I don't think—"

"Can you do it?"

"Well…"

"Can you?"

"Why Kuru?"

"Because it'll work."

"That's like playing football with nitroglycerin."

"I understand."

"Kyle, you know as well as I do—"

"I do. That's not the question. Can you get it?"

"I don't know. I've worked with streptozotocin, but Kuru's another matter. Think of those poor people in New Guinea."

"I understand, but if we're going to do this right, I need Kuru."

"All else aside, how do you intend to administer these entities?"

Kyle frowned. "They have to be given intravenously. It's the only way to get a high enough dose of streptozotocin and protect everybody from Kuru."

The creases in Tate's forehead multiplied tenfold. He turned to Nate Champion and Randy White.

The two ex-Navy SEALs always had good ideas.

"Gentlemen, I agree with Kyle. This has to be administered by vein, which leaves us with a major problem. How do we do it?"

"What about that dart pistol?" Nate suggested.

"Excellent idea," Randy replied.

"Tell 'em about it."

Randy clasped his hands and leaned forward. "Back in the service, we worked with a .06 caliber air gun that used minuscule darts. It was designed for the CIA by a doctor. The darts have an anesthetic on them and are shaped to penetrate the skin with little or no pain. Inside each one, there's a hollow compartment that carries drugs."

"Any drug?" Tate asked.

"Anything liquid."

"It's simple, then," Tate said. "Chloral hydrate. We'll give her concentrated chloral hydrate."

"A Mickey Finn," Tursi said with a grin.

Stenton sat up straight. "Damn it, Carlo, I see no humor here. We're deciding a person's fate."

Tursi's black eyes flashed. "Mr. Stenton, death is a part of my work, and

I find that levity helps keep my sanity." Tursi continued, his eyes meeting Stenton's straight on."But don't think for a minute that I take this matter with any less gravity than you."

Stenton returned Tursi's penetrating stare with equal resolve. "I'm glad to know that."

Tate jumped in before Tursi could speak again. "If I could clarify Carlo's comment, a 'Mickey Finn' is the layperson's term for chloral hydrate in alcohol. Chloral hydrate is a potent sedative that produces prolonged sleep. A dose of one gram makes an effective sleeping pill; a dose of eight grams is lethal. I suggest a dose of four grams—enough to put her out for at least twelve hours. I can concentrate it into a drop or two of fluid. Will the dart hold that?"

Randy thought for a moment. "It should."

Kyle looked at Randy. "I have a question."

"Yes?"

"What happens to this dart? Can it be picked up on X-ray?"

"That's the beauty of it. The thing's made of a protein with sugar that's absorbed by the body within hours. It's untraceable."

Kyle filled in the details. They liked her idea, she could tell from their faces. And it wouldn't take long to get off the ground. Now they just had to avoid carelessness. Anything short of perfection could leave them with a fate worse than death.

"Mr. Stenton," she said, "I suggest that one of the medical people accompany Nate and Randy on this case. Like I said, the drugs have to be given by vein while she's asleep. The technique is tricky, and there's no room for error with Kuru."

The other physicians nodded their agreement.

Nate and Randy remained silent but exchanged glances. Kyle knew they were used to working as a pair. She hoped they didn't think she lacked confidence in them. But they had no idea how dangerous Kuru was.

"I have no objections," Nate said.

"Me either," Randy agreed.

"Good," Kyle said, "because I want to be the one who goes."

CHAPTER TWENTY-TWO

Their faces fell, and neither spoke.

She'd expected this. She was regarded as a talented and maybe the brightest member of the group. But she was still a woman. Why should it be any different here than in the real world?

Nate and Randy fumbled with their pencils and avoided her gaze.

"I understand you might have reservations about my capabilities in a tight situation," Kyle said. "But I can keep up with the best."

"It's nothing personal," Nate said. "It's just that Randy and I are kind of, well… we're used to working together." He shrugged. "We'd consider it an honor to work with you."

Randy nodded. "Absolutely."

"Fine then." Stenton stood up to leave. "You three hammer out the details. And watch your sixes."

Kyle imagined freezing when she was needed most and getting her new friends mangled, maimed, or killed.

Just like she did with her brother.

A lightning bolt of pain exploded in her brain.

Chapter Twenty-Three

Eva Corman's Condominium

Center City, Philadelphia

Exactly five minutes after Eva Corman's car left the parking garage, Randy and Nate entered the lobby of her Franklin Arms condo building. Each had on a gray Philadelphia Electric Company shirt with a stitched-on red name over the white cloth rectangle above the left pocket.

They introduced themselves to the uniformed door attendant, then stomped off the mid-January snow onto the weave rug covering the marbled floor.

The stone-faced attendant had been notified that the electrical contractors would be doing repair work. He thus allowed the tool-laden pair to enter with a constipated smile and unequivocal disapproval of their boot-cleansing methods and general lack of etiquette.

They first went to the basement to disable the current to her condo, then proceeded to the third floor. Nate removed the elevator switch panel on Three and began to adjust and readjust the wires. It was mid-afternoon and, except for them, the hallway was deserted.

"Keep me posted," Randy said as he started down the hall.

"With all this traffic, I'll be calling every ten seconds."

"Wise ass. Just don't electrocute yourself."

In a matter of seconds, Randy picked the deadlock to Eva's apartment, stepped inside, and locked the door behind him.

He winced at the kitchen filth but wasted no time in getting down to business. The "enabled" and "disabled" lights on the alarm panel were both out, thanks to their little safari to the basement. It didn't get much easier than this.

Randy unscrewed the telephone mouthpieces in the bedroom and the living room and inserted a small, round disc beneath each receiver. He loved these little guys. They monitored incoming and outgoing calls, and could disable a phone in a blink if need be.

Since she likely had a cell as well, he planted a jammer under her bed, close to where she'd probably use it.

He gathered his tools and turned to the front door, then stopped to tap his earwig.

Damned static...

"Randy, don't come out. Cop in the hallway."

Cops? What were they doing here?

How could they have been so stupid? A battery backup. But in a guarded building? This Corman was one suspicious bitch.

The knock on the wooden door reverberated through the apartment.

"Philadelphia Police. Open the door, please."

Randy looked to the windows. Twenty feet or more to hard pavement, not even a tree close by. The chances of breaking a bone on the sidewalk were high, even for someone with skills and physical prowess. Besides, there were people on the street. It would look really great for some guy with a tool pouch to suddenly drop from the sky.

"Nate," he whispered, "are they trying to force the door?"

"No, just turning the knob. It's only one cop."

"The devices are set, but I can't get out the window."

"Let me see what I can do."

Randy heard a shrill sound, then the knocking stopped. He jammed the receiver into his ear to catch what was happening.

"Hello, officer," Nate said.

Randy let out a sigh of relief.

"What's that noise, buddy?"

"Just my electron polarizer."

"Your what?"

"It gives megahertz readings on the elevator."

"Huh?"

"That's how they run nowadays. By computer."

"Okay…you seen anybody come by here?"

"No, it's just been me for the past half hour. Been working solid."

There was a pause. "The doorman said there were two of you. Where's your partner?"

"In the basement. He had to cut the power circuits. Is there a problem?"

"The alarm to this apartment went off. I'm investigating."

"Hmm…probably because we had to fool around with the main circuit board. Happens all the time."

"Whatever. Let's see some ID, pal."

"Sure."

There were muffled noises as Nate searched for his wallet and Pennsylvania driver's license. Randy, for once, was thankful for Alden Booth's compulsiveness. He insisted upon impeccable credentials.

There was a pause after the cop called in the license.

"Alright, Mr. Davis, how about letting the station know next time you're working around lines that set off alarms. I could haul you in, you know."

"Sorry, Officer," Nate said. "Next time we'll call."

Randy waited for the all-clear from his partner. He reset the alarm and battery alarm backup, opened the door, reset the deadlock, then wiped the perspiration from his forehead as he hustled down the hallway. Nate already had the elevator panel back up, and the two walked down the stairs to the parking garage in the basement.

Geez, he hated getting his clothes soaked every time he went on a mission.

Waiting for Eva Corman would be the easy part.

He hoped.

Chapter Twenty-Four

Eva Corman's Condominium

Center City, Philadelphia, PA

Eva Corman fingered the .32 Smith and Wesson snub-nose revolver in her purse as her Buick pulled back into the parking lot. She sat for several seconds, scanning the area for anything out of the ordinary. Then she cautiously walked into the parking lot, opened the trunk, and tugged on a bag of groceries.

"Okay, William Tell," Randy whispered from their spot behind a red Olds. "Go for it."

"Right. A blind cyclops could hit this babe."

"Don't make me laugh," Nate whispered. He let a breath halfway out and squeezed the trigger.

"Bullseye."

Nate gave his partner a playful fist-bump in the chest.

Eva spun around, frowning, and grabbed her right buttock. Occasionally, the darts caused minor discomfort, but it was momentary, like an insect bite. She'd gotten the slow-release kind, so they had twenty minutes until the chloral hydrate kicked in.

"Look at that face," Randy whispered. "Pissed off at the world."

Eva rubbed her backside, then bent over to look under all the vehicles.

Randy and Nate jumped up and held onto the side of the car by grabbing the door handles.

After ten seconds, Eva shrugged and resumed her efforts to pull out the groceries.

The stage was set.

Chapter Twenty-Five

Pennsylvania Hospital

Center City, Philadelphia

Kyle jumped when her office phone rang at a deafening decibel level. Her respiratory rate jacked up double time, and sweat dripped from her hairline onto her blotter.

She took a deep, calming breath and connected. "Dr. McCann."

"In front of Independence Hall. Twenty minutes."

The receiver clicked. Kyle bit her lip and looked at her watch. It was four p.m. on the dot. Independence Hall was a five-minute walk at most. She had ample time to spare.

She signed out with the hospital operator and threw on Nittany Lion sweats over her street clothes so she'd be inconspicuous among the other runners on the Philadelphia streets. Before leaving, she grabbed a small package from her desk and tucked it under her loose-fitting top.

Outside the hospital, she headed toward America's birthplace. A gentle breeze ruffled the maples and caused the ice on their bare branches to sparkle in the waning rays of the January sun. The bells in the old Presbyterian Church on Pine Street bonged out the time—as usual, two minutes late. But Kyle had other things on her mind.

Traffic around Independence Hall was heavy, even for rush hour. Kyle stationed herself on the front sidewalk next to the nine-foot cast-iron statue of George Washington and waited.

Four-twenty.

She tapped her foot and scanned the oncoming vehicles for Nate and Randy's black van. Where the hell were they? What if something happened? Had her lust for revenge put her in the middle of a shitstorm that could blow up her world?

A blue and white police car pulled up straight ahead.

Oh my God!

She stopped mid-breath, heart pounding three times its normal rate.

Time to run?

Which way?

The passenger side cop was looking right at her, the sunlight reflecting off his mirrored glasses. He raised them and motioned.

A wave of relief swept over her.

Randy White, dressed in the smart blue of Philadelphia's finest, smiled from the open window. Officer Nate Champion was driving.

Kyle climbed in the back, her hands trembling.

"You okay?" Randy said, turning around. "You forgot about the patrol car, didn't you?"

"Yes." Kyle swiped her bangs. "I thought I was cooked."

Randy's smile broadened, and she could see Nate grin in the rear-view mirror.

"Don't worry," Randy said. "Happens to everyone the first time."

Kyle slipped out of her sweats. "First time? Does that mean I get to go on the next one, too?"

"Depends on this one, Wonder Woman." Randy flipped her a card for her wallet. "Here's your badge, double-oh-seven."

"Very funny."

They pulled up a block or so from Eva's condo and walked the rest of the way to the building. The doorman gave an obsequious smile as they entered. They'd waited until the change of shift to avoid the curmudgeon Nate and Randy dealt with earlier.

All three kept on their large sunglasses to throw off the camera behind the lobby desk. Without inter-pupillary distances, photo-ID software freaked out.

Kyle turned her back to the camera, flashed her badge, and folded her glasses in her hand. "Detective Smith, Officers Fisher and Iacobucci. Here to check out another burglar alarm."

"Christ, this is the second time today. Those electricians must have really screwed something up."

They took the elevator to the third floor. So far, so good. The phone monitors showed Eva hadn't made any calls.

Randy knocked hard.

No answer.

The hallway was still empty, but people would be coming home from work soon. Randy took out his pin-like picks and blew through the lock. He then checked to make sure the regular alarm and battery alarm were off.

The men entered and turned right into the kitchen, leaving Kyle behind. She felt like the kid sister being ignored by her older brothers.

Eva was slumped in a wooden chair, slouched over the table, her face lying in a half-eaten piece of custard pie.

Randy elbowed Nate. "Honest, Mama, I wasn't cheating on my diet."

"Stop it." Kyle pushed the two men aside. She pulled back Eva's head and felt her neck for a pulse. Thready, but there.

"Help me," she said. "She's blue. Look. She's suffocating in the pie."

Nate pulled out the chair, and Randy helped Kyle lay Eva on the floor. Her nose and mouth were clogged with custard and cream.

Kyle searched through the drawers and grabbed a small butter knife to excavate the debris. She stopped for a second to place one hand in front of Eva's mouth and the other on her pulse.

"Damn. She's really depressed."

"From the chloral hydrate or the pie?" Randy asked.

"Probably both. Give me some room."

Kyle knelt over Eva, pulled her chin backwards, and forced a breath into her mouth. Yellow custard blew out Eva's nostrils, hitting Nate right in the face.

"Ohhhh shit!" He wiped off the snot-like debris.

Eva's chest rose each time Kyle exhaled with CPR. Minutes passed until she finally began breathing on her own.

"What a disgusting job." Kyle looked up and shook her head.

"Copy that," Nate commiserated. "Good, you got her back to the land of the living. Would've been bad if the cops found a ton of chloral hydrate in her veins."

Randy remained silent, his arms crossed, jaw set as he stood over Kyle and Eva.

Nate dropped to his knees and examined Eva's arms. "Whoa… Where's a vein?"

"Let me see," Kyle said.

It was a common complaint of junior house staff when they attempted to put in IV lines. She just took the needle and eased it into a blood vessel. But Nate was right. Her veins were deep. They might as well be buried under a sand dune.

But there was no choice. The drugs had to be injected straight into the bloodstream. Kyle moved down toward the hands. Nothing. She hadn't expected this. Eva might be carrying a few extra pounds, but she was far from obese.

She smacked the back of Eva's right hand, then finger flicked it with rabid passion.

"What are you doing?" Nate asked.

"Trying to raise a vein. Gimme the alcohol."

Kyle rubbed the area she'd beaten until the surface was almost raw. A good alcohol rub would often raise a vein when all else failed.

It didn't.

"What do we do now?" Randy asked. "Give them as shots?"

"They won't work," Kyle said. "It's IV or nothing."

Kyle sat back and stared. Sometimes the external jugular vein on the outside of the neck was a good vessel. Not today, though. The last thing they needed was a large hematoma at the injection site to raise suspicion.

She stewed in silence for thirty seconds. "I've got it!"

She opened Eva's mouth and pulled out her tongue with a gloved hand. "You see them?"

"See what?" Nate and Randy said in unison.

"The veins under her tongue. This is one of the few places in the body you can give an injection without leaving a mark someone will see."

Kyle looked at them, pleased with herself. "If you ever want to commit suicide and let someone collect on your life insurance, give yourself an injection under the tongue with a tiny needle. Nobody will ever find it. They'll never look." She pulled harder on the thick organ to get better exposure.

"Thanks," Nate said. "Good intel."

Randy managed a wry smile. "Yeah, I'll remember that."

Kyle picked the largest vein, then let the tongue pop back into Eva's mouth. She drew up the syringes, one containing streptozotocin, the other the Kuru virus. She wanted to handle the Kuru as little as possible. Exposure to a fraction of a drop could be deadly. She laid them on a piece of newspaper from her pocket.

"Guys, put on gloves. Nate, help me hold her tongue."

"Sure." He donned a pair of blue rubber gloves and pulled on the organ.

The large purple blood vessels under Eva's tongue stood out in bold relief. Kyle took a small intravenous catheter, punctured the most prominent vein, and advanced the tip. There was good blood return.

"We're in," she announced.

She turned to Randy, careful not to upset the precarious IV line.

"Grab the syringe labeled streptozotocin."

Randy picked it up. The clear plastic cylinder contained a teaspoonful of a yellow fluid, viscous and malicious in intent.

"Now take the needle off the end of the syringe."

"Okay." He gingerly unfastened the capped needle with a counterclockwise twist.

"You don't have to be careful with this one," Kyle said. "It can't hurt you. Plus, you have on gloves."

"Yeah, but the needle could—"

"You call yourself a SEAL?" Nate snickered.

"Ex-SEAL."

"Just give me the damn thing."

Kyle grabbed the syringe from Randy's hand and held it up to the light, scrutinizing the calibrations. She handed it back.

"You'll have to fasten it to the line. I need two hands; I can't let go of the IV, or we'll lose the vessel."

Randy removed the cap from the free end of the IV tubing and connected the syringe with streptozotocin.

Kyle stared at the needle in Eva's tongue. "Now, inject. Slowly...no rush..."

The fluid entered the thin plastic tubing, pushing back a line of red blood trying to flow out. The yellow and red met, forming a distinct juncture moving toward the tongue. This was the point of no return.

The drug entered Eva Corman's body and disappeared, moving to every organ within sixty seconds. While most tissues were immune to its effects, within hours, the islet cells of the pancreas would selectively absorb the toxin and be rendered forever useless.

The next substance was the one Kyle respected and feared, loved and yet hated. Used in the right way, it had great research potential for neurodegenerative diseases. But it could also cause a fate so repulsive that the natives of New Guinea who formerly practiced ritual cannibalism preferred the blessing of death to its final stages. These included tremors, emotional outbursts, difficulty walking, trouble swallowing, and dementia, all eventually leading to death.

The extract had been carefully prepared with Lindsey Tate's help in Kyle's infectious disease research lab at the hospital.

Kuru prions in the solution, the transmissible pathogenetic agents...were a good bit smaller than most bacteria. They had the unique ability to bend proteins in the brain and kill neurons.

Unweakened.

Devastating to neurological function.

CHAPTER TWENTY-FIVE

Routinely lethal.

No direct contact was permitted, and the Kuru containers were only touched with latex gloves and gowns. It was safe when handled under a sterile hood, with laminar air flow and no access to the outside. Unleashed in an uncontrolled environment, it was worse than deadly.

A cubic millimeter, one fiftieth of a drop, contained enough prions to seal the fate of a hundred men if in the blood. The virus could theoretically enter through mucous membranes in the mouth, nasal or ocular tissue, or through the vagina or rectum. But those routes might well fail. An IV approach, however, virtually guaranteed success.

"Randy," Kyle looked up at him, "can you hold the IV and her tongue? I'd better handle this one myself."

"No argument there."

Randy and Kyle switched places.

She removed the spent syringe and replaced it with the Kuru syringe. Small beads of sweat broke out on her forehead. A spittle of a drop from a leak in the plastic line or syringe could finish any of them. With maximum pain. Her hands quivered as she tried to push the plunger, inject the solution into a human being she despised—yet a human being nonetheless. It went against all she stood for. Yet it also saved innocent lives.

And honored her dear, dead brother.

"Want me to do it?" Randy asked.

"N-no," Kyle said. "First-time jitters, is all."

"We understand," Nate said, "but it has to be done."

Kyle remained in a kneeling position. This was her show. She took a breath and mustered her strength to push.

This is for Nettie...and for Janice...and for everyone else who's been in your clutches. If only they could be here.

She pushed the plunger toward the base of the syringe, meeting resistance at the end.

Ninety percent of the drug went in. Then the plastic line flew off on the syringe end, and a fine spray misted from the opening.

The guillotine blade had dropped.

"Sweet," Nate said.

While Kyle tried not to freak out as she muttered, "Oh shit."

"What?" Randy asked, suddenly on high alert.

"No, not sweet," Kyle said. "Some liquid passed out from the end of the catheter. Avoid her face, neck, and upper chest when you carry her to her bed."

Kyle removed the IV, and Nate and Randy carefully lifted Eva by her arms with ease and lowered her onto the bed.

She ran to Eva's kitchen closet and rummaged through the contents with her gloved hands. She carried back a white plastic bottle of Clorox with a red-and-blue label.

"Sorry, "Nate said as he returned. "I shouldn't have said sweet."

"It's not that…"

Randy went to rub his nose.

Kyle grabbed his wrist in mid-air and held it.

"Hey!" he said.

"Do not touch your noses," Kyle commanded

"Why not?" Randy asked.

"Somehow the injection line became obstructed…and at the end a small amount of formula sprayed out."

"Did enough get in?" Nate asked.

"More than enough," Kyle replied. "I'm not worried about that. It's the Kuru that escaped."

Both men froze. They all looked at each other in a silent three-way staring contest.

Kyle finally spoke, having thought out her plan.

"We all take a shower here with Clorox. Then, when we go right home, drop all our clothes in full-strength Clorox and gently rub it on our skin in the shower again. Then wash it right off with soap and water after sixty seconds."

"We're going out of here looking like wet scarecrows?" Nate asked.

"No," Kyle said, already removing her blouse. "Take off your clothes."

Nate and Randy looked stunned, then blushed.

"Come on," Kyle said as she removed her pants. "You have two choices. Shower. Or don't shower, risk getting Kuru and dying a worse death than you could ever imagine. It's a bad way to go."

They whipped their clothes off and followed a now naked Kyle to a large stall shower.

She turned on the water and stepped in. "Watch me."

"Not hard to do," Randy whispered.

Nate nodded his agreement.

Kyle washed every place she could reach, then asked Nate to step in to do her back.

She next splattered Clorox on every square inch of her skin. "It's going to hurt anywhere unless you have open skin," she said. "And don't get any in your eyes."

"This could be an awful lot of fun if it wasn't for staring death in the face," Nate quipped.

"I was thinking the same thing," Kyle said with a half-smile, trying to lighten the situation.

She finished rinsing and stared at the two men. "Now, you both do the same."

Kyle left the shower and grabbed three towels from Eva's closet. She dried off, put on the clothes she had worn, and left two towels for the men.

Within three minutes, the men were dried off and dressed as well.

They picked up their belongings and the towels and stopped at the door to look over the apartment one last time. Kyle had already dried up any floor drips with paper towels soaked with Clorox and stuffed them into her small satchel.

No loose ends.

"What do you think?" Randy asked Nate. "All clear out there?"

Nate pointed his infrared scanner toward the outside hall. "Near as I can tell," he said.

Randy opened the door. They left the apartment and boarded the elevator for the lobby. Kyle waved to the doorman at the front desk, who returned a nominal wave without looking up from his "Elvis Spotted in NYC" page of the *National Enquirer*.

She felt a wave of crushing nausea leave her belly. She stopped outside and took in the cold air to help stop the nausea. She was still shaky, and her shirt was soaked from new sweat, but a great weight had been lifted from her shoulders. She threw her arms around Nate and Randy's shoulders.

"Hey guys, thanks," she said in a weak voice.

Randy patted her on the back of the hand. "O'Riordan's is just down the block."

"No way," Kyle managed. "Home to your showers for another Clorox bath. And let's make it quick before I puke on the sidewalk."

Randy steadied Kyle's arm and guided her into the car.

"Let's get you home before we all die."

"Excellent idea," Kyle grinned weakly.

Chapter Twenty-Six

Eva Corman's Condominium

Center City, Philadelphia

"Oh, fuck me!"

Eva opened her eyes and reached back to rub the kink in her neck, a pain that felt like the mother of all aches. Had she fallen asleep with it bent the wrong way?

She stared up at the jagged crack traversing her white bedroom ceiling. But she knew that no crack was there. A hallucination? She blinked for thirty seconds, and it disappeared. Thank the Lord. As if she needed anything else.

The morning sun had crept in, and she could hear pigeons squabbling under the eaves outside the window. Why couldn't they just shut up?

She lay in bed trying to remember what she'd been doing before she fell asleep.

She was sitting at the kitchen table, eating. Yes, a custard pie, that's right. What else? It was all so fuzzy. Did she call James at the pawn shop? Did she watch TV? Another *NCIS*? God, she must have really been dead.

Eva dozed in and out of consciousness for an hour, swearing each time she awoke that she'd get up. When the radio alarm exploded at eight, she tried to get up.

She made it on the third attempt, dizzy and struggling, but upright. She usually wasn't this exhausted in the morning. Maybe she had a cold, or even the flu. Sometimes a canker sore came before her colds, and she could feel a new one under her tongue. It hurt like a son-of-a-gun when she rolled the tip backward to feel it.

That had to be it, a cold. That's why she felt like crap. Better pop a few Tylenols and Sudafed before it got worse.

Cold or not, she had to get her ass in gear. Today was the first of what she hoped would be many prosperous visits with a new client.

Eva swung both legs over the edge. She shook her head from side to side, trying to clear it.

Did she have a few drinks? Was that it? God dammit, what the hell happened last night?

As her level of consciousness improved, she realized that her lower abdomen ached when she moved. It felt like her bladder was ready to burst.

That was it! She must have put down a few Jack Daniels and didn't remember. That's why she had this damn headache and slept for twelve hours. Now it all made sense.

She staggered into the bathroom. Mystery solved, she perked up.

None too soon either. If she could work the old Rosenberg widow like she expected, there'd be a lot more cash shares in the Eva Corman account.

Chapter Twenty-Seven

Pennsylvania Hospital

Philadelphia, PA

Kyle's heartburn was in the stratosphere, with hydrochloric acid gobbling up the lining of her stomach like some demented version of Pac-Man. Add to that, her nerves were frazzled to a cinder, any that were left. But the images of Nettie and Janice kept her going.

She excused herself from the rear of the Pennsylvania Hospital elevator and got off on Two. She was exhausted. Not surprising, since she hadn't slept more than two hours straight for the past two weeks.

Janice had deteriorated to the point that she needed a tracheotomy, a hole in her neck to connect a breathing tube. A machine pumped in air fifteen times a minute to keep her alive in a nursing home.

In a small town near Pittsburgh, no less, where her mother lived. The administrators had refused to keep her another day at Pennsylvania Hospital. And while Kyle disagreed, she understood that regulations were pushing them.

Regrettably, with her schedule, there was little chance she would get to Pittsburgh soon to see her. Not that Kyle could do anything they couldn't.

It was only a matter of time until Janice aspirated food into her lungs. Then bacterial pneumonia would move in. With any luck, the end would be swift, and she wouldn't realize it.

Today was Kyle's day to help the house staff, assisting the interns and residents who manage the incoming patients in Medical Clinic. They saw it all here: young, old, thin, fat. Good health to near death. Pennsylvania Hospital had the reputation of being one of the finest medical facilities in the City of Brotherly Love. And for good reason. The brightest young minds in the country came here. The clinic was therefore popular, and the patient load seemed never-ending.

Kyle walked into the waiting room and stopped in her tracks. Dead ahead was a woman in a blue-print dress.

Eva Corman!

Her head and heart pounded as she stood frozen in place. Eva, not six feet away, stared off with a vacant look.

Don't just stand there, McMann. Move!

Kyle cleared her throat, praying she wouldn't be recognized when she slipped by.

Eva seemed to frown, and Kyle thought she heard a soft grunt. But that was it. Eva had seen her face-to-face during Nettie's hearing, but it was obvious she didn't remember. Could it be the Kuru already?

Kyle retreated to the privacy of the back hallway. She rested against the wall and took shallow breaths. Her medical training had never prepared her for this. How could it?

Graham Kurland spotted her and couldn't stop a smile from spreading on his face. But as he studied her, he knew something was wrong.

Quite wrong.

And he wanted to make it right. So he hustled over.

"Kyle, you okay?"

"Couldn't be better." Even she could tell she sounded like a terrible liar.

"You look pale."

"Just weak for a second. I shouldn't have skipped breakfast. I'll be fine." She looked at her watch. "You better get moving. Looks like a real circus out there today. Let me know if I can help."

"Come on." Graham took her arm. "You don't look like that from skipping breakfast."

He walked her down to the attending physician's office, where they sat on a sofa. He felt her pulse, then listened to her chest with his stethoscope and felt her face for a fever.

"I'm okay," Kyle said. "Really."

"Then why are you sweating like you just came out of the sauna and look like you just had a near-death experience?" He took her blood pressure. "Low. Ninety over fifty."

"You haven't really seemed yourself the past couple of weeks," he said, resting his hand on top of hers.

"What do you mean?" she asked defensively.

"You don't smile. You're jumpy. And you seem to have difficulty concentrating...now this."

"It's just that I..." She looked into his eyes and had the almost overwhelming impulse to confess everything. "Have something we should talk about sometime."

"Kyle, it's me," Graham said with heartbreaking earnest empathy shining in his kind eyes.

"I've been..." But when she tried, the words just wouldn't come out.

"Talk to me. I'm worried about you."

"Thank you, Graham. Seriously. But not now." She rubbed the back of her free hand against his cheek. "I'm actually feeling better... Go to clinic. Or you'll be so far behind that you won't know which end is up."

"Do you have your phone?"

"Yes."

"Call me if anything gets worse. I'll be checking in on you."

She leaned forward to give him a kiss on the lips.

He returned a kiss to her forehead. "Call me later."

"I will," Kyle said as she watched him stride away on his long, strong legs.

Still shaken, she lay back on the sofa. It was two weeks since Eva's injections, but it had to be the virus. Things were moving much faster than she'd expected.

The next several hours in the clinic passed uneventfully, but by five o'clock, Kyle felt like she was going to explode. Graham had checked twice, and she told him she was fine.

He knew it was a lie. But she was grateful he didn't call her on it.

All afternoon, she'd been dying to get a look at that record. The residents and patients had gone, but the charts were still stacked on the counter by the registration desk.

At last, the clerk left.

She ran out to the pile.

Where was it?

Come on, it must be here.

She threw the top few charts off to the side, then leafed through the others like a woman possessed. Finally, it surfaced.

Graham had seen her himself. He wouldn't miss a thing. She flipped the pages and scanned the history.

Forty-five-year-old woman with sudden onset of increased frequency of urination—up four to five times a night—ten-pound weight loss over the past two weeks—marked thirst, drinking excessive water—increased appetite.

Kyle wet her lips. Excessive urinating, drinking, and eating: the triad of acute diabetes mellitus. Aretaeus, the ancient Greek, nailed it on the head when he named it "to run through" two thousand years before.

She scanned for today's blood glucose level.

Four hundred fifty!

Three times normal.

The streptozotocin had done its work well. There probably wasn't an insulin-producing cell left in Eva Corman's pancreas. She now had fulminant diabetes mellitus.

Just like Nettie Johnson.

But could anyone figure out why?

Only one person she could think of.

She wished someone other than Graham had picked up the chart.

Anyone.

Chapter Twenty-Eight

Washington Square

Center City, Philadelphia

Graham Kurland paced in Kyle's Washington Square apartment building lobby, tripping over the rug. Fidgeting with his collar, he glanced at the elevator, then looked at his watch for the tenth time in ten minutes. There wasn't much that made him nervous, but right now he felt like a teenager going to his prom.

The elevator bell rang. Graham took a last look in the full-length mirror and straightened his black tie. Grandma Meg was right. Nothing made a man in a tux look worse than a crooked tie.

The doors parted, and Kyle smiled as she walked toward him. She was radiant. The low-cut red dress accentuated her smooth skin and clung to her soft curves.

"Hi." Her voice was like an angel's.

"You look...wow!"

"Thank you. Sorry, I'm late, but it's not every night that a girl gets invited to a ball at the Union League. Quite a change from the lab coat, isn't it?" She half spun for his enjoyment.

"Yes and no. The everyday Kyle looks pretty good, too."

It was true. He'd thought she was special from the first day he saw her. Strange that they'd worked in the same hospital and never became closer.

Was he brain-dead? Or just had too much respect for etiquette and the fact that dating a respected attending physician as a junior house officer could be frowned upon.

But now, near the end of his internal medicine training, already with his Surgery Boards and numerous published papers, it was difficult to believe that even the old generation of docs would look unfavorably on their relationship. Until now, their rapport had been strictly professional, but with any luck, that was about to change.

Kyle imagined them in a house of their own. Cooking. Watching a movie. Reading. Making a kid's room. Making a kid.

"You ready?" Graham grinned at her.

She broke out of her sweet reverie and reminded herself not to let her imagination run away with her. She vowed to just cut loose and have fun with the one and only Dr. Graham Kurland.

In the cab, they sat in a silence charged with electricity, chemistry, and dreams.

She looked at him. He looked at her.

"How are you-"

They said at exactly the same time.

They laughed.

"Tell me about yourself," Graham smiled as they pulled away. "I realized I don't really know much about you, apart from the fact that you're a world-class doctor and care about your patients so much it puts the rest of us to shame."

"I've always been kind of…private."

"I understand. How did a genius like you wind up in Philadelphia?"

She smiled. "I got a good job offer I couldn't refuse. I don't have any roots, so moving was easy."

"What about your family?"

"There is none."

"None?"

"My Dad was a Marine who died in Iraq. I lost my brother right after med school, and Mom passed a few years ago."

"I'm so sorry."

"Thank you." She turned her head and looked out the window.

Graham took this as a cue to change the subject. "Where did you train?

"Atlanta."

"Nice city. Azaleas, dogwoods, Spring for six months."

"I know. I was a resident and infectious disease fellow at Grady Hospital."

"I hear it's wild down there."

"Like Tombstone in the 1880s."

"Good training though."

"The training was great. Quality of life, not so much."

"Like how?"

"Like helping a six-foot-four patient who stumbled in the ER holding his intestines after a knife wound…then hearing somebody yell, 'No, that's not the patient.' It was his brother in the cab, stabbed in the heart."

"Whoa, grim."

"A rape counselor raped in the Rape Crisis Center. Some guy shot his wife and child outside the ER door. Being so busy at night that you had to leave dead bodies for the morning shift—after you knocked off the cockroaches."

"Nooooo…cockroaches?"

"One drinking pooled blood from a dead woman's mouth."

"Sounds like a MASH unit. Or a horror movie."

Kyle shrugged, nodded, and grinned.

But Graham knew life in a big city hospital. He'd spent time at Cook County in Chicago, and still awoke in a sweat over the psych patient running toward him with a bomb strapped to his chest. Praise the Lord, it was a dud.

The cab stopped in front of the Union League. Graham hopped out and opened Kyle's door.

She stepped out onto the sidewalk and admired the red stone Civil War survivor. Three stories, with blue-gray shutters and a double stairway that curved up to the front door, it was surrounded on both sides by concrete skyscrapers.

It was here that Philadelphia's upper echelons controlled the city's way of life for the past hundred sixty years.

Graham offered his arm. She gladly took it.

Such a simple thing, but it made her heart stop for a second as a tingle shivered up her spine.

He glanced at her side-eyed, and something inside him melted seeing her all decked out and dolled up, on his arm.

This is what's been missing in my life.

Grinning, they climbed the stone steps to the second level. The doorman, polished and trim and grim in dark navy dress, nodded. "Good evening."

"Good evening," Graham and Kyle replied at exactly the same time. Then smiled.

"A little stiff," she whispered once they were inside.

Graham shrugged. "Welcome to Philadelphia high society."

They walked past the portraits of solemn Union generals, each in a classic Napoleonic pose. The mellow sounds of the orchestra playing Moonlight Serenade drifted down the wide hallway. Pity it couldn't brighten the generals' faces a little.

Tonight was the annual Pennsylvania Hospital Ball, each as elegant as the last. Elegance that Kyle appreciated. But that she could just as easily do without.

They stepped into the forty-foot-high ballroom, where paintings of past League presidents draped the walls and crystal chandeliers hung from the ceiling to light the gleaming oak floor. Where for decades men had dressed in 1920s tuxedos, and their women had sparkled in graceful ball gowns.

Graham and Kyle stepped onto the dance floor. The music and people faded. He pulled her closer. He could feel her soft warmth, the suppleness of her lithe body.

Again, he thought:

This is what's been missing in my life.

Chapter Twenty-Nine

Kyle's Apartment

Center City, Philadelphia

The Union League Ball was a blast that went by in a flash, full of dances and champagne as Graham and Kyle had the most fun they could remember.

Suddenly, it was midnight, and they were floating into her apartment lobby, kissing while the doorman snored behind the counter.

"How about an after-dinner drink?" she said.

"I thought you'd never ask." He paid the cabby and waved him off.

They took the elevator to her apartment, and she poured him a Grand Marnier. Graham sat back on the off-white sofa, while Kyle faced him from the side. Balancing a green crème de menthe, she kicked off her heels and drew her legs up under her.

"How did you like high society?" he asked.

"It could grow on me. But I'm not sure how it would be as a steady diet."

"I feel the same way," he chuckled.

"Sounds like the voice of experience."

"My father came from a poor family and joined the military. He became involved with computers in grad school and the Army and wound up doing quite well in the private sector when he retired."

"I see."

"So, I'm familiar with these society engagements."

"Are your parents still in the area?"

"No. My Mom and Dad died four years ago in an auto accident. I had a younger brother who passed away. So, I'm the only one left, just like you."

"Were you close to your brother?"

"I was. He was a police officer killed in the line of duty."

"I'm so sorry. I guess we're both members of a club nobody wants to join."

"Yeah. Can we talk about what's been going on with you the last couple of weeks?"

Kyle shrugged and avoided his gaze. "Yes, just…maybe. But not right now."

"Fair enough." He thought for a moment. "So, where are you from originally?" he asked after a moment.

She took a sip from her glass and licked her lips. "Kansas. I'm a farm girl. I used to milk the cows at five in the morning. We had horses, chickens, goats, all the barnyard animals you could think of."

"A farm girl? Fresh from the dirt?" He looked into her large brown eyes.

She put down her drink and slid over until she was snuggled up next to him. "Yes."

"So, what are you looking for?"

"Uh, well…" She smiled and ruminated. "I'm looking for a doctor who's Board Certified in Surgery and Medicine to sweep me off my feet with his rugged good looks and magical surgical fingers."

He grinned. "Well, this is your lucky night."

Graham leaned forward to meet her. Their lips touched at first, in a soft, chaste kiss. He pulled her closer, his big hands caressing the bare skin exposed by her backless gown. She leaned into him and enjoyed the feeling of being held.

The moment was perfect…

Until a rude, staccato beep arose from Graham's breast pocket.

"Mother of…" He grabbed his cell pager with a clenched fist.

Kyle sat back and laughed. "You better answer it."

He sighed as he dialed, muttering about duty. "I'm only kidding," he said with a smile and a wink. "You're right. It's just the timing."

"Mind if I listen?"

"Be my guest."

He held the cell away from his head so she could hear too. Kyle moved over and gave his ear a quick nibble.

"Kurland here."

"Sorry to bother you, Graham." It was Art Klein, the Surgery Chief Resident, who was rotating through Transplant Medicine.

"No problem, Art. What is it?" He motioned Kyle to stop.

She gave his ear another nibble.

"I know you're not on Transplant now. But Hugh Reinhart's traveling and Colin York, who's on call, just came down with influenza."

"Okay. What's going on?"

"We've got a twelve-year-old girl with congestive heart failure on a respirator. I'm not sure she has more than a week or two unless she gets a new heart."

"Right."

"And one's just become available. A perfect match. Our procurement team can have it here in an hour."

"Then bring her down to the OR now so we're ready to go. I'm only a few minutes away."

"You bet, Graham. Thanks."

Kyle sat back. "Should I call a cab?"

"It's only four blocks. I'll run."

"You're kinda my hero, transplanting hearts into little girls."

"Just another day in life."

Graham leaned over and kissed her. She smiled. They laughed and said:

"Rain check!" at exactly the same time.

She grinned as she watched him jog down the hall. There'd be time for them later.

She'd make sure of it.

But right now, someone's little girl needed him a lot more than she did.

Chapter Thirty

Eva Corman's Condominium

Center City, Philadelphia, PA

"Shit!" Eva jumped and snapped her head away from the bang of the truck outside as her left arm began twitching. She grabbed it with her right hand and stumbled toward her bathroom.

It was almost four weeks since she developed this damn diabetes. Everything was going to hell. Too much insulin, too little. Sugar too low. Too high. And the damn needle hurt.

And now, this problem with her arms shaking. Every time she heard a loud noise, one or both of her arms twitched out of control. Things were so bad that she'd been forced to stop visiting her clientele.

She took her insulin first thing each morning. She hated it, but she needed it more and more. This morning, she drew up the syringe to the 50-unit mark. Her trembling hands made it difficult to stop at the right spot.

She tried a stab with shaking hands.

"Ouch!"

Again.

"Fuck!"

She winced as the needle slid into a skin fold over her stomach on the fourth try. It hurt like a bastard when the stuff went in, but these twitching arm movements were even worse. It was like the devil was inside, taking control. She'd almost totaled the Mercedes yesterday when a taxi passed too close, and the crazy driver had honked his damn brains out.

She didn't care that her appointment was still a week off.

She was going to see that doctor today and tell him he better do something before she kicked his butt.

Chapter Thirty-One

Pennsylvania Hospital

Center City, Philadelphia

Graham had come to expect—and dread—at least two visits a week from Eva.

Obnoxious. Demanding. Crude. An impatient patient. Take your pick.

He'd never considered himself religious, but lately he'd taken up praying. Maybe if he started going to church on Sundays, she'd stop coming in on Mondays.

But part of his job was to absorb her hostility and allay her fears. Even so, he fantasized about an overloaded elevator dropping a few stories. Not enough to kill her, mind you. Just enough to get her transferred to Orthopedics.

He actually did feel sorry for her. The hardest job in medicine was getting someone to accept their problems. And it wasn't happening here at all. The silver lining? She made him appreciate his other patients more.

Graham paused, his hand on the Clinic door.

Please don't let her be there.

He opened it.

Should've gone to church.

He trudged out to pick up her chart, already two inches thick.

Graham turned to wave her over, but she was already in his face.

"Hi, Ms. Corman. Shall we go in?"

He ushered her into a chair in the closest room and sat on the adjacent table.

"How have you been?"

"Lousy."

"Why is that?"

"You're the freaking doctor. You tell me."

"How about a little cooperation? Just tell me what's happening."

"I keep getting these shakes in my arms. On the way over, I even had one in my leg. They start twitching, and I can't stop." She burst out with a shrieking laugh.

This was new and different.

Graham raised his eyebrows and jotted notes on her chart. It didn't seem like anything typically seen with diabetes.

"Do they come at any particular time of day?"

"No. They happen whenever I jump. Like when I hear a loud noise."

"Let's take a look."

Her description was unique, but somewhere in his head, he heard a bell distantly ringing. A Jacksonian seizure, the kind that started in one spot, then spread? Possibly. But damn peculiar. The neurologic exam wasn't much help either. Reflexes, sensation, cerebellar function, cranial nerves, eye exam—all normal.

Graham turned away, biting his inner cheek, and tapped his pen on the computer keyboard. Something was familiar about the history, a scenario he couldn't exactly place, but something he didn't like. And that laugh? Where in the world had he seen this? If he could just think.

"Well?"

"Ms. Corman, I'm not sure why you're having this problem. Let me see if my associates have any thoughts."

"Christ sake. I thought you were supposed to be the best here."

"I'll be right back." Graham resisted the urge to snap back at her, sighed, and said, "I'll be right back."

A minute later, he found Kyle in the attending physician's office reading a chart.

He had a flash of them together, just about to launch themselves into each other. What might have been, what could be, what will be, it all played through his head in a snap of his fingers.

She felt him watching and looked up. Confusion turned into surprise, which turned into delight, unadulterated.

"Got a minute?"

"For you? Anytime. Anywhere."

"Rightbackatcha," he replied with a smile of his own.

"How's the little girl with the new heart this morning?" Kyle asked.

"Giggling. Breathing without the respirator. She makes me feel like I justified my existence for the week."

"Oh, I'd say more than that." Kyle laughed. "What's up?"

Graham dropped into the chair across from her desk. "I have a forty-five-year-old woman here with adult-onset diabetes who just developed uncontrollable tremors, particularly when she's startled."

Kyle dropped the papers she'd been holding onto the floor where they landed with a SPLAT.

She bent down to retrieve them, almost knocking heads with Graham as he bent to help.

As she picked up her file, he saw her face plunge into a grim grimace of worry, which she tried to hide with a stiff smile.

"You okay? Graham asked.

"Yes, yeah, I think it's just a…migraine." She shrugged as she rubbed her temple in a way that was not entirely convincing. "What's going on, Kyle?" he asked with great concern. "One second you're the happiest camper and the next you have the worries of the world on your shoulders."

She reached into her desk drawer for what appeared to be a sumatriptan migraine tablet, but Graham noted that she just palmed it.

"Nothing, really, I just…haven't been sleeping well and…"

"Does it have something to do with that thing you wanted to talk about?

"No, I…let's talk tonight, or tomorrow, okay?"

CHAPTER THIRTY-ONE

Graham started to press. Then backed off.

Which made her like him even more. "Thanks."

"Of course," she replied.

They smiled. The moment passed.

"Any localizing neurologic signs?" she asked as they rose, trying to be careful, while being just the opposite.

"No, nothing like a stroke. They don't sound like seizures either. Frankly, I'm not sure what it is. An unusual manifestation of low blood glucose? Have you ever seen that?"

"Not that I remember. But hypoglycemia can cause bizarre behavior."

The term bizarre struck home for Graham.

"I'd hold off on a full neuro workup," Kyle continued, plopping her papers back on the desk. "Make sure the glucose is under control first."

"Sounds reasonable." Graham gave a small wave of thanks and headed back to the exam room.

She stopped him and gave him a small but potent kiss.

He nodded, appropriately jolted.

Kyle tried to ward off an approaching migraine and figure out how to stop Graham while making it look like she was helping. And of course, falling madly in love with him.

As he went back to Eva, he tried to figure out his next step with her. Great. He'd been hoping he could confine her to another section of the hospital for a few weeks. Now she'd be back bright and early in a couple of days. He was going to church next Sunday for sure. Maybe both services.

On the other hand, he saw the Otis truck parked by the maintenance entrance. Maybe an elevator needed testing.

Damn, he was going to burn in hell.

Graham opened the door and caught Eva wiping a stream of drool from her mouth with the back of her hand. He handed her a Kleenex and rested back against the wall.

"Ms. Corman, I suspect the trembling is occurring from low blood sugar. Cut the insulin to forty units and call me in a couple of days if things aren't better. If they are, let's see you in a week. And try to measure your sugars three times a day."

Graham knew the last request was as ridiculous as pissing into a hurricane. She hadn't measured her blood glucose once the entire time he'd been following her.

He was about to let Eva go when Kyle appeared in the doorway.

"Ms. Corman, this is Dr. McMann. Dr. McMann, Ms. Corman."

"Hello," Kyle said with a smile that seemed skin deep. Graham couldn't blame her; Eva's reputation had spread through the office grapevine like wildfire, snapping back to a proximity of her regular self. "Dr. Kurland told me about you, and I wanted to see how your progress was coming."

"Fine," Eva said. "Do I know you?" she demanded with a guttural voice. "You look like someone I don't like."

"I don't think so, my dear. It must be a coincidence. I would hope you'd like me."

Eva stared at Kyle, her frown increasing.

"Anything else you'd like to tell me?" Kyle asked as she assessed Eva. She relaxed a little as she saw what a mess the monster was. And that no one had a clue what was wrong with her. Not even Graham.

"No," Eva glared. "You look so fucking...but my memory's all of a sudden fucked."

"I'm sorry to hear that," Kyle lied.

"We good here?" Graham asked.

"Absolutely," Kyle said with what looked like absolute certainty.

"Uh, yeah..." Eva said like she had no idea.

Something seemed off here. Graham stored it in his memory bank to be unpacked later.

Chapter Thirty-Two

Main Line

Berwyn, PA

Kyle was all business as she tried to control the heartburn tearing her apart despite upping her Prilosec to the maximum dose and popping Tums antacids every hour. It didn't help that the monthly Tribunal meeting began at Stenton's later than usual.

Tursi rushed in panting, twenty minutes late instead of his usual ten.

"Good evening," Stenton said. "Now that you've decided to join us, Dr. Tursi, perhaps we can get started. Kyle, can you bring us up to date on the Corman case?"

"She's continuing with severe diabetes from the streptozotocin. It's been less than two months, and already the neurologic changes from the Kuru are incapacitating. She's developed severe incoordination, memory lapses, and loss of control of her muscle movements."

"What do you expect from here?"

"I'm not sure. The primary data we have on humans comes from the cannibal tribes of New Guinea. The women and children acquired the disease because they ritually ate the raw brains and bone marrow of fallen enemy warriors. They also practiced endocannibalism, eating the brains of dead relatives as part of funeral rituals. Eventually, the Kuru caused them to lose control of their body movements, swallowing, and then their minds.

"In those cases, it took years for the symptoms to develop. I suspected that giving IV Kuru would speed the course, but it's progressing much faster than I expected."

"You think she'll still develop dementia, correct?" Tursi asked.

"I'm certain," Kyle said. "We're already seeing it."

"And there's no way this is transmissible?"

"It's very difficult to transfer unless someone eats her, drinks her blood, or gets a transfusion from her. We had to worry about the purified virus in liquid form, like when Nate, Randy, and I administered it. But all three of us are negative for any type of antibody or other biochemical response, so that's not a concern now."

"What do her doctors in the Clinic think?" Lindsey Tate asked. "Any suspicions?"

"None. Graham Kurland follows her. He's our Chief Resident, the best. But I'm sure he doesn't suspect Kuru. There's probably one case in a lifetime in Philadelphia. And even if he figures it out, he won't be able to say how she got it."

"Good," Stenton said. "Alden, what about her other activities?"

"We're fine. Other than going to doctors, she hasn't visited anyone for over a month. She's a hundred percent engrossed with her physical ailments."

"Outstanding. I believe we'll be able to close this case soon. Are there any further developments with Mancini's associates, Randy?"

Randy was seated in his usual laid-back fashion in his Dartmouth University jacket. "There are rumblings in South Philly. DiNunzio thinks his uncle may have been poisoned, that it wasn't just some act of nature."

Tursi sat forward. "When did this pop up?"

"Just last night. We grabbed it from the bug on his phone. They've contacted a pathologist, Victor Samuelson from Boston, to review the autopsy specimens. Anybody know him?"

"I do," Tate said. "He's nobody's fool. He was a year behind me at Harvard. What did he say?"

"He confirmed that Mancini's blindness was caused by methanol. And he thinks the skin disease came from a drug reaction."

Stenton emptied the bowl of his pipe into the ashtray. "I doubt DiNunzio can trace us from that information alone. His family already knew that he'd gotten methanol."

"I agree," Randy said, "That's why we didn't notify people last night. Let me caution you, though. DiNunzio's a bloodhound. Once he's gotten the scent, he doesn't quit. He'd try to kill any of us if he had one molecule of evidence. I think we're safe for the time being. But I also believe it would be a serious mistake to relax our guard."

"Without a doubt," Stenton said. "Keep us posted. And remember the emergency alert. If anyone discovers *anything* even resembling a threat, call the hotline right away." He looked around the table.

Kyle could feel the sweat on her palms. DiNunzio was nitro waiting to blow. She shivered at the thought of the pain that monster could inflict.

Stenton filled his pipe with fresh tobacco and tapped it down. "It would be foolish to ignore even the slightest possibility of exposure."

Carlo scowled. "You think?"

Stenton ignored him. "There's an old Chinese proverb that says you should dig a well before you're thirsty. Since this group was my creation, I feel responsible for the ill winds that might blow in our direction. I've therefore asked Alden to outline a contingency plan. You'll be well taken care of if this blows up in our faces."

He rose and walked to the door, turning before he left. "Our next meeting will be in two weeks, rather than four. There's an important development in a case that needs our attention."

The group was silent as the door closed.

"Jesus Christ! I thought this damn thing was foolproof," Tursi said, slamming his fist on the table.

"Nothing's foolproof," Tate argued.

"People, can we please get on with business?" Booth said. "We have other issues."

"Shut up, Alden." Tursi turned to Kyle. "Is there any way they can trace that sulfa?"

"Calm down, Carlo. Like I said before, there's no way they could find the sulfa drug in his blood. It's broken down by the liver and excreted in the urine. A little in the feces and sweat. His body eliminated it within days after the final dose—and there were no sulfa blood levels drawn during that time."

"And the hair?"

"They might identify the sulfa, but they have no idea where it came from."

Tursi fell back in his chair and gave a loud sigh. The mood in the room remained tense as he waved Booth to go on.

Kyle was glad that Booth took over as chair.

She was also glad that she had held off getting socially involved with Carlo Tursi.

She understood his concerns. Concerns they all had.

But he was a real pain in the ass about it.

That said, deep down, she still worried about the sulfa drug and the fatal allergic reaction it caused in Frank Mancini. She didn't know exactly why. But she'd keep her eyes and ears open to make sure it didn't come back to bite them.

DiNunzio would leave no stone unturned when he smelled blood.

Chapter Thirty-Three

Medical Clinic

Pennsylvania Hospital

Eva sat in the Clinic waiting room, squirming in her chair, pissed off at the world. For a moment, she couldn't remember why or how she had come. She started to get up to go home.

When she sat forward, it dawned on her that a Quaker Cab brought her in because of the jerking in her arms and legs. The twitches were coming seven or eight times a day, with episodes lasting ten to twenty minutes. At times, she was close to blacking out. Her entire body shook, and sweat poured down her face.

Any attempts to stop the spasms only made them worse. She felt like a maniacal marionette flailing on crack. Her body was no longer hers, and she was afraid. Sorely.

An elderly gentleman with a wooden cane passed in front of her and brushed against her outstretched leg. "Excuse me, I'm sorry," he said, and moved on with a shuffling gait.

Eva sprang up with a scream that was heard all the way to New Jersey. "You cocksucker! I'll tear your fucking balls off!"

The small man froze and cringed. She lumbered toward him, her arms outstretched, fingers curled in anticipation of wrapping her hands around his emaciated neck.

Without warning, her right arm twitched so that it smacked her own face.

"God dammit!" She groped at the arm and took another step before her knees went out from under her.

"Shit!" Eva grabbed the back of a chair, her legs shaking like she was wearing roller skates on ice.

"Help. Help me, old man!"

The frail man went into express shuffle mode and escaped out the Clinic door.

Chapter Thirty-Four

Medical Clinic

Pennsylvania Hospital

Kyle and Graham heard Eva screaming at the elderly man. They ran out and steadied her under each arm, guiding her into the closest exam room and sitting her in a chair.

Kyle winced at the smell of composting feces encircling her like a reprehensible shield. Strands of her greasy hair stuck out at acute angles, and her blouse was half buttoned and saturated with saliva from intermittent drooling. Freakish remains of lipstick were streaked across her cheeks and forehead, giving her the look of a full-blown lunatic.

When Graham wasn't looking, Kyle allowed herself a satisfied smile. It had been days since Eva's last visit, a little over two months since the onset of diabetes.

It was obvious that the Kuru was destroying her inhibitory center. The frontal lobes of her brain were going downhill at Olympic speed. Underlying basal urges, until now repressed, were no longer under her control.

If only Janice Parker was here. She wished that somehow Eva's victims were able to see these final stages.

"Geez, look at her," Graham whispered. "She's checked out of the planet."

Yeah," said Kyle like she really meant it, "it's sad."

Eva's face contorted into a wild grin, and her head rolled back, with only the whites of her eyes showing. It snapped forward again in twenty seconds as she regained consciousness with senseless, manic laughing.

Kyle wanted to time the seizures to see how long before her next episode of incoherency. No matter, Eva's grasp on reality was intermittent at best. It would soon slip away forever.

"Maybe we should call an exorcist," Graham muttered. He turned to Kyle and put down his stethoscope. "Could you watch her for a minute? I'll grab some tubes for blood work. I think we should admit her."

"Absolutely."

"Be right back." Graham shut the door behind him.

Kyle looked at Eva, who was now only suffering minor tremors.

"Do you think Nettie Johnson felt this way before she died?"

Eva's eyes flew open, and her hands began to shake. It wasn't the Kuru this time.

"W-w-w-what do you mean?"

"I think you know. Just remember that there is justice in this world. And you should stay the hell away from here before something even worse happens to you. Like what you did to Janice."

Kyle turned and gritted her teeth as she left.

Stupid, McMann. Just damn stupid. What is the matter with you?

What possessed her? The thought of Nettie? The horror of Brian? No matter, it was senseless and selfish to take that kind of risk and endanger the others.

She felt like being an avenging angel was making her into her worst self. Instead of her best. No impulse control. Fight urge turned up to eleven. She had to do something to rein herself in. But she had no idea what that might be.

And what if Eva had a moment of cogency and blurted out what Kyle had just said?

No. No one would believe her mad ravings. And the fact that she now knew made revenge all the sweeter.

That said, the heartburn in Kyle's throat rose to Pike's Peak level.

As a headache wrapped its bony fingers around her skull and started squeezing.

Eva remained silent after the lady doctor left, but her mind raced. How the hell did this woman know about Nettie Johnson? And Janice. She felt sweat trickle down her forehead, and she tried to calm her quaking hands before they triggered another convulsion. What in God's name had that woman done to her?

During the lull between the spasms, she was still able to move herself. Best to get away before she lost it again. Before that woman did anything else. She wasn't sure what was happening, but when she got better, that bitch doctor was in the surprise of her life.

Kyle watched with relish as she saw Eva rush out, then went back to her office.

Graham returned to the exam room and opened the door, only to find it empty.

Where was she?

And where was Kyle?

He ran to the attending physician's doorway. Kyle was seated at her desk.

"What happened? Where is she?"

"Gone. Her tremors stopped, and she was more lucid."

"Then you let her go?"

"I tried to talk her out of it."

"We've got to get her back. I doubt she can even give her insulin."

Kyle put down her pen and looked at Graham straight on. She kept her hands resting on the desk to prevent shaking. "The woman made her own decision. We're doctors, not our brothers' keepers."

"She can't make a rational decision."

"She did. At least from what I could tell."

"Kyle, that's not like you."

"I'm trying to prioritize patients who are most likely to recover. There's only so much we can do, and better to help those who try to help themselves."

"Well, that's true," Graham admitted. But there was something else going on here, and he knew he had to get to the bottom of it. "Kyle, we never talked about—"

"I know, I've been slammed. We will, I promise. Look, it wasn't my first choice. But I couldn't keep her against her will. Not when she was coherent."

"But what about when she's not?"

"I suspect she'll be back. I'll try to contact her at home. If I can't get her, we'll send the police over."

"But she—"

"She what?"

"Never mind." He stared down the hall toward the elevator. "We'll talk later."

Back home, Eva lay on the living room floor, the side of her face pressed against the carpet.

She looked at her watch with hazy vision, but she could still see the fluorescent numbers. She'd only left that damn clinic an hour ago, dropping to the floor a half dozen steps into her home.

Vomitus pooled around her mouth and cracked lips. She could feel the diarrhea and concentrated urine saturating her slacks and the bottom half of her blouse.

But that was minor compared to the tremors and painful muscle spasms that wracked her body. She tried to pull herself along, but her body said no. The devil had finally taken over.

And she was so damned thirsty. When she looked up, she could see a glass of water across the room on the coffee table. If she could have a drop to wet her lips.

Just one. If only someone would come to the door and find her.
Please!

Eva was down and, somehow, through the ramblings and incoherent thoughts, knew this was the end.

A black fly landed on her exposed cheek, decided it was safe, and laid a batch of eggs.

Chapter Thirty-Five

Stenton's Main Line Manse

Berwyn, PA

Kyle tried to get control of her racing breath and make sure her I'm-okay-face was plastered on.

"Please, people!" Booth waved his hands to no avail at the far end of Stenton's dining room table as the last rays of the March sun started to fade. "Please! Can we please have quiet here?"

She noticed that the murmurs continued until Stenton himself leaned forward to speak. Booth really got no respect.

"Thank you all for coming this extra Friday," Stenton said. "You all know how Eva Corman died, and the situation is stable on the South Philly front. So, let's get right to the case I mentioned last time. Randy White did the research and will give us the details."

"I can't wait for this one," Kyle whispered to Carlo. "Wonder why we didn't get a report before the meeting?"

"He was talking before you got here. Something about too much in writing, less paper trails from now on."

Randy picked up the projector remote while Booth walked over to the wall and dimmed the lights.

"This is the man of interest," Randy said.

He clicked the remote, and the face of a well-groomed, bearded man appeared on the screen. His dark eyes were deep and penetrating, his nose and cheekbones sharp. Kyle's first guess was that he was a college professor. Or perhaps a businessman.

"Jonas Erozan began as a hoodlum in Baltimore. Following a meteoric rise to drug world stardom, he runs a narcotics empire that covers Maryland and West Virginia. It's been cocaine and crack, but recently he's launched into fentanyl, a synthetic drug with fifty times the potency of heroin. He's known for his ruthless brutality and has the conscience of a rabid hyena. Last month, he beat a fifteen-year-old kid to death for trying to quit his organization."

Randy changed the photo to a heavier man in his late thirties or early forties.

"This is William Ferguson, a well-to-do stockbroker, who lived in Towson, a comfortable suburb outside Baltimore. Bill was a casual user of coke, but when the bottom dropped out of the Market in 2022, he became an occasional dealer to make up his losses. He was never big-time, sold only to friends in his firm and their friends. His problems started when he spent profits before Erozan got his cut."

Randy faced his colleagues. "In spite of the drug use, Ferguson was a devoted husband and the father of three children."

Another photograph came up, this time of Ferguson and his family. Randy pointed to the petite brunette standing next to Ferguson.

"This is his wife, Marie. A bright, loving mom. These are Jason, Gailyn, and Jessica, ages nine, five, and three. Jessica developed neuroblastoma, a bad cancer requiring expensive medical care. Another reason Ferguson ran into financial trouble.

"We've been able to reconstruct what happened a year ago, last April. Ferguson had come home from work, and his family was getting ready for dinner when the bell rang. Marie opened the door for a young woman in a FedEx uniform. Erozan was right behind with a half dozen thugs.

"They forced Ferguson, his family, and the housekeeper into the basement. Ferguson offered cash and valuables, but Erozan wanted blood. He needed an example."

Kyle tried to relax the tension in her forehead. But it was too late. The pain had already penetrated into her brain. She reached into her bag, pulled out a sumatriptan migraine tablet, and swallowed it.

"He ordered his men to attack Marie," Randy went on. "She was gang raped in front of her husband and children, while Bill pleaded with Erozan to stop." His voice rose and tempo quickened. "Instead, Erozan slit little Jessica's throat and let her bleed out like an animal in the slaughterhouse."

Another picture appeared on the screen. Kyle gasped and turned away, her stomach twisting into a knot.

"Ay, Dios." Ramos was on his feet.

"This is how they found her when the police arrived," Randy said.

Kyle couldn't look. She didn't need to. The image of the tiny, near-decapitated corpse surrounded by a pool of blood was frozen in her mind. She tried to turn back the wave of nausea. To fight an awful cancer, then die like this? Before she had any real chance at life?

"This is the quintessence of demoniacism." Randy paused with a blank look at the picture, then took a deep shuddering breath. "While this small girl was being slaughtered,

Someone was able to set off a silent alarm."

Kyle could see tears in Randy's eyes.

"Ferguson tried to fight, but that only infuriated Erozan, who ordered both his arms cut off. The blood from his mutilated limbs spurted high enough to stain the ceiling.

For Marie, it was different. They cut off her right breast and put a bullet in her head. By the time help arrived, all three adults and the two remaining children had been shot in the back of the head.

"The police arrived right as Erozan and his sick scum were leaving. There was a gun battle, and the two officers who answered the call were killed by shotgun blasts. Each had a family with small children."

Carlo raised his hand but spoke before being acknowledged. "Are you telling us this homicidal maniac walked?"

Randy nodded. "The band escaped before more cops arrived. Erozan wasn't picked up until a month later."

"What about the FBI?"

"No witnesses lived."

"Why didn't the Justice Department take a giant shit on him?" Ramos, the ophthalmologist, interrupted.

"Money buys judges, top lawyers, and good alibis. We've all seen that. The housekeeper didn't live long enough to make the mug shots, and the circumstantial evidence was minimal. Their guns disappeared, their cars were stolen, and clothes with blood were burned."

Randy made eye contact with each of the members. "Some of you may be wondering why I seem to have a personal interest in this case. Marie Ferguson is my younger sister. Her family was killed, but she wasn't as fortunate. She's still paralyzed in a coma with irreversible brain damage. I pray every night for the Lord to end her living hell." He lowered his head.

A deafening silence followed.

Kyle could only stare at Randy, feeling his grief. At least Brian had died. They never caught his killers. But thank God he wasn't lying around like a vegetable. How could Randy live knowing his sister would never wake up? And that Erozan escaped unpunished?. She wanted to scream, to hit something. Anything. Instead, she squeezed her hands till the nails drew blood.

After a chair shuffled, Kyle broke the uncomfortable silence. "Randy, why didn't you tell us about this before?"

"I was waiting for the right moment."

"Oh, brother," Carlo said under his breath.

"Let me explain why Randy and I decided that now was the right time," Stenton interjected. "Reports have recently surfaced that Erozan is expanding his operation to northern and western Virginia.

"Now he's into prostitution and sex-trafficking too, particularly with younger girls. He treats them all like sex slaves. His drugs and sex trade will ruin more lives, destroy more families, and cause more misery. The man has no soul. It is my opinion that we're dealing with the epitome of evil."

He pounded his fist on the table. "This subhuman beast must be destroyed!"

Kyle had never heard such anger in Stenton's voice. He always seemed so detached, so reserved, even when they discussed the most heinous criminals. Nice to know the man was human.

"He's completely rational and understands the consequences of his actions," Stenton continued. "But as a psychopath with no conscience, he could kill one or a million without remorse… I propose an immediate vote."

Booth collected the ballots, and Stenton examined them. The vote was a mere formality.

"It's time to plan a course of action," Stenton said. "Suggestions?"

Carlo raised his hand. "I have a thought. Though it's hard to imagine retribution severe enough to match this crime."

"Tell us."

"I've been using a new method of micro-stereotactic surgery that's not widely appreciated." He walked to the blackboard off to the side and began to sketch. "It involves passing a wire-thin plastic fiberoptic laser into the brain with the help of a CT scanner. The laser can destroy small tumors and microscopic areas that cause seizures without damaging adjacent structures. There are no large incisions, just a tiny hole through the skull."

Carlo elaborated his thoughts as the meeting went into the early hours of the morning. The plan would be difficult, but the horror of the crime resulted in a unanimous agreement that it was fitting.

Suppressing a four a.m. yawn, Stenton faced Nate Champion and Randy White. "Gentlemen, can you deliver this monster to the medical team?"

"No problem," Nate said. "We'll just do it."

Randy added a thumbs-up. "Consider it done."

Chapter Thirty-Six

Sixth Street Antique District

Center City, Philadelphia, PA

Saturday night. No patients. The end of a week from hell.

Kyle lay on her back, allowing herself to sink into the soft green sofa in Graham's top-floor apartment. Peering through the French doors to the balcony, she could see the white marble stairs rising to the massive columns of the Philadelphia Art Museum. The only thing missing was Rocky.

It was a relief to lie back with a Merlot. Her third one was doing wonders for her current outlook on life.

The Tribunal was dominating her activities to the point of losing control. There wasn't an hour during the day when she didn't think about it, obsess over it in some way. In the beginning, over a year ago, she was so gung-ho. So smug. Anything to avenge Brian and the others. She thought it would give her life meaning.

Now she wasn't so sure.

Treating a baby for staph sepsis in the neonatal ICU gave her meaning. Knowing the child could grow up to have a normal life, rather than be wheelchair-bound in an institution? That was meaning.

What they were doing was revenge. Justice, yes. But what if they ever exacted their toll on someone who was innocent? The thought gnawed at her more and more. She kept reminding herself that they were stopping evil people from inflicting harm on more innocents.

None of them was perfect. No one was. It was only a matter of time until a mistake happened. And if it did, she didn't know if she could live with herself.

Now, there was her relationship with Graham. Smart. Honest. Honorable. Caring. World-class surgeon. The last thing she wanted to do was get him involved in their dangerous game.

Tribunal protocol discouraged family or romantic ties for all members. She wasn't sure how her involvement with another doctor would be viewed.

But she could guess. It wouldn't be good.

She rested her feet up on the arm, her thin blue dress slipping up to mid-thigh.

Graham stuck his head around the corner from the kitchen and stared. "It's hard to concentrate with a half-naked woman lying on my couch."

"Really?" Kyle bent her right leg, and the dress slipped up further.

Graham walked to her, rested his hand on her knee, and leaned over for a long, sensual kiss. He pulled back and stared into her eyes. "I predict that once you taste my love potion, you'll fall under my spell forever."

Kyle laughed. "Okay, Merlin. I hope it's better than Army rations."

He moved his hand a little higher and came toward her again—until the loud sizzle in the kitchen sent billows of steam through the door.

"Son of a…!"

Graham jumped up and ran into the fog.

"Ouch!"

The clang of a large pan hitting the floor echoed through the apartment. "GOD DAMN PIECE OF…!"

Kyle heard another loud BANG, like a pot smashing into something glass that shattered.

Startled and scared, she ran into the kitchen.

Graham looked like a maniac, eyes on fire, face red, rage veins popping.

The kitchen was a mess, brown liquid splattered and glass shattered. A metal pan had clearly been tossed at high speed into a tall glass pasta holder, which had broken and fallen onto the floor.

Kyle couldn't believe what she was seeing. Mild-mannered Clark Kent had turned into a violent Incredible Hulk.

Graham turned to face her like a soldier ready to rip the throat out of his worst enemy.

Kyle shrank, horrified, terrified, afraid for her life.

Graham's eyes met hers. His face went from hard to soft, like Mr. Hyde turning back into Dr. Jekyll. He looked like his soul had returned to his body.

A look of guilty shame came over him. He took three very deep breaths. "Oh God, Kyle, I…"

He stopped, let out a sharp breath, and his head fell into his hands as he tried desperately to stop from breaking down. His legs buckled, and he fell to his knees in the kitchen, gasping.

Kyle's fight/flight/freeze instincts vanished, and her medical training kicked in.

She observed. Processed. Evaluated. Concluded.

PTSD.

Had to be.

Slowly and carefully, she stepped around the mess and gently stopped in front of him.

He felt her there and looked up into her eyes.

She saw the tears, the fear, the humiliation, the longing, the self-loathing, the loneliness, the exhaustion of carrying the weight of his dark secret.

She saw the need to be loved.

Kyle was intimate with all of those feelings. She wanted with all her heart and soul to hold him in her arms and take away the pain.

But she knew enough to let him come to her. So she did.

Slowly, he moved towards her, like he was steel and she was a magnet pulling him to her.

Until he was so close she could feel the heat of his body.

His head rested on her belly.

It felt so good, Kyle had to stop gasping. Slowly and silently, she let out a long, slow breath.

Again, she stopped herself from holding him like her life depended on it.

Graham loved the way his head felt against the warm, taut muscle of her core.

It released something that had been festering inside him for as long as he could remember. The war, the killing, his best pal Eddie Severs blowing up right in front of him, identifying his parents on the slab, getting the news about his dead brother.

Graham collapsed into her. Ever so slowly, Kyle put her arms around him.

A wave rose up from inside him.

This time, he didn't stop it. It flowed out of him as his shoulders shook and the tears poured out of him and into her.

It was so good.

Cleansing. Releasing. Like a baptism washing him clean from the inside out.

Kyle was ecstatic. She loved helping Graham unload all the toxic poison that was clearly eating him alive.

It made her own knots loosen, and she felt her venom flow out of her.

Neither could say how long they lived in this moment.

But eventually Graham's wave subsided, and his storm passed.

He felt a lightness, a calmness, a peace that was unprecedented.

He pulled back a little, smiled up at her, and said with soft, warm gratitude:

"Thank you."

Kyle returned her smile and whispered:

"It was my pleasure."

He rose to the standing position and sheepishly asked, "Still hungry?"

She laughed. "Famished. But we don't have to-"

"No," he said, "It was only the soup, everything else is okay. Just gimme ten minutes to right the ship, and we'll be good to go."

"Are you sure? We could order out and-"

"I'm sure," he said, like he was totally sure.

"Well, at least let me help with the clean-up, it's the least I could—"

"You've already done more for me than I could ever say. I'm sorry, it's the PTSD—"

"I know, I suffer from some of that myself, my brother died, lots of trauma, but that's a story for another night."

"Yeah, of course," he said, full of empathy. "I want to talk to you about all this, but let me clean up and get dinner, it'll give me time to regulate and gather my thoughts. Is that okay?"

"Of course," she said, "you take all the time you need, I'll snuggle up with my new best friend Monsieur Merlot, and if you need me, I'm ten seconds away."

She kissed him lightly but deeply on the lips and took her leave.

Graham smiled and shook his head like he was the luckiest man alive.

Kyle poured herself an extra generous glass of Merlot, collapsed into the luscious couch, and let out a sigh with a smile, like she was the luckiest woman alive. She shook her head and smiled to herself as she pulled the dress back down.

Her mind drifted back to last night's meeting. She found herself wondering whether Nate and Randy would have trouble with Erozan. The man had a brigade of bodyguards, and Stenton said he was never left alone for more than five minutes. But their guys hadn't failed yet. And she believed in Louis Pasteur's dictum. "Chance favors the prepared mind."

Her train of thought was derailed by the sound of Graham tidying, straightening, and cooking.

She took another deep pull of Merlot and focused on the warm, happy feeling spreading down her throat into her belly, down her arms, through her pelvis, into her legs, and tingling her toes.

Graham walked into the dining room and placed a large bowl on the table.

"Salad a la Kurland. From Grandma Kurland in Vienna."

"Looks good."

"Good? It's fabulous."

Graham yawned as he sat in a plush wing chair kitty-corner to Kyle's.

Like it was contagious, his yawn triggered Kyle, and she let out an epic yawn of her own.

They chuckled. The chuckles turned into laughs.

"Tired?" she asked.

"A little," she answered. "You?"

"A little." He looked away and grinned. Looked back and said, "But I feel good."

"Me, too," she said.

They stared into each other's eyes for a long moment.

"Merlot?" she asked, handing him her glass.

"Sure," he beamed, and took a pull. "Yeah, that is good. Okay, ten minutes to launch."

"Good." She yawned again as he headed back into the kitchen.

Again, without her consent, her brain presented her with the image of the little girl with her throat slit to the backbone by Erozan the Terrible. Then Mancini and DiNunzio. No matter how hard she tried, each toss and turn brought another worry.

Would it ever stop?

Maybe they should leave a calling card after they finished Erozan to scare the others.

In fact, why not just do the others?

Was she turning into someone as bad as them?

How long could the Tribunal go on?

It couldn't be forever.

And when it ended, what would happen to them all?

What would happen to her?

And how could she bring Graham into it without his knowledge?

"Earth to Kyle."

She beamed back into her body and regained control of her brain, which made her say:

"Sorry. Just thinking."

"You wanna talk about the thing we haven't been talking about?"

"Uh, Yeees? But..." she started tentatively.

"But not now..." Graham finished her thought.

Kyle nodded, embarrassed and relieved at the same time.

"We don't have to. Not tonight. Sometimes it's better to just give the old brain a rest."

"Thanks, yeah,"

"Let's discuss your upcoming birthday instead. After all, you're going to be thirty-four, right?"

"Thirty-three! And I'm not interested in talking about birthdays."

"Of course. Old people never are."

Kyle smiled despite herself. "You're terrible."

"I'm the worst," Graham agreed before he disappeared into the kitchen. "Four more minutes."

"Sure." Kyle lay back on the green sofa. She was in no rush.

Graham checked the roast. Perfect. The potatoes. Divine.

He couldn't believe he'd lost it in front of her. Revealed he was a mess, a wreck, a lunatic. But even more, he couldn't believe how good he felt not lugging his misery around inside him. Trying to start a relationship with a lie of omission. Even though he couldn't believe she still liked him. Maybe even loved him. What a world!

"We're ready," he called. If he ever retired from body reconstruction, it was the restaurant life of a chef for him.

He rounded the corner, tray in hand, and stopped short.

Kyle was fast asleep. A surprise. But not really. He set the tray on the table, grabbed a blanket from the bedroom, and covered her.

She was so beautiful sleeping there. He wanted her on her couch, in his home, in his life, for the rest of his life. He was falling hard and beginning to realize it more than ever.

Kyle woke up hours later in utter confusion. Where the hell was she? Alone in a big bed. In a white room. Unfamiliar. He felt lost and disoriented, alone and frightened.

Then she remembered. Graham. She was at Graham's. But she couldn't remember coming to his bedroom.

She peeked under the covers. Her blue dress and panties were on. Graham was a gentleman. Was there really any doubt?

Where the heck was he?

She hopped out from under the covers and tiptoed to the door.

He was asleep. Under a green blanket that matched the green sofa. A man with taste that actually went beyond the color of his most recent Phillies cap.

It took her only seconds to decide. Removing her dress, bra, and panties, she tiptoed to the couch ahead and lifted the green blanket. Graham's back was facing her. She slipped in and pressed herself against him.

He stirred minimally. Was he still asleep?

A "hmm" answered the question.

"Am I dreaming?" he asked. "Or is this a commando raid by a beautiful woman?"

"You might say that," Kyle murmured as she pulled his T-shirt up over his head. He flipped over, and suddenly his boxers were off.

Later, as they lay facing each other, they basked in the afterglow. He gently stroked her thigh and she his chest.

Neither wanted the moment to end.

Chapter Thirty-Seven

International Airport

Philadelphia, PA

Ralph DiNunzio opened his window and spat at the retreating car, "God damn New Yawkus! Where'd ya learn to drive, ya jabroni! Shoulda hit him, Lou."

Lou Gennaro adjusted his white golfer's visor and stared straight ahead down I-95 South. Lou was a good man. Never did anything to annoy Ralph. Unlike the fucking tourists.

DiNunzio sighed and shook his aggravated head. It had been over five months since Uncle Frank's death, and he still didn't have any answers.

Poisoning. Maybe. But how? They'd checked every bottle of booze in the house and squeezed the owner's balls in every liquor store Frank ever looked at. And for what? Nothing.

He began to wonder whether the lady doc was right. It was some bizarre act of nature. If today's meeting with the pathologist didn't shed any new light, he was ready to pack up the whole damn thing.

"Come on, Lou, step on it."

"What's the rush, Ralph? The Doc's sitting in the airport waiting for us."

"Punch it anywayz."

Lou pushed the Caddy's gas pedal to the metal.

The black Cadillac screeched into the "No Parking" zone outside the

American Airlines Terminal at Philadelphia International. Alarmed passengers turned to look.

DiNunzio placed a crisp fifty in the uniformed porter's hand.

"Don't let da cops get it. We'll be back in half an hour."

"Yes, sir." It was Friday afternoon, and Terminal B was packed. The two men walked in and looked for the pathologist.

DiNunzio scratched his head. Where was he? Half the people there were short, dumpy men with no hair. Just like the Doc.

"Mr. DiNunzio?"

"Huh?"

"Dr. Samuelson."

DiNunzio turned around. He'd only met the man once before, two months ago, when he was in town to review tissue specimens from the autopsy.

"Hey, Doc. Yer not exactly a standout in da crowd." He nodded to Lou. "This here's my business 'ssociate, Mr. Gennaro. Let's go to da lounge. It's a better place to tawk."

The airport bar was filled mostly with businessmen in suits. DiNunzio picked a small round table in the far corner, out of earshot from the clientele.

Under the NO SMOKING sign, DiNunzio lit a Havana cigar and tossed the match on the floor.

"Let's hear it, Doc. Wha'cha got?"

Samuelson waved away the cloud of smoke, pulled a pile of papers from his briefcase, and pushed them across the table.

"This is the final report, Mr. DiNunzio. Your uncle died from loss of blood due to an ulcer just beyond the stomach. The ulcer was brought on by his severe skin disease and overwhelming secondary infection."

DiNunzio slapped the table. "Doc, yer not telling me nu'tin' I don't already know. You spent my money and wasted all dat time just to tell me this?"

"I'm not finished. If you can't be civil, you can read the report yourself."

Lou stood menacingly. The pathologist drew back in his chair. DiNunzio halted him with a raised hand.

"Sorry, Doc. T'ings been a li'l' tense 'round here. Go 'head."

Samuelson looked at them suspiciously, maintaining as much distance between himself and the two mobsters as possible.

"The most relevant results came from the studies that arrived this week. It was like looking for a needle in a haystack, but I think we have something."

"Good. So, tell me."

"I was unable to find any evidence of toxins in the body tissues that normally contain them, like the liver and kidneys. Because the toxins had long since been eliminated. That is, from everywhere except the hair."

"What toxins?"

"Open to page ten."

DiNunzio flipped through the pages until he came to one with a photograph of a magnified hair. It had discrete dark rings along its length.

There was something big here. He could feel it.

Samuelson pointed to the picture. "Each of these bands in Mr. Mancini's hair corresponds to a drug that he ingested on separate occasions."

"What drug?"

"Likely a sulfonamide derivative, an antibiotic."

"But dat's good, right?" Lou said. "Antibiotics are good."

"In the right dosage, yes. But sulfonamides are a known cause of toxic epidermal necrolysis, the skin disease that led to Mr. Mancini's death. I believe that his body became sensitized to the drug over a period of weeks. This leads me to believe he was poisoned."

Frank Mancini hadn't seen a doctor in years. DiNunzio's suspicions were right.

"Is dis a perscription drug?" DiNunzio asked.

"Yes. You can't get it over the counter anywhere in the States."

"But I also suspect it was altered to make it more allergenic. The spectrograph showed it was attached to some form of albumin-like protein. That worsened the allergy ten times over."

"When'd he get it? Can you gimme da times?"

Samuelson pulled out another copy of the report.

"At times, he got it every day. But there were others where he went a week in between. One point of interest is that his last dose was a whopper."

Samuelson pointed to the darkest ring at the bottom of the hair strand. "That's the one that pushed him over the edge. He must've received it just before he was admitted to the hospital."

"Any idea how he got it?"

"I can only tell you that he probably ingested it by mouth. But where it came from originally? No clue."

DiNunzio stood and handed the doc a roll of hundred-dollar bills.

"Le's keep dis awff da record, Doc. 'kay?"

"Of course."

"You been a 'uge help. T'anks."

DiNunzio hurried for the car. Lou had to jog to catch up.

"Lou, we're gonna get dose motherfuckers, if it takes every man we got. I'm gonna cut da bastards into li'l' pieces and feed 'em to da fishes in the Schuylkill."

DiNunzio stopped short, and Lou almost ran into him.

"Aw, crap!" He yanked the parking ticket from under the wiper blade. "Looka dis." He slapped the hood.

"Lou, come back tomorruh wit' Nicky an' break dat fuckin' porter's arms. Got it?" He held the ticket directly under Lou's nose.

"Den shove dis so far up his ass that he pukes it out."

Chapter Thirty-Eight

Stenton's Country Estate

Middletown, MD

N ate Champion couldn't shake the feeling of gloom and doom as he drove the Maryland State Trooper car past the glorious dogwood blooms and flowering azaleas and down the oak-lined drive from Stenton's country estate.

Nate glanced at Randy staring out the passenger window. It was quiet like this before missions. The more dangerous, the quieter. That's how they liked it.

The ledger of Nate's life events had been spinning through his mind. Strange how memories popped into your head when you thought your number could be up.

The early days in the Detroit ghetto with his Aunt Etta had been rough. Peer pressure aside, he'd worked like a dog to maximize his talents in a climate that made it difficult for young black men to get ahead. None of that street corner bullshit for him.

He built those skinny legs into championship hurdler quality in high school, then went on to play linebacker and graduated magna cum laude from the University of Michigan. After that came his MBA at Harvard.

Between the two degrees, he'd spent four years as a Navy SEAL. That was when he met Randy White. In the Navy and after, he never neglected his love of sports. He liked to believe he could still run the hundred in ten flat and pass for a pro middle linebacker. Wishful thinking, maybe, but the image came in handy when he started his chain of successful athletic stores.

Randy had done well, too, though from a different background. Born into a well-to-do WASP family on the Philadelphia Main Line, he graduated from Dartmouth at twenty.

After his SEAL stint in the Navy, he took his master's from MIT before hitting it big in the high-tech field. Like Nate, he kept the same sinewy physique he had during college football days.

Back then, Nate never would have guessed that he'd be involved with a Tribunal-like group. But not a night went by that he didn't remember how his kid brother, Marvin, was stabbed to death in a Detroit cab. As far as he knew, the perp had never been caught.

The murderer remained free, while he was condemned to no family and recurring nightmares for the rest of his life.

He gave the car a little more gas.

They sped through hillier terrain west of Baltimore toward their rendezvous. Except for an occasional truck heading in the opposite direction, the countryside was quiet.

"Think they'll be packing heavy-duty heat?" Randy asked.

"Probably an artillery battalion."

"Yeah." Randy sighed and frowned.

A quarter mile after the sign for Hagerstown, Nate pulled off on a side road and turned around. "Let's wait here," he said. "They'll have to pass us to get to Thurmont."

"Why did you pick Thurmont?"

"Isolated. No cops."

"Okay."

Nate looked at his watch. "We've got a half hour to kill."

"Think he'll show?"

"For five hundred thousand and a chance at a new market? Yeah, he'll show."

The question was, who would show up with him? If he had two or three goons, fine. If he had eight or ten? That could be nasty.

They both strained to catch a glimpse of the passengers in the passing cars. Dusk was settling in, and each vehicle was harder to see.

"Crap," Randy said after forty minutes. "For all we know, he's already gone by."

Nate leaned forward and squinted as three more cars passed.

Ten minutes later, a black Mercedes limo zoomed by.

"Oh, you magnificent greedy bastard."

He hit the lights and siren, threw a cloud of gravel and dust into the air, and spun out.

The darkened windows hid the passengers. But Nate knew who was inside. It slowed and pulled over to the shoulder.

"Please open your window and have your licenses and registration ready," Randy announced over the loudspeaker.

Nate put on dark glasses with a metallic sheen and walked up to the driver's door.

The driver rolled down his window and handed Nate the registration. He could see three other men in the shadows.

Nate returned to the squad car and faked calling in the info. By the time he returned, two of the men were looking out open windows at him.

"What's the problem, officer?" someone asked from the back seat.

"Just checking the registration, sir. There are outstanding violations on this vehicle."

"Can't that be taken care of later? We have an important meeting."

"Afraid not. Could you please all step out of the car?"

One of the men reached inside his jacket.

Nate tensed.

The spokesman restrained his sidekick and peered through the window. *Erozan.*

A little heavier, and the beard was gone. But it was him.

"Officer, I have some important friends in the State Police who wouldn't appreciate this type of treatment. I suggest you just let us go on."

"Sorry, sir, can't do that. I suggest you all get out of the car. We've already called for backup."

Nate hoped his last statement would keep them in line.

It did.

Erozan looked at the others and gave a loud sigh.

Nate stepped back from the door as the men got out, two on each side.

"Let's see some ID, please. From everyone."

With pained looks, they reached into their pockets, while Randy joined his partner.

Erozan was now out in full view of the police cruisers' high beams. 5' 10", olive complexion, coal black eyes, Roman nose that had its own zip code.

It was him all right.

Nate reached for Erozan's license, looked closely at the photo, and then at his face. It was all he could do to hold back from smashing it in.

"Sorry, sir," he finally said, handing back the license. "I didn't realize who you were." He turned to Randy. "They're okay, Harry. We can go."

Erozan's smirk broadened into a Cheshire cat grin of satisfaction.

"Just be glad I'm willing to forget this unfortunate episode."

The men turned to climb back into the limousine. Randy pulled out his pistol and silently shot a dart into the buttocks of each of the three associates.

The first two didn't notice, but in the third, it hit a nerve. The man winced and reached inside his suit jacket.

Erozan grabbed his arm. "What are you doing, Sal?"

Sal looked down at his back. "I think they just shot me."

"I didn't hear anything." Erozan fired a questioning glare at Nate and Randy.

Nate held up his hands. "In less than a minute, this place will be crawling with cops. Think it over before you make any rash decisions."

"What the fuck?"

Erozan watched as his bodyguards dropped to the ground. "What's going on here?"

Randy fired a Taser at Erozan's chest. The needles struck him in the left shoulder. His arms and legs spasmed and jerked as he fell back. His eyes rolled up as he lay twitching and shaking.

Nate yanked him up, and together they shoved him into the back seat of the patrol car, where Randy injected a syringe of chloral hydrate through his pants into the upper thigh.

He'd be hopping mad when he awoke. But that wouldn't be for hours.

And by then it would be too late.

Chapter Thirty-Nine

Stenton's Country Estate

Middletown, MD

Jonas Erozan lay on his back, arms and legs restrained by thick leather straps attached to the operating room table. Two halogen lights shone down on the top of his clean-shaven head.

The blue-tiled room was quiet except for cardiac monitor beeps, while the air was filled with the pungent smell of antiseptic cleanser. Inside the cabinets, the glint of surgical steel reflected off the glass.

Lindsey Tate, as anesthesiologist, approached Erozan from the right. The veins on the back of the hand stood out in bold relief. Tate cleaned the area with alcohol and pierced the skin with an intravenous catheter.

"Ow!" Erozan winced. "What the hell are you motherfuckers doing? I'll have you all killed when I get out of here! You sons-a-bitches. You hear me? KILLED!"

Tate stared at him until Erozan quieted and stopped pulling on the restraints.

"Sir, very soon you'll know what we're doing, because I intend to let you observe it. A little advice, though. It's not especially wise for a man in your position to be making threats."

"Fuck you."

"Oh no." Tate smiled. "You have that backwards."

Erozan stared at him with saucer-wide eyes.

Tate left the room. Let Erozan stew in his juices.

Kyle and Tursi were lathering up at the scrub sink. Her icy stare at Erozan reflected the raging hatred that had continued to grow since she first heard about him.

Tate joined them but kept his eye on Erozan through a window.

"You know," he said, "I've been thinking about a technique I wanted to run by you. I got the idea from a case they presented to me when I was lecturing in Boston last month."

"Let's hear it," Tursi said.

"A woman was admitted for an appendectomy. They gave her anesthesia with an initial dose of curare to paralyze her, and at the same time, put her on a barbiturate drip for pain. The barbiturate should have kept her unconscious and pain-free, but someone mixed the wrong dose, and she only received a tenth of what she should have."

"Ouch," Kyle and Tursi said in unison.

"Right. The curare paralyzed every muscle in her body, but she was still conscious. Able to think and feel when they cut into her, but unable to respond."

Kyle looked at Tate from behind her face mask. "The pain must've been excruciating. Is that what you have in mind for our friend?"

"Yup," he smirked.

"Sounds about right for this sadistic deviant," Tursi said, adjusting his mask on his shoulder.

"Good Lord, you are an evil genius," Kyle said with admiration. "But I'm not sure we should deviate from what the Tribunal agreed upon.

"Okay, just a thought," he said with a little bow.

They stared at the figure struggling against the leather straps.

Tate pulled up his face mask and pushed the swinging door open with his shoulder. He surveyed the room and marveled at Stenton's miracle.

It was an extraordinary feat, building an ultramodern operating room beneath his house in the Maryland countryside. There were major hospital CEOs who would sell their firstborn for half the equipment he had down here.

"Hey!" Erozan shouted. "If it's money you want, you got it. You name it."

"It's not money."

"What is it? Drugs?"

Tate snickered.

"Our next shipment from Miami's got enough coke to keep Baltimore high for a month. It's all yours."

Tate lubricated the clear plastic endotracheal tube that would maintain Erozan's breathing while he was paralyzed. He injected half a teaspoon of curare into the intravenous tubing.

"The next two shipments…six months' shipments. Whatever you want."

"Don't want your drugs," Tate nodded.

"What the fuck do you want? I'll give you anything."

"I want your soul, Jonas Erozan."

Erozan recoiled, then pursed his lips and spat. He missed. "Fuck you, scumbag!" he shrieked. "I'm going to fucking…"

The words trailed off as Erozan's tongue fell back into his throat. He stared like a corpse at the white ceiling.

"Mr. Erozan, I know you can still hear me and that you're quite awake. I assume you're having some difficulty breathing." Tate fitted a needle on a plastic syringe.

"Oops. I guess you're not breathing at all." He glanced at the silent man before turning back to the syringe.

"It's quite an interesting drug, this curare. The South American indigents in the upper Orinoco River Basin used it in poison darts to kill animals and their enemies. It's derived from the plant Chondrodendron and was first used in anesthesia in 1942. Blocks the nerve endings. Lasts at least an hour."

Tate snapped his fingers. "You don't really care about this trivia, do you?"

He leaned over to relish the terror in Erozan's eyes.

"Suffer, you bastard."

He knew the man's vision was getting blurred from lack of oxygen. Every cell in his imprisoned body was screaming for it. Tate allowed himself a brief smile.

Inserting the curved metal laryngoscope into the back of Erozan's throat, he pulled hard to expose the pathway to the lungs. Next, he thrust the plastic endotracheal tube into the airway and connected it to the respirator.

With the curare alone, Erozan was experiencing an incredible urge to gag. Sensation was intact, but ability to react was nil.

"Yes, a fascinating drug."

Tate switched on the respirator and saw the panic in Erozan's eyes ease after three surges of oxygen. The machine would pump it in every six seconds, converting the blue lungs back to their normal pink. He pulled up each lid and placed a small amount of lubricant in both eyes to keep the corneas from drying.

"You didn't think we'd let you go that easily, Mr. Erozan, did you? No, we have much grander plans for you. That was just a taste of what lies ahead."

Tate pushed a needle into a vial of sodium pentothal, filled the syringe, then paused and squirted most of the usual dose into the wastebasket. He injected what was left into the IV line.

"No doubt, you'll soon feel a warm flush and be drifting off to sleep—for a few minutes."

The image of Tate's baby girl lying in that crack house was still vivid.

Chantelle, barely a day over sixteen, a prisoner of the drugs and men who killed her. Where that happened, no one knew. And the chances of finding the murderers, much less bringing them to justice? Nil. They found her body in a Baltimore dumpster, put out like a piece of trash.

Sorry, Kyle, this one's personal.

Kyle and Tursi entered the operating room. Art Ramos, who had joined them after Tate left the scrub sink, followed close behind. Each put on a light blue gown and tan gloves.

Tursi scrubbed Erozan's shaved head with iodine solution, giving his skin a bronzed nicotine sheen. He'd placed blue plastic drapes over Erozan's face and chest, leaving only the right temple of the head exposed and facing the ceiling.

He sat on a stool at the end of the table.

Kyle and Ramos took positions on his right and left, respectively.

"Has he gotten the Pentothal?" Tursi asked.

Tate held up the empty syringe.

"Good. Scalpel, please."

Kyle handed the blade to Tursi. He made a tiny, horizontal incision down to the bone along the right side of the scalp and pulled the flaps of scalp apart. Bleeding arteries squirted blood into the air. Ramos hit them with the cautery, and the odor of burning flesh spread through the room.

"Ready for the drill," Tursi said.

Kyle passed him the electric drill, and Tursi bored an eighth-inch burr hole through the rock-hard bone on the right side of Erozan's skull.

The sickening, sweet smell of hot bone particles permeated the air and made Tate's stomach turn. Over the years, there were two things he never got used to in the OR: the smell of powdered bone and the odor of pulverized teeth. Both were nauseating. That is, unless you were an orthopedic or oral surgeon. If they bothered you enough, you needed a new job.

Through the small hole, Tursi cut through to the meninges, the membranes covering the brain, to get to the gray matter.

"I actually made this sound a bit easier than it really is," he admitted.

"How so?" Ramos asked.

"We need to destroy the upper two-thirds of the pons. But if we damage the adjacent structures, it'll be over fast. If we're successful, there should be minimal changes in thinking and memory."

Tursi maneuvered for a better view.

"Good thing we decided to leave him under," Tursi continued.

"The meninges are the most sensitive tissues in the body. It'd feel like someone was sticking a hot iron into his head and juicing it with 220 volts. He might deserve it, but I don't know if his body can take it."

Tate checked the vital signs. The Pentothal should have worn off just before Tursi's first incision.

Once through the meninges, Tursi eased the sharp tip of the wire-thin, fiberoptic laser scope into the soft temporal lobe of Erozan's brain. There was little resistance.

He held it in place while Kyle and Ramos pushed and pulled the OR table, positioning Erozan's head inside the torpedo-tube opening of the CT scanner in conjunction with the movements of the scanner itself.

Kyle switched on the CT, and the overhead screen revealed the inner structures of the brain. The medical group watched from the operating room, while Stenton, Randy White, and Nate Champion looked on from the amphitheater above.

"We're in the midbrain, just above the pons," Tursi said. He pushed the laser scope deeper, glancing back and forth at the CT monitor to determine what type of tissue he was in. A small amount of bleeding developed but was stopped with the laser.

"The composition of the pons is different from the surrounding tissues. We should be at the right spot...now. We'll find out in a minute...if I'm half an inch off, we'll have an early supper."

Tate looked at the screen too. Sudden death would be far too merciful.

Tursi stepped on the foot pedal. There was a crackling inside Erozan's head as the laser seared his brain cells and denatured their protein. The tissue changes appeared on the black and white screen of the CT scanner.

"If he was awake," Tursi said, "he'd be experiencing the brightest flashes he'd ever seen." He pushed down the pedal and destroyed more neurons.

Tate looked at the EKG monitor and frowned. "Carlo, you almost finished?"

"Just about. Why?"

"He's got some EKG changes. Step it up if you can. His heart doesn't like what you're doing."

Tate's brow furrowed as he watched the EKG.

"Aw shit! Ventricular tachycardia," he said, looking at the fast cardiac beats.

Kyle broke the scrub and rushed for the defibrillator.

"We've got to cardiovert him, Carlo," Tate said. "Can you stop?"

"Yes...I'm done." Tursi pulled the fiberoptic cable from Erozan's skull.

"We're losing him," Tate said. "Now he's in ventricular fibrillation." He watched the irregularly irregular beats skitter across the monitor.

Kyle ripped the drape from Erozan's body and pulled the stretcher away from the CT scanner.

Ramos squeezed lubricating jelly onto the defibrillator paddles and handed them to her.

"Everyone back!" she yelled. "No need to shock us into V-fib too."

She slapped the paddles on Erozan's chest and hit the red button. Despite the paralyzing effect of the curare, his body jumped off the table, then fell back with a thump.

Tate checked the EKG rhythm monitor.

Still FUBAR.

"Hit him again," he shouted.

"Everyone back!"

Erozan's body spasmed a second time.

Kyle fixed on Tate's monitor and whispered under her breath.

"You're not going like this, you bastard."

Tate pushed a three-tablespoon vial of sodium bicarbonate into the IV line to combat the lactic acidosis building up in Erozan's tissues.

The current surged a third time.

This time, the convulsion was followed by regular beeps on the EKG machine.

Kyle stared at the pattern on Tate's screen.

She loosened her grip on the paddles, and a look of relief swept across her face.

"We're back. Normal sinus rhythm," Tate reported.

"That was close," Kyle said. "We almost lost him."

"Let's sew things up," Tursi said. "Art, how long will it take you to cut the eye muscles?"

"Twenty minutes, tops."

"Good. We need another ten. Then we can get the hell out of here."

Tate pushed more sodium pentothal and a good dose of fentanyl into the IV line to dull Erozan's consciousness and kill the pain.

No, Mr. Erozan. Not that easily.

Chapter Forty

West Baltimore

Maryland

John Greco had thought a lot about how he was going to make these pimps, hustlers, dealers, and number-runners bend to his will. He took a long drag on his Camel, then blew a thin stream of smoke toward the disparate crew assembled in the back room of Chico's Bar & Grill in West Baltimore.

It was a motley crew. Sixteen to sixty, they'd crawled out of numerous holes to be there. With khaki fatigues and suits, jeans, and Raven's sweatshirts.

More of a ragtag horde than a church-boy choir.

But who cared?

What mattered was that they'd swim through a sea of shit for the right price.

Greco raised his hand for silence. "In case you haven't heard, Jonas Erozan is missing," he said in the deep voice that earned him the nickname Lurch. "He was kidnapped last night, fifty miles west of the city. We don't know who did it, but we're following leads."

Gasps erupted into wild speculation.

Greco paused for another puff. Let them fly in all directions before he grounded them.

And they did.

Three more puffs and Greco continued. Though a thug to many, his IQ was 140, the same as many of the sociopaths he admired and emulated.

"I expect the same cooperation you gave him. Not one bit less. We'll run this as a business organization. If we work together, we'll all make more money. I wanna make money for everybody, not just for those at the top."

A few disquieting murmurs erupted. Not unexpected, since Erozan still had friends. But the overall tone was positive.

"What about the percentages?"

"We'll start ten percent higher."

The tone of the murmurs improved. Already, his position was solidifying.

"But our first job is to find Erozan. No attack on this group goes unanswered. And when we catch who did it, I guarantee that I'll cut their hearts out with this very knife."

He brandished an ugly eight-inch stiletto. "And their heads will hang until the flesh falls from their faces." He flung the knife toward the far wall, where it impaled a wooden beam and quivered.

Greco dropped the cigarette and crushed it into the hardwood floor. "We're offering two hundred fifty grand to anyone who can lead us to whoever took him."

Great excitement spread through the group

Greco smiled. He knew that kind of money would bring the maggots out from under every rock in Baltimore.

"One last thing," Greco said. "It might've been kidnapped by State Troopers, or someone dressed like them. We don't know yet whether the cops are in our pocket on this one or not."

There were sighs of consternation. Everyone there had a record, and few were eager to enhance it by confronting cops.

"No wonder you're giving so much."

Chapter Forty-One

Stenton's Country Estate

Middletown, MD

Erozan awoke with a start, looking straight ahead at the wall clock above the foot of his bed. In fact, it was the only place he could look.

10:30.

A beam of sunlight fell across the green blanket and warmed his body. His throat was sore, and the right side of his head throbbed.

Although he could only see it out of the corner of his eye, he could sense a bathroom or sink off to the side. A whiff of soap or air freshener drifted in, and he could hear birds chirping and leaves rustling outside his window. An intermittent tractor hum was audible in the distance.

Where the hell am I?

He tried to pull off the covers with his right hand.

It didn't move.

Must have slept on it. It'll wake up in a minute.

A large green fly circled overhead and disappeared off to the left. Angry buzzing waxed and waned as it bounced off a window for the umpteenth time.

The insect zipped past his ear, then circled above before lighting on the tip of his nose. It marched back and forth in an erratic fashion, inspecting for threats and opportunities. Meeting no resistance, the little beast had the balls to walk up his left nostril.

Oh, that itches! You little shit!

The fly inserted its stinging proboscis and started to feed.

He tried to swat it.

Nothing moved.

You bastard!

He tried to swat it again.

The arm was still asleep. He couldn't twitch a finger.

He tried to close his mouth and breathe it out through his nose.

Nothing.

The insect struck a second time, feeding higher up on the mucous membranes of his inner nose.

Son of a fucking bitch!

Erozan stiffened, but his body lay limp.

All he could do was stare straight ahead and watch the clock tick off time.

Ten seconds.

Fifteen seconds.

Twenty.

You little bitch!

The itch was intolerable.

He wanted to scream.

Agh!!!

Every fiber in his body ached with the desire to shriek at the top of his voice.

He tried to jump up.

To swat the thing.

Anything to get the little mother out.

Only one scream.

Please!

Just one!

At last, the fly had its fill and flew on.

With the torture over, Erozan forced himself to retrace what had happened. They'd been on their way to that meeting. Then the cops on the highway…a black one and a white one…and that electric thing in his chest. It was a setup, for sure.

Were the Warlocks behind it? They were crazy enough.

Those cops would suffer. A quick call to the governor was all it would take.

Maybe he should handle this himself. You didn't screw with Jonas Erozan. Unless you wanted to swim with cement shoes in the middle of the Chesapeake.

What a greedy idiot he'd been to get trapped by those scumbags. Well, that would change. He'd plan better the next time.

But the stretcher.

Where did that come in?

Then the odor.

Antiseptic. In the operating room.

The IV line.

The plastic tube in his throat.

The one he couldn't get out, no matter how hard he tried.

And the incredible pain. Felt like someone lit a blowtorch in his head. They were heating it—no, frying it—to the point where it was exploding.

Then those horrible flashes.

Like looking at the sun. Only a thousand times brighter.

Then nothing.

But wait a minute. That hard-ass doctor. What did he say? A taste of what lies ahead?

Dear God, what did they do?

He couldn't even talk!

He tried harder.

Nothing.

Erozan couldn't remember anything else. But from what he saw, he was in some recovery room…a hospital room?

Yes, that was it! This was a hospital. He had to be healing here.

Just wait until Greco finds them. Then their asses were his.

An eternity passed.

The wall clock read 10:40.

Erozan mobilized every muscle in his body to move his legs.

His toes.

His fingers.

His mouth.

His eyes.

He looked for a door. His eyes didn't move.

What the fuck was wrong? He knew his arms and legs were there; he could see them.

But he couldn't move them.

Two men and a woman entered the room.

"Scalp wound looks good," the taller man said. The shorter man pulled up Erozan's right lid first, then his left. " I can't even see the eye incisions. Imperceptible."

Eye incisions?

Scalp wound?

The woman switched places with the shorter man. "I was just about to give him a neurological," she said.

She picked up Erozan's right leg. It gave a jerk after a tap with a small rubber hammer at the knee joint. She tested his other leg and his arms. They all did the same. Arms too.

They moved!

There's hope!

"They're intact," the woman said.

"Just what I'd expect," the taller man said. "Voluntary movements are gone for good, but the spinal cord reflexes are unaffected."

What?

Gone for good?"

The woman put her face in front of his. "Look at me, Mr. Erozan."

Erozan gasped.

She knows I hear her.

You fucking bitch!

He stared, unable to avoid her eyes, unable to close his own. They only blinked intermittently, no matter whether he wanted them to or not.

"Mr. Erozan," she said, "I know you can understand what I'm saying. Up to now, this whole event has been a mystery. But in a few minutes you'll learn all about it."

The three people turned and left the room.

After they left, Erozan willed his right hand to move. Just like he did every day of his life.

Nothing.

Nada.

He willed harder. If he did it hard enough, the hand would move.

He rested for a few seconds.

This was exhausting.

He wasn't moving a damn thing.

Now his hardest! He screamed at the same time.

But nothing came out.

While a headache moved in.

His head was splitting.

He relaxed and breathed more heavily. The exhaustion was overwhelming.

Now he was sweating too.

He should blink. Yes. He could communicate that way.

No use. His eyelids just did what they wanted.

He had no control.

One last try.

Every ounce of his energy went into moving his hand.

MOVE, damn you!

Nothing.

Please, God. PLEASE!

He'd give his entire fortune for just one twitch.

He collapsed back, his energy sapped.

10:50.

He couldn't even shut his eyes to block it out.

CHAPTER FORTY-ONE

A second green fly circled overhead.
GOD HELP MEEEEEEE!!!

Chapter Forty-Two

Stenton's Country Estate

Middletown, MD

"I liked what we saw in there," Kyle said to Carlo Tribulsi and Art Ramos in the hallway of Stenton's Maryland estate. "Not only was he one hundred percent paralyzed, but he couldn't move his eyes one nanometer."

Both men nodded their agreement.

Kyle knew people with the locked-in syndrome Carlo had created were essentially paralyzed, though they could still look up and down. And that would have allowed Erozan to communicate with the outside world. Now that Art Ramos cut the muscles that moved the eyes, there was no possible way the man could interact again with another human being, just like Randy White's sister in her coma.

Entombed in an immobile prison, his body was a vessel to keep his brain alive. He was excommunicated from the rest of humanity for eternity. Like Randy's poor sister in her coma.

Was she becoming the evil she was fighting against?

Kyle couldn't get the image of the murdered little girl out of her mind. If there was ever a person who deserved such retribution, it was this human scum.

No. She was serving justice against evil. He was evil to innocents. She was saving lives. He was destroying them.

"It would've been risky to tell him anything before the surgery in case things didn't turn out the way we wanted," Carlo said. "Now that we're two days post-op, we can be confident this is permanent."

"Good," Ramos said. "Then today's news should hit him like a brick in the face."

Kyle concurred. "Like my Daddy would say, hooh-rah!"

Stenton's face was somber as he marched down the hallway from the far end. Booth traipsed alongside him, pushing aside the green taffeta drapes with his clipboard.

"Good morning, team," Stenton said. "Your accommodations were adequate?"

"Refreshing," Kyle volunteered, knowing the others cared little about pleasantries.

"How's our patient?" Stenton asked.

"Bedridden forever," Carlo said. "Like Marie Ferguson. Only he'll be fully conscious. A fitting twist for the son-of-a-bitch."

"There's no possibility this can be reversed?" Stenton asked.

Carlo shook his head. "Impossible."

Stenton's worry melted away. "Then he can only be released by death."

"That's right."

"How apropos."

The five entered the room and formed a semicircle around the foot of the bed. Erozan lay with the head of the bed elevated. Stenton positioned himself at the foot, in Erozan's field of vision. Placing his hands on the end of the bed, he bent forward.

Kyle saw a thin smile touching the corners of his mouth. A little flash of the glee he felt over Erozan's situation.

"Mr. Erozan, we've come to explain why you are here. I imagine you might well be able to guess. You've stolen life's happiness from so many that I'm uncertain whether any retribution could repay you. The misery you've bestowed upon not only your victims, but their families and friends as well, is incalculable."

His tempo quickened and his face flushed. "You and your kind are a pestilence, a paradigm of moral bankruptcy. For these reasons, we've condemned you to a living hell. Death would be much too kind for you."

Stenton leaned closer. "I trust that even someone like you will remember this small piece of God's Bible. 'Ye have heard that it hath been said, an eye for an eye, and a tooth for a tooth.'"

"And by the way," he turned to Randy White, who'd just walked in, "you remember Marie Ferguson, Bill Ferguson's lovely wife. I thought you might like to meet Marie's brother. He's had a great interest in your career."

Randy towered above Stenton, his face devoid of emotion. Kyle knew if he had Superman's X-ray vision that Erozan's eyes would be exploding in their faces. Though he remained silent, the crevices on his forehead showed the incredible stress he was feeling.

Stenton straightened up with an icy stare. "With these thoughts, Mr. Erozan, we leave you. Forever and an eternity."

They walked out of the room and let the wooden door close.

Erozan had no choice but to stay exactly where he was.

With the clock.

And the buzzing fly.

Chapter Forty-Three

Stenton's Country Estate

Middletown, MD

The next evening, Kyle shivered, feeling a draft of late March air sneaking in through the cracks around the tall French windows, and the threat of death in the air as Stenton nervously peered over his half glasses at the other seven members of the Tribunal sitting in the oak-paneled conference room of his Maryland estate.

"I called this additional meeting to bring you up to date on DiNunzio," Stenton said. "We've heard from the wiretap that he's still convinced outside factions, possibly medical, are responsible for his uncle's condition.

"A second doctor, a dermatologist, Dr. Myles Mihalke, was consulted. Mihalke also suggested sulfa as the cause of Frank Mancino's toxic epidermal necrolysis. Just like Samuelson, their first consultant. Does anyone know, or know of, this man?"

"I do," Tursi said. "Myles was a classmate at Columbia. He's competent, but I'm not sure what else he can tell them that Samuelson didn't."

Kyle frowned. "Are you suggesting we do something?"

"Yeah," Randy interjected. "Smoke DiNunzio before he does us."

"Not yet," Stenton said. "We have no hard evidence. I want us to keep our eyes open and our guard up. As you know, a shark is predisposed to a frenzy once it has the scent of blood."

He turned his chair at the head of the rectangular table to face Nate and Randy. "Gentlemen, once more, do you see a possibility that any of us can be linked to Mancini?"

"I don't see how…" Nate answered. "Unless there's an internal leak. The evidence was removed right after they took Mancini to the ER."

Stenton's face was still painted with concern. "So, we have little to be concerned about. There is, however, one additional point to discuss. Nate?"

"Yesterday, a contact of mine in the downtown courthouse told me that DiNunzio's lawyer got a court order a week ago to exhume his uncle's body."

"Oh, my Lord." Kyle held a trembling hand to her mouth

"What?" Carlo questioned. "What are they up to?"

"They are going for more hair samples," Kyle said. "That's how they first got onto the altered sulfa drug that caused the toxic epidermal necrolysis."

"How? I thought you said his body eliminated that stuff."

"It did," Kyle said. "Totally. Except from his hair. They probably needed more hair to refine the analysis."

"Damn!" Carlo sat back and smacked the table.

"But even if they identify the sulfa," Kyle said, "they can't track it to us."

"True," Ramos said. "But it brings them one step closer."

The room turned silent.

When the discussion resumed, Kyle could only half listen. She rehashed the facts as she leaned back in her chair. Had they missed something? For the life of her, she couldn't think of it. But she hadn't called the hair either. What if there were other clues? Or worse yet, a leak like Nate said?

Everyone was feeling it. She watched out of the corner of her eyes. Even Art Ramos was eyeing his neighbors. She snapped her lids shut. Now she was doing it too.

"Can we please have a progress report on Erozan, Carlo?"

"It's been almost six weeks since the surgery. His vital signs are stable, and his neurological condition's unchanged. The nasogastric tube feedings are working well, thanks to Alden here, and he hasn't lost any weight. The scalp wound is virtually invisible, and with several weeks' growth of hair, the chances of it being discovered are nil.

He looked at Ramos. "The same goes for the eye incisions. Right, Art?"

"Yes. They're invisible to the naked eye. If someone suspected surgery, they'd have to sit him up at a slit lamp. That alone would be an incredible feat. Since you need the magnification to find the wounds, I believe we're safe."

"Coming back to the skull," Tursi resumed, "an X-ray taken from the right angle might detect the hole. Nonetheless, it's minuscule compared to the normal burr holes we make to drain blood or remove a plate of bone. A careful CT or MRI would also pick up the damage to the pons. But that looks just like a stroke from any number of causes.

"So," Stenton asked, "the chances of someone putting this together are?"

"Still close to zero. Even if the burr hole and brain damage were discovered, I don't see anyone connecting the dots. Only a handful of people know about my micro-laser."

"Then I believe it's time to find permanent placement for Mr. Erozan," Stenton said.

"We could put him in a nursing home," Nate suggested.

Kyle shook her head. "That won't work. One of the docs or his family would have to admit him. There'd be a direct link."

"Then what?" Nate asked.

"We should drop him off where he'll be picked up and brought to the nearest hospital. Let me qualify that. The nearest hospital where we have a modicum of control."

"Good idea," Randy said. "What about the Claridge Apartments down the block from Pennsylvania Hospital? Nate and I can make sure he'll be found at the right time to arrive on your service, Kyle."

"I can go with that," Stenton said. "Kyle?"

"Okay by me."

"Good. How soon can we move?"

"As soon as the technical aspects are worked out," Tursi said. "From a medical standpoint, he can leave at any time."

Stenton turned to Booth. "Alden, will you please coordinate?"

"Of course. I'll need Dr. McMann's schedule."

"Easy," Kyle said. "I'm on service starting tomorrow. He'll have to be found and brought in sometime during the night to be on my service. More exactly, from six p.m. tomorrow, Saturday, to six p.m. on Sunday. Let me know what time you drop him off and when he's found."

"Any objections?" Stenson asked.

None were forthcoming.

"Then it's settled." He lit up a huge cigar and blew an extended puff into the air.

Kyle groaned internally. *As if the pipe wasn't bad enough.*

Now, her main worry was whether Erozan's drop-off would go as planned. No matter how cautious they were, and how much they strategized, there always seemed to be some land mine. They'd avoided them or cleaned up the aftermaths to date, but as a statistician, she knew that eventually there would be an outlier they couldn't fix.

And in this situation, whatever you couldn't fix could kill you.

After too many grueling, excruciating hours, the meeting adjourned. The members walked down the blue hall toward the other end of the ground floor, physically and emotionally exhausted.

Faces with black hats and white bonnets in the Renaissance wall paintings stared as they passed. Even they seemed suspicious.

Carlo and Kyle left the building and said nervous goodbyes to their colleagues. They climbed into their separate cars and drove east to the Maryland House rest area on I-95 North.

She parked her new Miata in the lot and hopped in the passenger's side of Carlo's white Jeep. She'd pick it up in a few days when they came back to see Erozan.

Tursi sped out of the lot and under the sign for Philadelphia. The soft leather of the reclining seat felt good as Kyle lay back to rest.

She tried to sleep, but it was useless.

Who in their right mind could sleep after that?

"Do you think–" they said in unison. They chuckled.

Carlo reached over and gave her hand a gentle squeeze. "There's a leak?"

"Anything's possible. Have you thought about what might happen if we're exposed?"

Carlo's face went taut. "Only every day. I've been meaning to talk to you…I have—"

"I don't want to hear it."

"Are you serious?"

"Yes, I don't want to know."

"You can't bury your head in the sand. Come on, Kyle, be realistic."

"I am."

"You're not. Have you been talking to your transplant buddy?"

"No. Like I said, forget it. And keep Graham Kurland out of this. He has nothing to do with it. Nothing whatsoever."

"Is he the reason you won't go out with me?"

"Graham and I have been going out for a while. But no. I just don't think you and I are compatible."

"He's still a house officer."

"And a board-certified transplant surgeon with a fund of knowledge greater than anyone at the hospital. He also happens to be a war hero who won the Distinguished Service Cross and other medals."

"What the HELL!" he yelled.

"See. You fly off the handle at the slightest provocation."

She thought Tursi might be more upset at her last comment. But he seemed calmer.

"Fine," he said.

"Okay," she replied.

"Dammit," he whispered, followed by a few more blunt but unintelligible phrases. She leaned over and rested her head against the passenger window as they passed a convoy of National Guard headed for weekend maneuvers.

Times like this made her wonder whether they all had any real future.

Especially her and Graham.

Was she doing this for her brother?

Or ruining her life for revenge?

Chapter Forty-Four

Pennsylvania Hospital

Center City, Philadelphia

Graham Kurland was worried about Kyle. After their night—and morning—of falling in love, he'd thought it would be clear sailing. But she was edgy, distant, removed. And when he tried to talk about it, she shut him down. He didn't know what to do. And since they weren't public, he couldn't talk to anybody about it.

Patience, Graham, he reminded himself. *Focus on the job.*

He was covering for the senior medical resident on call for the Pennsylvania Hospital ER on Saturday night. While he spent most of his time now on the Transplant Service, as Chief Resident, he was always ready to help when they were really stuck.

Just like in his military days, it was the best people who volunteered. The ones you knew you could count on. And he wanted to stay in that cadre.

If he had to be here, tonight was as good as any. An April sleet was slicking the Philadelphia streets with black ice, reducing the clientele and the chaos. Even the knife-and-gun club should keep it down to a dull roar. He might actually catch a few Zzzs.

He yawned until his jaw popped, pressed himself into the blue vinyl chair in the doctor's lounge, and picked up the tattered April 2nd issue of the *New England Journal of Medicine.*

He scanned a couple of dull articles until…

Kyle McMann walked in and sat kitty corner to him, smiling big and wide.

He gave her a full smile with the high beams on. His night just got a thousand times better.

Graham started to rise.

"Sit," she said, waving him down.

"Yes, ma'am." Graham leaned forward, elbows on knees.

"Hey. I thought you were still at that Maryland meeting."

"No, thank God I'm done." She felt awful about lying to him about being at the Tribunal. Slowly but surely, it was turning her into someone she didn't like very much.

"I'm glad." He nodded, happier by the second.

"What brings you here on a Saturday night at this ungodly hour?"

"You."

She leaned in and gave him a soulful kiss. He gladly reciprocated.

When the kiss ended, they pulled back, faces flushed and blood pumping.

Kyle clicked into work mode. "Okay, I've been a little off…I know that. But I've been thinking. And now I want to talk to you about that thing…"

"The thing you've been wanting to talk about?' he grinned.

"Exactly," she grinned back. I've been…"

But try as she might, she couldn't spill the beans about the Tribunal. She couldn't risk putting Graham in the middle of the madness. And honestly, she was worried that he'd think she was a monster. Like she was as bad as the monsters she was destroying. So she pivoted.

"We've never talked about your long-term plans."

He breathed a sigh of relief. It wasn't something dark and horrible. It was something warm and lovely. "Great, yeah, okay, I've been thinking about that, too. A lot, if I'm honest."

"Really?" she said with a sly grin of her own.

"Well, I just took my Internal Medicine Boards and passed."

"Oh, my God! Congrats…"

"Thanks."

"Though I didn't think they would be much of a problem for you. You're the only human I know who has Boards in both Surgery and Internal Medicine, and you've got a search engine brain that puts Google to shame."

Graham aw-shucked with a humble shrug, which just made him all the more adorable. The hospital grapevine was already spreading the word that Kyle spent most of her nights at his place. It was one of the few communication methods faster than the Internet. But he didn't care, as long as she didn't.

"I've talked to the Transplant Team here, and there's definitely interest."

"Is that what you want?"

"Transplant suits me. And I like it here. People are friendly. And smart. And this is where I've done my research. Plus, there's you. I'm not about to go anywhere without you."

Kyle gave a heartwarming smile that Graham would remember forever. "I feel the same."

"I was thinking about making our relationship more permanent."

"Does that mean what I think it does?"

"I think it does." He gazed into her eyes, sparkling and wide.

"I think I'd like that," she said.

Kyle came over and sat on his lap as they kissed deeper and sweeter.

"What if I ever had to leave here?" she asked.

"Without me? No way. Wherever you go, I'm going too."

They stared into each other's eyes. Her sparkle changed to tears.

"What's the matter?" Graham asked.

"Just tears of joy."

"Are you sure?" He was great at reading people.

Before she took the next step with him, she knew she had to tell him about the Tribunal. Let the chips fall where they may. She couldn't start this with that six-hundred-pound gorilla in the room with them. She had to tell him about the Tribunal and the life-and-death danger that required an emergency exit plan.

Graham's beeper rang.

Saved by the bell!

CHAPTER FORTY-FOUR

Graham stared at the text and sighed. "ER. That was the Psychiatric Institute."

"What is it?"

"Remember the guy who ate a Philodendron plant a couple of months ago?"

"Hard to forget. Did he eat another?"

"Nope. He ate a light bulb."

"Regular or fluorescent?"

Graham chuckled. "Wiseass."

Kyle looked at her watch. "It's time for me to go anyway. But I want us to be together. To take this to the next level."

"Me too. I love…" He stopped, suddenly shy. "Being with you."

"Me too."

Graham stood with her and accompanied Kyle to the door.

"I'm happy," he confessed.

"Me too."

Another deep, sweet kiss shook them both. Graham smiled.

"This is exciting," he said sheepishly.

"I'm excited," she said with all her heart.

Kyle walked to the elevator as he gazed from the doorway.

From somewhere he couldn't remember – maybe the movies? – he knew that if a person had more than a passing attraction to whomever they just left, they'd make it known with a final parting turn.

He watched and waited.

The elevator rang, and the doors parted.

Just romcom propaganda.

Kyle bowed her head and started to walk in, then stopped in mid-step, turned with a smile, and blew him a kiss.

Wide-eyed, he smiled back and gave a small wave.

Graham's brain showed him a sweet daydream where he and Kyle were setting up their own home. Making dinner. Making love. Maybe even making a kid together.

That would be great, he thought with a smile.

Chapter Forty-Five

Pennsylvania Hospital

Center City, Philadelphia

Dr. Cindy Burke traipsed down the dim hallway in her green surgical scrubs, trying to stop her brain from showing her the image of a guy who ate lightbulbs taking a bite of her cheek. Graham was a good guy, despite the occasional lapse into dark Army Ranger humor. He had a brilliant mind. More importantly, he cared about his patients' welfare, especially those unable to help themselves. And he was always there to help.

His battlefield brotherhood often crossed over to the medical arena. Win-win for everybody. She wasn't surprised when she heard he won medals. His desire to help others was so strong that it couldn't be repressed, no matter what he was doing.

Flooded with outpatients during the day, the corridor was stone quiet at night. It would be nice if Graham was here right now.

She looked behind and picked up her pace until she rounded the corner and saw the welcome lights of the ER. The double glass doors parted as she approached.

"Hi, Cindy." Nancy Dugan, the head nurse on night shift, fell into step with her and the two walked down the hall.

"Hey, Nance. What's up?"

"Got a new one for you," Nancy said.

"The crazy who ate the light bulb?"

"No. He's still being checked in."

Cindy's forehead creases relaxed, and she smiled. "What is it?"

"Middle-aged man. He's in a coma, but his vitals are stable. The police found him lying in a stairwell in an apartment building. Said they got an anonymous call from one of the residents. They figured he must have fallen."

Nancy pointed to Cubicle Three, and they walked in. As she had been trained, Cindy began her exam at the doorway.

Maybe forty. Forty-five at most. Thin. In no apparent distress.

Lying on the stretcher, he stared straight ahead, no expression. Like he was sleeping or dead, but with his eyes open. His periodic blinking made his blank stillness even more disturbing.

"He gives me the chills," Nancy whispered in her ear. "He looks like a robot the way he blinks."

"Any name?"

"No. No ID, no family. No nothing."

Cindy gently shook the man's right shoulder. "Sir, look at me."

No change.

She shook harder. The face remained expressionless and the eyes unchanged.

"Sir, can you talk? Talk to me."

Nothing.

She gave him a major shake. "Talk to me!"

Nothing.

After noting the vital signs on the chart were stable, Cindy felt the pulse and listened to his heart.

There didn't appear to be a cardiac problem. Besides, he wasn't that old. Drug-induced? Neurologic?

She aimed her flashlight at his eyes. "At least the pupils react."

She leaned in, and with her ophthalmoscope, she looked at the optic nerve in the back of each eye. "No evidence of increased intracranial pressure."

She tapped the knee and arm joints. "The reflexes are intact, maybe even a little hyperactive."

Cindy leaned back against the cubicle wall and watched the intermittent blinking. A drug couldn't cause this. At least not one she knew about

"Nancy, I think this man's likely had a stroke. Would you please page Dr. Kurland?"

"Sure. Be right back."

He sure as heck couldn't have been lying around like this for any length of time.

He would have been dead in three days without water.

And he was well-shaven and cleanly manicured.

What is Heaven's name?

Three and a half minutes later, Graham loped into the ER and asked. "What've we got?"

"I'm not sure," Cindy said. "An unidentified man in his mid- to late forties who appears to have had a neurologic insult. Maybe a stroke."

"What's the history?"

"The ambulance drivers said they found him like this in an apartment stairwell."

"That's it? Nothing else?"

"Nope. We checked again with the cops. They had nothing."

They walked to Cubicle Three, and Graham leaned over to feel the scalp for signs of trauma, external blood, or a wound.

"Seems normal," he said. "With that history, though, we should rule out intracranial damage, possibly from a fall down the stairs. I wouldn't be surprised if he's had a brain bleed."

Graham studied the man. His eyes were open, and he blinked, although it appeared more automatic than voluntary.

He seemed to be conscious, but why didn't he move? Was his neck broken? Possibly, though it had to be below the C5 level, the fifth cervical vertebra, or he would have suffocated since his diaphragm wouldn't work and he couldn't breathe. But he should still be able to talk with that kind of spinal cord injury.

And the poor muscle tone, the flabby limbs. The pieces didn't fit. Muscles started to deteriorate rapidly after days of paralysis. But it had to go on for weeks to produce muscle atrophy to this degree.

"Any Battles' sign?" Graham asked.

"Blood behind the eardrum? I haven't looked yet."

Graham grabbed an otoscope off the wall and looked in the man's ears. "No sign of what you can see with a basilar skull fracture, suggesting intracranial bleeding. It can look like blood behind the eardrum or raccoon's eyes from blood around the upper face."

"Sorry, it's late."

"No problem. Any optic nerve swelling suggesting increased intracranial pressure from a ruptured intracranial blood vessel?"

"No," Cindy said. "I got a great look with the ophthalmoscope. I'm sure on that one."

"Let's get cervical spine x-rays and an MRI of the head," Graham said. "I'll ask the operator to page the radiology resident and get things moving."

No matter how much you saw, whatever you read, or how long you had been in the medicine business, there were always new and baffling issues.

That's what keeps it exciting, Graham thought with a grin.

"What do you think?" Cindy asked as if expecting an immediate answer from the man universally acknowledged as a genius.

"Beats me," Graham said, wiping his brow on his sleeve.

"Oh," she said, surprised. "I thought you'd—"

"Hey, life's no different than medicine. Full of mysteries."

"Could it be contagious?" she asked, backing away from the stretcher.

"Highly unlikely," Graham said, smiling. He scanned the bloodwork reports that just came in. "I think we're safe there."

They silently wheeled the motionless man through the dim hallway to Radiology. Her face was tight and drawn, and he could tell she was freaked out. Understandable, since it looked like the set of a slasher film.

By the time they reached the magnetic resonance imaging room, Howie Stone, the resident on call, had already turned on the unit. The humming, almond machine was the size of a small car, had a three-foot hole in the center, and a black rectangular stretcher passing through it.

"Hi folks, what's your pleasure?" Howie said, nodding toward the stretcher.

"Altered consciousness and paralysis," Graham said. "Could be a stroke, trauma, or maybe an intracranial bleed."

"You've really narrowed it down, huh?"

"Sorry. That's all we have."

"Any history?'

"None."

"Great."

"Hey, if it was easy, anybody could do it. We may also need a CT scan, too, depending on what the MRI shows."

Howie rolled his eyes despite knowing full well that this was the case. "Oh, yes. In case I forget, let me thank you for this fascinating consult—*in the middle of the night*!"

Graham smirked.

A petite brunette technician pushed the transporting stretcher next to the MRI machine. Graham noted her lipstick was a bit smeared. Howie's work? The four of them lifted the paralyzed man onto the MRI stretcher.

"Can you guys get plain skull and neck films first?" Graham asked.

"Can we do that, Susie?" Howie asked with funny fake formality.

"Why of course, Dr. Stone," she replied with a flirtatious smile and tone more appropriate for an online chat service than a hospital setting where the difference between life and death was measured in nanoseconds and millimeters.

Susie manipulated the MRI switchboard that looked to Graham like it belonged at NASA. She then went back and forth between the patient on a stretcher and the machine to adjust his head and her control panel.

She was tiny. Graham imagined a little ant moving a giant tree. She snapped multiple pictures from different angles, then hit a switch to pull the stretcher out of the MRI unit.

Howie looked at the X-rays on the MRI view box with a white background light. He ran his index finger down the side of the neck. "No spinal fractures."

"That's one plus for him," Graham said. A bone in the neck that impaled or severed the spinal cord connecting the brain to the rest of the body was bad. Really bad. If the injury was high up toward the head, breathing stopped. Then you were dead. If it was lower, you'd lose movement in one or more limbs. And your body could shrink to a fraction of its normal size over time.

He prayed for the day they'd have neural growth factors that could bring broken nerve endings back together. Until then, the prognosis was grim.

Howie changed the film. "This skull shot looks pretty good, too. No evidence of a fracture… Hold on." He moved closer. "Whoa, look at this." He pointed to a small, circular spot in the bone. "See it?"

"What is it?' Graham asked.

"I'm not sure. Almost looks like a burr hole neurosurgeons make when they want to take off a piece of skull to get to the brain. Much too small, though."

"How often do you see a single burr hole?" Graham asked.

"Not very. They usually make several, then connect them." Howie called to the technician. "Susie, let's run the MRI."

The mobile stretcher slid the patient's body farther into the cylindrical torpedo tube. The screen on the control panel clicked on, and the machine clanked and scanned sections of the brain from top to bottom. Even Graham, with his greenhorn radiology skills, could tell there was no evidence of a blood clot pressing on the brain.

After several minutes, the clanking stopped, and the machine pulled the stretcher back out of the tube.

Howie leaned forward and pointed to a shot with something in the center of the screen. "Look! This area's abnormal. Distinctly."

"Where?"

Graham stared at the image. That's why radiologists spend four years after their internship. To see things that no one else did. At least they'd get some answers.

"Here." Howie poked the screen with his index finger. "It's subtle, but it's real. This region of the pons has a different density than the surrounding tissues."

"Isn't that normal?" Graham said.

"Yes, but not to this degree. This looks like scar tissue, like what you see after a stroke. Let's give him some contrast and check it out."

Susie injected a colorless liquid into the patient's IV line. It reached the brain in a minute.

Graham watched the monitor as the dye turned several structures white on the screen.

"Yep, that proves it," Howie said. "This guy has scar tissue in the region of the pons. It's not a tumor or multiple sclerosis. I guess that you're right, he's had a stroke."

"When?" Graham asked.

"Hard to say. Weeks ago, maybe months."

"Any idea how it happened?"

"Hey, I just find 'em. You internists are the so-called geniuses, remember?"

Graham frowned.

"At least we don't have to drag a cranky neurosurgeon out of bed to crack his head and drain blood."

"True," Graham said, though he would've liked to have Carlo Tursi's opinion. Let him sleep. What he really wanted to know was how this man had an incapacitating stroke weeks or months ago and was still alive. It didn't add up.

He looked to Cindy. "Any ideas?"

"Nope. I've never seen one like this. Have you?"

"Not exactly. Although I've had a couple of patients with the 'locked-in syndrome.'" Graham turned away from the man. "A horrible thing. A person can see, hear, and feel everything. But they have a hundred percent voluntary muscle paralysis except for up-and-down eye movements."

He came back and put a finger in front of the man's face. "Sir, follow my finger," Graham instructed. He slowly moved it up and down.

The eyes remained frozen.

"Sir, blink."

CHAPTER FORTY-FIVE

Nothing.

"Blink!"

Still no blink response to Graham's command

"He blinks as if he's awake, though," Cindy commented.

"True, though not to command. But sometimes blinking on command returns with time. We'll have to watch." Graham scratched his head. "I wonder if he can hear us. Though I suppose there's no way we can find out."

"Bizarre," Cindy said. "How about if we run a tox screen on his blood and urine?"

"Fine with me, but I can't recall any toxin that could cause this. Let's get him up to the floor and think about where to go from here. Who's the attending?"

"Kyle McMann."

"Great!" Graham lit up. Maybe a little too much. Trying to cover his tracks, he shrugged and said, "I mean…she always has, uh…good…ideas."

Cindy gave a wry smile, like she knew they were an item. "Yes, she certainly does."

Graham started to defend himself. And her.

Cindy chuckled.

Graham smiled: Busted! "Okay, well, call me for the light bulb guzzler," he said as he shut the MRI room door behind him.

Looking forward to seeing Kyle, he headed to the on-call room. He ran the variables on their blind, paralyzed patient and ended up at a dead end. Again.

Dammit, he hated unknowns. They made him feel so useless.

His temper flared, lizard brain took over, and he lost control, violently kicking a metal garbage pail down the hall.

The noise jolted him out of his PTSD fit. He took three deep breaths and asked himself if he wanted to be the guy who lost his shit and violently kicked trash cans down halls.

He replied to himself that he most certainly did not want to be that guy.

His frontal lobe took over, and he went back to doing what he was born to do.

He diagnosed.

A long-term stroke, yet somehow, he was kept alive. How? And by whom? *No fucking idea.*

Chapter Forty-Six

Pennsylvania Hospital

Center City, Philadelphia

Kyle pulled into the Pennsylvania Hospital parking lot and stepped out of her yellow Miata. Some days she walked there from her apartment, but today, with her mind spinning, she wanted to get to the office early.

Monday morning, Philadelphia traffic was infuriating. She slammed the car door, thinking about the Neanderthal who drove her onto the curb. One shot, that's all she wanted. Just enough to break every bone in his nose.

She shook her head at the violence that coursed through her. The Tribunal was getting inside her head. She'd never let these maddening impulses get to her in the past. But she also rarely had stress like this.

Were they related?

Foolish question.

The hospital lobby doors whooshed open. She walked past the hallowed picture of Benjamin Franklin, the founder of Pennsylvania Hospital. Shaking her head, she realized how bone tired she was. Yet this bespectacled guy started a newspaper, discovered electricity, invented bifocals, and gave birth to a hospital, likely in his spare time. While she could barely make it through the day.

It was seven-twenty, ten minutes before patient rounds with the house staff. Kyle key-carded the lock to her office and placed a chocolate mocha coffee in her Keurig. She watched the brown ambition stream into the Philadelphia Eagles mug and leaned back against the counter.

She was excited about seeing Graham, who'd been gone for three days to take care of the company he inherited. But it was a real shame Graham had picked up the case. As Chief Resident, he had the option to follow any medical case he wanted. He'd stick with this one because it was a real mind-bender. She'd have to do some clever sidestepping to keep him off track. Anyway, no sense worrying about it.

She took a cautious sip of the brew, burned her tongue anyway, then whipped on her white lab coat.

The phone rang.

"Hello?"

"Kyle?"

"Carlo. What's up?"

"How's our patient?"

"Haven't seen him yet."

"Let me know what happens when you do. If you run into problems, call a neurosurgery consult, and I'll get right on it. But that's not the reason I called."

"What is?"

"Booth phoned. He was in a rush. He couldn't reach you, so he asked me to do it."

"What did he want?" she asked, looking at the recent calls on her iPhone and realizing she had slept right through Booth's call.

"Some of Erozan's people have been nosing around hospitals and nursing homes in the area."

Kyle's stomach churned. "You think they suspect us?"

"No. I think they're shotgunning. But it's only a matter of time until they get here. Even if they find him, though, they can't trace him to us."

"Right, that's what we thought with Mancini."

"Anyway, I wanted to warn you. In case one of them shows up."

"Thanks."

Just what I need, a bunch of drug-crazed maniacs chasing me with machetes. What next?

Kyle headed toward the second floor, rehearsing her approach to Erozan's case. The team was already waiting at the nursing station, all in a line: Crystal James, senior resident, Brian Quinn, the junior resident, Cindy, and four medical students.

And Graham at the head. He gave her a tiny nod and smile. She returned them both.

"Good morning." Kyle smiled at the rest of the team. "What have we got?"

"Several run-of-the-mill cases," Graham said, "and one fascinoma,"

"Okay, tell me about it, and then we'll go see him."

Graham looked at her. "How did you know it was a man?"

Kyle swallowed, realizing she had slipped, and started tap dancing as fast as she could. "Because, as everyone knows, female patients don't give diagnostic problems. AND, I was using 'him' in a non-gendered sense. Instead of *it*." She did a one-eighty and led the group down the hall.

Everyone managed to squeeze into the wooden chairs around the conference table. Cindy related the patient's history and physical findings. The house staff were baffled. The med students drew total blanks.

Kyle suppressed a smile. The case was overwhelming. A series of dead ends. Just what she'd hoped. They were looking for a natural explanation. The truth was as far from natural as you could get.

Graham stood up with the MRI films hanging from his hand. "You can see why this one's a mystery. It seems to me a variant of the locked-in syndrome from a pontine stroke. I tried to get you at home last night for advice, but your answering service said you were unavailable until this morning. So, I took the liberty of getting a neurology consult."

Damn it!

Kyle started and spilled her second cup of coffee. She loved the guy, but should've known he'd pull something like this. He was too good. She grabbed a handful of Kleenex tissues and wiped up the mess.

"What did they say?"

"Not much that added to our working premise. They agreed that a pontine stroke was most probable. They weren't sure about the timing either—why the stroke looks chronic on MRI."

"What do you think?"

"I don't know."

Good. Graham was still confused.

"Let me see the films." She could assuage him with a reasonable story. The tension in her neck and shoulders eased.

Graham placed two composite films on the view box and turned on the light. Kyle came close to look at them. The others crowded behind.

She stared for a long while. She and Carlo had gone over this.

"It does look like an old stroke," she said, tapping her index finger against her lip. "But don't be fooled. You all know that a myocardial infarction in the heart can extend for days to weeks. Right?"

There was a muddled positive consensus.

"The same thing can happen with a stroke. I suspect this man had a pontine stroke a while ago, but that it wasn't bad enough to cause serious functional impairment. More than likely, another stroke extended the area a tiny amount. That's why acute changes aren't visible on our MRI—at least not yet. In the right place, even a smidgen of additional brain tissue loss can cause drastic functional changes.

Graham rubbed his chin. "Good point. A small change could be difficult to detect with MRI. Any thoughts on the underlying cause of the stroke?"

"It could be any number of things. Does he have high blood pressure?"

"Not now," Cindy said. "We don't know before the stroke."

"Were the retinal arteries narrowed? That's an early sign of hypertension."

"I'm, uh, not sure."

"Then look again."

Cindy bowed her head.

"What about cholesterol passing up from the carotid artery in the neck?" Kyle asked, happy that all her rehearsals were paying off. "A little embolus, a piece of calcium or cholesterol from hardened arteries, can break off and fly through the bloodstream into the brain or the eye, inside the retinal arteries. The same can happen if a piece of calcium breaks off one of the heart valves. Cindy?"

"I'll look harder."

"Good." Kyle liked that answer.

"His retinas were fine," Graham said. "No evidence of hypertension or emboli."

"How old is he again?"

"Probably in his forties," Cindy said.

"Then a congenital blood vessel malformation," Kyle continued. "Or a ruptured aneurysm. I'd also make sure he doesn't have any clotting problems or giant cell arteritis. People who clot too well can have one in the brain. They can also have a hole in their heart between the right and left upper chambers that didn't close at birth and lets a clot pass from the venous side of the blood stream to the arterial side without being filtered out by the lungs. The clot can then travel right up to the brain."

"Good thought in a younger person," Graham said.

He took down the MRI film and put up the skull x-ray. "What do you make of this, though?" He pointed to the tiny hole in the temporal skull bone.

Kyle looked at the black-and-white film. "I'm not sure. It seems atypical for an old surgical scar, but maybe. Old trauma? What do you think?"

"It could be, but I hate to just write it off to that. I can do a little research tonight."

Good. Not perfect. But good.

She'd sold him on the extended stroke, though he wasn't buying the trauma tale. Even so, the puzzle had to be too much for him. For anyone. In all likelihood, he'd have to add it to his growing list of medical imponderables. But she loved his determination. And how his jaw set when he was deep in thought.

"Why don't we see the patient?" Kyle said.

The group walked to Erozan's room and assembled around his bed while she thumbed through the chart.

Nothing incriminating. Nothing whatsoever.

"Hmm…too bad we don't have any additional history," she said. "This isn't much to go on."

"The physical findings are just like we discussed," Cindy said. She uncovered a leg and pointed to the poor muscle tone. "I wish there was more we could do, but I don't think we have much to offer."

"Yes, I'm afraid this case is hopeless," Kyle said, as she stared right through Erozan's open eyes. "Let's watch him for a few days to make sure he's stable. I'd contact Social Services now to get them working on nursing home placement."

She wondered how Erozan felt to hear himself given the status of a vegetable, nothing more than a piece of furniture.

Living death is a cold, lonely place, Mr. Erozan.

The group dispersed at the end of rounds, and Kyle walked down the hall. She stopped by the stairway and called back to Graham. "Let me know if that man's family comes in, will you?

"Oh, I forgot to mention. We called back the police to see if they could help with identification. They're sending someone over to fingerprint him now."

"Great," Kyle said with a flimsy smile.

Really great. That would just bring the authorities and Erozan's psychopathic hellions one step closer to them all.

Change the subject, her mind told her.

"I've been thinking about our…conversation. Maybe we could look for a place. Together."

Graham smiled. "Or maybe you could move into my place."

"I love your place," Kyle smiled back. "I could totally see myself there."

"Really?" he asked like a kid about to get a great Christmas present.

"Really," she replied. "Maybe I could come by when we're done here, and we could explore…the possibilities."

"I would really like to explore all the possibilities."

She reached up and gave him a kiss.

He kissed her back.

Chapter Forty-Seven

Center City

Baltimore, MD

J ohn Greco sat in the office of his Baltimore penthouse, leaned back in his swivel chair, put his feet up on the desk, and smiled as he tapped his fourteen-hundred-dollar, black Oxford Ferragamo shoes together. With a half-dozen Cayman accounts teeming with cash, and a bevy of eager-to-please females vying to give him anything he wanted, he was living the life.

But unless Erozan was either dead or crazy, exclusive control was tentative. Until they found him, or what was left of him, he had to pretend to give a crap about the scum sucker.

A sharp knock sounded on the wooden door.

"Who is it?"

"Leon Weiss."

Greco took his feet off the blotter, grabbed a pen, and sat up. "Come in."

The young man barged in breathless. "I have great news! We've found Mr. Erozan."

"Where?" Greco, suddenly on high alert, bolted up from his chair.

"In a hospital in Philadelphia. I found this clipping in the *Baltimore Sun.*"

"Let me see that." Greco grabbed the tattered piece of newsprint.

MISSING DRUG LORD IN HOSPITAL

PHILADELPHIA, May 15 — Police announced today that a man found in a coma in a Washington Square apartment complex has been identified as Jonas Erozan, alleged chieftain of a Maryland-based drug ring. Erozan abruptly disappeared two months ago. It was estimated his influence extended throughout Maryland, into Northern Virginia, and beyond. A Pennsylvania Hospital spokesperson indicated the patient's condition is guarded.

Greco looked out the window, concealing the smile that crept across his face.

"Good work, Leon. I'm very pleased." A comatose Erozan was as good as a dead Erozan.

Leon beamed. "I can sure use the money."

For a damn news clipping?

"Sure, Leon. We're going to Philadelphia right away. Tell Clinch and Sullivan we're leaving in fifteen minutes."

The black Lincoln and his men were waiting downstairs. It was suddenly a very good day. If this were Erozan, he was probably close to terminal. And if not, an arrangement to have him meet his maker sooner could be made. If it wasn't him, they could still spread the word that it was and that he was brain-dead. Either way, John Greco was the King.

It's good to be the king, Greco thought as he smiled.

Chapter Forty-Eight

Pennsylvania Hospital

Philadelphia, PA

"DR. GRAHAM KURLAND, CALL SECOND SOUTH, STAT!"
The mechanical voice echoed through the corridor with sonic boom intensity.

Graham picked up the phone and dialed the nurse's station.

"Dr. Kurland here."

"Mr. Armistead isn't responding."

Graham ran to the elevator. Armistead would be in rigor mortis by the time that piece of junk arrived. So, he switched to the stairs, taking three steps at a time. He practically fell down the six flights.

Graham burst through the second-floor hallway door and swung around the corner into Armistead's room. Four hundred pounds of man lay on his back, motionless. His eyes were closed.

Two medical students and three nurses stared at the cardiac monitor.

"Dr. Kurland, it just went flat," someone said.

Graham looked up. Dead flat.

He shook Armistead's shoulder.

"Mr. Armistead."

No response.

"Mr. Armistead!"

He shook harder.

Nothing.

No pulse in the arms or neck.

Graham lifted his right arm and brought his fist down with all his considerable might in the center of the man's chest.

Armistead's eyes popped open in an instant.

"OH, SHIT!"

He wheezed and tried to sit up, his arms and legs flailing in four different directions.

"You killed me. I'm dying." Then he erupted into a fit of coughing.

Graham knew he hadn't hit him hard enough to kill him. But he also knew that the KGB trained its assassins to stop the heart with one savage punch.

Graham fished around in the bed and came up holding a small green wire that was meant to be attached to Armistead's chest.

"You were awake the whole time and too lazy to answer?" Graham barked, waving his hands. "You're lucky we didn't shock you with the paddles."

"Whose patient is this?" Graham asked.

A small, redheaded nurse meekly raised her hand. "He's mine, doctor."

"And you are?"

"Helen Schmidt."

He was about to bawl her out.

But when she saw her watery eyes, his anger turned to empathy. "Happens to the best of us. Next time, please check the leads."

Graham walked towards the nurse's station.

A thin man, easily 6'4", looking like Count Dracula in a black tailored suit, blocked his way.

"Can I help you?" Graham asked like a man in the heat of battle.

"You're Dr. Kurland, aren't you?"

"Yes."

"You're taking care of Jonas Erozan?"

"I am."

"Good. I'm John Greco, a close friend and business associate. I'd like to see him with you if that's possible."

Graham had learned of Erozan's vile reputation after the cops IDed him. He visually frisked the man's suit jacket and saw that the man was packing heat.

Graham extended his right hand.

They walked to Erozan's room, followed by three men built like Sherman tanks with the IQs of exhaust pipes. Only two visitors were allowed at the same time. Graham thought that under the circumstances, it was best to let this rule slide.

Graham stood by the patient's head, and the others surrounded the bed.

"We visited an hour ago and tried to talk to him," Greco said, "but he just stares into space like we don't exist.

"Unfortunately, we believe Mr. Erozan has had a stroke."

"How bad?"

"Very. The chances for recovery are grim." Graham scanned the group.

Their expressions didn't change. Though he thought he caught a glimmer of glee dance in Greco's eyes.

A tense silence followed. One of the men lowered his eyes and crossed himself.

"How did he get to this particular hospital, Doctor?" Greco asked.

"Mr. Erozan was found like this in a nearby apartment building by the Delaware River. The police questioned the locals, but no one knew him or saw how he got there."

"How did you identify him?"

"Fingerprints."

"Do you suspect foul play?"

"There's no evidence of it. Why do you ask?"

"Mr. Erozan disappeared under strange circumstances. We had no idea where he was. It's unlike him." Greco nodded to his crew, who nodded their heads. "We all wondered whether someone could've done this to him."

"I don't know how. He's severely incapacitated, but only a small part of his brain is affected. Unfortunately, it's the area of the pons, a critical pathway that multiple nerves travel through. Those nerves are irreversibly damaged. There's no evidence of any external trauma. We believe he had an unusual stroke due to natural causes."

Graham hated to use the term *natural causes*. He knew there was a definitive reason for every stroke. They just couldn't find it.

"I see," Greco said. "You said he won't recover?"

"We believe he'll probably remain like this for the rest of his life."

One of the younger men wiped away a tear and blew his nose like a foghorn.

Graham sighed in the sad silence as the four men stood poker-faced, staring at Erozan.

"Any other questions?" he asked.

"Do you think Mr. Erozan can hear us?" Greco said.

"It's entirely possible."

"Give me a minute alone with the doctor. Please," Greco said, waving his associates out.

After they left, he turned to Graham. "I wanted to speak alone because I don't think my colleagues are prepared to deal with this tragedy."

"As are we. I'm sorry we can't do more. Our best people are on his case."

A barely visible smile crossed Greco's lips. "Have you ever seen anyone recover from this?"

"Never. We're planning to transfer him to a nursing home this week. Unless he has family who want otherwise."

"There is no family."

"Are any of you his legal guardians?"

"No. He has none. He always thought of himself as indestructible."

They looked at Erozan, who blinked in return.

Greco folded his hands in front and shook his head. "I suppose we must persevere, mustn't we?"

"I suppose we must."

"Doctor, do you mind if I spend time alone with Mr. Erozan? We're like brothers."

Graham nodded, pleased to be done with John Greco. There was something creepy about him, the way he looked at the patient, the weirdly inappropriate smile. The man said the right things. But the vampire voice didn't match his words. Fortunately, Graham hadn't spotted any fangs, and the man didn't seem to be concealing a wooden stake. So he left, closing the door behind him.

He reminded Graham of a Taliban chieftain who pledged allegiance to him and his unit, then stabbed them in the back the first chance he got. Fortunately, Graham's sixth sense put his unit on the alert so that the chieftain and his zealots would never do that again—to anyone. They provided fertilizer for good food nourishing future generations of Afghan children.

Chapter Forty-Nine

Pennsylvania Hospital

Philadelphia, PA

Greco waited until Graham was gone before pulling a chair up to the bedside. "Hello, Jonas. I hope you're not mistaking me for somebody who gives a fuck."

He laughed and sparked up a fresh Camel. Resting his feet on Erozan's stomach, he leaned back to blow a trademark smoke ring over the inert man's head.

"You always hated other people's smoke, didn't you?" He puffed a cloud into Erozan's nostrils. " I hope to hell you can hear me."

Greco took his feet down, rocked on the front legs of the chair, and leaned forward. "You know, I hated your ass right from the beginning. I would have shoved my foot up there years ago, but I knew you'd enjoy it."

Greco took a long drag and exhaled a full breath up Erozan's nose. "Must be nice being retired. No work, no worries. Nothing to do but relax in bed all day and watch the wall."

He blew another puff up Erozan's nose holes. "Don't worry, I'm taking care of everything. And don't worry, your favorite girl, Sofia, is taking real good care of me. You never mentioned her world-class BJs. I'll give her your best tonight." He stood up, leaning on Erozan's testicles.

"Well, gotta go. Take care. And keep in touch."

He crushed the butt in the sink and slammed the door on his way out.

Erozan lay as still as the air in an underground cavern at midnight.

A single tear slipped from the corner of his right eye and plummeted to the pillow.

Chapter Fifty

South Philadelphia, PA

Jeffrey Jackson walked fast past boarded-up storefronts, burned-out shells, and piles of drifting litter on South Street, careful to avoid eye contact, smelling danger in the dank air as he imagined his night with Marla Turner, the girl he loved with a thousand hearts. Who'd have thought that skinny little kid he used to tease in the fifth grade would turn out to be his dream come true? Soon as he was done at MIT, he was going to marry her.

Jeffrey knocked on her front door. Herbert Turner opened it. Same old green sweater with a hole in the left elbow.

"Come in, Jeffrey. How are you?"

"Good, sir. And you?"

They shook hands warmly.

"Just fine…Marla!" he yelled up the open stairway. "Jeffrey's here."

Marla entered the room, looking lovely in a simple blue dress. She smiled at Jeffrey, clearly overjoyed to see him. "Good evening, Mr. Jackson," she said in a funny faux formal way. "I do hope you're very well."

"Good evening to you, Ms. Turner. I am very well, thank you for asking."

They shook hands and did silly little bows.

Turner winked at Jeffrey. "What's so important about this fellow?"

Marla walked over and sat on the arm of the sofa. "Good question." She looked into Jeffrey's large brown eyes. "He's simple, but he's entertaining.

And he doesn't drool much." She glanced at her father. "Except when he's hungry."

Jeffrey grinned and looked down. Marla took his upper arm and kissed his cheek in feigned apology.

"Enough beating up the innocent," Turner said. "Get outta here." Her father ushered them to the door. "Have a good time. Any problems, call me."

Marla took Jeffrey's hand, and they walked along South Street.

Jeffrey stopped in the middle of the sidewalk and held her at arm's length. "You look good, girl."

"Good? Is that all?"

"Great."

"You're getting warmer."

"Sizzling?"

"Now you're hot."

"How about deliciously edible?"

"Now you're steaming."

Marla giggled and squeezed his hand.

The night was warm for mid-May. The nice weather brought a large crowd to the concert. Jeffrey and Marla unrolled their blanket between two thirty-something couples and stretched out on the soft grass. Overhead, the moon shone a smile on them.

Olivia Rodrigo on the stage by the Art Museum was just a speck, but a nearby loudspeaker made up for the distance.

The concert ended two hours later, and Marla kissed Jeffrey's cheek as the applause for Olivia faded.

"Let's go for a soda."

"Where?" he asked.

"Polito's."

She gave him a quick peck on the cheek.

"Let's do it,"

The crowd thinned once they were away from the Museum area. On a Friday night in the downtown sidewalks were deserted at eleven o'clock.

"Let's go a little faster," Jeffrey said, once they reached Washington Square Park, six acres of tall sycamores, clumps of bushes, and historical markers.

"What's your rush?"

"Don't turn around," he said with dark urgency. Marla looked out of reflex, but Jeffrey jerked her forward and kept her moving.

"Guys have been following us for the last few blocks. Hold my hand and let's move it."

Four predatory scumbags hunted them from a block behind. If they could cut through the park, they could beat them. The other side was poorly lit, but three blocks further were crowded streets.

They picked up their pace, race-walking through the park.

So did their pursuers.

Jeffrey glanced back. "Can you run in those shoes?"

"I think so."

"Then let's go."

Jeffrey stopped short. Dead ahead, standing side-by-side with crossed arms, three more wild animals disguised as humans blocked their path.

Chapter Fifty-One

Center City

Philadelphia, PA

"Shit!" Jeffrey said under his breath. He glanced behind. The others were coming up fast, cutting off their escape.

"Hey, Black boy," the biggest sneered. "We wanna party with you and your mad hot lady friend."

They wore dirty, ripped jeans with chain belts and their drawers hanging out. Emilio Solas, aka Blade, was 6' 3", with an open black vest displaying cut abs and beefy pecs. Blood drop facial tattoos and screaming, blood thirsty eagles with huge, sharp talons were tatted on their faces and forearms.

"We don't want any trouble, man," Jeffrey said. "We'll just walk away and-"

"Don't call me man, Black boy. You call me Mr. Solas. And my Diablos just wanna get better acquainted with your hotty girlfriend." Solas grinned and hit his lackeys in the chest with the backs of his hands. "Don't we, boys?"

Jeffrey heard the men behind him break into a run. If they were going to do something, it had to be now.

He put himself between Marla and Solas. "Run toward Walnut for help," he whispered. "I'll hold them off."

He shot a glance to the left, then the right. The streets were deserted.

Jeffrey lunged at Blade as Marla broke into a run. Solas went down, and Jeffrey grabbed him by the throat and squeezed as hard as he could.

He could hear Marla running and the shouts of the other gang members. She was fast. Thank God.

Chapter Fifty-Two

Donatucci's Café

South Philadelphia, PA

Maybe DiNunzio wasn't coming, Jimmy Crawford thought as he sweated bullets. Shifting from one foot to the other, he stood outside Donatucci's cafe in South Philly. He wondered what the hell he was getting himself into, meeting with a man who'd once threatened to tear someone's head off and shit down his neck.

It was late Friday night, and he glanced down at his watch for the fourth time in three minutes. Ten years ago, he'd never have taken this scumbag as a client. Today, he needed the cash. But he knew in his gut that if you swam long enough with sharks, you eventually got eaten.

A black Caddy pulled up to the curb. DiNunzio was fifteen minutes late, but at least now he could give the 411, take his blood money, and never lay eyes on this monster again.

DiNunzio stepped out from the passenger's seat like Death incarnate.

Crawford greeted them with a tight-lipped smile.

The big man swaggered to the cafe and waved his hand. "Come on."

Crawford sighed, swallowed, and followed. The main dining room was empty.

DiNunzio sat at a square wooden table with a red-and-white checkered tablecloth at the back of the room. His bodyguard stood behind him like a human Doberman pinscher.

Al Donatucci and a young woman appeared out of the blue.

Jimmy Crawford was told to sit. He sat.

"Mr. DiNunzio, so good to see you again." Donatucci smiled and turned to the girl. "This is my daughter, Nina. She'll bring you anything you need."

DiNunzio smiled. "T'anks Al. We just need cawffees an' privacy."

"Absolutely." He flagged Nina to bring the drinks as he walked to the front door to hang out the "CLOSED" sign. "Stay as long as you want."

"We 'ppreciate it." DiNunzio turned to Crawford. "Whatchew got bettah be good, considerin' what I'm payin' youze."

Crawford tried to act normal as his heart pounded and he pulled a dozen photographs from his tattered brown satchel. "When you thought doctors were involved in your uncle's death, I checked out everyone who had had any contact with him. You told me he hadn't seen a doctor in years."

"He di'n't trust doctuhs."

"So that left the ones who took care of him in the hospital. It took me a long time to get the records, then identify the names," Crawford said. "The hospital wasn't very helpful. And the docs don't write their notes so well."

"No shit."

"There were three who mostly took care of your uncle." Crawford handed three glossy prints across the table.

"I remember 'em."

Crawford pointed. "Kyle McMann. She's the big mahoff."

"Yeah. She ran da show. She knows her shit, but she's a bitch an' a half."

"Graham Kurland was the Chief Resident. That's the one in charge of all the docs who graduated from med school but are still training."

"I know what a fuckin' Chief Resident is, ya mook."

"Sorry, Mr. DiNunzio. I didn't mean to insult you."

"Fuggetaboutit. Gimma da rest."

"Then there's Harry Turner, the intern."

"Bozo da clown. Only skinny."

"Yeah, that's him."

DiNunzio licked his lips. "Dese are da ones who done it?"

"I don't think so. I followed Kurland and Turner for weeks. I think they're clean."

"What about the chick?"

"She's another story. I followed her for the past couple of months. Seems her brother was murdered ten years ago. They never found out who did it."

"So?"

"Motive."

"What?"

"She's got some kind of vendetta."

"Whatta youze tawkin' about?"

"She had a reason to kill your uncle. Plus, three times she's gone to a meeting at a mansion on the Main Line. It's owned by Stenton, L.C. Stenton. He's a multimillionaire. A group of half a dozen doctors and ex-Navy Seals meet at Stenton's place. Seems on Fridays. I don't know who they all are yet. Here are their pictures."

He passed the rest of the photos.

DiNunzio studied each one in turn.

"Yer pretty fuckin' good wit' dat camera, ya numbnut. Where'd ya take dese?"

"Outside the drive to Stenton's. Got them when they came in and out in their cars."

DiNunzio looked up. "So, how do we find out who dey are?"

"I know two of them," Crawford pointed to the photos. "This one is Alden Booth, Stenton's gofer. And this is Lindsey Tate, an anesthesiologist at Temple Hospital."

DiNunzio leaned back and thought for a minute. "How'd you get da make on 'em? You di'n't drop my name, didja? 'Cuz if any word of our meetin's gets out, dere's no place on Earth I won't find yer sorry ass."

"God no, of course, no, I didn't, I wouldn't…" Crawford wiped his sweaty brow and wondered if they could tell that his shirt was soaked.

"Don't shit yerself, ya dumbfuck. Get me da names of de rest of dese fuckfaces. Pronto, capiche?"

So much for being finished.

"And their families?"

Crawford nodded too hard. Yeah, he could see this guy cutting off somebody's head and shitting down his neck.

"If I hear from youze soon, I'll t'row in a li'l bonus."

"Great, thanks, I'm really..."

But DiNunzio and his meaty bodyguard were already headed for the door.

Crawford walked back to his beaten-up Olds and toe-kicked a parking meter.

Was he out of his fucking mind?

He had a wife and two kids, for God's sake.

Well, a divorced wife. And his kid hated him. But still.

Life was too short to deal with this shit.

And death was too long.

Chapter Fifty-Three

Washington Square

Philadelphia, PA

One of the Diablos pummeled Jeffrey's back and head, trying to pull him off as he choked Blade Solas.

Jeffrey back-fisted the weasel in the mouth, and he went flying. Another jumped on Jeffrey's back, and someone else pushed him to the ground.

Three stainless steel blades in his face convinced Jeffrey it was time to stop fighting. He looked up to see Marla being dragged back with a six-inch stiletto to her neck.

Blade stood, wiping blood from his lower lip and sad goatee. He rubbed his neck and smiled at Jeffrey, who was being held by each arm.

He whipped around and buried the heel of his hand in Jeffrey's face.

Jeffrey reeled backwards and felt warm blood pour from his nose.

"Stinking jigaboo! What the fuck is wrong with you?" Blade screamed. "Didn't you hear? We just wanna get to know your lady friend better."

He walked over to Marla and lifted her chin with a finger. "She's real pretty, eh? You think, boys?"

Jeffrey looked around desperately. There were several high-rise apartments, but the park was dark, and nobody could see them through the trees and thick bushes.

"Let her go. Please!"

"Shut up, you darkie scum!" Blade yelled.

"What do you want to do with this son-of-a bitch? Eh, Blade?"

"Put him on the pole, Paco." Blade pointed to a lamppost with a shattered bulb.

"You try to scream or get away," Blade's #2 Paco whispered through his two missing eye teeth, "and we'll slit your girl's throat."

He and another Diablo dragged Jeffrey to the pole, one on each side. Each pulled an arm back in one hand, and Blade held a knife over Jeffrey's kidney with the other.

Jeffrey was closer to Walnut Street now. A quick push and he was gone. Paco reached inside his pocket and pulled out a pair of handcuffs.

Jeffrey tensed to run.

But no way in heaven or hell could he leave the love of his life with these scumbags.

Paco slapped on the cuffs, tightening them until Jeffrey winced. He grinned and patted his victim's shoulder. "Don't worry."

He slammed his right foot into Jeffrey's groin. "And don't ever hit Blade. Nobody hits Blade unless they wanna get cut." He laughed as the thugs walked away.

Jeffrey slumped forward, unable to breathe, his vision dimming.

He squeezed his eyes shut and bit his lower lip to keep from passing out.

His legs buckled beneath him, and the handcuffs dug deeper into his wrists.

When he opened his eyes again, the thugs were back in the group, thirty feet away. Paco put his arm around Blade's shoulder and gave him a quick one-armed hug. "This is one fine looking chickie, eh? We're going to have fun with her, no?"

"Great fun, Paco." The others laughed as they lined up behind Blade and Paco.

Marla was out of her mind, sobbing, tears pouring out of her eyes, blue makeup streaking down both cheeks. She looked at Jeffrey, her eyes crazed and white in the darkness.

"Dammit!" Jeffrey pulled on his wrists wildly.

Marla stumbled forward. The two men holding her arms yanked her right back up.

Blade stepped in front of her, rubbing a shiny stiletto against the ball of his thumb.

"Girl, we want you to show us a good time. If it's good enough, we may even let you and your boyfriend go. If not, well, these boys are hard to control when they get mad."

He laughed and put away the knife. Then he put away his smile.

"Take off your clothes, bitch."

Marla shrank back. "No, please. Please don't do this. I'm begging you."

Blade shook his head and moved in closer. A sharp nod, and in an instant, two men ripped off Marla's blouse and bra.

Marla recoiled and crossed her arms over her chest.

"No!" Jeffrey wrestled against the cuffs until he felt warm blood on his hands. "No! Leave her alone."

Blade looked over at him. "You keep quiet, or this is what we do to her." He made a fake slash at his neck with the stiletto, then turned back to Marla. "Now the pants."

"No!" she screamed and grabbed her belt.

Blade smashed her face with the back of his fist. "Bitch, you scream like that again, and I'll kill you myself." He held the sharp tip of his stiletto blade to her breast. A small trickle of blood rolled down.

"Now take 'em off."

Marla glanced at Jeffrey, then shut her eyes.

Jeffrey fell to his knees.

It was over.

He saw it in her face.

He could only pray it would end soon.

She slid her pants to her knees and kicked them off each foot. Paco grabbed Marla's panties from the rear and yanked them down to her ankles with one thrust. She covered herself and tried to back away, but the two men on either side pulled her arms out straight.

"No, please don't. No."

Blade pointed to the grass behind her. "Lie down, bitch."

"No, no, no, no." She staggered back.

He pointed again, and his men threw her down on the grass.

While one held her arms, two others grabbed her legs and spread them.

"This is where I come in."

Blade released the chain belt and pulled down his filthy jeans. He jumped on her and thrust himself into her body.

Marla screamed and tried to kick.

Jeffrey turned away, looking for somebody, anybody.

Dear God, if only...

He looked back, and Marla lay still, her eyes closed, while Solas continued to grunt and satisfy himself.

Finished, Blade stood up and buckled his pants with a grin.

"Hombres, I have initiated this young lady into our club. I'm sure she'd like to be welcomed by the other members, too."

Marla fought to free herself, but the efforts were useless. Man after man, they had her.

Jeffrey saw her bite her lower lip until her chin and cheeks were covered with blood.

Blade clapped for his friends. "Jose, you are the last."

He looked first at Jeffrey, then at Marla. "Then we start over."

Jose was smaller than the others, five-six, maybe sixteen. He unbuckled his pants and removed his penis, holding it directly in front of her face.

"You like?"

Blade stopped him. "Hey, you ain't putting that scabby thing in there if I'm going again."

Marla winced and screamed.

"No! Oh God, STOP!" She sobbed again, her entire body shaking.

Jeffrey pulled against the cuffs, his wrists numb to the pain.

It was no use.

The smaller man backed off, and the thugs holding her down released her, and she rolled to the side, whimpering and drained.

"Okay, amigos, that was a good first round." Solas rubbed the palms of his hands together. "Now for round two. Get up bitch."

Marla didn't move.

Blade raised his voice. "Get up bitch, or I'll kill you and your lover boy. I swear to God."

Marla sat up slowly, teetering. Jeffrey couldn't believe she was still conscious.

"Okay, girl, this time I want you to open your mouth wide and start right here." Solas pointed to his crotch and pulled his pants to his knees.

Marla swooned and gagged, covering her face.

She took his penis in one hand and paused.

She bit down with all her strength.

Then she lurched forward onto her hands and knees and vomited into his pants.

Blade screamed, grabbed his crotch, and fell backward, blood dripping around his hands.

Marla lay on her stomach, the side of her face pressed flat against the ground, still retching and gasping for air.

Jeffrey buried his mouth into his shoulder and shook his head to clear the tears from his eyes. He looked up and saw Blade writhing on the ground, screaming.

His men watched as Blade wailed in pain.

He pointed to the nearby fountain with a bloodied hand and croaked, "Drown her!"

Two of the gang members dragged Marla across the pavement. Paco followed.

"No!" Jeffrey screamed, pulling against the cuffs and the pole. "Let her go, you bastards!"

"Shut him up." Paco waved the rest of the men toward him.

One strode over and buried his fist in Jeffrey's stomach.

Jeffrey collapsed, unable to breathe.

"Come on, asshole, stand up." The man kicked him in the jaw.

Jeffrey heard a thump and looked up.

The two men had hurled Marla forward by the arms, but she didn't clear the cement side of the fountain.

Blood squirted from a deep gash in her forehead and spilled onto the pavement, pooling within the cracks.

"Again," a voice from somewhere shouted.

The two picked her up again and shoved her over the edge of the fountain. One leaned over the side and pushed her head under the surface.

An arm shot up.

Within seconds, it fell, and all movement stopped.

Jeffrey bowed his head.

Marla.

"Up, you bastard, up," someone screamed in Jeffrey's ear. A hand grabbed him by the hair and pulled him to his feet. Tears streamed down his face, but he could still see Blade crying as he rolled and held his privates.

"You see what happens to people who don't cooperate?" Paco said.

Jeffrey looked up. What was left to live for? He stood up as best he could and spat into Paco's face.

Paco screamed a string of Spanish expletives and punched wildly. Only when Jeffrey fell to his knees, half-conscious, did he stop.

"Manuel, you bring it?"

"Si, Paco." The man took a Coke bottle filled with a white liquid from a knapsack.

"Good. We'll turn him white before we cut him, just like the others." Paco laughed. "You know, we're doing him a favor. Once he's the right color, he can get a better job."

Jeffrey lifted his face and looked at Paco through the cracks in his swollen eyes.

"What did we ever do...why are you..." His voice trailed off as Blade continued to scream in the background.

Paco stared at him. "You want to know, Black boy? One of your fucking bros, he killed Blade's baby brother with a knife. What do you think of that, eh? And you're going to pay for it, just like the others."

He turned to the man with the bottle. "Give me that stuff."

The minion removed the top from the bottle and handed it to Paco, who walked toward Jeffrey and stood over him. "Look at me, you bastard."

Jeffrey didn't move. Just let this end.

"Look at me!"

Jeffrey struggled to raise his head.

Paco poured lye into his eyes.

A searing hellfire lit him up.

They sloshed lye all over his face.

He screamed, thrashing his head to avoid the excruciating pain, fighting to free his hands to claw at his eyes and scrape the skin from his face.

Then he choked, gagging on the liquid as vomitus pooled in his mouth and throat.

"Well, what do you think, men? Time to cut?" Paco leaned close to Jeffrey's head. "Like I said, one of your brothers killed one of ours with a knife. So, we're going to cut you up, too. But you, we'll do piece by piece. And I get to go first."

Paco backed off. "Gag him. We don't need no more noise."

Someone stuffed a cloth into Jeffrey's mouth.

"I think it's time for an ear," Paco said, coming closer again.

Paco grabbed an ear and partially cut it before Jeffrey jerked his head away, causing his attacker to sever his own thumb.

Paco shouted and lunged forward, aiming for the groin.

The knife sank in between the hip and thigh.

Blood gushed out, and Jeffrey felt himself slipping away.

Peace settled over him.

His eyes fluttered, and he could hear his attackers scattering...

A siren.

There were flashing lights.

Then gunshots.

Then blackness.

Chapter Fifty-Four

Pennsylvania Hospital

Center City, Philadelphia, PA

Kyle was already on Six West studying a chart when Graham and his big, wide smile arrived early the next morning, making her heart skip several beats.

"Hey," he said. "Missed you last night. You're a sight for sore eyes."

"Are your eyes sore?" she teased.

"Yeah, from not seeing you," he said as his grin got bigger.

"I know a great doctor who could take a peek," she beamed. "She's very busy, but I could put in a good word for you."

"That would be great." He moved in close, and she felt the heat of his body.

She looked around. With the hall empty, she gave Graham a quick but meaty kiss.

But as they pulled back, her panic attacked, and her face clouded.

She caught herself and tried to smile. She failed.

"That bad, huh?" Graham said sympathetically. He started to ask what the real problem was. But again, this was not the time or the place. And he knew to wait for her to come to this with whatever dark secret was lurking beneath the surface.

"No, it's fine, I'm fine, everything's…fine…" But the more fine she said it all was, the less fine it all seemed. "How about you?" she asked, hungry to skirt around her Tribunal struggles.

"Good, but you know, exhausted. The emergencies made it hell here the whole night. I barely got from one patient to another. But you know me. I leap tall buildings in a single bound."

"Just one of the many things I adore about you. Your delusional optimism is inspirational."

"It's one of my best features."

A colleague walked by and side-eyed them with a little smirk.

"We have to stop meeting like this," Graham whispered.

"Indeed," Kyle smiled back, then snapped into work mode. "Let me give you a capsule summary on this one. Jeffrey Jackson, eighteen-year-old kid, was out in Center City with his girlfriend when they were jumped by a gang. The girl was gang raped and drowned, and he was doused with lye, mutilated, and stabbed. They got his femoral artery."

"I read about this in the *Philly Inquirer*," Graham said.

"That's the one."

"Made me sick."

"Me too."

"Did they get the psychos who did it?"

"The one who knifed him was shot in the head by a cop."

"Justice," Graham whispered under his breath. He knew head shots were fatal ninety percent of the time.

"Pardon?

"Just mumbling."

"There were others, too. They brought in a couple more but didn't have enough to hold them."

"WHAT?" Graham snapped, looked like he was ready to kill. "Don't you ever just wanna make these fuckers suffer?"

If only you knew, Kyle shook her head. "You okay, Graham?"

Graham re-entered his body. Took a breath. Looked her in the eyes. "Sorry, Kyle, I just feel...sorry, I didn't mean to..."

"Don't apologize, I know exactly how you feel."

"Do you?" he asked, pleading in his voice.

"I do." She stopped for emphasis. "I… really do. I mean, really."

"I guess both of our brothers…"

"Yeah," she said. "And the fuckers got away with it."

"They almost always got away with it."

Kyle sighed. "And now this kid. They got his eyes-"

"Lye, right?"

"Yeah, lye. What kind of disgusting human does that?"

"The worst kind."

"And there's probably not much we can do about it. They also cut one of his ears, and now the second one's disintegrating from the lye. On top of that, he suffered a cardiac arrest in the ambulance and developed kidney shutdown. He's still not putting out a drop of urine."

Graham knew Jeffrey had acute tubular necrosis, ATN. When the blood pressure dropped too low from the bleeding, in conjunction with the cardiac arrest, the kidney cells that made urine got no oxygen and died. If they didn't come back within ten days, the prognosis was catastrophic.

"He's on dialysis?" Graham presumed.

"For now. We have him on the transplant list."

"Getting a kidney is tough."

"His mom may be a match."

"That's good."

"True. But this poor kid is so screwed."

Graham could see tears welling up in her eyes. He wanted to give her a hug, but stopped when a cadre of house staff and medicine students showed up in the hallway. "I'm so sorry," he whispered. He hated to see her so broken up. He knew all too well what that felt like.

Kyle brushed her right eye with her sleeve and handed him Jeffrey's chart. "Like Harry said, we called you because lye went down his throat. His esophagus is narrowed."

"How bad?"

"Bad."

"Can he get down soft solids?"

"He can't even get down liquids."

"Are you nourishing him intravenously?"

"Yeah. We were wondering if you could go in with the endoscope and break up the stricture. If not, then we'll have to stick a feeding tube through his abdominal wall."

"We'll do it. I can't guarantee the results, though."

"Of course. You'll keep me apprised?

"For sure."

"Thanks." She smiled and walked into another patient's room.

Graham already knew what would happen. They'd put the endoscope down the boy's esophagus and break up the scar tissue.

The procedure would work at first, but in a matter of weeks, the lye would shrink the tissue all over, and they'd have to repeat the process.

In the end, the kid would still end up with a feeding tube poking out of his stomach wall. No way to live.

He sat at the computer reading the chart. No other revelations about the esophagus. But he was riveted by the ophthalmology report. Kyle had called them over from Wills Eye, two blocks northwest on Ninth and Walnut.

Vision: bare light perception in each eye. The corneas are opaque in both eyes. The retinas may be non-viable. An electroretinogram will tell. Have ordered it.

Visual prognosis: Dismal. Sodium hydroxide (lye) forms irreversible soaps with corneal tissues in the front of the eye. These remain for years and can destroy a human donor corneal graft if attempted in the future. If there is retinal function remaining in two months, the patient may be a candidate for a plastic (methyl methacrylate) prosthetic cornea.

Arturo Ramos, MD

Wills Eye Hospital

Graham shook his head. He remembered the old medical school dictum—lye in the eye, wash it out with water on the spot. If you rushed to the ER first, you'd be blind by the time you arrived. It was too late in this case. At least there was hope with a prosthetic corneal implant.

He flashed back to Eddie Severs stepping on the IED. He lost both eyes and never recovered psychologically. His only peace came when he hung himself from a rafter.

Graham closed his eyes, cleared his head, closed the chart, and walked to Jeffrey's room. He stopped at the doorway and swallowed the wave of nausea that swept through him.

Jeffrey lay on his back with his head elevated. His handsome facial features were intact, but the skin on his scalp, face, and neck was snow white. Graham knew no matter what they did, the early shallow folds would soon contract into rigid scar tissue and give him a hideous Freddie Krueger look.

Concentrated lye burned, only worse than fire. It stayed forever and kept burning. And there was no way you could cut off the flesh to get rid of it. On the face, you'd have to go down to bone.

Where the colored part of the eyes should be, Jeffrey had snow-white centers surrounded by swollen scarlet tissues. All hair was gone, burned off his head, eyelids, and face. His left ear was missing, and only a fragment of the right remained.

His face had innumerable hemorrhages from the lye breaking down the tissues, and now they were appearing on his arms and chest. In combination with the blood he lost from the knife wound, his blood count was going lower and lower.

His hands were all scar. Like he was wearing white gloves with corrugations that looked like flippers. He was sure the hand surgeons kept separating his fingers with black-out level pain.

He had a vision of himself and his M4 lining up those subhuman pieces of shit against a wall.

Graham swallowed again and took another deep breath before stepping into the room.

"Jeffrey?" He laid his hand on the young man's right arm.

Jeffrey started at the touch. The white globes of his lifeless eyes scanned the room without success. He raised a hand and felt for Graham.

CHAPTER FIFTY-FOUR

"Jeffrey, can you hear me?"

No response.

Of course. His outer ears were damaged. How could he hear well?

Jeffrey made a series of guttural noises, then shook his head and turned away.

Damn, the lye got his vocal cords, too.

With his hand on Jeffrey's shoulder, Graham touched the young man's mouth, indicating that he wanted to look in.

Jeffrey nodded and painfully opened his mouth. The inner linings of his cheeks and throat were inflamed beyond recognition. Irritated scarlet areas blended with patches of dying gray tissue. They'd have to give him heavy sedation to pass the endoscope.

"Hello, may I come in?"

Graham turned to see a middle-aged Black woman standing in the doorway.

"I'm Mrs. Jackson, Jeffrey's mother," she said.

"Hello. I'm Dr. Kurland, one of the gastrointestinal doctors."

"How's he doing, doctor?"

A choking feeling arose in the back of Graham's throat. How could he say death would be a blessed relief? He looked at her disfigured son, knowing the boy she loved was forever sealed inside a grotesque, shriveled, pain-drenched shell. Only years of practice and seeing the worst on the battlefield gave him the tools to stop his voice from cracking.

"Ma'am, I'm not his regular doctor, so I can't give you a full report. I'm a specialist they asked in because of Jeffrey's difficulty eating. He's losing blood and weight, and his doctors are worried about his nutrition."

The woman gazed at her son with hopes and dreams. "Thank you for coming, Dr. Kurland. That's why I brought him these cookies I baked." She pulled a small box from the grocery shopping bag in her right hand.

Graham managed a smile. It was small. But it was real.

"I've always told Jeffrey he needs more meat on his bones. He's got to put on weight so he can recover."

Graham's heart sank in agony.

"That boy's got a bright future ahead of him," she said. "He's going to MIT on a full engineering scholarship. He's a good boy. Ever since his Daddy died, he's been working dawn to dusk, weekends, and still getting the grades. Too bad about his girl, Marla. They were in love, you know."

She blotted her eyes with a crumpled tissue. "One day, he came home from school and said, 'Mama, after I get out of MIT and take you out of this ghetto, I'm going to marry that girl.' He was so proud of her. So proud."

Graham could feel the tears welling up in his own eyes. What could he say? And what had Kyle and Harry told her? They must have told her the truth—that her son's prognosis was grim. She either didn't understand or didn't want to understand. Or a little of both. On the other hand, hope was a powerful force.

The soft smile on her face disappeared without warning. Her eyes widened, and her jaw fell open.

"Oh, Lord." She pointed toward her son. "His ear! His other ear!"

Graham looked again at Jeffrey's head. He saw that the right ear was just a stub. But he didn't realize this was a new development.

She pointed to the floor. The remainder of the misshapen organ lay by the bedside, still recognizable as an ear despite its ghostly white appearance. The lye had dissolved the last shred of tissue, attaching it to his head.

Graham tried to escort the woman to a seat at the nurse's station, but she kept turning, shaking, and yelling.

Ramona Velez, Jeffrey's nurse, came running up.

Thank goodness. Ramona was the best at consoling grieving relatives. Graham was relieved to leave Mrs. Jackson in her hands.

"Oh, Ramona, oh Lord. It was there, right there…"

Graham walked back to Jeffrey's room with a 10% formalin bottle and picked up the ear with a tissue to send to pathology. Four years in the Army, all the tragedies he'd seen in medicine, and still the new ones caught him in the pit of his stomach. He thought he'd learned to detach himself.

The poor woman. Had the roles been reversed, he would have been just as horrified. He couldn't imagine seeing a piece of his child's body lying there.

He stood outside the room and rested his forehead against the door frame as Kyle appeared down the hallway.

"Graham, what's wrong?"

"Oh, God. Just an…episode with Jeffrey Jackson's mother."

"What happened?"

"The rest of his outer right ear, the necrotic one…it fell off. He held up the formalin-filled bottle. His mom was the one who found it."

"Oh, no." Kyle took the bottle and stared at the snow-white piece of ear bobbing up and down.

"I'm sick about this one," Graham said. "I mean, I am physically sick. I wish I could get my hands on the bastards who did it, especially if they're going to get away scot-free. There's no way this kid could ever identify them. He can't see, can't talk, can't hear, or write…and he'll probably be dead in a week from loss of blood."

Kyle handed back the bottle and looked in at Jeffrey. "Don't worry, I have a feeling that whoever did this will pay."

"Excuse me?"

She realized she'd said too much and backpedaled. "I mean, uh, karma. You reap what you sow… Anyway, do what you can for his esophagus. I'll check with you later. And I want to see you soon, you know, not here, okay?"

She said with such longing that it moved something all the way inside Graham,

"Yeah, absolutely, I'll text you."

Then she was off to fight her next battle.

Graham watched her walk down the hallway, always a pleasure. But…

Pay?

What did she mean, whoever did this will pay?

Chapter Fifty-Five

Carlucci's Cafe

South Philadelphia, PA

Angelo Carlucci had been Ralph DiNunzio's sworn enemy for years. But now that someone else was operating on their turf, both found it distressing and had vowed to whack those responsible. Now they just had to work out the details.

Carlucci fancied himself a self-made scholar. He knew Sun Tzu stated in *The Art of War* that "the enemy of my enemy is my friend." That was fine for the history books, but if they were after one Sicilian family, it was only a matter of time until they came after another.

Carlucci's South Philly Cafe was as good a place as any to meet with DiNunzio. Fifteen or so square tables, each covered by a white tablecloth with bird images elegantly stitched in, were separated by socially acceptable distances. Though it was after hours, blue candles still burned in the center of each tabletop. They cast faint shadows and a bayberry scent throughout the room.

This was Carlucci's base of operations. It was where all his important deals had taken place over the past twenty years, where the fate of a score of men had been sealed. All in a day's work at the South Italian restaurant.

Carlucci was smaller and more refined than DiNunzio. A good half-foot shorter and slighter in build, he nonetheless carried himself with the confidence of a self-made man. As usual, his gray-black hair was combed without a flaw and just the right amount of mousse.

"Tell me, Ralph, what have you got?" Carlucci said as he rested back in his chair from across the table. Other than for Lou, DiNunzio's right-hand man, and Carlucci's personal bodyguard, the room was empty.

"We finally gotta break, Angie. Da doc from Hahva'd dat my internist buddy recommended put me on to it."

"What?"

"Uncle Frank was poisoned wit' a sulfa drug, some kinda antibiotic." DiNunzio leaned forward, tucking his shirt tail into his pants. "It made his whole body 'llergic an' turn on itself. So basically, he self-destructed."

"But that doesn't tell you who did it, does it?"

"No, but it turns out dis medicine's a perscription drug. Only doctors can get it."

"You want anything bad enough, you can get it, doc or not."

"Yeah, but da stuff hadda be changed to do what it did. And who would know dat besides a doc?"

"Okay, so yer sayin' doctors did dis?"

"Dat's exactly what I'm sayin'."

Carlucci raised his eyebrows and took a long drag on his cigarette. Thugs, assassins, and crime bosses were his fare. But doctors?

"Dis is unusual, Ralph."

DiNunzio smiled. "Makes life in'erestin', Ang."

Carlucci felt like slapping DiNunzio's mouth right off his face. He hated that fake smile, the way he put it on before the kill.

"I thought dem docs on Uncle Frank's case was actin' funny," DiNunzio went on. "So, I had 'em tailed by a private dick. One goes to a meetin' every month wit' a group outside da city. Some mansion on the Main Line."

"What kinda group we talking about?"

"Not sure yet, but I may need yer boys to help."

DiNunzio savored his red wine, staring at Carlucci with flamethrower eyes that made most men's blood curdle.

Carlucci stared right back, not flinching for a second. He'd been around long enough to know how to play these mind games. DiNunzio finally broke gaze and leaned back from the table.

"Ang, I just wanna be sure yer wit' me. Look, whoever got Uncle Frank is gonna come after youze too. And like we said before, if yer boys start hittin' us, dere's gonna be an all-out war."

Carlucci took another drag. He suppressed a shiver at the thought of going like Frank. And nobody wanted a war.

"Ralph, I'm with you. You got my word. We're not going to interfere."

"Good, cuz dere's one more t'ing."

"What's that?"

DiNunzio sat back, ran a hand through his stringy hair, then felt his pocket for a smoke. "If I don't succeed, I want you to finish da job."

"That's quite a favor you're asking." Carlucci tossed him his pack of Winstons.

"I know, but it's in yer bes' in'erest. Who knows whose payroll dese docs are on? And if youze don't wanna do it for me or for yerself, do it for Uncle Frank. He woulda done da same for youze. He respected you."

That wasn't entirely true. Frank might have sought revenge, but not for any love of Angelo Carlucci. He'd have done it for the thrill of the kill. Frank Mancini didn't learn to like killing. It was genetic.

DiNunzio slid the pack back, and Carlucci lit another smoke with the table candle.

"Ralph, I'll do my best."

"No." DiNunzio slapped the table.

"Whadda ya mean?"

"Swear on yer mother's soul that ya'll kill every las' one."

Carlucci hesitated, tapped his fingers on the table, then finally said,

"Alright, I swear on my mother, me and my people are gonna finish them."

DiNunzio leaned back, his half smile gone. In its place was a genuine one, a satisfied smile Carlucci rarely saw the man give.

"How are you going to find this group?" Carlucci asked.

"I gotta lead on a inside snitch. Da dick tells me one guy's mudder lives by herself up in da Poconos. Once we find her, he'll tawk. And when he does, we finish 'em to da las' man. And woman."

"Woman?"

"Yeah," DiNunzio said like the devil himself, "woman."

Chapter Fifty-Six

Kyle's Apartment

Center City, Philadelphia

Kyle awoke two hours later at 2:10 am.

Graham was still asleep, facing her on the other side of the bed. A true gentleman, as always. She loved the way he looked asleep, sweet and peaceful. For the life of her, she couldn't understand why it took her three years to realize that she was working with her soulmate. Sure, she was impressed when they first met. Brilliant surgeon, great teacher, compassionate, patient. Not to mention the photographic memory that allowed him to help so many people and enabled him to become double-boarded. Men didn't come any better.

But would he feel the same way about her if he knew she was a murderer?

Probably not.

What if she dragged him into the middle of a war with the likes of DiNunzio?

And the burden of keeping this secret from the man she loved?

Or should she quit the Tribunal? Had that ship already sailed?

If she really loved him, shouldn't she just walk away now?

As she stared at him, Graham opened his eyes and smiled.

Kyle couldn't stop herself. She moved across the bed, kissed him on the lips, and did a full-body embrace. She loved how they fit into each other.

So did he.

"Wow," Graham said. "I could do that for the rest of my life."

"Me too."

They kissed again, and he held her close in his muscular arms. It felt so good. All she wanted was to stay in bed with him all day.

But she knew he had rounds at 6:30 and surgery at 7:30. And she had to be in by 7:00.

"Graham, I'd love nothing more than to stay here for the rest of my life, but we've got lives to save," she said before going for another kiss.

"Can I have a rain check?'

She laughed. "Yes, I am prepared to give you a rain check. A S A freaking P."

"A S A freaking P it is."

Chapter Fifty-Seven

Stenton's Main Line Home

Berwyn, PA

Kyle's angel and devil were fighting it out furiously as she pulled into the oval driveway in front of Stenton's Main Line house. Should she quit the Tribunal? What about all those evil monsters walking around scot-free? The innocents, they would punish and kill? Then she had to break up with Graham. The thought of it made her physically ill. He was the love of her life. She couldn't walk away from that. From him. The rock and the hard place were squeezing the life out of her.

Kyle sat in her spot next to Randy and Nate, who nodded hello. It felt good to have these two superhumans as her new besties.

"Enough!" Stenton barked. "Let's get down to business," Stenton said with magisterial authority as he rested his elbows on the table and made a pyramid with his hands. "I have news to report on the Jeffrey Jackson case. Randy and Nate have been investigating. Marla Turner's murder and Jeffrey Jackson's mutilation were almost certainly committed by a gang led by a man named Emilio "Blase" Solas. Solas was questioned by the police because of his record and ties to the man shot at the scene of the crime. Unfortunately, they lacked sufficient evidence to bring an indictment. Seems the semen DNA reading was inconclusive."

"That's it?" Kyle said. "Inconclusive?"

"Something about contaminants," Nate Champion said. "I personally think they botched the samples. The defense attorney for Solas also came up with photos suggesting Marla Turner was a flirt. Even promiscuous."

"SON OF A BITCH!" Kyle slammed the table.

The entire table was taken aback. They'd never heard Kyle speak like that.

"Sorry," she said, reclaiming her composure. This whole situation was making her into a hot mess of a crazy woman. She had to get it together. They had work to do. "You don't gang rape a woman, murder her, and then call her a slut. Not if you want to live in my world."

"It's horrific," Stenton said. "Beyond comprehension."

"I have another point," Kyle said.

"Go ahead."

"Jeffrey's voice was a mess, but he was trying to say Solas. I know it. He also tried to write it, but all I could make out was the 'S.' It makes sense now."

"What other evidence do we have?" Stenton asked Nate.

"First, he was boasting in his neighborhood when this hit the papers. We have statements from two of his "esteemed" colleagues. And you'll like this," he said, directing his attention to Kyle.

"What?"

"Before she died, Solas forced her to perform fellatio."

Kyle shuddered, a bilious taste coming up her throat.

"But instead she bit off three-quarters of his penis."

Kyle's frown morphed to a grim smile of satisfaction, while the men winced. "There's some justice," she mumbled.

"What if they talk with Solas and tell him you were looking?" Carlo asked.

Randy White smiled. "They won't. Both decided to leave town—fast and permanently."

Kyle knew the ex-SEALs had ways of reducing people to quivering protoplasm and tattooing terror into their souls. She never asked for details but understood that their talents were an absolute necessity.

Nate continued. "Number two, we have a witness."

"Who's the witness?" Kyle asked. When they'd discussed the case, there was no mention of a witness.

"Randy and I found a homeless woman who saw the whole thing. Her description matches Jeffrey Jackson's injuries and the autopsy report on Marla Turner to a tee."

"How can we be sure?" Kyle asked.

"We went over the autopsy report," Nate said. "Even if she read the papers, she wouldn't have been able to provide the details she did. She knows things nobody else knows. We also showed her random photos."

Kyle leaned forward. "And?"

"Each time she identified Solas. Hands down."

"Why haven't the police questioned her?" Carlo asked.

"She refuses to speak with the police. Doesn't trust them."

"Did they talk with her?"

"She was adamant," Nate said. "No cops. If they came, she said she'd clam up and disappear for good."

Having a witness assuaged the nagging thought lurking in the minds of the eight people at the table; someday, they might hurt the wrong person. It was an unfathomable nightmare. But there was no doubt here.

"More questions?" Stenton asked.

Silence.

"Then I'll turn the floor over to Art Ramos. He's reviewed Jeffrey Jackson's hospital records and has a plan."

"Thank you," Art Ramos said in response to Stenton's introduction.

He'd remained quiet to this point at the July Tribunal gathering. And for good reason. Deciding the fate of another human being was no easier for him than for anyone else in the room.

"As with the other cases," Ramos said, "the principle of equitable justice must prevail. For a decade, I've been working with biochemical compounds, one of which I believe can be effective here."

He hit his laptop, and the projector illuminated the salient features on the wall. The presentation lasted twenty minutes. When it was finished, no one spoke. Kyle wasn't sure whether it was because Ramos was so complete and compelling, or whether they were all stunned.

It was good.

No, it was perfect for this human sewage.

She had brought Jeffrey's case to the Tribunal and still lay awake agonizing over his death. That said, the thought of doing this to a living person played havoc with her moral compass. Again. Was she turning into the evil she was trying to destroy?

"Alden," Stenton said, "you've been over this man's record with a fine-tooth comb. Your comments?" Stenton insisted upon psychological profiles to confirm their opinions.

"I have no reservations," Booth said, taking off his glasses. "To call him a monster is an understatement. Solas was a sociopath from an early age. Certainly, his environment enhanced it, but he had a character disorder from the moment his father's seed fertilized the egg. He will strike again. And again. There is also evidence that he has committed similar crimes. It is my opinion that he's a sadistic killer who should be incapacitated to protect innocents."

"Discussion?" Stenton asked.

"What about medication?" Kyle asked, wanting to make sure all bases were covered. "Is there any chance the newer anti-psychotics could alter his behavior?"

"None," Booth said. "Character disorders this severe almost never respond to pharmaceuticals."

Stenton moved for what was a perfunctory vote. It was unanimous.

Coordinating the plan lasted well into the night.

Jeffrey and Marla's tortured souls would soon be avenged with medical advances never conceived nor intended for that purpose.

Kyle was satisfied.

For the moment, anyway.

Chapter Fifty-Eight

Gallery Mall

Center City, Philadelphia

Nate Champion strolled the breezeway of Philadelphia's Gallery Mall at Ninth and Market Streets. Home to Aeropostale, American Eagle, Eddy Bauer, Kate Spade, and Ulta Beauty. The glamorous fifty-year-old façade belied the history of name changes, shootings, looting, vandalism, and ransacking.

Nate regularly maintained eye contact with Randy White. Not more than fifty feet apart, they pretended to take in the window displays and back-to-school sales.

It was a weekend, and the mall was overflowing with the late August crowd. Noisy teenagers enjoyed their last weeks of summer freedom, while hassled mothers dragged their precious offspring into jam-packed clothing stores as they whined and threw tantrums.

Their phone tap revealed Solas would be here in the early afternoon. The sheer mass of people camouflaged the two large men, but also made it difficult to catch every passerby.

Nate spotted him first, down by McDonald's. Joking, laughing, flitting around like a drunken barfly, with two of his pond scum pals, grinning like his own shit didn't stink.

Nate seethed. *After the misery they inflicted, it just wasn't right.*

He wanted to knock that toothy smile off the bastard's face. But he was too good to let his emotions get the better of him and endanger the mission.

Randy joined him several steps back, and they watched Solas move towards them. They stopped in front of opposite ends of Brooks Brothers but kept close to the store. The crowd was so dense that it could easily sweep them into the throng.

Solas passed a yard away. He was wearing tight-fitting polyester pants. Perfect for their purpose. Nate fell into step several feet behind, waiting for Blade to stop and allow the mass of shoppers to move on.

The hardest part had been finding him.

From here on, it was simple. The pellet gun would fire the S-antigen into Solas's backside, and they'd be on their way.

Nate pulled the small pistol from his jacket pocket, palmed it in his right hand, and aimed at his passing victim.

From out of nowhere, someone grabbed his arm as he squeezed the trigger.

The shot went wide.

The gun slipped away and skittered across the floor.

Damn!

A plainclothes cop.

Who else could it be?

Where was Randy?

Nate lunged forward and dragged the cop with him, but not before the man already had a cuff on his right wrist.

A nearby woman screamed. The crowd panicked and surged away.

Where was the pellet?

A little boy had been walking with his mother next to Solas.

No!

Where was it?

A telltale liquid spot on the floor.

Thank God.

The security guard regained his balance in a flash.

He went for Nate's other arm and tried to shove it into the open end of the cuffs.

Nate pulled back and yanked his free hand away before the cuff closed. His momentum carried him back two yards.

The cop reached into his jacket.

Nate tensed.

It was over.

Before he could draw his gun, Randy's grip on the man's neck from behind brought him to his knees.

The man's heart rate dropped from compression of his carotid sinus, his blood pressure crashed, and he collapsed forward into a pile of newspapers.

Nate scanned the staring crowd. A young man with stringy hair held up his hand, his fingers separated into a V. "Live long and prosper, dude."

Nate and Randy broke through the inner ring of people and melted into the crowd, keeping their heads down. Nate sprinted for the Ninth Street exit, while Randy ran towards Tenth Street. They'd meet four blocks away, among the masses always outside City Hall.

After fifty yards, Nate slowed to a fast walk. The mall congestion was still the best cover.

The cop never saw Randy, which was good. And there was no video monitor nearby. They'd checked.

What if they'd missed one? The cops could already have a BOLO out.

He turned his blue jacket inside out to make it yellow and stuffed his hands inside the pockets to hide the cuffs. Slipping outside in between five or six people leaving through the triple set of double glass doors a block down, he avoided both an exit camera above and the gaze of the man in a Philly's jacket off to the side.

Hey, buddy, why not just hold up a big sign saying "COP"?

Mr. Phillies started toward him.

Oh no.

Nate stiffened.

Play it cool, man.

He kept coming.

Closer.

Closer yet.

Nate tightened his fists.

The man walked on by.

Thank you, Lord.

He headed for City Hall at a normal pace, resisting the overwhelming urge to run. Periodic looks revealed no Philly's jackets.

Nate spotted Randy and took a deep breath.

Alone.

No cops.

"Randy, over here." Nate waved across the pavement.

It was a shitty break, for sure, but they were trained for this type of thing. Today, he made Navy SEALs look like lifeguards. Not only had Solas escaped, but he'd also lost the pellet gun. A gun that, of course, could be traced.

"Hey, if you're not living on the edge, you're taking up too much space."

"Thanks for your wisdom, Plato. What do we do now?"

Randy raised an eyebrow. "Let's see. You can start by carrying your own damn gun." He palmed the pellet pistol from his sweatshirt and slipped it to his partner.

"Sweet. Hey, thanks, buddy." Nate dropped it into his pocket and broke into a relieved grin.

"Forget it."

"Now we have to regroup to get that bastard again."

"I don't think so."

"Why?"

Randy smiled and patted his shoulder holster. "I told you it was a good idea for both of us to have one. I got him."

Nate responded with something he rarely did.

He gave Randy a big hug.

Chapter Fifty-Nine

Third Floor Apartment

North Philadelphia, PA

Emilio "Blade" Solas woke with a terrible, relentless itching where his penis used to be. There was only a nubbin left after they sewed it up. How could that little piece itch so much? At least the pecker docs told him he could get a new one. Some prosthetic gizmo. But who wanted to walk around with a plastic dick? He was glad he'd drowned the fuck out of that bitch.

His apartment sat across from a row of homes that had seen better days. The crumbling stucco on the outside walls encased windowless window openings, half of which were boarded up with three-eighths-inch plywood sheets. Several had been occupied until kids smoking crack got careless and let the flame escape into the trash, where it went berserk and spread exponentially.

The early sun was just over the tops of the North Philadelphia row houses when Solas awoke the next morning. It was still cool. The day hadn't yet given in to the persistent late summer heat.

He stood, stretched, and shuffled bowlegged to the window, where he pulled the blinds apart.

"Ay, Jesus!"

The light!

He winced at the piercing glare and shielded his face with his forearm. A knife-like pain shot through his head, and he staggered backwards.

"Mi Dios!"

He pushed the heels of his hands into his eyes, fighting back the tears. Groping to yank the blinds shut, his eyes opened to bare slits. No further, no matter how hard he tried.

Elena sat up in bed and pulled the sheet to cover her breasts. Even though he couldn't have sex, he still wanted her to sleep naked with him. A small girl with a round face and a pleasing smile, her long black hair flowed down her exposed back.

"What's the matter, Emilio?"

"That light, it's killin' my eyes." He tried looking toward the window again, but met with the same result. "I can't see nothin'," he screamed. He groped for the wall for support. "What the hell's going on?"

"I don't know, Emilio."

"I gotta get to a doctor. Put on your clothes. I need to go to the hospital."

He opened his eyes just enough to peer through the lashes. Was she still in bed? He couldn't even tell.

This was hell on earth.

He heard her get out of bed and pull on her underwear and jeans.

"Come on, let's go." Solas tried to pull on his pants, but the zipper stuck. Elena finished dressing and tried to help him.

He pushed her aside. "Leave me alone, woman. I can dress myself."

"Where are we going, Emilio?"

"Wills Eye Hospital." That's where everyone in Philly with bad eye problems went.

"Get moving. You drive. Vámanos!"

Solas clung to Elena's arm for guidance. She led him down the steps to the first floor and onto the street. His red Firebird was parked a block away.

Without her help, it might as well have been a hundred miles. He walked with one hand over his eyes, tears streaming down his face. He could hear an occasional car, but didn't dare open to the light again. They'd better get him good medicine for this.

Pronto.

Chapter Sixty

Wills Eye Hospital

Ninth Street, Philadelphia, PA

"You can spot pubic lid lice from across the room. They leave large crusts and itch like crazy. They also leave tiny white eggs that stick to the lashes." Rudy Garcia, the second-year resident in charge of the Wills Eye Hospital Emergency Room, had brought in his best pictures. He liked teaching and projected them onto the screen in the conference room.

Today, it was only for Liz Dobbs and Brian Bartlett, his first-year resident charges. Early Monday was often slow. Yet by mid-morning, the pace would be frenzied as people from all walks of life rolled into the mecca of visual rehabilitation.

He brushed a piece of his short blond hair from his right eye, admired his photographic prowess, then faced his mini-audience.

Liz made a face and groaned at the grotesque picture Rudy was so proud of.

"Remember," Rudy continued, "lice don't appear without good reason. They're often associated with infections of—" the intercom buzzed—"the genitourinary tract."

Rudy leaned over and hit the 'talk' button. "Yes?"

"Dr. Garcia?"

"Yes?"

"We have a man out here in a lot of pain. Ms. Burke would like you to see him."

"We'll be right there."

Rudy headed toward the doorway. So much for his big chance on the lecture circuit. "Let's go see this guy."

The three residents entered the exam room. A thin young man in a faded *Scarface* tee shirt sat in the exam chair at the opposite end. His head was bowed, and his hands covered his eyes. A young woman at his side rested her arm on his shoulder.

Rudy picked up the chart. "Mr. Solas, I'm Dr. Garcia. This is Dr. Dobbs and Dr. Bartlett."

Solas didn't look up.

"Doctor, fix my eyes. They're killing me."

Rudy read the history.

Twenty-five-year-old male with history of awakening with

marked vision loss and severe pain in both eyes.

No previous ocular problems...

Vision: finger counting at one foot in each eye.

This was big-time serious. The man couldn't even see the big "E."

Rudy moved the slit lamp microscope in front of Solas' chair and pointed to the chin rest. "Put your chin up here, sir."

With his eyes still closed, Solas moved his head toward the slit lamp. He winced when he hit his forehead on a sharp edge of the instrument.

Rudy guided him in more carefully and attempted to open his lids. Solas squeezed tighter.

"Sir, you have to open your eyes."

Solas relaxed his grimace enough to allow Rudy to raise the right lid with a Q-tip.

"Wow," Rudy mouthed. The white of the eye was no longer white, but confluent scarlet.

"Fuck! That light burns, man." Solas squirmed in the slit lamp.

"I know, but I need a good look if we're going to help you."

Rudy beckoned for Liz and Brian to take a look through the eyepiece for a magnified view.

"Severe uveitis," Rudy said. "Those little dots in the anterior chamber, just behind the cornea in front, are white blood cells. Too many to count. Notice they're not moving. That means there's an outpouring of protein from irritated blood vessels. The protein makes the eye fluid thick and holds the cells in place."

Solas pulled back from the machine and continued writhing. "Cut the bullshit, man. What the hell's wrong? Tell me in English."

"Give me a minute." Rudy pulled Solas's head forward again and looked at the other eye.

Just as bad, fire engine red.

He rolled his stool back, pushed the slit lamp off to the side, and leaned forward with his hands on his knees.

"Mr. Solas. You have something very unusual. A severe inflammation in each eye. It's called uveitis."

"What's inflammation?"

"Irritation. Same thing."

"What's it from?"

"I don't know yet. We have to do some tests to look for things like tuberculosis, something called sarcoid, and a few others."

"Like what?"

Rudy glanced at his female companion and lowered his voice. "Like, uh...syphilis, and HIV, and..."

"AIDS! No fucking way."

The young woman's eyes widened, and she bit her lower lip.

"I didn't say that."

"What's HIV then?"

"You're jumping to conclusions. Many times we can't even find a cause."

"Then what?'

"We still treat it the same way. Something is making your body attack your eyes. There's a war in there. The white blood cells are the soldiers, and they are coming by the millions to fight whatever is doing this."

"Okay, there's a damn war. Call for peace."

"That's what we intend to do. You need large doses of cortisone drops in each eye, and I suggest we give you an injection of cortisone behind each one to help."

"Does it hurt?"

"Compared to what you have now? You'll hardly feel it."

Rudy turned to the charge nurse. "Alice, could you please get me two retrobulbar setups with a vial of triamcinolone?"

Rudy reclined Blade's chair to flat and drew the white fluid into two syringes through inch-and-a-half needles. He cleaned the lower right lid with an alcohol swab, then slid one needle through the lid and buried it to the hilt behind the eyeball to inject the medication.

The girlfriend's legs buckled, and she leaned against the wall for support. The thought of having that long needle behind the eye by the brain often brought on that reaction.

"Okay. One more," Rudy said. He used a similar injection to give the cortisone variant to the other eye.

He removed the needle and flicked the switch to return the chair to an upright position. "That wasn't so bad, was it?"

Solas muttered something in Spanish under his breath.

Rudy was just as glad he couldn't hear. He filled out the ER record and handed two prescriptions to the girl as he spoke to Blade.

"Use these drops just like they say on the labels. One drop in each eye every two hours while you're awake, and the other twice a day. In a couple of days, he'll be as good as new."

"Are you sure?" Solas asked.

"Positive."

"No me joda."

Translation: Don't fuck with me.

"Huh?"

"Forget it."

"Let's see you in the Uveitis Clinic in two days."

Dr. Ramos would be there then. This was right up his alley. In addition, he'd be on the service himself and could see the patient in follow-up.

The nurse stayed behind to put more drops in Blade's eyes and get him to the lab for blood work, while Rudy led his disciples back to the lecture room.

He loved it when the first patient of the day had interesting pathology. Better yet, it was good to know that the uveitis would respond like a miracle to the injections and the drops.

God, it was great being a doctor.

Chapter Sixty-One

Wills Eye Hospital

Philadelphia, PA

Art Ramos stepped into the back entrance of the Wills Eye Hospital Uveitis Clinic and dropped his umbrella in the porcelain stand behind the door. He had the premonition that it was going to be a highly unusual day.

Joanne Chung sat behind the front receptionist's desk, surrounded by neat stacks of paper.

Ramos liked Joanne. A lot. She'd worked for him in the Clinic for almost two years and cared about the patients as if they were family. When they cried, she consoled them, and when they laughed, she laughed with them.

Despite a fondness that lingered above the norm, Ramos treated her with professional dignity. He was, after all, twenty years her senior. Besides, he didn't want to involve her in the dangerous game he was playing.

It was bad enough to hear Nate Champion and Randy White say that Kyle and Graham Kurland were dating. He couldn't believe she'd be so foolish.

He walked out to the reception desk and smiled. "Good morning, Joanne."

"Hi, Dr. Ramos."

"Do you have today's list?"

"Sure." She pulled it out from a pile of papers.

"I'm looking for…" He ran his finger down the names. "Ah, here it is, this one. Will you please let me know when Mr. Solas comes in? One of the residents called me about him, and I want to see him myself."

"Of course, sir."

She smiled sweetly. He smiled sweetly. He retreated to the back office, put on his white lab coat, and sat down at the desk. He pulled two glass vials from his pocket. Each was an inch long and contained a contact lens floating in a clear solution. He held the containers up to the window to get a better look at the small pieces of methacrylate polymer.

The tiny lenses danced in the liquid, their carefree movements belying their deadly intent.

"Dr. Ramos?"

It was Rudy Garcia, early for a change.

"Good morning, Rudy. How are you?"

"Fine, thanks. I wanted to catch you before patients, so we could discuss the patient I saw in the ER. The one in his twenties with the nasty uveitis?"

"Sit down." Ramos motioned to a red chair. "What have you done in the way of a workup?"

"Well, the chest x-ray didn't show sarcoid or TB. No history of arthritis, another thing we thought about."

"What about HIV?"

"The blood work is pending."

"Good. Did you check for syphilis?"

"Yes. We drew an FTA, but it's not back. This guy was a bit on the nasty side. I wouldn't be surprised if it was positive."

"Nice people get syphilis, too."

"You're right," Rudy said, regretting his comment. "I'll let you judge for yourself."

Ramos knew that no cause was found for many uveitis cases. He hadn't considered whether Solas had syphilis. If he did, and it was believed to be the cause of his uveitis, so much the better.

A crackle erupted from the intercom on Ramos' desk. "Dr. Ramos, that gentleman you asked me about is here. He seems pretty uncomfortable. I think someone better come and look."

Ramos and Rudy walked out to the screening area. A man in dirty jeans sat bent over, face between knees, head in hands. An attractive and worried young woman stood next to him.

Ramos looked at Rudy's sheet from two days ago. "Mr. Solas?"

"Yeah?" Solas raised his head and looked toward the voice.

Rudy took a step back, and Joanne covered her mouth to suppress a gasp. Between the swollen lids were globes that had lost any resemblance to normal eyes. Fiery red tissues choked and engorged the normal whites. The clear corneas in the center had turned pure white, blocking any view of the brown iris.

Ramos waved a penlight in front of each eye. Blade reacted like he could see a difference between on and off.

"Let's get him to the slit lamp."

Together, they led a fumbling Solas to the exam chair. Ramos sat behind the slit lamp opposite him. He pried open the right eyelid, then the left.

The S-antigen air gun pellet had done its job well. The corneas in the front of the eyes were opaque and already appeared to be melting. Behind them was solid pus, the result of a mass migration of white blood cells from all parts of the body. The enzymes from the white cells were digesting the ocular tissues and turning Blade's eyes into a battleground of Waterloo proportions.

Relinquishing his chair to Rudy, Ramos said, "Take a look."

Rudy sat and peered through the eyepiece. His jaw hung open, and he shook his head.

Ramos motioned him to the back office, and they excused themselves to Solas.

"He didn't look anywhere near that bad two days ago," Rudy said. "I've never seen anything like it."

"It is unusual," Ramos said, searching his memory to recall someone who looked this bad in both eyes. "What do you want to do for him?"

"Admit him."

"Then what?"

Rudy paused. "Even though we don't know the cause, I think we should give aggressive treatment."

"Such as?"

"High dose intravenous cortisone, cortisone drops every half hour, and subconjunctival injections."

Ramos rubbed his chin. "I agree with the first two, but I think we can do better than the injections. You know they're incredibly painful."

"What's the alternative?"

Ramos reached into his pocket and retrieved the two glass vials.

"These." He held them up to the light.

"Contact lenses?"

"Yes. They've been treated with a large amount of a cortisone derivative for a prolonged release. Perfect for this case."

"Cool," Rudy took the vials and looked at the floating lenses. "I'll be glad to put them on."

Ramos pulled them back. "No, that's okay. This whole concept of treatment is somewhat new. I think it would be better if I applied the lenses myself."

Rudy shrugged. "Okay. Whatever you say."

They returned to the exam room together. Ramos explained the plan to Solas, then removed one of the malleable lenses from its container with small plastic forceps. He leaned Solas back in the reclining seat and placed the lens on the front of his right eye.

"That's interesting," Rudy said. "Why can't you just put it in with your fingers?"

Ramos stopped, pausing to wipe sweat from his cheeks.

"Because this lens is going to stay in place for a while. I'm worried about bacterial or viral contamination. Particularly since it holds so much cortisone."

"Ah, good point."

Ramos relaxed after he put in the second lens. He motioned Rudy into the back room again.

"When you write this man's hospital admission orders, I want it perfectly clear that no one, *I repeat, no one,* is to remove either of those lenses. In order for them to work, they have to stay in constant contact."

Rudy nodded. "Yes, sir. I'll make sure your orders are followed."

The physicians returned to Blade, and Ramos knelt down to his face level. "Mr. Solas, you have a very serious problem. I can't guarantee we can save your vision, but we're going to do our best. We should admit you to the hospital for a few days so we can treat you the best way and observe your progress. Is that okay with you?"

"Yeah, anything." Blade didn't raise his head.

"He's a good deal more manageable than the other day," Rudy whispered as he and Ramos left the examining area.

"Losing your vision is a terrifying event, even for the bravest. Why don't you get him upstairs to a bed? I'll be by to see him in the morning."

"Sure thing."

"Thanks, Rudy."

"What do you think?"

"Tough call at this point."

Though Ramos knew the real answer.

This was invisible justice.

Chapter Sixty-Two

Wills Eye Hospital

Philadelphia, PA

"What the FUCK are you doing, lady?"

Rudy Garcia heard the fury in the voice and stepped up his pace down the stairs to the eighth floor of Wills Eye Hospital. It was a slow week, which suited him fine. That meant more hours to read journals, stay sharp, and talk with each patient.

This Solas case was gnawing at him. He'd done a ton of research, but so far, they had nothing.

Judy Sellers, the night-shift nurse, had just called, concerned that the eyes were getting worse.

He felt so helpless. If he could only figure out why this was happening.

Rudy could hear the familiar voice halfway down the hall.

"Leave me ALONE, BITCH!"

"Please, Mr. Solas."

"Those drops are killin' me! Dey hurt like a bastard. And dey don't do crap."

Rudy picked up his pace.

"Tell those FUCKING doctors to get up here. I gotta talk to 'em."

Judy came out of Blade's room and scanned the hallway. Rudy raised his hand, and she marched toward him.

"Hi, Jude, what's up?"

"What's up is that scumbag in 715. He refused his drops. Then he knocked me against the wall. I called you before it happened because he was uncomfortable, and his right eye was looking worse."

"Are you okay?" Rudy asked, full of concern.

"I'll live."

What an asshole!

Rudy headed toward Blade's room. Judy was a nice girl, kind to patients, no threat to anyone. She couldn't be more than five feet tall. There was no excuse, no matter how bad the situation. Rudy stormed in. "What's the problem, Mr. Solas?"

Solas turned toward his voice, scowling. "You doctors ain't doing jack SHIT for me. I'm worse than when I came the fuck in here."

"You're on the best medicines we have. And there is NO excuse to EVER lay a hand on a nurse," he spat angrily.

Blade clenched his jaw, made a fist, and searched around to no avail.

Rudy wondered if anyone used shock therapy for uveitis.

After half a minute, Blade sighed, deflated, and relented. "Okay. Sorry, doc, I won't do it again."

"I understand your frustrations. You have to remember that fixing something this serious takes time."

"Yeah."

"Come on. Let's examine you down the hall."

Rudy led Solas to the exam room and guided him to the swivel chair at the far end. He sat on the rolling stool, pried apart the lids at the slit lamp, and shone the light into Solas' right eye.

"Ugh." Rudy felt a wet blob hit him in the face, some landing in his mouth. "What the…?"

What the FUCK!

The taste was beyond disgusting. He spat into a Kleenex, wiped the warm liquid off his cheek, shuddered, and looked back into the slit lamp.

The right cornea had melted to nothing. The eyeball had ruptured with a large empty hole dead center. The pus-like contents had splattered onto

Rudy's face and mouth. Now some were dribbling down Solas' cheek.

"What's going on, doc?" Blade pulled back and ran his hand across his face. "What's this sticky shit?"

Rudy wiped sticky wet matter from the corner of his mouth.

"Hard to tell," he said, as he spit again and wiped away the mucoid debris with a fresh wad of Kleenex. "It may just be something from your eye. I think we better patch it for now and let Dr. Ramos look."

Like Ramos could do anything with this shitshow.

Rudy's stomach churned as he stared at Solas, then at the sticky green slime on the clump of white tissues. He spat again. Not even a miracle could save this eye.

He was about to look at a reddish-purple patch on Solas's forearm, but passed it off to the shadows and the subdued light.

Besides, he wanted to check the chart again to be extra sure the HIV titer was negative. That would be a nifty first, getting AIDS from a huge inoculum flying in through the mucous membranes in his mouth, like a giant pus fireball shot from a catapult.

God, sometimes it sucked being a doctor!

Chapter Sixty-Three

Emergency Room

Pennsylvania Hospital, Center City, Philadelphia, PA

"Dr. Kurland!! Quick!" Life-and-death urgency filled the hallway as Graham hurried towards it. He suspected it was coming from the room where that Solas character had been transferred from Wills Eye.

Bizarre case, the kind that left an imprint on your brain. And Graham's huge cranium had been working overtime trying to wrap itself around the facts of the case.

Plus, the similarities between him and Jeffrey Jackson were uncanny. He would have written it off to coincidence, but those haunting red and white eyes, and the loss of blood in each man. What were the chances of seeing two patients like that in a lifetime, much less within weeks?

Could it be something contagious?

Maybe…no.

No micro-organism he ever heard of could do that. Anyway, Jeffrey's main problems came from the lye.

But the real kicker was Kyle. She wasn't her normal self around Solas.

There was something off, something that bothered her deeply. He could tell it was lurking under the surface. But what?

She never failed to follow a lead. Never. But not here. She seemed too eager to dismiss further workup for his incessant oozing, even though he was going straight down the toilet. Over the past few days, Solas had developed constant drainage of blood from his nostrils, mouth, rectum, and penis, what was left of it.

And that look he saw on her face. Like a lioness ready to pounce. Jaw clenched, eyes set, a menacing, steady stare. What was her problem? He thought about calling her, but she was probably trying to save some poor soul, so they called the resident genius because no one else had any idea what the hell to do.

He'd only seen her act like this once before. Now, who was that with?

Joey Eisenberg, one of the ER interns, waved his arms from across the room.

Graham sprinted over. "What's the problem?"

Joey pointed to the open hand of a man standing in front of him with a bloodied patch over one eye. In his palm was a round object that resembled a red walnut. Graham looked closer.

Holy shit!

An eyeball. An intact eyeball. Covered with blood.

Graham grabbed Joey by the shoulder and pulled him aside. "What's going on here?"

"This guy got into a fight. The other guy pulled this guy's eye out of the socket."

"No!"

"Yes!"

"That's impossible." Occasionally, the globe popped forward and became trapped in front of the eyelids in people with prominent eyeballs. It hurt like a son-of-a-bitch and made you panic like being face-to-face with a curled cobra. But the eyeball remained attached to the muscles that moved it and the thick optic nerve connecting it to the brain.

"I thought the same thing," Joey said.

"Then how?"

"After he pulled the eyeball in front of the lids, he put it in his mouth and bit it out. Some deranged animal actually bit this fricking guy's eye out of his head and then spat it out."

"That's…unbelievable and disgusting."

"What do you think we should do?"

"What can we do?"

"He wants to know if we can put it back."

"Is he serious?"

"Deadly."

"Tell him the truth." Graham turned and lowered his voice further as the man looked toward them with his remaining eye.

"There's no way to connect the optic nerve. Contact the ophthalmology resident to sew him up. And call the cops."

Graham stepped out of the ER for fresh air. At times, he missed the excitement. But this wasn't one of them.

The drizzle of the cool night was refreshing compared to the hotter-than-Georgia-asphalt day. Except for an occasional passing car, the midnight streets were deserted. Graham stared at the streetlight overhead.

The image of the poor man holding his eye in his hand made him shudder. There was something about eye injuries, eye problems in general…. He couldn't get Solas out of his mind.

And the bleeding, all that bleeding. It was a wonder that Solas had any blood left. He hadn't seen bleeding like that since when? Since Mancini. Yes, that was it. Frank Mancini.

Come to think of it, Mancini had gone blind, too.

Strange coincidence. Or was it?

Mancini had gone blind, although it was nothing like Jeffrey or Solas. And Mancini didn't die from DIC. He died from a bleeding ulcer.

On the other hand, he vomited up every drop of blood in his body, just like…just like the cop who was burned and blinded by Mancini's thugs. Mancini wound up with the equivalent of a burn and died the same way as the young cop he had executed: blind and exsanguinating from the gut. And now, Jeffrey Jackson and Solas? Both were blind. With Jeffrey losing so much blood that his kidneys failed. And Solas losing it from a hundred plus puncture holes and a strange coagulopathy they still hadn't identified.

Could this really be a coincidence?

Maybe. They happened all the time.

But here?

This seemed too much for chance.

One in a million?

Hell, one in a billion.

Maybe he was just being paranoid. On the other hand, maybe he wasn't. Maybe the one set. But two?

Something very odd was going on here. His spider senses were tingling the way they did when his unit was about to be ambushed in Fallujah.

He had to talk to Kyle. She has been so tense and upset lately. Maybe there was some way he could help.

But the first chance he got, he was going back to see Solas. He was getting close to the answers he needed. Just a few more pieces to the puzzle.

And being Graham Kurland, he couldn't rest until he solved this life-and-death puzzle.

Chapter Sixty-Four

Intensive Care Unit

Pennsylvania Hospital, Philadelphia, PA

"What happened?" Graham brought his hand up to his forehead as he studied Solas lying inside the room, an endotracheal tube in his mouth connecting him to a ventilator. The slow ooze of blood into his lungs made it impossible for Blade to breathe on his own.

Clear fluid dripped through an IV line into one arm. A second line in the other transfused blood back into his bleeding body.

Despite everything, Solas was awake. He couldn't speak with the tube down his throat, so he wrote notes to the nurses on a yellow pad.

Graham walked over and stood next to Amy Roth, Solas' nurse. She'd just read one of the notes and was passing a long, thin plastic line down Solas' endotracheal tube to suck out the blood and mucus secretions.

"He had a bad night, Dr. Kurland."

"That's an understatement." Graham stood in the doorway of the first glass enclosure in the ICU, looking between the patient and the computerized portable chart.

"What did he say?" he asked.

"Told me he couldn't breathe."

Solas lurched forward with a cough that expelled bloody debris through the tube in her direction.

"Geez!"

Graham stepped back into the hallway, leaving Amy to wipe the secretions from her hair. No need to be exposed to the body fluids, much less her wrath.

He turned to the laboratory section of the chart. The values were appalling. The clotting factors were nonexistent. No wonder this guy was hemorrhaging from every orifice.

He looked back through the glass. Solas was a pathetic sight. His purple body was bloated to twice its normal size from blood leaking into the tissues. A reddish discharge oozed from the corner of his mouth and dribbled around the endotracheal tube.

The sheet below had a magenta stain from the blood seeping through his rectum. The dozens of puncture sites in his arms where they'd drawn blood or given IVs spread red polka dots across his gown.

The worst, though, was the dripping scarlet patch covering the socket where they removed the ruptured eye. It was only a matter of time until the blood flowing out exceeded the blood they could push back in.

Graham sighed. This was like trying to hold water back with a sieve.

Almost two weeks had passed since Solas developed disseminated intravascular coagulation, and the course had been relentless. Unless they could find and correct the underlying cause, he was a dead man.

To date, they'd had no success. Zero.

Kyle arrived as Graham walked back into the room.

"Give me an update," she said, flat and detached.

Graham shook his head and looked away from Solas. "He's coherent. I hate to say it, but I'm afraid he's bought the ranch." He turned back to Solas and raised his voice. "Are you in pain, sir?"

Solas nodded.

"We'll give you something for it. Hang on a minute."

"Give him morphine," Kyle said as they headed to the door.

"I will. Almost wish I had the guts to give him an overdose so he could go peacefully, poor devil."

"Graham, you can't do that," she said with too much vehemence.

"I know. Just a thought. It won't be much longer anyway. He'll be dead in twenty-four hours."

"Make him a no-code and take him off the cardiac monitor," Kyle said with a sinister edge. "It's all we can do."

They were about to leave, then stopped when Solas tried to rise and sit up. His body was wracked by another attempt to cough and clear the bloody mucus. The powerful lurch expelled the contact lens from his remaining eye.

Graham reached down to pick it off the floor.

Kyle grabbed his arm. "Don't touch that!"

"Why not?"

"I-it may be contaminated."

"With what? Anthrax?"

"Bacteria."

"Come on, Kyle, give me a break. It's only cortisone." He picked up the lens and held it between his thumb and forefinger, looking at it from different directions.

"Graham, listen to me. Put it down."

What was wrong with a contact lens?

Graham laid the piece of plastic on the table next to Solas' bed and met her eyes in a straight-on stare.

"We have to talk," he said as he looked at her with puzzled concern.

"Is it urgent?"

"Yes."

"Well, uh, now's not the best–"

"When?"

"You know my schedule's awful for the next twenty-four hours, plus I'm on call. I probably won't even get home tonight. How about we meet on the second floor right after the cardiology conference tomorrow morning?"

"That's fine. Come to my place tonight if it quiets down to a dull roar here."

"I will."

"Are you okay? Graham asked urgently. "You seem so…"

"I'm…" Kyle stopped herself from saying something vital and dangerous.

"What is it?" Graham insisted.

She sighed, stopped whatever was trying to come out of her, and put on a painfully fake smile. "I'm good, I'm… yeah, I'm okay." She gathered herself and said, "Sorry, I guess the stress is getting to me. We'll talk tomorrow, I promise."

Kyle blew him a kiss and walked away.

Graham almost grabbed her arm to stop her. But he didn't.

Solas coughed, and Amy inserted the suction catheter again. The near-dead patient moaned and shuddered. His face contorted in pain, but after the spasm passed, Graham could see something other than blood streaming down his face.

Tears.

Graham hung his head and shut the door behind him.

Only the Devil himself deserved to go like that.

The terror continued for twelve more hours. Thinned blood filled Emilio Solas' windpipe and tributaries, ultimately drowning him. He died two hours before Jeffrey Jackson.

Death was a blessed relief for both.

Chapter Sixty-Five

Stenton's Estate

Berwyn, PA

Kyle's mind was spinning out of control, danger and death closing in on her from all sides as she tapped her pencil on the table, and her leg restlessly thumped on the floor.

Carlo flashed her a disapproving look. She had the almost uncontrollable urge to lash out at him. Somehow, she managed to restrain herself.

She looked around at her colleagues' faces attending the August Tribunal meeting. The events were taking their toll on everyone. She recognized the medical signs. Randy looked gaunt, like he hadn't slept in weeks. Nate told her he'd developed an ulcer, and Carlo was more short-tempered than ever. Now Booth's left eye kept twitching.

It was only a matter of time until someone cracked.

Kyle thought about the boiling frog parable. Throw a frog into boiling water, and it jumps out. Throw it into lukewarm water and slowly turn up the heat? It stays where it is and dies every time.

That's what was happening here. The temperature was slowly rising. Would they be able to get out in time?

She had no idea.

Alden Booth worried her the most. He sat at the far end of the table, shuffling and reshuffling his papers like he'd lost something important. He could be an abrasive pain in the ass, but he was always a well-organized abrasive pain in the ass. Until now. And the psoriasis on the back of his hands was spreading like wildfire. One more indicator of pressure getting to him.

Like she was one to talk. Her periods had become irregular, and her bouts with migraines had turned into daily battles in a war she was losing.

Last week, she'd started buying Tylenol in bulk. This thing with DiNunzio had her constantly looking over her shoulder. She jumped at the slightest sound, awaking in cold sweats in the middle of the night.

She hoped somebody tonight would say something to allay her fears. All of their fears. But she was doubtful.

And Graham was suspicious about Solas. She could feel it. What if he finally put two and two together and came up with four? He would see her for the monster she had turned into. It would ruin her. Destroy their lives together.

Kyle glanced at her watch. Almost eight thirty. Come on, Lindsey. She couldn't help thinking it, but what if he was dead?

Tate walked and dropped his briefcase by the side of his chair. "Sorry. Ruptured aorta. It took the surgeon longer than he expected."

"It's alright, at least you called." Stenton glared at Carlo.

Carlo glowered back. Kyle's stress level skyrocketed. Why did the two men clash? Was this a testosterone slugfest? That was the last thing they needed.

"Alden, you have the agenda," Stenton said.

Booth ran his finger down his brown clipboard. "I b-b-believe Art is first."

Ramos cleared his throat. "Just to refresh you, S-antigen is normally present in the human retina and is associated with uveitis, a severe inflammation in the eye. The S-antigen in the pellet Nate and Randy shot into Solas caused his immune system to create antibodies to attack it. The antibodies crossed over and attacked the S-antigen normally present in the retinas of his eyes. The battle created a vicious uveitis in both eyes, the worst I've ever seen."

"Pity you can't publish the results," Carlo commented.

"Quite," Ramos said. "His body went on a mission to turn his eyes into pockets of pus. One actually ruptured and had to be removed, and the second was only a day or two away from the same thing when he died. The contact lenses worked well, but I think Kyle can elaborate on their effects better than I can."

Kyle's tone of voice was matter-of-fact. "Solas also developed DIC—disseminated intravascular coagulation—within days after Art placed the contact lenses. The proteins in the Crotalid snake venom in the lenses caused clots to form throughout his body. When his clotting factors were exhausted, he bled from every conceivable spot. We kept replacing the blood, but as long as the lenses kept releasing venom into his system, it was hopeless."

Lindsey Tate gave a wry smile. "Then the miserable bastard died the same way Jeffrey Jackson did, right?"

"A fair assessment," Kyle said, cool and calm, as a deep satisfaction swept through her. She pictured her brother. No, of course, it didn't bring him back. But it was justice. An eye for an eye.

"I doubt even his lice will miss him," Tate said.

The members murmured their approval. She knew this was the moment they savored, the post-mortem, the time when they could relish in the fact that justice had been served.

She stiffened as the reality of what they'd done hit her. The consequences. The danger they'd put themselves in. The migraine attacked like an atom bomb. She rubbed her head hard. Trying to stop the pain that relentlessly invaded her brain.

"Enough for now," Stenton announced. The murmurs slowed and then stopped. "Let's move on."

Booth stared up from his agenda. "Nate's next."

Nate licked his lips. "I have disturbing news. Our tap on DiNunzio's phone was discovered this afternoon."

Kyle closed her eyes as the agony spread through her body and a lump filled her throat. No matter how many times she swallowed, it wouldn't go away.

"How do you know?" Ramos asked.

Nate pulled a portable tape recorder from under the table and pushed a button.

"Lis'en good, youze ass-wipes. We gotcher tap an' it won't be lawng 'fore we get youze." There were scratching sounds and a loud click. Then silence.

"How did he find it?" Kyle asked.

Nate shrugged. "SWAG?"

"What's that?"

"Sophisticated Wild Ass Guess."

Kyle felt the noose tighten around her neck as the pain wracked her brain.

Chapter Sixty-Six

Ralph DiNunzio's Office

South Philadelphia, PA

Ralph DiNunzio picked his teeth with the sharp end of the wooden toothpick, trying to dislodge the little piece of beef stuck there. As he fantasized about the slow death he was going to inflict on the scumbag doctors who killed his uncle. A half dozen of his closer associates sat around the office amidst tattered old issues of *Hustler*, cigarette butts, and used Styrofoam cups.

To the uneducated eye, it was nothing more than the DeFrancesco Trucking Company. And to an extent, that's what it was. But it was really a command center for DiNunzio's business dealings. A few legitimate. Most nefarious.

With a desperate lunge, he freed the piece of steak and flicked his prize off to the side. Now he was ready to talk.

"I cawled youze boys here 'cuz we gotta break in Uncle Frank's case. Crawford linked a buncha docs dat meets out on da Main Line. He helped Lou and me make one of 'em. We got to his mudder, and he's cooperatin'." DiNunzio gave a grin of satisfaction. "Seems he don't want his old lady trashed."

Several of his men snickered.

"Anywayz, da snitch woul'n't tell us names, but we know where dey meet.

Soon we'll know when, too. We're gonna be able to take 'em awll out together."

"What kinda group is dis?" Al Romano asked.

"Vigilantes. So we gotta get 'em awll. Down to da last man…and woman."

"Woman?" one man said.

"Jeez," DiNunzio said, "youz jokers sound like fuckin' Carlucci. Yeah, dere's a woman. She's da doc who took care of my uncle."

"Holy shit," Vinnie Russo slapped the side of his head.

"Lou and I t'ink dese fuckers whacked more dan Uncle Frank. We don't know who yet."

"Dey coming after you too, Ralph?" Vinnie asked.

"I don' know, but dat's anudder reason I wanna get 'em first."

Al Romano flicked his cigarette onto the floor and stomped it. "What's da plan?"

"Da same thing we used for dose Colombian pricks in Sout' Jersey. First, we light 'em up, then we mop 'em up.'"

The men nodded and smiled, excited about shedding blood and spreading death.

"Does dat mean we kill da woman too?" Vinnie asked.

DiNunzio rolled his eyes. "Vinnie, I'm glad yer here to see how we run t'ings. If we get da chance, we fuck her up first."

Vinnie fell silent and looked away.

Shit. Vinnie was a greenhorn and didn't realize that when push came to shove, nothing was sacred. He'd learn.

"Listen up," DiNunzio said. "I heard dey meet at dis guy Stenton's mansion. It's us'ally on a Friday, an' da snitch said dey're havin' a meetin' in a week or two. So, we got plentya time to get ready.

"I t'ink we can do this widdout Carlucci, which is fine, 'cuz I don' wanna owe dat son-of-a-bitch nuttin'. Lou's gonna give each of youze yer 'ssignments. I don't want no screw-ups. Un'erstood?"

There was silent accord.

Lou looked at DiNunzio. "You ready to go, Ralph? Da snitch is s'pposed to meet us at nine."

"Good. We'll keep it to ourselves, but after he gives us da time of dat meetin', he's as dead as da rest of 'em."

Yeah, DiNunzio thought, *it's good to be the King.*

304

"Good. We'll keep it to ourselves, but after he gives us da time of dat meetin', he's as dead as da rest of 'em."

Yeah, DiNunzio thought, *it's good to be the King.*

Chapter Sixty-Seven

Auditorium

Pennsylvania Hospital, Philadelphia, PA

Graham's mind kept wandering back to Kyle, trying to fit all the pieces together and figure out the answer to the most important question in life: What should he do?

He always found the first hour of the cardiology lecture tedious, the second interminable. The third would be fatal. Silverberg was a decent clinician, but his slow delivery made Graham suspect a sluggish metabolic rate. A few guest lecturers were as entertaining as Lady Gaga. But many were like corpses at a funeral. You needed them for the ceremony, but you couldn't expect much excitement out of them.

When Graham's beeper shrieked, half a dozen senior physicians clutched their pockets. Graham chuckled at the pained looks of envy as he left through the side door.

"Hello, Dr. Kurland?"

"Yes?"

"This is Priscilla, the operator. It's eleven thirty. I'm calling, like you asked."

"Thanks, Priscilla. You're the best." Graham smiled and hung up the wall phone.

He took the stairs to the second floor and scanned the long hallway for

Kyle. It didn't take long to spot her in the distance.

"Kyle? Wait up." He ran toward her.

She stopped and looked up, chart in hand. She smiled instinctively, happy to see her man. Then she was hit with the heaviness of the situation. She tried her best to act normal. "Hi, Graham. Sorry, I was in a rush the other day. Is everything okay? What's up?"

He shuffled from one foot to the other. "I'm not sure just how to say this, but I have to. I've noticed strange similarities over the past few months among several patients. All of them were under your care at one time or another."

"I'm not sure I follow you."

"Remember the young cop who was burned a year and a half ago?"

"Vividly."

"He died later from a hemorrhaging stress ulcer. Almost the same way another patient died, Mr. Mancini. Remember?"

"Of course."

"Mancini also died from the equivalent of a burn. And both men were blind, too."

"Okay. What's your point?" She said it too hard and sharp. *Tread lightly here,* she reminded herself.

"My point is, don't you think it's a pretty strange coincidence?"

"It's not unusual for different people to die from similar pathology," she said in a very measured tone. Maybe too measured. "We see it all the time."

"I suppose. But the night Mancini came in, a plainclothes cop came too. Sergeant Rossi. He said Mancini was responsible for blinding and burning a young cop."

"So?"

"So, at first, I wrote it off to chance." Graham paused. "But the similarities between Jeffrey Jackson and this Solas fellow also seem like way more than coincidence, too. Both go blind and then bleed out? I don't think you'd see a case like that in a lifetime, much less two in two months. After I looked at the incidences of the diseases, I'd put the odds at one in millions for each. What's up?"

"What do you mean, 'what's up'? Nothing's up." Kyle looked back at her chart, trying to avoid eye contact. She was afraid she looked guilty. She was right. "Stranger things have happened."

"Then there was Erozan and his muscle tone."

Kyle's head shot up, and her eyes met his. "Are you accusing me of something?"

Graham stared back. This was harder than he'd expected. "Yeah, uh…I guess I am. Look, all I want to know is what's going on."

Kyle went back to flipping through the chart. "Nothing is going on."

"Come on, I know you too well. You can't even look at me when you say that."

She met his eyes again. But behind the stare was the look of a scared child. "I, uh…"

"You can trust me. What's going on? I can help you."

"You don't want to know," she said as she rubbed her temples in pain. "I can't get you involved."

"What's wrong? Another migraine?

"Yeah, but it's…" She groaned as another wave of pain lashed into her brain.

"You're getting them every day. And they seem to be getting worse. Are you in some kind of trouble?"

"No. I mean…the best thing you can do is ignore any coincidences. Just forget about them."

"I can't do that."

She frowned. "Come on. Some place private."

Grabbing him by the arm, she walked him to the elevator and pressed "B." Once they reached the lower level, she led him to a booth at the back of the hospital cafeteria. Three nurses were talking two tables away, but they were well out of earshot.

Kyle sat across from him and put her head in her hands, trying to squeeze the ache out of her skull. It didn't work. She let out a gust of troubled air and folded her hands on the table.

"I don't have to tell you how unfair life can be," she said in a quiet, calm voice. "Children drown, people die in the prime of life from cancer. We hate to see these things. But they're out of our control."

"Yes, of course. What are you getting at?"

She leaned in and lowered her voice even more. "There are events in our control. Events for which we should be accountable. A person murders another in cold blood, or rapes and tortures, or—"

"Burns someone alive and gouges out his eyes?"

"Yes."

"I'm still not sure what you're driving at."

"Horrible crimes are committed by evil people who go free. Only thirty to fifty percent of murders are solved. Lots of these criminals go out and do the same thing to other victims. The police admit they can't protect everyone. The legal system's far from perfect. Hell, you can shoot the President, call yourself crazy, and practically get away with it. Most people throw their hands in the air, but some individuals are willing to do something about it."

"Are you telling me there are people out there acting as vigilantes?"

Kyle shrugged. "Remember what Edmund Burke said. The only thing necessary for the triumph of evil is for good men to do nothing."

"You can't do that!" Graham said much louder than he meant to. The table of nurses chatted on.

"You can't do that," he whispered

"I'm sorry, Graham, I've already said too much."

"You have to let me in on this," he said. "How else can I help you?"

She shook her head. "Graham, I can't get you involved in this. At least not now."

"Okay. I've always trusted you." He took her hand in his. A tear came into her eye. "There's no reason to stop now."

"Thank you, Graham."

"Before you leave, there's one other thing you should know."

"What's that?"

"A couple of months ago, a guy was in here asking me about Mancini and the doctors who took care of him. Said he was a cop and flashed a badge, but he didn't act like one. I didn't think much of it at the time. I didn't tell him anything. But he was asking about you in particular. So…be careful. Okay?"

"Thanks." Kyle squeezed his hand. "Why don't you come and spend the night at my place tonight?"

"I'd love to." He wanted to give her a hug, but this was neither the time nor the place.

Kyle took off. Graham stayed behind for lunch. He was torn in two by the idea of Kyle, a doctor sworn to help and heal, being a vigilante who tortured and killed. But, he'd seen enough innocents suffer to know that the predators who got away with their violent attacks just kept hurting the weak and the meek. He couldn't tell anyone what he'd just heard from Kyle.

At least not for now.

Chapter Sixty-Eight

Seventh Street

Center City, Philadelphia

"I want out!" Kyle practically shouted as she placed her hands on the back of her head and pulled forward to relieve the tension jabbing at the base of her skull. "I can't keep doing this."

"NOT POSSIBLE!" Carlo Tursi, her fellow Tribunal doctor, spat angrily, scanning up and down Locust Street as they walked past LaBuca Restaurant near Independence Hall. "This isn't the Girl Scouts. You don't just drop out because you're having your first period."

"Don't be an asshole, Carlo. This is destroying all of us. Look at yourself. Your rage is out of control, you explode over the tiniest things, and your limp has gotten worse."

"My limp has nothing to do with this. I'm fine."

"No, you're not. You've also developed a twitch."

"A twitch?"

"Yes. Don't you realize it? Your right eyelid fires off like a strobe light in a disco. I noticed it the other day at Stenton's. That comes from stress."

"You're telling me a neurosurgeon doesn't tolerate stress?"

"Not this kind. Our lives are going down the toilet. And I don't want to wait around for the final flush."

"What do you suggest we do?"

"Tell Stenton. The Tribunal meeting is in two days. Tell him we can't go on like this."

"This isn't like you. You always had more resolve and guts than anyone in the group."

"I'm sorry, I can't do it anymore. I have violent thoughts, I snap at people who don't deserve it, I can't sleep, I've lost my appetite; I get screaming migraines that make me want to cut my own head off. I'm done."

"I'm taking you to Mellon Bank." Carlo fished around in his pants pocket. "Here's the key to a safety deposit box with a collection of bonds." He handed over a small aluminum safety deposit box key. "Once you meet the manager, you'll have the same access I do."

"I don't want them."

"In case something happens. In case one of us makes it, and the other doesn't."

"What about your family?"

"All I have is a grandmother who's ninety-five. She lives in a nursing home, has severe dementia, and doesn't even know me. Her funeral expenses are already covered. What I don't want is to have the government grab it."

"But why me?"

"Despite our differences, I'm closer to you than anyone else in the Tribunal."

Very true, Kyle thought.

They passed a Philly cop, and Kyle shuddered at what it would be like at the station house. Or behind the barbed wire and high walls of prison, or heaven forbid, even worse.

On the other hand, there were times when she felt like it would be a blessing to let this end.

Even if it was the end of her.

"Kyle," Carlos said, "I know this DiNunzio thing has you all bent out of shape. Maybe we can talk to the others, brainstorm, and come up with some type of counterplan. The man's a depraved killer. You heard what Randy said. 'The best defense is a good offense.'"

"Are you suggesting that we do DiNunzio, too?"

"It's a reasonable thought."

"But we still have nothing solid on him. If we move without any proof, we're no better than he is. It was different for Mancini and the others."

"He's got more notches on his gun than Pol Pot."

"Can you name one?"

"No, but—"

"If we ever went after the wrong person, I couldn't live with myself. "And it's not just DiNunzio. If he's gone, another killer will pop up to take his place. Don't you understand? There's only one possible ending if we keep walking down this road to ruin."

"Maybe you're right."

"I know I'm right," she said.

"Then how about I bring it up at the next meeting?"

"I don't think we have much choice."

Carlo tucked his brown satchel tighter under his arm and held the glass door for her at the Mellon entrance off Independence Square.

They waited at the reception desk until a balding man with legs too short for his trunk ushered them into his office. The meeting was business-like and pleasant, but Kyle's head pounded, and the lights flashed in her eyes so badly that his high-pitched voice seemed a hundred miles away.

Back on the street, she struggled to hold back her pain, fears, and tears. She didn't want to give Carlo the satisfaction. "Here," she said, handing his key back. "Keep it. I can take care of myself."

"I don't want it. I want you to keep it."

"It's not worth fighting over," she fumed, sticking the key into her purse. If anything did ever happen, the money was going to a fund for crime victims in his name.

The walk back to the hospital was shrouded in icy silence.

A crystal clear thought penetrated the haze of ache in Kyle's brain, *Maybe I should get the hell out of Philadelphia.*

Chapter Sixty-Nine

Pennsylvania Hospital

Philadelphia, PA

G raham was so overwhelmed by the confusion running riot in his head, heart, and soul that he didn't bother to look at the name on the hematology consult slip he grabbed from the Department of Medicine office.

It'd been over twenty-four hours since they talked about the vigilante thing, and he still couldn't wrap his mind around it. Was Kyle the person he thought she was? As a soldier, he had killed in the name of justice and the American way. Was she doing something worse than that?

But he could see the toll it was taking. He was still haunted by the toll it had taken on him. The toll it was still taking. He saw it in her face. Circles around her eyes, deep folds on her forehead, and a palpable melancholy that made it seem as if she might burst into tears at any moment. She snapped irritably; her sense of humor was gone, and her stiffness around patients and staff was so unlike her.

He didn't know what the hell to do next, but he knew he couldn't let it lie. He'd had to get answers. Figure out a plan.

Four-thirteen was just down the hall from the elevator. He rested against the wall outside the room and turned to the history and physical section of the chart.

Hmm, Emily Mancini. Any relation to the old man who died last year? There couldn't be that many Mancinis. He moved further down the chart.

Admitting diagnosis: acute leukemia

Attending physician: McMann, K.

Chief complaint: increasing weakness for six weeks.

A common enough history in people with leukemia, particularly the acute forms. When the leukemic cells replaced normal red blood cells, the body's tissues couldn't get their oxygen to function and survive.

Graham flipped through the pages. The woman had been hospitalized for almost four weeks, and her record resembled *War and Peace*. Where was the darn bone marrow report? That should tell him something. Kyle would have ordered it. Or at least the normal Kyle would have.

There it was, the yellow pathology slip near the back of the chart.

Specimen most compatible with acute myeloblastic leukemia (AML).

Graham frowned. AML was the second most common form in adults, but by far the deadliest. Abnormal white blood cells reproduce with no limit until they destroy the body's ability to fight bacteria, form blood clots, and function as a coherent unit. The end would come from severe internal bleeding, overwhelming infection, or any number of other horrors.

The progress notes weren't encouraging. She had high fevers, and the chemotherapy wasn't touching her. There were still large numbers of blasts, immature white cells, in her bloodstream. No one survived unless they could be eradicated.

Graham knew what to do. Which drugs to recommend? But they'd just be buying her time. And probably not much. He tucked the chart under his arm and entered the room.

The woman was as pale as her sheets. A unit of blood dripped into the IV line attached to her arm, and a young woman of about eighteen sat holding her hand. She opened her eyes as he entered.

"Mrs. Mancini?"

"Yes?"

"I'm Dr. Kurland."

The woman turned her blanched face toward him. "Dr. Kurland," she said in a raspy whisper. Graham leaned closer to hear. "It's so good to see you. I remember when you took care of my husband."

He was right. She was related to the old man. Graham smiled and gently placed his hand on her shoulder.

Mrs. Mancini turned her head toward the younger woman. "Dr. Kurland, this is my granddaughter, Susan."

The girl said hello, then excused herself, wiping her eyes as she closed the door behind her.

"When did you start to feel sick?" Graham asked.

"Four weeks ago. I tried to contact Dr. McMann, but the hospital said she was out of town. Then I came to the emergency room, and they admitted me."

The woman's face was a mask of pain. The leukemia had aged her twenty years since Graham had last seen her. Her hair was turning white, and her once-smooth skin was chiseled with wrinkles. Her eyes reflected the deep sadness of one surrendering to death.

"Doctor?" she said in just above a whisper.

"Yes, Mrs. Mancini?"

"I'm going to die, aren't I?"

"That's a difficult question, ma'am."

"Damn it, son, answer me! Am I dying? Dr. McMann told me I was, but I want to hear it from you, too."

"I'm afraid things don't look so good right now."

"For God's sake, just say yes or no."

Graham paused. Sighed. He hated extinguishing hope. But if a patient demanded the unvarnished truth, he felt obliged to give it.

"Probably yes."

Relief filled her face. Graham looked at the countless needle marks and purple bruises on her arms, the blood dripping into her veins, and the oxygen cannula in her nose. Clearly, the truth gave her peace.

"How much longer do you think I have?"

"To be honest, it could be days, maybe weeks, depending upon how heroic we get."

"Spare me the heroics."

She opened her mouth for a couple of breaths. "Dr. Kurland, you remember my husband, Frank, don't you?"

Graham nodded. "Of course."

She smiled. "You were so kind to me when he was dying. I'll never forget you for that."

"Thank you."

"My husband was not a nice man. Neither are his associates. They've done awful things to people, things I can't even talk about."

He patted her hand. "You don't have to talk about it. Save your strength."

"But I do. I can't hold it in any longer."

She took several labored breaths and waved Graham closer.

"As a dying woman, I know I can trust you. Do you know where Dr. McMann is? I've been asking the staff to contact her for an hour. No one's been able to reach her."

Graham looked at his watch. Kyle said she had a departmental meeting. That could be anywhere.

"I'm sorry, Mrs. Mancini, I don't know."

She shut her eyes. "I think she may be in danger."

"What do you mean?"

"Frank's nephew, Ralph DiNunzio, is looking for her."

The Neanderthal.

Mrs. Mancini grasped Graham's hand. "Dr. McMann means a lot to me. She put her heart out for me over the past few weeks, and I'm sure she's helped so many more people than my husband hurt. We need to help her. I don't think there's much time."

"Why do you say that?"

"I don't know all the details, but last night Ralph DiNunzio had a meeting at my house. My granddaughter could hear them talking. Ralph thinks doctors had something to do with Frank's death, and she heard him mention Dr. McMann's name."

Graham gripped the bed railing to keep his hands steady. "How did he find out about this group?"

"I think he had a detective follow them. Someone in the group turned on the others."

"What's he planning to do?"

"Kill them."

"When?"

"I don't know. Maybe tonight."

"What time?"

"I don't know, *I don't know.*"

"Where? Do you know where?"

She shook her head. "A house out on the Main Line. A man named Stenton owns it, but I have no idea where it is."

Graham bolted for the door, then turned back. "How are they going to do it?"

She looked up with a half-laugh and half-cry.

"The same way they murdered my cousin Albie. With a bomb."

Graham's central nervous system activated, and he clicked into Warrior Mode.

Chapter Seventy

Pennsylvania Hospital

Philadelphia, PA

Kyle drilled her thumb into her right temple. She'd managed to keep the migraine at bay for two or three hours, but the Tylenol finally succumbed to the headache. She punched the elevator button. She said a quick prayer that the pain would pass during the ride to Stenton's.

She'd tossed and turned all night with a suffocating sense of dread. Tribunal days had gone from stressful to panic-attacking.

But it was more than that. Everything was wrong. Terribly wrong. She'd been in anxiety overdrive since Graham told her about the man nosing around, asking questions about her.

Then there was Graham himself. She desperately didn't want him to get involved with Tribunal problems. She felt terrible lying to him about the departmental meeting tonight. She couldn't let it go on anymore. That by itself could destroy their future together. The whole situation was crushing. It had to stop.

Did anyone else know? Or were they guessing?

Harry Turner?

The nurses?

Tensions had reached a boiling point at Tribunal meetings over the past few months. This would only fan the fire.

Kyle remembered when Stenton had first contacted her almost two years ago. She was stunned by his proposal, but the hatred that burned inside her for the years following her brother's brutal murder drowned out her objections. While she knew joining would change her life, she never really anticipated it would also destroy her.

The elevator bell rang.

Kyle was about to step on when she heard the page. Someone had been trying to reach her for an hour. With the migraine and everything else in the ICU, she'd forgotten to return the call. She looked at her watch, then down the hall at the staff phone on Five East.

"In or out?" a lab tech said, holding the door.

"Go on. I'll catch the next. Thanks."

Damn. She was fifteen minutes late as it was, and Randy and Nate were no doubt already waiting. Booth, Carlo, and the others would be furious, but it had just been one thing after another the whole day. At least when she'd called, Stenton actually sounded forgiving.

She stopped in front of the phone, picked up the receiver, and dialed the operator. "Hello, this is Dr. McMann."

"Hello, Doctor. Someone's been trying to reach you."

"Look, I hate to do this, but call Dr. Kurland. He's covering emergencies. I have my own problems down here."

"But—"

Kyle hung up and ran for the stairs. Whatever it was, Graham could more than handle it.

She took the stairs two at a time and heard her name repeated over the intercom. If someone was that serious about contacting her, they could call the stat number on her pager. She felt her front pocket.

Dammit! It was in her locker.

Chapter Seventy-One

Pennsylvania Hospital

Philadelphia, PA

Graham sprinted as fast as his long legs would take him down the hall, yanked the phone off the hook, and punched O.

"Operator."

"Please page Dr. McMann again."

"Boy, she's popular today. Just a moment, I'll put you on hold."

Graham's leg bounced, and he shoved a knuckle between his teeth so he could bite it.

"Come on, come on."

"Dr. McMann, please call the operator," a metallic voice sounded over the loudspeaker. "Dr. Kyle McMann, call the operator."

"I'm sorry, sir," the operator said, "she doesn't seem to want to be reached today."

"Do you know if she's gone home?"

"I don't know…oh, wait a minute, this could be her. Hold on."

The operator clicked off, and something by Bach started up.

"Please, Kyle, be there." His fist banged into the wall over and over.

"I'm sorry, sir, she hung up on me. She said she has an emergency, and you should contact Dr. Kurland."

"THIS IS DR. KURLAND!" Graham yelled. "Sorry. Please page her again.

This *is* an emergency."

"Dr. McMann, stat," a frustrated voice boomed. "Dr. Kyle McMann, phone the operator, stat."

The operator came back on after another verse of Bach. "I'm sorry, she doesn't answer."

"Thanks."

Graham slammed down the phone and took off at breakneck speed for the stairwell.

At least she might still be in the building.

He banged out the door and sailed through the stairwell. Far below, he heard another door bang open, someone else in a hurry. He raced up two flights to the ICU and pushed in the door. A nurse jumped back.

"Kyle," he said. "Have you seen Kyle McMann?"

The startled woman pointed to the nurses' station. Graham ran for it.

"Have you seen Dr. McMann?"

"You just missed her," the ward clerk said. "She couldn't have left more than two minutes ago."

"Where was she going?"

"I don't know. She left in a hurry, though. Didn't even wait for the elevator."

"Damn."

Graham ran back to the stairs and practically dropped the five flights to the first floor. He smashed open the door and barreled down the hallway to the main lobby. If he couldn't catch her, maybe he could spot her as she passed in front of the hospital and flag her down.

The automatic door didn't open fast enough, so Graham shoved it. A black van was waiting to pull into traffic.

It was her. It had to be. He'd seen her get into a van like that before.

"Kyle!" he yelled as it pulled out and sped off. He tore out after the van.

"KYLE!" Graham screamed as loud as he could and waved frantically.

"Shit!" He stomped his foot as the van sped away.

Bent over, hands on his knees, he took rapid breaths. He hadn't sprinted a quarter mile like that since the Army.

What should I do now?

He jogged back to the hospital and rushed into the ER.

"Any emergencies?" he asked the head nurse.

"No, pretty quiet."

"Good. Call Dr. Harry Turner and ask him to cover for me. Tell him I have an emergency. He should be on one of the floors."

"You sound out of breath. Are you okay?"

"I'm fine, thanks. Just call Turner."

"Okay."

Graham sprinted to his car.

All he could see were body parts spread far and wide. He had a flash of an 81 mm mortar round exploding in a training camp in Afghanistan.

Not even the organs of those nearby were identifiable.

Chapter Seventy-Two

West River Drive to the Main Line

Philadelphia, PA

The dusk fog created halos around the army of oncoming headlights on the West River Drive as Kyle tried to squeeze the agony out of her aching brain and stop the doomsday fantasies of the Tribunal—and Graham—being blown to smithereens. On the opposite shore of the Schuylkill River, lights on the frames of the rowing houses made it look like something out of the Magic Kingdom.

But Kyle knew this was no Magic Kingdom. There was only dark magic in her life today.

She leaned back into one of the captain's chairs in the customized Dodge van. She was dead tired but knew she couldn't nap with her head exploding like a hydrogen bomb. Being with Nate and Randy was somehow comforting. Safe even. They'd become close friends. Maybe it was better to spring the news about Graham on them before she told the others.

Randy was sitting in the front passenger's seat and spoke before she could open her mouth. "What did you think about Lindsey Tate's case?" he said.

"Interesting."

She'd read it once, but that was enough. The thought of the Russians amputating victims' hands sent shivers down her spine. A good dose of enhanced leprosy bacilli would fix them.

She stopped herself. She already had them in their graves before she even knew the details. Hunting and punishing monsters was turning her into a monster.

"Is that all you can say, interesting?"

"It made me sick. It was awful. But we're going to talk about it at the meeting tonight. Anyway, there's something else I wanted to tell you before we get there."

Nate leaned his head back from the driver's seat. "What's that?"

She bent forward. "There's a doctor in the hospital, Graham Kurland, who's taken care of a good number of my patients. The other day, he questioned me about the similarities between them."

"Which ones?" Randy asked.

She told them what she'd said to Graham.

"Have you told anyone else?"

"Just Carlo."

"What did he say?"

"Nothing I care to repeat."

Neither Nate nor Randy spoke. These were her confidantes. If they reacted like this, what would Stenton and the others do?

"How did you leave it?" Randy asked.

"I told Graham I'd talk to people and get back to him. He'll stay quiet."

Nate looked into the rear-view mirror. "Can you trust him?"

"Yes, he's a good friend."

"How good."

"Very."

"I hope so," Randy said.

They crossed into the Main Line west of the City. The moonbeams silhouetted the large homes and tall sycamores that buffered them from the outside world. Within ten minutes, they'd arrive at Stenton's, possibly the grandest of all manors.

"I'll let them know we're close," Randy said, dialing his cell. A minute later, he pocketed it.

"No answer," he announced in an even, controlled voice.

Kyle had no idea what to do. And it was killing her.

Chapter Seventy-Three

Pennsylvania Hospital Parking Lot

Center City, Philadelphia

Careening down the ramp from the doctors' parking lot on two wheels, Graham hit the curb and barely missed a concrete post. He slammed on the brakes at the bottom to avoid a snail-like SEPTA bus.

"Come on, damn it! Get your thumb out of your ass!"

Even with minimal traffic, the trip would take the better part of thirty minutes. To make matters worse, he wasn't sure where he was going, and they had a good five-minute head start.

He tried again to reach Kyle's beeper from his cell.

"FUCK!"

Stenton had to be involved. Kyle had mentioned him in the past. He remembered how indignant she was when an editorial in the *Inquirer* denounced the man's lack of community spirit. She claimed he had given more money to cancer research than Gates.

He'd shrugged it off at the time, but now realized there might be another reason for her passion. It would take both money and power to run a vigilante operation below the radar. Stenton had both.

The Friday exodus from Center City made traffic a nightmare on the West River Drive. Graham weaved in and out of the other cars, ignoring the honking horns and flashing headlights.

Running a gauntlet of red lights, he shot a glance at his dashboard.

7:00 pm.

A white flash of a Philadelphia Electric repair vehicle erupted off to the right. Graham had a triggering flashback of an artillery flash like the one that shredded his cousin Lucas in the Marine Darkhorse Battalion in southern Afghanistan. His heart pounded, and his brain erupted as PTSD invaded.

Graham used his training. Took his three deep breaths. Asked himself three questions.

Do I want to be the guy who loses his mind when he's trying to save the woman he loves?

No.

Do you want to be a useful soldier who smites the bad guys and saves the girl?

Yes.

Do you want to be a kind, loving person in a kind, loving universe?

Yes.

And he was back in the saddle.

How the hell was he going to get Kyle out of the shitstorm she'd gotten herself into?.

All he could see was an image of Kyle's body being blown to pieces by C4.

He was still ten or fifteen minutes from Stenton's house.

He pushed the pedal all the way to the metal: eighty, ninety, one hundred mph.

He squealed around a corner onto the street he thought was Stenton's, activating his world-class memory bank to the time he was on vacation as a kid, and his parents pointed out Stenton's mansion on the hill in the distance. But it was dark now, and there were a few mansions up on the hill.

The black van he'd seen in the hospital parking lot came over a small rise and roared past him going past him in the other direction, barely missing his Subaru.

He hit the brakes and spun a 180.

Seconds later, Graham caught up to it. He flashed his headlights: on, off, high beams, low beams. Like a man possessed.

BLAM!

He was blinded by bright red lights. He slammed on the brakes with every bit of his considerable torque; they squealed in protest, and he barely avoided climbing up the van's rear end.

The van catapulted ahead at top speed and left him in its wake of flying dust and gravel.

What's under that hood? A rocket?

He hit the gas and followed. There was no way he could catch it.

Wait!

From the crest of the hill, he caught a glimpse of a taillight as it disappeared from the main road.

Thank God for the darkness! Another ten yards and he would have missed it.

He pulled the wheel as hard as he could and screeched onto the side road.

Adrenaline pumping, he was calm and on fire at the same time.

He remembered why he loved being a warrior on his way to war.

Chapter Seventy-Four

Stenton's Estate

Berwyn, PA

The migraine was so bad that it was making Kyle's hair hurt. She bit the nail of her index finger, and this time tasted blood. They were getting close to Stenton's, but the seconds became minutes that felt like hours.

Twice now, Randy had tried to reach security on the phone, and each time there was no answer. Somebody always answered at Stenton's.

"Step on it, Nate." Kyle urged.

Something was wrong.

Very wrong.

The van surged ahead, pushing them back into their seats.

Randy stared into the passenger's side mirror. "We have company."

Kyle turned around to see a car just behind them flashing its headlights frantically. "Looks like he wants us to pull over," she said. "Anyone recognize it?"

Nate glanced in the mirror. "Tough to tell with the light show."

"DiNunzio?" Randy said.

Kyle squinted as she looked back. "I can't tell. Don't stop, Nate. Just go."

"Hang on."

Nate hit the brakes hard. The van's front end dipped, and Kyle heard a screech of brakes from behind. Nate stomped on the gas. The tires squealed, and they flew away, making the chasing car eat their dust.

"Did I ever mention we have a police interceptor engine in this baby?" Nate said.

Kyle was breathing hard. "Uh, no."

The van closed in on Stenton's estate.

"Phones are out." Randy pointed to the dangling phone lines in the small gatehouse by the driveway entrance.

Kyle shut her eyes. "Please, God, please," she whispered.

Everything else was quiet and ordinary as the van turned onto the winding road. Stenton's mansion lay two hundred yards up the hill. They leaned forward, straining for a view. From where they were, they could only see the roof.

Kyle bit her lower lip. *Please let them be okay.*

Nate slowed to a crawl and killed the van's lights. The full moon illuminated the twisting white concrete drive like day.

Headlights appeared in the drive behind.

Oh shit! Kyle thought as a lightning bolt of agony shot through her head.

Chapter Seventy-Five

Stenton's Estate

Berwyn, PA

"Stay here," Nate said as he jolted the van into Park before coming to a complete stop by the driveway off the side of the road.

Randy threw him an M4A1 Carbine that matched his, and the two of them were out and running toward the car behind.

Kyle watched out the back window. The car skidded to a halt as Nate pointed his gun into the driver's side window. He waved the driver out.

The driver opened the door, and the light shone on a familiar face.

"Graham!" Kyle yelled as she fumbled with her seatbelt, her hands shaking with relief.

"I'm Dr. Kurland," she heard. "I'm looking for Dr. Kyle McMann. It's a matter of life and death!"

Kyle opened the side door and saw Graham facing the wrong end of Nate's Carbine.

"It's okay," she said. "He's the good friend I was talking about."

Nate lowered his gun.

"Graham, what are you doing here?" Kyle asked.

"Thank God I found you. Someone knows about your group."

"Our group?"

"Yes, your group."

"What group?"

"Dammit, there's no time to play games."

"Tell us then."

"You know Mrs. Mancini?"

"Of course, she's my patient."

"Then you know she's on her deathbed."

"Yes."

"She told me tonight there's a leak in your group, and that Ralph DiNunzio thinks you had something to do with his uncle's death. Mr. Mancini, remember? DiNunzio's uncle?"

"Of course. But why did you rush out here now?"

"Because she said they're coming to kill you all tonight."

Kyle's lip began to quiver. "How did she know?"

"Her granddaughter heard DiNunzio and his men talking. They're planning to set off a bomb. They're gonna blow up Stenson's house and everybody in it."

Kyle glanced up at the estate house. The rest of the Tribunal was in there.

She looked behind her and saw Randy drop.

The ground around them exploded in front of him.

"Get down!" he yelled.

Four large dark Range Rovers rumbled toward them, high beams lighting up the van, thundering automatic weapons firing from their windows.

Kyle counted again. She was right; there were four.

DiNunzio!

Kyle fell to the ground, looking for cover. The mobster was taking a chance showing up here. He obviously wanted no survivors.

He was going to kill them all.

She rolled towards a bush, realizing as she did that it was precious little protection. Another round came close to Randy as he crawled around the van.

"Stay down!" Nate screamed from inside the van.

Kyle heard a swoosh and saw a flash of something heading towards the Range Rovers.

The lead vehicle ripped apart and erupted with a thunderous roar, twisting into the air. The two men in the front seat were hurled out, while a man in the back lay half in and out of the splintered rear window.

"Yes!" Nate celebrated his direct hit then fired a volley of shots with his M4A1.

Randy leaped into the van and knelt to get a bead on the following car with another rocket-propelled grenade.

Lead rounds zinged in at twenty plus per second, throwing pebbles and dirt into his face.

Ignoring the blitz, he stood tall to get better aim.

Another whoosh.

An RPG erupted just in front of the second car, creating a large excavation.

It swerved and turned broadside to avoid the crater, lead rounds still teeming from the windows.

Separately, two of DiNunzio's soldiers swooped in from the back, stopped, and aimed pistols at Randy from twenty feet away.

"Oh my god," Kyle said. At that distance, Helen Keller couldn't miss.

She squinted as both gangsters went down at the same time, and a cannon blast deafened her.

She turned in awe toward the shot as Graham came running from the direction of his car, holding a huge rifle.

"Holy shit," Nate exclaimed.

"Is that a Barrett .50 caliber M107A1?" Randy asked.

"Military sniper rifle," Graham said.

"That puppy can penetrate 1.2 inches of steel plate."

"Thanks, man, I guess we owe you a life," Nate said with a grin.

"Let's get out of this first so you can pay me back," Graham said.

"Hell yeah!" Nate turned and fired another RPG.

This time, he caught the second car in the back end, a direct hit in the gas tank.

The trunk and rear wheels blew into the air in a fiery conflagration, flames flooding the interior.

Kyle spotted DiNunzio outside the car next to the passenger's seat with a blown-out window.

His convulsive movements slowed over seconds to twitches as he slumped to the ground next to the charcoal remains of the three other men still in the car.

She could hear fat under their skin crackling in the intense heat.

Their blackened forms stood out in stark contrast to the surrounding yellow-orange flames.

She realized Graham was helping her up.

"Who are these guys?" he asked.

"DiNunzio. Gangsters. Frank Mancini's nephew."

Graham put his arm around her as Kyle stared at the grim, burning spectacle.

"Oh, you bastards," she said, sobbing and covering her eyes with her hands.

Nate and Randy threw their weapons into the rear of the van. But before they could shut the doors, incoming bullets from the remaining two cars pinged off the side of the van. They flattened themselves onto the floor of the van to grab their M4A1s

The two cars were sixty yards away, at most.

Randy shimmied back out.

Nate was hit, and as he came back out, he slumped to the ground.

The cars slowed.

Randy crawled over to Graham and Kyle. He pointed to a hill for Graham's benefit, then to where he was going to situate himself behind another hill to create a crossfire.

Graham grabbed Kyle's arm, and they scurried below a hill and saw the eight or so gangsters pouring out of the two remaining cars, while Randy did the same.

Randy set up his M4A1 tripod just behind the ridge of the hill, ninety degrees from Graham, while Graham did the same with his Barrett M107A1 tripod.

Graham handed Kyle a .357 snub-nose Smith & Wesson revolver from his pocket. Small but powerful. "Remember when I showed you how to use this?"

"Yeah, uh…yes," she stammered, rattled.

"In case you need it. There are five shots. It's a revolver; all you have to do is pull the trigger. Use both hands because there's a decent recoil."

Eight thugs charged, pistols spitting hot lead.

Randy gave Graham the signal to fire.

Randy got onto one knee and fired his automatic .556 M4A1.

It spat out 750-900 rounds a minute.

Three thugs flew back.

They died before they hit the ground.

Suddenly, Randy jerked backwards as a bullet hit him dead in the chest.

Graham fired once. A fourth man flopped backwards.

The other four thugs stopped. Graham nailed another one with a kill shot to the head.

The three remaining thugs took refuge behind a rusted tractor.

Graham pulled the trigger again and put a slug right through the metal of the tractor into a thug.

He fired again, hitting a DiNunzio soldier in the arm. The powerful .50 mm bullet took off his arm at the elbow, eliminating him from the firefight.

Now there was just one.

Graham got another shot off, and it hit the tractor

The last remaining gangster fired a round.

A 9 mm slug caught Graham in the chest.

The man thug jumped up and sped down the hill like a cheetah.

Graham collapsed, his eyes fluttered shut.

"Graham. NO!" Kyle cried and ran towards him.

A familiar voice behind her shouted:

"Now yer gonna get whatchoo deserve, ya murderin' bitch! For killin' my Uncle Frank!"

She turned to see DiNunzio, who had circled the hill and crept behind her.

Clearly, he wasn't dead.

Her mistake.

"Me?" she spat indignantly. "You and your Uncle Frank are the murderers. Torturing innocent people, stealing, killing. We were stopping human scum like you and your uncle from doing it again."

DiNunzio half-smirked and half-laughed as he raised his pistol to shoot her right between the eyes.

She flashed back to her baby brother Brian bleeding out in front of her as she froze and let him die. Killed him. Or so she thought. Was she going to do it again? Not with so many lives depending upon her. She willed herself to take action.

"Please don't!" she begged DiNunzio. "Please!"

DiNunzio just laughed and spat, "Fuck awff, bitch! You know what, I'm gonna fuck with you real good before I kill the fuck outta-"

As DiNunzio monologued, she grabbed the Smith & Wesson .357 and fired.

The kick from the pistol was so hard that it flew out of her hands.

The .357 copper-jacketed bullet flew at 955 mph and penetrated DiNunzio's lower abdomen just below his pubic symphysis.

She smiled, knowing he would never reproduce again.

DiNunzio's face was wracked with horror and shock, and he managed to raise his pistol.

"NOT THIS TIME!"

Kyle grabbed the .357 and squeezed off a second shot.

This one hit DiNunzio in the chest.

This time, the monster crumbled, fell to the ground, and stayed there.

Kyle ran over to Graham.

He looked dead. She felt his neck for a pulse. Nothing.

"NO!" Kyle screamed.

She plugged his nose, opened his mouth, then blew air in.

Then she began rhythmically pressing into his chest over his heart.

"Come on, Graham, stay with me. You got this."

He lay inert.

Kyle filled with an inhuman strength and shouted:

"NOT AGAIN! NOT ON MY WATCH!"

CHAPTER SEVENTY-FIVE

She pounded on his chest over and over.

Graham's eyes shot open, and he gasped, his lungs sucking in oxygen like his life depended on it. Because it did.

"Oh my god, oh my God!" Kyle exclaimed, overcome by relief and joy. "You're alive."

"I think I am. I guess I owe you a life now."

"You already had my life."

She covered his face with kisses.

Then looked at his chest wound. Blood bubbled out from his protective vest just below the right clavicle. The bullet missed his heart. But it had to have hit the right lung apex, the very top, of the upper lung. Not good.

"Are they all down?" Graham asked, slipping into Warrior Mode. "The bad guys?"

"I think so…YES!"

"Good. See if you can warn the others in the house."

Kyle ran as fast as she could towards the house.

She was going to save her friends. All of them.

Or die trying.

Chapter Seventy-Six

Stenton's Estate

Berwyn, PA

Kyle raced as fast as she could towards the house. Two hundred yards away. One hundred and fifty. One hundred.

BOOOOOOOOOOM!

A roar of fire engulfed Stenton's house.

The explosion was deafening.

Flames shot a hundred feet into the air.

A series of new blasts ripped through the house.

Kyle screamed in horror as she was thrown back, landing with a thump.

She shook her head to clear it and looked at the conflagration that once was Stenton's stately mansion.

He was dead. They were all dead. Kyle sank inside herself.

She had failed again. Only this time she knew it wasn't her fault. They all knew this was a possible outcome when they started the Tribunal.

The worst-case scenario had happened.

Kyle snapped back into Doctor Mode.

Randy and Nate were down. Graham needed immediate care.

She sprinted back to them as fast as her legs would take her.

She got to Randy first.

"What's the damage?"

"I'm good," Randy said, wincing. "Check on Nate."

Randy struggled to pull himself up into the van driver's seat, leaving Kyle to deal with Nate. The van shot up the hill and parked a hundred fifty feet kitty corner to the front door.

Kyle rushed to Nate on the ground. He was alive, moaning and trying to right himself. He was barely conscious, but his Kevlar vest had stopped a life-ending bullet.

Kyle helped him get to his feet and into the van, where he collapsed onto the floor.

She hustled over to Graham, who was limping forward, having made yet another remarkable recovery.

Or maybe it wasn't remarkable for Graham Kurland, Warrior Surgeon Superstar.

"Look at you, a medical marvel," Kyle said as she helped him towards the van.

"Just lucky I had my lifesaver with me," he replied, leaning on her for support.

When they got to the van, Randy asked, "Can you patch up Graham without going to the hospital?"

"Yeah, I think so," she said.

"Good," Randy said. "You guys go to this address." He scribbled a number on Spruce Street in downtown Philly and handed it to Kyle. "It's a safe house. We'll meet you there later. If you're stopped by the police, deny any knowledge of what you've seen. You were coming to a casual gathering at the Stenton estate and found this mess. Got it?"

"Copy that," Graham muttered.

"The cops will be here any second. Then it'll be too late. We'll catch you there."

Randy hit the gas and quickly disappeared.

Kyle helped Graham limp to his car, helped him in, and then got in the driver's side. The searing flames from the Range Rover were close enough that he had to shield his face. Graham noticed blood on her hands.

From where?

He was having more difficulty breathing.

Kyle thought about DiNunzio, dead as dead could be. Or so she assumed.

What a bastard.

He should burn in hell for a thousand years.

This invisible justice felt good.

The main road at the bottom of the hill was still quiet as Kyle followed the van down the drive and took the turn out on two wheels.

The van made a right at the next crossroad, leaving them alone with the orange reflections of the inferno shimmering in the rear mirrors.

Graham kept his eye on Kyle and saw the source of her bleeding. But from the way the blood was pulsing through her blouse and jacket, it had to be at least a small artery in front of her elbow.

"You got shot," he said.

"Did I?" she sounded surprised.

"Yup," he said. "In the arm."

She followed his look down, not even feeling the wound in her arm.

"Like Ronald Reagan. Shot without even knowing it."

"Damn!" she marveled. "I guess I'm a badass now. I think you must be rubbing off on me."

"God, I hope not," he chuckled. "I need you to rub off me, not the other way around."

Graham grabbed a newspaper from the back seat and pushed it under her jacket until there was considerable pressure on the elbow. While not completely sterile, the newspaper was surprisingly clean and should prevent clinically significant hemorrhaging until they reached Pennsylvania Hospital.

Within a mile, two black-and-whites approached, their red-and-blue beacons flashing. Graham's mind spun, thinking of the best story to explain their blood if they were stopped.

Broken glass injury?

Knife wound?

Neither one would fly if the cops had more than a single neuron.

To his relief, they sailed past.

Graham's breathing was becoming still more labored with quick and short breaths.

"What's going on?" Kyle asked.

"Can't breathe," Graham shook his head. "I may have a tension pneumothorax." He was breathing eighty times a minute, five times the normal rate.

Kyle slammed on the brakes, pulled into an alcove, and put her ear against his chest. She heard no breath sounds on the right, and the left lung had negligible sounds.

But Graham already knew that.

The air from the right lung escaped through the bullet hole into the pleural cavity, the space between the lung wall and the chest wall. When Graham breathed out, some of the air went into that space until it built up into an area of air under pressure that compressed the lung. To his detriment, the hole closed when he tried to breathe out. Eventually, the compressed lung could no longer inflate when Graham breathed in.

As his breathing became more and more restricted, he started to turn blue.

What she didn't tell him was that the air surrounding the compressed right lung was so expansive that it also compressed the other lung.

But he already knew that.

He had minutes.

IF THAT!

Kyle pulled a utility pen from her pocket, one she had always carried around since college. Shiny on the outside, it resembled a writing pen. And indeed it could write.

But the outer layer was composed of anodized aluminum. With a tungsten tip, it could penetrate a cement block – or a chest wall if needed to incapacitate an attacker. An ingenious disguised weapon, if the situation arose.

Kyle opened it, pulled out the central ink cartridge, loosened the tip, and then punched a hole in the back end with the pen, leaving an open tube.

She tapped on Graham's chest to see where the air had built up, positioned him, then pushed the narrower end of the utility pen over the edge of the right sixth rib from the right side. Going on the underside of the rib could cause perforation of the blood vessels that normally travel under the rib, leading to a severe hemorrhage.

She pressed the utility pen with both hands and put steady pressure over the sixth rib. It slowly penetrated. She kept up the pressure. Finally, it broke through the musculature in the chest wall with a pop and an abrupt decrease in the pressure needed to push it. She stopped pushing, not wanting to penetrate the lung itself as it expanded.

A whoosh of air initially escaped from the external end of the utility pen. She held it in place for five minutes until Graham's blue color lessened and his respiratory rate decreased to forty per minute. At this point, his level of consciousness started to improve as well.

"Can you hold this in?" Kyle asked. "It's a chest tube."

Graham just nodded a weak yes as his lids fluttered.

Even with her rudimentary chest tube, she knew they likely had minutes at most.

Graham gasped, and a strangulated death gurgle groaned out of him.

She took off in a flash.

She'd lost her brother. She'd lost her Tribunal partners.

She was not going to lose the love of her life.

Chapter Seventy-Seven

Kyle stepped from the cab to the curb on the Ingelstrasse, a picturesque street on the pastoral outskirts of Bern, Switzerland, an iconic landmark city with Gothic cathedrals, spectacular fountains, and a 16th-century clock tower whose mechanical puppets performed before the hour.

Any other time, she would have been delighted to be there. But now? Starting a new life alone in a foreign country?

She was afraid.

No. Terrified.

The unknown had always made her uncomfortable.

And that was all she could see when she tried to see her future.

The New York Times lay open to the obituary section in the back seat of the taxi. The article on Stenton dominated the page. His death in a fiery inferno, along with a dozen other bodies in the house and scattered around the grounds, had become international news.

The police, with help from the FBI, had tentatively identified many bodies, but other bodies burned beyond recognition remained unknown.

There was no mention of DiNunzio.

But she knew the identities of everyone in the mansion.

At least money wasn't a problem. Stenton had invested five million for each of them in a Swiss account in case of something like this.

The thought that the others wouldn't need it brought tears to her eyes. She thought she was done crying. But apparently, there was an infinite pool of tears waiting to come out.

Carlo's bonds had already been sent to a non-profit, the *National Center for Victims of Crime*, after she checked on his grandmother.

Leaving Graham had been harder than she'd thought. He'd cover for her in Philadelphia, take care of her paperwork and patients, provide excuses, and legitimize her leave.

She knew she'd miss him. She didn't know she'd ache for him with every fiber of her being.

He'd taken a terrible risk getting her into Pennsylvania Hospital, having his vascular surgeon colleagues fix her arm, his shoulder, and avoiding the mandatory reporting directive to the police.

She was afraid he'd have to pay for her sins. He could lose his license. Go to prison. He'd done it all for her. She couldn't stop the waves of guilt that were drowning her. She was responsible for making him break the law. She couldn't even be sure whether he might face charges for shooting the murderous hoodlums. Putting his entire future in jeopardy. She was going to make it up to him. Every day and in every way.

If she ever saw him again.

Once they were sure the threat from DiNunzio's people was over, Nate and Randy were going to leave town as well. But until there was some proof of DiNunzio's death, no one—especially her—could rest without worry. It was exhausting always looking over her shoulder.

She prayed this thing would someday blow over.

But after shooting DiNunzio, and all the murders she'd planned and executed in the name of invisible justice, she knew there was a good chance she'd never see home again.

Fall had come late in Switzerland this year. For most, it was a happy time. A time when high school girls giggled as their beaus carried their books. When college lovers canoed and canoodled on the lakes with swans under the midday sun.

But not for her. All she felt was numbness shrouding her body like a veil.

It was after six, and the sun's final rays were being snuffed by the massive peaks surrounding the city. An uncomfortably cool breeze blew over the avenues, and Kyle shuddered when she thought of the coming darkness.

"Miss? Excuse me." The cab driver leaned out the window. "Do you need help?"

Kyle suddenly realized she'd been standing there for a minute or more.

"No, thank you. I'm fine."

She handed him the fare and a tip, then turned and hauled her blue suitcase up the walkway toward the front door. It was painful to think it contained all her worldly possessions.

Set at a good distance between two other homes, each with window boxes brimming with red geraniums, Graham's Bern house was larger than she'd expected. The size of a four or five-bedroom home in the States, it was hardly her idea of an Olde World chalet.

Then again, she had no idea until a week ago that he was rich from inheriting Kurland Industries and building it into a major US chipmaker after his parents died in an auto accident. Just like he never talked about the horrors of his war experiences or the bravery that earned him medals, he never boasted about his meteoric medical career. He was that kind of quality act.

Kyle stared at the brass knocker on the ancient, stained door, then rummaged through her purse for the key Graham had given her. She clutched it so hard that her hand whitened and the teeth bit into her skin. Her hand shook as she fumbled with the lock.

Tears welled up again and tumbled down her cheeks. She couldn't do this without Graham. Wouldn't it just be easier not to do this? To walk away from it all. To end the suffering. And not inflict her damage on Graham, bring him down with her.

NO! A voice from all the way inside her screamed. She wasn't going down that rabbit hole again. She'd made her own life through hard work, a life of accomplishments and triumphs. She'd saved countless people. Comforted the sick and ailing. And a good man loved her. No. A GREAT man LOVES her. And by hell or high water, she'd get him back to her and start a new life, an even better life.

She steadied her hand on the door handle, but before she even turned the key, the door opened.

It wasn't locked.

Maybe someone just forgot to lock it.

Or someone had broken in and was waiting to ambush her.

Or maybe they just didn't lock doors here. The magazine on the plane said the crime rate was close to zero.

Her heart raced. Was this a trap? But who could possibly know she was here?

She swallowed her fear and stepped in.

Kyle jumped as the tall grandfather clock in the foyer bonged for six-thirty.

Was there someone in the house waiting to ambush her? Maybe one of DiNunzio's thugs was there looking for revenge.

Heart pounding, adrenaline pumping, breath shallow, she silently crept through the foyer that was larger than her old apartment, twenty by twenty-five feet, and elegantly done in an eighteenth-century colonial motif. She crept through the huge, generous living room and the sitting room in the back. She peered into the dining room and snuck a peek at the modern kitchen in the rear.

No one. Nothing.

In the living room, a portrait hung over the fireplace. She stopped and stared. A handsome couple. They had to be Graham's parents in their younger years.

She was being paranoid. There was no one in the house. She had to let go of the fear.

She took a deep breath and stared at the painting. The woman had Graham's eyes. The man had his tall, powerful build and bearing.

She suddenly realized she was weeping.

She missed him so much that an ache filled her. She wondered if she'd ever see him again. He could be arrested. Killed by one of DiNunzio's avenging devils.

STOP!

Worry is living in the future. Live here now. You're in Switzerland.

You escaped. You're free. A world away from Philadelphia.

Kyle dropped her suitcase in the foyer and started up the stairs. The second floor was less formal than the first, with a Swiss Laura Ashley version of wallpaper. A canopied mahogany bed graced the center of the master bedroom, bordered by two white marble end tables, each with a Chinese lamp.

She turned on a lamp and sat on the bed. A puff of dust arose.

Of course, there was no one here.

I guess they don't lock their doors in Bern.

Kyle smiled. She liked the idea of living in a place where you didn't have to lock your door. And she loved the house. It already felt like home.

The only thing missing was Graham.

Her stomach gurgled. She rubbed it to ease the heartburn that left a bitter taste in her throat. Why should that be surprising? She hadn't eaten more than a few bites since the explosion.

Maybe there was something in the kitchen. She headed back down and opened the refrigerator. A jar of pickles and a half-empty bottle of ketchup.

She slammed the door and leaned back against it.

"Damn it, damn it, DAMN IT!"

She jammed the heels of her hands into her eyes to stop the tears before they came.

But she couldn't.

Kyle wiped away the tears. She'd call a cab to grab a bite. She picked up the phone receiver and then let it drop.

Dead. Dread surged again.

No. She wouldn't allow herself to panic about DiNunzio's people every time a floor creaked. Or a phone had no dial tone.

Holding her painfully empty stomach, she turned out all the lights and walked downstairs to the front door. She remembered passing a cafe on the way in—Peruto's, Peruti's, whatever—it was only a half mile down the road. She slipped on a blue windbreaker.

At the end of a ten-minute walk, she was greeted by the Italian equivalent of "Closed on Monday." With no other restaurant in sight, she continued toward downtown.

The lights of the closed shop windows illuminated the sidewalk. She felt oddly comforted. They lined each side of the quiet streets that became narrower as they converged upon the older section of the city.

Except for an elderly man on the opposite corner, she was alone. She looked back to see how far she'd come. Headlights in the distance dimmed, then snuffed.

She froze for a moment.

Coincidence?

Get it together, girl.

She was a million miles from Philadelphia. No one she didn't trust with her life knew she was here. She'd used the fake passport and credentials Booth had given them all in case of something like this. He was too good at that kind of thing to slip up. She had to get a grip.

She continued another quarter mile. Nothing. Time to give up. She was tired and had barely slept on the plane.

A pair of headlights appeared again.

Fifty yards behind.

The car moved at a slow speed, the rate of a brisk walk.

She picked up her pace, trying to look unafraid. She couldn't spend the rest of her life suspicious of every car that went under the limit. DiNunzio might be powerful in Philly, but he wasn't global.

The headlights came closer. She looked back and caught the outline of a black sedan with a dark figure in the driver's seat.

The car moved closer.

The nervousness in her legs made it hard to walk.

Instinct told her to run, but she wasn't sure she could.

Then the car passed.

Thank God!

The car pulled over, and the front passenger window rolled down.

"Dr. McMann?" a deep voice boomed.

Chapter Seventy-Eight

Old City

Bern, Switzerland

Kyle's wobbly legs found new strength, and she bolted into a narrow alleyway on the right behind the car.

Only someone who had followed her from the States would know her whereabouts and name. Even her plane ticket had been purchased with cash and the fake ID.

He had to be one of DiNunzio's. Or could Erozan's people have found her, too?

Tires squealed on the cobblestones. She ran deep into an alley until she couldn't breathe. She stopped and tried to catch her breath.

It was cave-dark, the only light coming from the beams of the pursuing car.

Kyle darted to the left, hoping to lose her assailant in the maze of old city streets. She spotted an overpass ahead in the moonlight. A bridge, one story above. She groped up the narrow stairway, praying she hadn't been spotted.

The car moved on. She could just make out the driver's face.

It was big.

Unfamiliar.

Sinister.

And he was looking right at her with a stare that curdled blood.

He'd be up the stairs in a matter of seconds!

Please!

As he jammed on the brakes below, she grabbed a large potted plant and lifted it with strength she never knew she had.

She threw the pot at the car with all her might.

A sharp pain shot out of the wound in her arm.

The windshield crashed.

She ran for the park on her right.

From the bridge, it was a short jog to Graham's. Her arm ached, but she kept going.

A mobster or a hitman, or a lunatic could be lurking there, too. But there was no other choice. Everything she had, including Stenton's account number, was in the suitcase. Without that number, she was finished.

She slowed at a hundred feet.

The downstairs lights were on.

Had she turned them out?

Or hadn't she?

She shook her head and tried to remember, but couldn't.

Her mind was racing.

She cracked the front door and peered in.

Everything seemed normal.

The suitcase.

Where was it?

She couldn't think.

What was wrong with her?

Gathering her last drop of courage, she tiptoed into the foyer.

The suitcase was gone. She must have taken it upstairs.

No. She knew she hadn't taken it upstairs.

That suitcase was the difference between life and death.

She heard a noise from upstairs. Or was it?

Kyle stopped breathing and froze.

Yes, there was a noise up there.

Faint, but unmistakable.

Had the thug already beaten her back? After all, he had a car.

She grabbed a carving knife from the kitchen drawer, then silently inched up the stairway.

Her heart raced as she clutched the knife.

Light from the master bedroom seeped into the hallway.

Had she left that on, too?

She couldn't remember.

Was she losing her damn mind?

She inched forward, listening, not even breathing.

The water was running.

She definitely hadn't done that.

The silhouette of a large man with a white face appeared in the doorway.

He stepped into the dark hallway.

She raised the knife.

The thug grabbed her wrist.

She screamed.

He pulled her arm down.

Her vision was blurred from tears.

"NOOO!" she shouted, kneeing him in the groin.

The man dropped and fell back onto the floor.

Kyle reared back to kick the mobster in the head. Until…

"Heck of a greeting," a familiar voice rasped.

She stopped.

And collapsed in throes of combined laughter and tears. Grabbing Graham's arm, she helped him up and kissed his lathered face.

"Oh god, it's you. I never expected…" She broke into sobs and hugged him tighter. "I can't believe it. How did you get here so fast?"

"Give me a second." He grimaced, grabbed a white towel lying on a chair to swipe at the shaving cream, then pulled her over to the bed and sat next to her.

"I grabbed a military flight. They still like me because I do recruiting events for them."

"I thought you were gonna wait, what are you doing here?"

"I haven't been especially happy lately. Well, honestly, ever since you left. Seeing you so distressed made it much worse. So, I asked myself what I could do to make myself happier?"

"What was the answer?"

"Be with you.

She pulled Graham toward her and hugged him as hard as she could.

"I should have come on the same flight."

"I'm so happy you came. How long can you stay?"

"Forever."

Kyle hugged him again with a smile as wide as the Nile.

"What about your job?"

"The one you helped me get?"

"I what?"

"The one is Africa. As far as Pennsylvania Hospital is concerned, you and I are both on an extended sabbatical. I told them we'd be in Africa together for missionary work for at least six months."

"I bet that raised eyebrows. Missionaries, huh? I had no idea we were such good people."

Graham smiled.

"Oh yeah, we are the best. I suspect they're just envious."

They kissed. Long, slow, and sweet.

"I could get used to this," Kyle purred.

"Me, too," Graham agreed.

"Have they come after you legally?"

"Nope."

"What about Nate and Randy?

"Same. We believe the fire destroyed evidence of the meetings and any video. The place was leveled like Gaza."

Kyle looked toward the stairs. "There is a problem, though. A man here was following me. He even knew my name."

Graham laughed.

"What's so funny?

"He was the detective I hired to look after you."

"So he was following me?"

"Ever since you left Kennedy."

"He was the one chasing me?"

Graham grinned. "O'Hara was supposed to be guarding you, but you gave him the slip."

"Why didn't he tell me who he was?"

"You knew the plan. Trust nobody. Talk to no one. I thought it would be better if he didn't confront you. He'd have greater leeway if something happened. He was helping to keep you safe. At least that's what he was trying to do until you dropped a pot on his car."

"Is he okay?"

"He is." Graham pointed to his pocket phone on the bureau. "He called me ten minutes ago, he's fine."

"I'm so sorry," Kyle said. "But he scared me to death."

"No worries," he smiled. "I gave him a very generous parting bonus. From now on, I've got your back. And don't forget, I owe you a life."

"Trust me, I will be holding that over your head until the Earth hits the Sun in sextillion years."

"I look forward to that."

Then a darkness came over her. She bit her lower lip. "What about the others?"

Graham hung his head. "No one in Stenton's house made it out."

Tears ran down Kyle's cheeks. They were good men, people who spent their lives helping others. They were friends. They'd become part of her.

What in heaven's name ever possessed them to get involved in this wretched business in the first place?

She looked out the bedroom window and caught a glimpse of a man under the streetlamp across the street. He stared up at her, then moved on. She snapped the curtain shut and frowned.

"Graham?"

"Yes?"

"Are we safe here?"

"Well, the authorities don't know who's dead and who's alive."

"Right," Kyle nodded.

"But there's a…" Graham sighed dark and heavy, "…a problem."

"What's that?"

"They never found DiNunzio's body."

"But I killed him. I know I did."

"The body was gone. I don't know how. Maybe he crawled away, or someone picked him up."

"So his whereabouts are uncertain."

"Correct."

Graham knew that if DiNunzio was still alive, it meant that he would always have to be on high alert for Kyle.

"Don't worry about it," he said. "We're far from Philadelphia."

"Why did I ever get involved in that damn Tribunal?"

"You were angry. And rightly so. The authorities were as helpful as a Pet Rock. But you're in a different world now. You don't have to listen to the Tribunal anymore. All that's behind you."

"What about the authorities?"

"The people your group eliminated were all considered PSKs."

"PS… what?"

"PSKs. Public Service Killings. Homicides where the people you neutralized were the worst scum, People they're happy to see gone, so they won't commit more heinous crimes. They probably won't follow up. I wouldn't if I was a cop."

She peeked out the curtain one more time, then let it fall back. The street was empty.

"Who was the traitor?" she said.

"Booth. Wasn't he Stenton's chief aide?"

"Why would Alden turn on us?"

"Randy said his mother was in a nursing home and that she'd been visited recently by some rough-looking types. I suspect they threatened her life and held it over Booth's head. But in the end, they killed him, too."

Kyle felt better. If Alden had betrayed them, it was good to know it was because of his mother, and not for money.

"Do you think we'll ever go home?" she asked.

Graham shrugged. "I hope so. Randy and Nate are getting out now that you're here. For how long, I don't know.

"O'Hara, my PI, he's an ex-cop. He's going to nose around and find out what the police know, then try to follow up on the extent of any leak. He'll check in with me from time to time."

"Good."

"I think we'll be able to go back sometime, but for the moment, we're persona non grata. We'll…make the best of it."

Kyle tossed her windbreaker on the floor, pushed him back on the bed, and brought her lips to within an inch of his.

"I already am."

A Note from the Author

Dear Reader,

I have treasured writing from an early age. In the sixth grade, I wrote an unsolicited 250-page history of the US Civil War. It was of considerable interest to me since I had visited the battlefields, and my great-great-grandfather lost a leg in battle and eventually died from his wounds.

As a first-year ophthalmology resident at Wills Eye Hospital in Philadelphia, Dr. Jerry Shields, the world's premier ocular oncologist, stimulated my interest in research and taught me an incredible amount about writing scientific manuscripts. That led me to author 12 medical books and more than 650 papers (over 325 peer-reviewed), chapters, and editorials.

Ever since the fourth grade, however, I wanted to write fiction. I began to write more earnestly at the beginning of my ophthalmology residency following an exhilarating internship at Grady Memorial Hospital in Atlanta, getting up at 4:30 am to do so. I always carried my small notebook to write down interesting ideas and keep track of human events. Virtually all of the medical scenes in my books have occurred as a result of events I have seen or experienced, as well as those in the news. I feel that actual events are almost always more electrifying than what authors make up. I sent my work out, but I was rejected by twenty-five publishers. Nonetheless, my interest never dulled, even though other events got in my way.

You might say what other events? 1) My busy vitreoretinal practice at Wills Eye Hospital, and 2) my own physical ailments.

The latter began with terrible abdominal pains at age 36. The first episode occurred after I sneezed. It was so abrupt that I wondered if I had been shot. I had a mass in my abdomen that turned out to be blood. Ever the eternal optimist, I naturally assumed it was a bleed into a malignant tumor.

Thank goodness, it was not.

It was a large bleed into one of my kidneys due to something I was born with and never knew about, polycystic kidney disease. The anomaly causes large kidney cysts that put pressure on the internal kidney arteries and veins, causing them to rupture. Boy, does that smart!

Each of the many times it happened, I had to be admitted to the hospital for pain control. It seems like I spent every Christmas in the hospital. Lissa, my wife, also an ophthalmologist, ran for US Congress, and at times it was rough, with my pain, to help her. Shortness of breath eventually came as well from the large kidneys pressing on my lungs. I never thought it would come, but at age 52, my kidneys completely failed. My wonderful sister, Gayle, was a match and gave me one of her kidneys.

Two to three months later, I developed Guillain-Barré Syndrome. I spent four months paralyzed in the University of Pennsylvania Hospital, the first two weeks on a respirator. During that time, Lissa had to go by herself to a crosstown hospital for cancer surgery, though she showed up the morning after surgery in a wheelchair at my bedside. How's that for love?

I was able to walk in 6-7 months, but I still had little feeling in my lower extremities and painful neuropathy in my feet. It's as if they are always waking up. I developed two subdural hemorrhages surrounding my brain after a fall. But thanks to the great talents of neurosurgeon Jay Howington in Savannah, I have fully recovered.

Working with David Sterry and Arielle Eckstut from Book Doctors has been a godsend for me. These folks have published many important books themselves and are most knowledgeable, generous, patient, and adept at sharing their skills with others.

When I retired from my clinical practice at age 66, I was finally able to devote the time to put my trilogy of books together. And I am so excited to be published by Level Best Books, an excellent organization. Despite rejection and the many brushes with death that have complicated my life, I never gave up the idea of publishing fiction. From the medical point of view, I believe fiction serves as entertainment to improve quality of life and healing. It allows those who might be infirm or just frustrated with everyday life to forget their personal difficulties and immerse themselves in a different world. Since doctors only do two things: help people to live better or longer, I believe that entertaining reading is therapeutic.

For older writers or discouraged writers, I say, "Never give up." Time enhances your experiences. It is your experiences that determine what you write about. And don't use hardships as an excuse not to write. Look at me. As a professor told me in third-year medical school, "Never leave the hospital each day without learning something new." I have tried to apply this to all aspects of life, including writing, and it has helped me greatly.

As Lester Holt says on every evening news, "Please take care of yourselves. And each other."

Gary Brown

Acknowledgments

I wish to express my grateful appreciation for the superb book editing of acclaimed authors David Henry Sterry and Arielle Eckstut from Book Doctors, in addition to agent Alice Tasman at the Jean Naggar Agency, and editors Dave King and Mark Anderson for helping me to develop writing skills, what little I may have. Drs. W. Reed Kindermann, David Randell, Timothy Olsen, Ms. Janet Gorton, and Ms. Ramanda Bellegia were also of great help as readers

As well, I want to thank my incredible wife, Melissa Brown, MD, MN, MBA for her advice, wealth of scientific and political knowledge, human relationship expertise that far exceeds mine, patience, and the hard work she consistently and good-naturedly put in to allow me time to write.

About the Author

Dr. Gary Brown is a retired professor and vitreoretinal (eyeball for civilians) surgeon. He performed over 40,000 operations in his award-winning career. Among his honors are inclusion in *Marquis Who's Who in the World and The Leading Physicians of the World.* He served as the editor of three medical journals and has 650 publications and 12 medical/economic book authorships. This is his debut novel.

AUTHOR WEBSITE:

Coming Soon: www.garybrownbooks.com

Also by Gary Brown, MD

12 medical textbooks; over 600 articles

9 798889 201494